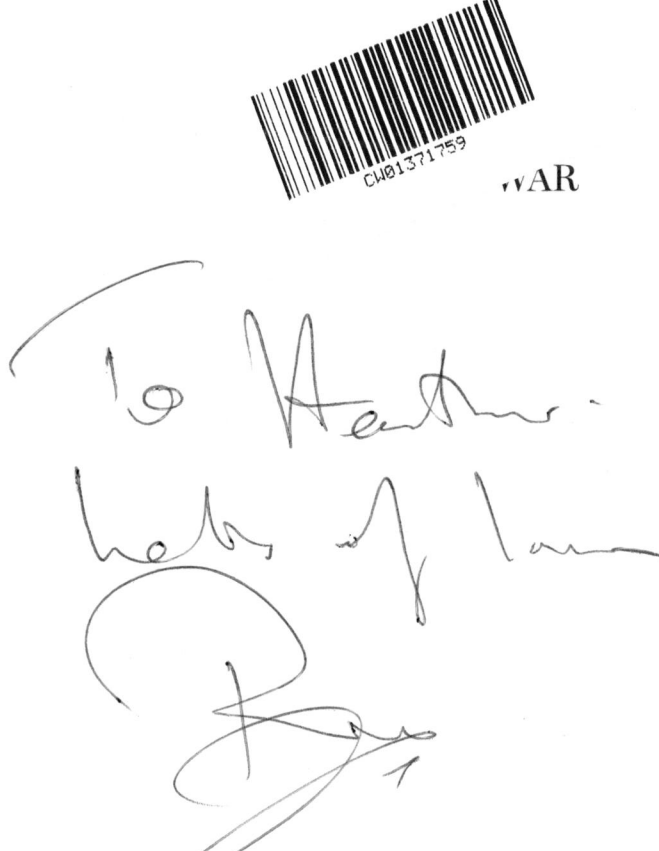

THEATRE OF WAR

ROY GOULD

The Book Guild Ltd

First published in Great Britain in 2023 by
The Book Guild Ltd
Unit E2 Airfield Business Park,
Harrison Road, Market Harborough,
Leicestershire. LE16 7UL
Tel: 0116 2792299
www.bookguild.co.uk
Email: info@bookguild.co.uk
Twitter: @bookguild

Copyright © 2023 Roy Gould

The right of Roy Gould to be identified as the author of this
work has been asserted by them in accordance with the
Copyright, Design and Patents Act 1988.

All rights reserved. No part of this publication may be
reproduced, transmitted, or stored in a retrieval system, in any form or by any means,
without permission in writing from the publisher, nor be otherwise circulated in
any form of binding or cover other than that in which it is published and without
a similar condition being imposed on the subsequent purchaser.

This work is entirely fictitious and bears no resemblance to any persons living or dead.

Typeset in 11pt Minion Pro

Printed and bound by CPI Group (UK) Ltd, Croydon, CR0 4YY

ISBN 978 1915603 692

British Library Cataloguing in Publication Data.
A catalogue record for this book is available from the British Library.

I started writing this novel the day after theatres around the country were closed down in 2020. A great many in the business lost their livelihoods that day. So I dedicate this book to all my friends and colleagues in the theatre game, past and present.

Prologue

He saw both of them die within a minute of each other.

They must have hit the fuel tank on the first one's aircraft – a direct hit; it exploded in a fireball.

Thank God, he thought, *at least the poor devil would not have known anything about it.*

They had joined on the same day, learned the art of being a fighter pilot together; now he had gone, in an instant.

Then they came again and he watched in horror as the bullets strafed the sides of his brother's plane and flames started to lick the fuselage. *Dear God, let him be alive; let him be able to get out of there.* He held his breath as he waited for the boy he had played with, teased and bullied, his little brother, who had joined up to emulate him, he prayed to God that… and then he saw the small figure plummeting towards the ground before the silk of his parachute opened and he began to float, gracefully. Thank God he was alive; yes, he would have to spend time being the enemy's prisoner, but at least you had to be alive to be a prisoner. They'd see each other again when the war was over – surely that couldn't be long now – and they could stand in a bar and impress the girls with tales of their death-defying feats whilst toasting the memories of their friends and colleagues who did not return.

Then the fighter came round once more. *Dear God, no.* He saw the flashes of gunfire from its wings; he looked in horror as the bullets cut into his brother's defenceless body as he drifted downwards. His head dropped, the lower half of his body almost severed, only hanging on by the threads of his flying suit; the bastard had cut him in half. His heart nearly stopped beating; his eyes filled with tears. Their mother's grief would be unbearable to witness. He would have to hold her hand and explain, it was his duty, but he would never be able to bring himself to tell her what he'd seen, the reality. It would kill her to hear the barbaric details, details that he knew he would never be able get out of his own head, a sight that would return to him nightly as he closed his eyes from now on.

He wanted to go after that bastard, that coward; he wanted to chase him down and come in close so he could see the horror on the murderer's face as he pressed the trigger button on the top of his joystick to strafe him into oblivion. He wanted another mother to be burdened with the same never-ending grief. Yes, let another mother grieve.

His own survival, however, was quickly brought into focus when he lifted his goggles a moment to wipe the tears from his eyes and he peered at the dials in front of him. The hand of the fuel gauge was dropping away at an alarming rate and he knew he had to get back. He hadn't even had the chance to drop his payload but he knew he had to get away before he ran out of fuel; he'd have to evacuate the bombs in the sea when he reached the coast to lighten the aircraft or he'd burn off too much fuel and end up in the water himself. He looked out to see where the enemy fighters were and, almost too late, he saw one coming in from below him. Throwing his joystick back, he hauled his aircraft up into the clouds, hoping to lose the pursuer. The clouds were thickening now and a nasty storm was brewing, which wasn't good news, but the move seemed to have worked and he was alone. It was just him amongst the dense blackness. He needed to stay hidden, perhaps in the worst part of the weather. He dreaded the turbulence that would throw his aircraft about fiercely, but it would be his only chance to get back home.

Those bastards would pay for what they'd done; they'd pay for their butchery. Yes, they'd pay. The phrase "Theatre of War" came into his head. Who could call this carnage a theatre? What sort of sick joke was that? Theatres were places of entertainment where you went to on leave with your latest girl, where they made you laugh or cry, where the war was forgotten for a couple of hours. Another world.

Now, as he started to be buffeted by the storm, he tried to steer his aircraft and struggled to keep his bearings for the coast. He'd done this trip three times now so knew that he just had to keep flying due east if he could.

The anger had surged up from his belly and took a stranglehold in his throat as he headed for the coast.

'The bastards will pay for what they've done. Someone will pay. Yes, I shall make sure of that.'

1

Act One – Beginners

Randolph Laine closed the door of his home and proceeded north, up Perrymead Road, towards the New Kings Road. He and his wife Hester had bought the house for a song when they first married in the early years of the century but, to be frank, he wasn't sure how much longer he could afford to stay in it. For a start, it was far too large for just himself and Sam, and now Hester had gone it seemed a dreadful waste. A great deal of the best furniture had been sold off along with his prized Savile Row suits and Hester's couture frocks. His funds had dwindled to almost nothing, having spent so much on Hester's nursing costs during her last few years; not that he begrudged spending the money – he would have done anything for her – but now her fight with dementia had been lost, the place felt as empty as his bank account. The only problem now, of course, was this: who would wish to buy a house in London while the Luftwaffe kept dropping bombs all around it?

That morning, Randolph was dressed in what was now his only respectable suit, a suit he had, unintentionally, packed into his suitcase on the last night of a production of the young Noel Coward play *Blithe Spirit* at the Theatre Royal, Worthing, in 1938, instead of returning it to the wardrobe department. Draped over his shoulders was a rather moth-eaten overcoat with a fur collar – again, something he had picked up during his many years in the business. At a distance the coat looked rather smart but, on closer inspection, one could see the evidence of the humble clothes moth and the stitching and patching efforts of various wardrobe ladies, of differing levels of skill, from theatres up and down the country. Perched on his head was a Homburg hat that had also seen better days but was an investment, when times had been better, purchased from Lock and Co in Savile Row. In his hand was a silver-topped cane, purchased from James Smith and Sons in Bloomsbury, which he tapped on the ground or swung nimbly in front of him as he went along his way. All in all, Randolph had the look of an archetypal theatrical actor-manager, which, indeed, he was.

Reaching the Kings Road, he paused and wondered whether he should walk its length up to Sloane Square and past the little Royal Court Theatre or follow the road down to the Thames and amble along the Chelsea Embankment. Even though London boasted, even in a time of war, many modes of transport, Randolph preferred, if possible, the oldest one of all, Shanks' Pony – his own legs. London, he thought, was the most perfect city for walking, and so, pointing his cane as if to show the world his intentions, he decided to take the river route. Turning right down Cremorne Road, he strode out with an air of confidence, and before long "Old Father Thames" hove into view. The road then bore left onto the Embankment itself and here Randolph stopped a moment to look down at the boats in the Chelsea Yacht and Boat Company's yard below. Shipwrights were busy refitting or repairing vessels, which, Randolph surmised, only a few months before may have made the dangerous journey across the English Channel to pick up those brave boys from the beaches of Dunkirk. Randolph tipped his hat in remembrance and respect and then continued on his way. Stepping out, he passed Chelsea Old Church, a place he had visited many times over the years to marvel at the magnificent monuments housed within. He looked across to the old building

– did he have time to pop in before his meeting? He took out his pocket watch – seven forty-five; still around an hour's walk ahead of him – next time perhaps. What he didn't know (and how could he?) as he stood marvelling at the old place on this sunny late summer morning in nineteen-forty was that, in less than six months, the Luftwaffe would visit London again and drop a parachute bomb directly onto it, reducing it to a pile of rubble. There were lots of things that Randolph didn't know that morning. If he had been more of a believer, perhaps divine intervention would have... intervened. If, perhaps, he had had a little faith, he may have popped into the church and got down on his knees and contemplated the Almighty for a moment or two; perhaps God would have sent him a sign, a sign that would have caused him, almost certainly, to turn around, head back home and pour himself a large brandy, no matter how early the hour. However, this morning, his lack of faith – or just plain fate – decided to let things take their own course, and so, tipping his hat to the old church, Randolph continued on his way, none the wiser.

As he made his way along the side of the river, Randolph's mind turned to the man he was making his way to see, Sir Peregrine Worsley – Porker Worsley, a rotund toad, to say the least, and a year above him at Eton. Never the instigator but a hanger-on who would stand in the shadows while his classmates pranked lesser mortals such as himself. One such prank, Randolph remembered – how could he forget it? – changed his life forever. Having been cornered by a gang of older boys, who had, no doubt, spent time in one of the local taverns and were out for some sport, they bound him hand and foot and lashed him naked, save for his vest and long johns, to the railings of Windsor Castle, just a mile from the college; an event that was bad enough in itself but that was made so much worse by the fact that it was enacted on one of the few times that the aged Queen, who was not known to be amused at the best of times, was in residence. Discovered by a passing policeman, Randolph remembered, with a shudder, being led by the ear to the headmaster's office, where the formidable Mister Warre, CB, CVO, the holder of both the most honourable Order of the Bath and the Royal Victorian Order, lectured his younger self on morality whilst swishing his birch cane ahead of him as he paced his study, then gave him six of the best with that same instrument of torture and "sacked" him on the spot. Sobbing uncontrollably, his backside throbbing with indescribable pain, he staggered out along the corridor. Young Porker Worsley, rather ashamed that he had been party to his misfortune, whispered that he was 'really awfully sorry' and mumbled that, had he tried to interfere, he would undoubtedly have found himself stripped and lashed to those self-same railings next to him. For this act of abject cowardice, Porker gave a solemn promise that should young Laine require his help in the future, then he must get in touch. 'Us chaps must all stick together; *Floreat Etona* and all that eyewash.' It was this promise that Randolph was on his way to call in.

It came as no surprise for Randolph to discover, many years later, that Porker had become a Civil Servant; Eton College was, after all, the Civil Service's sausage machine, and young Worsley was to the manner born, destined to push paper about for the rest of his life and to retire on a jolly good pension. The reason for his knighthood wasn't clear, but Randolph reasoned cynically that it was for nothing more than turning up at the office on time and keeping his nose clean. Of course, Randolph mused, as he made his way along the banks of the river, there was some likelihood that Porker would have no memory of him or the promise. It was all so very long ago and they hadn't seen or heard from each other since that fateful day. Randolph shook his head as if to banish the thought from his mind. No matter, he would play it by ear. *You're an actor. Give the performance of a lifetime; convince him of your cause.*

'When the blast of war blows in our ears, then imitate the action of the tiger,' he called out, giving his best Henry the Fifth and scattering the pigeons into the London sky.

On he ambled until he found himself on the edge of theatre land itself, his spiritual home. Up he went, through Victoria Embankment Gardens and into Carting Lane, past the back of the Savoy Theatre and up the steps by the Coal Hole public house, where WS Gilbert and Arthur Sullivan had reputedly put on the odd entertainment for the customers before returning to their theatre next door for a full-length performance. Crossing the Strand, Randolph found himself outside the Vaudeville Theatre. It was on the stage of CJ Phips' snug little playhouse that Randolph and his wife, Hester Simmons, had hoped to make their West End debut together in Somerset Maugham's *The Breadwinner* in 1931, taking over the parts from the two stars, Ronald Squire and Peggy Ashcroft. But sadly, the management suddenly withdrew the offer having decided, on reflection, that Hester Simmonds and Randolph Laine were not going to put enough "bums on seats" even in this sweetest of theatres, so up went the notice at the stage door and down came the curtain on the last night.

With his cane rhythmically tapping the pavement in front of him, Randolph continued his promenade along the Strand and into the curve of the Aldwych, where the dear old Gaiety Theatre lay, dark and empty, ahead of him, stripped of its finery and stranded at the entrance to the crescent. Passing the Waldorf Theatre, above which Mister Ivor Novello lounged in his apartment writing what were, to Randolph's mind, rather sickly sweet musical entertainments; and then past the Waldorf Hotel in all its glory, quiet at this time of day but where, in the evening, Al Bowlly could be heard crooning *Love is the sweetest thing* and *Goodnight Sweetheart* to the pampered clientele in its ornate ballroom, accompanied by Howard Godfrey and his Waldofians; and finally Randolph ambled past the Aldwych Theatre, home of Ben Travers' gloriously crafted farces. Following the arc of the road, he turned left into Kingsway and then proceeded along its length until he reached his destination, number one hundred and twenty-three, where the newly formed Council for the Encouragement of Music and Arts (CEMA) was headquartered, directly opposite Holborn Underground Station.

Not wishing to be questioned by some officious, inquisitive majordomo on his way in, Randolph hovered outside on the pavement for a minute or two, looking around as nonchalantly as he could, leaning on his cane, nodding and tipping his hat to the odd passer-by whilst taking the occasional peek through the glass door, ready to seize the opportunity of ducking in when the smartly uniformed, one-armed concierge standing with military bearing behind his reception desk was looking the other way. Then, as chance would have it, after only a minute or two, the old soldier, having one-handedly sorted through a pile of folders, picked them up and, placing them under his one arm, crossed the foyer, dextrously opened the door to a side office and entered, leaving his post unmanned for a moment or two. Without further ado, Randolph pushed open the main door and strode in. Not risking waiting for the lift, he made his way into the stairwell. Having it on good authority that Porker – *No*, he thought, *I must stop thinking of him in that way* – that Sir Peregrine Worsley's office was on the top floor, he put his best foot forward and started to climb the concrete steps. On the top landing two young men were smoking cigarettes and sharing a joke; Randolph wondered if he should hang back and wait for them to go but then, trusting his luck, he decided to take his chances.

'Excuse me, I'm most terribly sorry to trouble you,' he said getting his breath and tipping his hat to them both, 'but is this the correct floor for Sir Peregrine Worsley's office?'

'Yes,' said one of the young men, without taking much notice of him. 'Room 4045, I think. Marked as Annex B, isn't it, Rodders?'

'Yes, that's the one, old chap,' replied the other. 'Down the corridor on the left, but be careful of old Finchy, she bites.'

The young men laughed.

'Finchy?' asked Randolph.

'He means Miss Finch, Sir Peregrine's secretary,' said the other, nudging Rodders and making a face.

'Amongst other things,' mumbled Rodders, turning away, dropping his cigarette and coughing to hide his sniggers.

Randolph thanked them and doffed his hat once more. Pulling open the heavy oak door, he found himself in a dingy, dark and very long corridor. Brushing down his coat and straightening his collar, he strode off, his shoes squeaking on the worn and cracked linoleum that covered the floor. Peering short-sightedly at the numbers on the doors as he went, he eventually arrived at the correct one, Room 4045. On the wall next to it, a wooden sign had the legend 'The Council for the Encouragement of Music and Arts, (CEMA), Annex B'. He looked at his pocket watch – eight forty-five; he'd made good time. Shooting his cuffs and steadying himself for his entrance, his opening lines ready to be spoken, Randolph raised his hand to knock but then stopped as he heard a telephone ringing and a woman's voice from within. He smiled, remembering the young men; this could only be "old Finchy".

'Good morning, Sir Peregrine Worsley's office, this is Miss Finch speaking.'(He was right). Pause, a rustling of paper. 'No, I'm afraid Sir Peregrine's diary is full for the foreseeable future. Good morning.' Ping, as the telephone receiver was replaced on its cradle. She certainly sounded formidable.

Straightening his back and taking a deep breath, Randolph knocked on the door. No answer. He waited a moment and knocked again; this time the rather haughty voice of Miss Finch responded.

'Come in.'

He turned the brass handle and entered the room. Behind a

desk, writing something down in a large book, sat a rather austere woman with her hair in a tight-fitted bun, sporting heavily framed spectacles. She wore an immaculately ironed blouse in what one would describe as beige, with a tweed jacket on top. In fact, Miss Finch looked almost exactly as Randolph had imagined a British Civil Servant's secretary would look like.

'Yes, how may I help you?' she asked, closing the book and eyeing the stranger up and down. It was abundantly clear, by the way she looked over the top of her spectacles, that she wasn't overly taken with what she saw in front of her.

'I have an appointment with Sir Peregrine Worsley at nine o'clock,' he said in his most convincing manner – so convincing, he thought, that had he been giving evidence in court, he would have been acquitted on the spot. Unfortunately for him, Miss Finch was not to be so easily swayed.

'Your name, sir?'

'Randolph Laine.'

Miss Finch took another look at him and reached over to a large appointments diary. Slowly and very meticulously, she ran her fingers down the page. Having reached the bottom, she repeated the process and then, looking up with what could be described as a weak smile playing across her lips, said, 'I'm afraid, Mister Laine, that your name doesn't appear to be in Sir Peregrine's appointment diary for nine o'clock.' She paused a moment, then continued, 'Or, indeed, any other time.'

'Really?' replied Randolph, putting on his most sincere, concerned look. 'But I telephoned only two days ago and…' He was about to chance his arm and he knew it. 'I believe I spoke to your good self, Miss Finch.' It was worth a try. He noticed that there was no nameplate on her desk and as far as he could see her name wasn't in evidence anywhere. How on earth could he know her name unless he'd spoken to her?

She looked at him again, quizzically. It was very unlike her not to remember everyone that called and she prided herself on what Sir Peregrine called her photographic memory.

'I don't recall a telephone conversation with you, Mister Laine. Are you quite sure?'

'Oh yes, quite sure, Miss Finch.' He repeated her name as crisply as he could, letting it roll trippingly off the tongue. 'I distinctly recall how you answered the telephone. I remember thinking how efficient you sounded. Now, how was it?' Randolph was getting into his stride. He put his hand to his ear as if holding a telephone receiver and spoke. 'Good morning, Sir Peregrine Worsley's office, this is Miss Finch speaking.'

She was momentarily all of a fluster; this was indeed exactly how she answered the telephone, but try as she might, she could not recall a Mister Laine. This was most unlike her.

'Hmm, one moment.' She leaned across the desk once more and this time picked up another large book, the one that she had been writing in when he entered. Opening it, she flicked through the pages. 'If you called, it would be in the telephone book. What day did you say you telephoned again?'

Damn, thought Randolph, *this woman is the queen of efficiency.* 'Where are we today? Thursday? It would be Monday, or perhaps Tuesday.' He gave what he thought to be a charming smile. Miss Finch did not respond kindly to charming smiles.

'Monday or Tuesday,' she said again, dragging her finger once more down a page. 'No,' she stated firmly after going through the exercise a couple of times and then once more for luck. 'No, I'm sorry, Mister Laine, but I have no note of your telephone calls on either Monday or Tuesday.'

'Perhaps it was yesterday,' said Randolph quickly. 'I've been so busy, I lose track of time.'

'No, Mister Laine, I took the precaution of looking under Wednesday also. There is no note of a telephone call from you then either.'

'How odd,' he responded. 'Oh well, no matter, perhaps I can wait to see if he has five minutes later in the day?' He looked hopefully at her.

'Sir Peregrine will not have five minutes later in the day, I can assure you.' She looked rather fiercely at him.

'Ah,' said Randolph. 'I am, in that case, at my wit's end. What to do?' he added piteously; it was corny, but it might work. Miss Finch shook her head and drew the appointments diary closer and picked up a pencil.

'You'll have to make an appointment. Let me see.' She started to turn the pages, daintily licking her finger every so often as she went from page to page, running the finger down it each time. Randolph looked on; was there a human being behind those glasses and that formidable exterior? What sensitive heart beat beneath that tweed jacket and beige blouse, he wondered? After what seemed to be an age, Miss Finch looked up.

'Yes,' she said.

'Yes?' queried Randolph.

'Yes,' she repeated, and licked the lead of her pencil in order to make a note in the appropriate place. 'I have a three o'clock on Tuesday the fourteenth of November.'

'November?' snapped Randolph, his charm temporarily suspended. 'That's months away.'

'Sir Peregrine is a very busy man,' she answered curtly. 'Would you like me to book you in or not?' Her pencil hovered over the page.

He regained his composure and sighed. 'November will be far too late, I'm afraid.'

'It is the only date I have.' Miss Finch had thrown over her last offer.

Beaten, or so he thought, Randolph let out another sigh, whereupon the door behind him opened. He turned and there, tightly framed in the doorway, was the rotund boy; larger than he remembered him, yes, but without a doubt it was Porker Worsley.

'Good God. Norman Laine!' exclaimed Sir Peregrine.

'Perry!' exclaimed Randolph back.

Behind him, Miss Finch took a deep breath and looked down her nose at the man's brazen familiarity.

'Well, well, well, young Norman Laine,' chuckled Sir Peregrine, and around three of his chins wobbled up and down, his jovial pomposity being almost Pickwickian.

'I'm flattered that you recognise me,' Randolph said, bowing his head slightly towards him.

'Oh yes, oh yes, I'd recognise you anywhere; you haven't changed a bit, even with your clothes on.' Randolph breathed a sigh of relief – the incident had been remembered – and they both laughed. Miss Finch, on the other hand, looked down at her desk and started rearranging her ledgers.

'Ah, I seem to have embarrassed the dear lady,' chuckled Sir Peregrine, moving round the desk and putting his hands on her shoulders. 'Nothing untoward, I assure you, Miss Finch, just public school japes.'

Randolph doubted she thought that any more edifying by the way she looked up at her senior.

'So what brings you here?'

'To see you, old boy.'

Another flinch from Miss Finch. *Old boy, indeed. Sir Peregrine, a knight of the realm, and this man, walking in off the street with his untruths and a very badly patched overcoat.* Without doubt, Miss Finch was the biggest snob in the room.

'Are you in the diary?' asked Peregrine as he looked down at the desk.

'It seems that my name was omitted, Perry.' Miss Finch looked up at him, her eyes, sabre-length daggers, stabbing him repeatedly. Randolph gave her a sympathetic look and then turned a dagger back at her. 'But I'm sure that it isn't Miss Finch's fault; mistakes happen even to the best of us.'

She wanted to open her mouth but Sir Peregrine put his hands back upon her shoulders, and squeezed them ever so gently.

'Miss Finch is my trusted Sancho Panza, always loyally at my side. No matter, no matter.' He squeezed her shoulders once more, as if to say, *I perfectly understand that the man is lying through his teeth but one mustn't rise to such things. Turn the other cheek; we're British, after all.*

Miss Finch, understanding the signs, took a deep breath and adjusted her spectacles.

'Now, my dear Miss Finch, what time is my first meeting?' he asked kindly.

'Nine-fifteen, Sir Peregrine, you have an appointment with Mister Harrison in accounts.'

'Ah, yes.' The word "bugger" came into his mind. 'Well, I think I may be a little late for my appointment with Mister Harrison in Accounts, but no matter.'

She bowed her head as if to say, *Whatever you say, Sir Peregrine*; however, she was under no illusion that Mister Harrison in Accounts would be at all happy about it.

Randolph smiled and Miss Finch straightened her brooch; not that it needed straightening, but it stopped her first impulse, which was to strangle the odious man on the other side of the desk.

'A pot of tea for two, I think, my dear lady,' said Sir Peregrine in his best ice-breaking manner; he could feel the frostbite coming through his fingers from her shoulders as he held her there. 'And some biscuits from the secret rations,' he stage-whispered in her ear.

Within a few minutes, Randolph was sitting in a wing chair in Peregrine's office, sipping tea and eating a custard cream biscuit.

'Do have another,' Peregrine said, pushing the plate over towards Randolph, 'take two.' He leant in. 'Miss Finch and I have our own unofficial supply. Between you and me, a friend who is high up in Huntley and Palmers keeps me stocked.' He winked.

Randolph took two.

'You can dunk it, if you like, just as we did at school. Do you remember? Of course you do.' Sir Peregrine was back, dressed in his starched collar and ill-fitting Eton tails, with top hat on the table beside him, in the dorm as he dunked his own custard cream into his tea.

'Yes, yes,' replied Randolph.

'Of course it wasn't the done thing for a boy to dunk his biscuits at Eton,' said Peregrine, continuing his thoughts and laughing, 'but then again, it wasn't the only practice that wasn't thought the done thing, but the boys got round those as well, when the masters weren't looking.'

Randolph shifted uncomfortably in his chair, remembering the boys who wanted to do certain things to him, certain things he resisted but rarely succeeded in avoiding.

'So, Norman,' started Sir Peregrine.

'Sorry, Perry, if you don't mind, my professional name is now Randolph,' said Randolph.

'Randolph?'

'Yes, Randolph, as I'm here in my professional capacity.'

'Oh really?' said Peregrine, interrupting. 'I thought you might be here to call in that favour.'

'I am. I wasn't sure you'd remember.'

'Remember? Well of course I remember, dear chap. Oh yes, I've lived with the sight of you walking up the college driveway, pulling your box behind you. I shall never forget it.'

Nor should Randolph; he remembered it all too vividly, dragging all his belongings down South Meadow when his parents refused to meet him through shame; a shame that cut so deeply that when he got back to his parental home, he was immediately admonished, thrashed and disinherited (his father being the

Honourable Charles Laine, second son of the Earl of Pangbourne – or some such place, he could never remember) and, sobbing uncontrollably, put into a hansom cab to Waterloo Station and told to board the next train to Folkestone, where, he was informed, he was to stay with a distant relative. Upon arrival he discovered that the said relative ran a boarding house for, amongst others, theatricals and variety acts who were playing the Pleasure Gardens Theatre. In short, after a few weeks, he realised that he had never been so happy in his life. He never saw or heard from either of his parents again, not even on his birthday.

'So, Norman – sorry, Randolph,' said Sir Peregrine, bringing another custard cream to his mouth and wiping the crumbs off his waistcoat, 'do go on – how may I help you?'

Randolph smiled and took a sip of his tea.

'The thing is, Perry, about this touring theatre idea...' Randolph started.

'Which touring theatre idea is that, old chap?' asked Peregrine with a frown.

'The one outlined on this sheet of paper,' Randolph replied on cue, producing it with a flourish and passing it over, whilst trying to sound calm.

'Ah.' Retrieving it, Peregrine sat back in his chair, put on his spectacles and, biting into another biscuit, read through Randolph's proposal, taking time out for the odd sip of tea and another biscuit. It was, most definitely, a two custard cream proposal.

Randolph waited for his response. Would the old Etonian honour his debt with this?

'Yes,' Sir Peregrine said finally, laying the sheet of paper down on his desk.

Randolph could hardly breathe. 'Yes?'

'If I understand this correctly,' Peregrine continued after what seemed like an age, 'you want this department to hand over some of the Treasury's money in order that your troupe of players can tour the country in aid of the war effort. Have I got that right?' He said this very matter-of-factly, giving nothing away, and then took another sip of tea and leant back in his chair, clasping his hands over his large chest, a Civil Service Buddha. The only sound was the ticking of the clock and the odd rumble of Sir Peregrine's stomach.

Randolph leant forward in his chair. 'Well,' he said, a slightly nervous waver in his voice. He knew that this could go either way. 'The Old Vic Company is being subsidised, I believe that's the word – subsidised – to mount productions in parts of Wales, from what I hear.'

Sir Peregrine pursed his lips and smiled an enigmatic smile. 'And where, pray, did you hear that?' he asked, peering over his half-moon spectacles.

'The theatre business is full of gossip, Perry. Actors are incapable of keeping a secret.'

The Buddha let out a laugh. 'Well it can't be worse than the Civil Service; leaks like a sieve.' And then they both laughed and sipped their teas. 'The thing is that the Old Vic Company are seen by the department as cultural ambassadors, you see, and if they were going off on tour – and I'm not in any way confirming that they are, you understand…'

'Perfectly,' said Randolph.

'Indeed.' Sir Peregrine shrugged his shoulders and stood up. 'So, if this department were to be funding the Old Vic Company, it would be to bring Shakespeare and… who else was it? Who was the chap who wrote that rather strange play about stratagems? I remember the Upper Fifth did it once but I couldn't understand what the stratagems were.'

'The Beaux Stratagem, George Farquhar,' prompted Randolph knowingly.

'That's the chap. Old George Fucker, as some of the boys called him.' He chuckled at the memory. 'Yes, plays by him. It would, as I say, bring culture to the masses, not just raucous entertainment.'

'Raucous entertainment?' Randolph put on a show of righteous indignation.

'My dear chap, I'm only making my assumption from what you state in your little paper.' He picked up the proposal and scanned it quickly. 'Yes, here it is… *"to produce plays to take the public's mind off the war for a couple of hours by giving the local audiences good populist fare."*' He popped an entire custard cream in his mouth by way of a full stop.

Randolph took a sip of tea. 'What needs to be understood, Perry, is that the masses do not necessarily have any interest in Shakespeare or the convoluted antics of the Restoration period; their tastes, shall we say, are much more basic.' He also took a custard cream and popped the whole thing into his mouth, firmly, as an exclamation mark!

Sir Peregrine chuckled again. 'You mean those light comedies from Mister Coward and Mister Travers, I suppose?'

'Amongst others, yes.'

'Well,' said Sir Peregrine as he pulled himself out of his chair and started to perambulate around the room, his hands behind his back and one hand tapping the other as he hummed a tuneless tune. 'I feel, at this juncture, I should let you into a little secret, my dear Norman.' He blew out his cheeks and then stood with his back to the fireplace. 'Although it would never be freely admitted, lest the great British public balk at the idea, the Council for the Encouragement of Music and Arts, the reason it exists – its whole ethos, in fact – is to educate the masses under the guise of, if you will, entertaining them.' He smiled across to Randolph. 'I trust you understand me?'

'Educate?' said Randolph. 'But what if they don't wish to be educated, just entertained?'

Sir Peregrine nodded, 'I'm with you, old chap; yes, yes, quite.' He walked back to behind his desk as he continued, 'The problem is that I am but a very small fish in CEMA's very large pond. As you must yourself have noted, this Whitehall office is not housed in that great historic thoroughfare. CEMA itself is not a large enough fish to have its aquarium there; wherein you find us slumming it out here in the wilds of Holborn. Would you like a cigar?' he continued, changing the subject. 'Genuine Havana. Don't ask me how I got them because I won't tell you.' He proffered the box towards him, laughing.

'No thank you,' replied Randolph, wishing to get the conversation back on track. 'So what do you think about my proposal?' he said, grabbing the bull by the horns.

'The proposal, yes, the proposal.' Sir Peregrine picked up the paper and waved it in a similar vein to Mister Chamberlain coming back from Munich. On seeing this, Randolph hoped for better success.

'You've put me in a bit of a difficult situation, Norman, I must say, but a promise is a promise and must be honoured.'

'*Floreat Etona* and all that eyewash,' Randolph mumbled, sitting himself down again.

'What? Oh yes, quite.' Peregrine laughed before continuing, 'So, do you have any idea of what the repertoire would be?'

'I'm putting that together now,' stated Randolph, although he hadn't got round to pinning any particular plays down as yet.

'Wait.' Peregrine banged his hand on the desk, which startled Randolph a little and rattled the cups and saucers a great deal. 'What was the name of that very silly play you all did at school? You were in it, I'm sure of it. You know, the one when a good few of you chaps dressed up as girls and one of you was an old woman. What was it called?'

'*Charley's Aunt*,' said Randolph, recalling this old chestnut of a farce, which seemed to have been around forever.

'Yes, that's the chap, *Charley's Aunt*,' repeated Sir Peregrine, and then they both said in unison, 'From Brazil, where the nuts come from,' a line that was repeated throughout the play to raucous laughter, if done properly. They both laughed heartily – so heartily, in fact, that Randolph imagined Miss Finch in the outer office throwing her eyes to the heavens and considering applying to another department.

'Yes, yes, a jolly romp, I recall. Four or five of you boys in skirts skipping about the stage.' Perry laughed again at the memory although Randolph did not recall any skipping going on, just a lot of running about in and out of doors and around a garden. 'Well, it's no wonder that a few of you boys became a little confused as you were going through puberty.'

Randolph shrugged; he had never felt in the least bit confused, then or now. 'You made a particularly attractive young woman yourself, I seem to remember, and were I that type, I'm sure we could have had a lot of fun together.'

Randolph shuddered at the thought of he and Porker Worsley "having a lot of fun together".

'Strange as it may seem, *Charley's Aunt* was just the sort of entertainment I was thinking of. I shall put it at the top of my list.'

'It was?' said Sir Peregrine, cheerfully.

'A first-class suggestion, Perry, thank you.' He knew it was a mistake but if he was to get any money out of the old boy then needs must when the devil drives. *May I be struck down for such brazen grovelling*, Randolph thought, taking the old Etonian by the hand and grinning from ear to ear. How in God's name he'd cast up a play about undergraduates from the group of actors he had access to, whose average age was around forty, was beyond him, but the theatre was a place of magic and illusion and he'd work that out later.

Sir Peregrine was so pleased with himself that he clapped his hands wildly, like a little boy who had just got what he'd always wanted for Christmas, 'Well, well, how wonderful. I say, what fun.'

Randolph tried to suppress a triumphant smile, whilst holding his breath.

Act One – Beginners

Had he pulled it off?

'Well, I don't have access to vast amounts of the department's cash,' Peregrine continued, pacing the room with his thumbs in his waistcoat pockets. He knew that if Mister Harrison from Accounts had anything to do with it, he wouldn't have any of the department's cash. 'But perhaps a small subsidy to start with.' He put on a serious look and peered at Randolph. 'Of course, one must tie this up with something educational, just for appearances, you understand?'

Randolph understood and had the answer ready. 'I will be needing to employ and train up a young person for the position of Assistant Stage Manager. My son, Sam, who is an expert in such things, will teach this young person all there is to know.'

'That sounds just the ticket,' said Peregrine, glad to have got that formality out of the way.

'So, is that a yes, Perry?' Randolph had his fingers crossed behind his back.

'Oh, I think so, don't you?'

Randolph marched over to him and grabbed his hand and pumped it. 'Thank you, Perry, thank you.'

'Think nothing of it, dear boy,' he said, nodding his head and making his chins wobble merrily, 'us old Etonians must stick together after all. I fear that after this little disagreement with Herr Hitler, we privileged few may become a dying race.'

'That's wonderful news,' said Randolph, referring to the beginning of Peregrine's speech and not the end. 'Thank you, Perry... or should I say Sir Peregrine?' And he bent his knee and bowed to one of His Majesty's Knights of the Realm.

'Oh no, no; no titles between old school chums behind closed doors,' Peregrine smiled.

Randolph relaxed. A good performance.

Sir Peregrine turned and placed his finger on a large map of the British Isles. 'Now, you can have a trial run of, let's say, ten weeks?' He looked round at Randolph, who nodded. He turned back and ran his finger up the east coast over Suffolk and Norfolk. 'Good. Well, I think the Norfolk coast,' he tapped the map near the North Norfolk coastline. 'The locals deserve a good laugh between the Luftwaffe dropping their bombs into the North Sea. A couple have landed on one or two of the towns, I hear, so there's a risk you all might cop it.' He turned and half smiled at Randolph, who half smiled back, thinking that he didn't relish the thought that he "might cop it" in East Anglia when he'd almost "copped it" in Chelsea on a few occasions, but beggars couldn't be choosers.

'Still, up here,' said Peregrine, tapping the map, 'there isn't much risk of anyone from this department popping up and taking a shoofty at what you're up to; I don't think they'd travel any further from London than the Chiltern Hills, do you?'

'This is marvellous, Perry.'

'Think nothing of it, old boy,' Perry said, squeezing him on the shoulder as he passed and looking at his pocket watch. 'Goodness me, look at the time. Oh dear, Mister Harrison from Accounts will, no doubt, have his quill pen quivering over a ledger, ready to take me to task over some minor expenses discrepancy, I'm sure, so I really must get on.'

Randolph nodded and then added a few more words of thanks.

'Now, you pop off. I'm sure you'll have lots to do to get your company of actors together,' Peregrine muttered as he herded Randolph through the door.

'Not in the least; I already have them,' stated Randolph.

Peregrine stopped and turned to him and let out an explosive laugh. *The little blighter's played me like a fish and I've taken the bait,* he thought. 'Well, bless my soul. Yes, I remember now,' he said, turning to Miss Finch, who had followed their exit from the main office over the top of her spectacles. 'This boy always was an optimist, Miss Finch.'

That was not the word that she would use.

'That's exactly what we need in time of war, wouldn't you say?'

Miss Finch decided that it was best to say nothing, but nodded as the man in the badly patched overcoat tipped his hat towards her and left.

Alone in the outer office, Sir Peregrine gave Miss Finch a kiss on the cheek, to which she did not demur, and then left for his meeting with Mister Harrison from Accounts. She looked around at the office and then let her mind wander to their little meetings every Thursday afternoon at a little hotel off Bedford Square, where they could forget the rigours of the war for an hour or two.

Randolph Laine came out of the lift and strode confidently across the foyer, tipping his hat to the smartly uniformed, one-armed majordomo, and made his way into the morning sunshine, affording himself a wry smile. A good job well jobbed, as his father used to say. He strode off, swinging his silver-topped cane, towards the Strand.

2

THE COMPANY

Phyllis Campbell-Bennett pushed through the heavy brass-furnished doors of Liverpool Street Station. She was wearing a full-length fur coat, which was far too hot for this late summer weather but was too large and heavy to be packed into her suitcase or the large carpetbag she was carrying. Being an old pro, she knew that when 'on the road', one had to bring clothing for every eventuality. On her head was a fur hat, which for some reason of fashion had a feather stuck in the top.

'May I take that for you, madam?' asked a railway porter, giving a rather half-hearted salute. 'May I help you with your bags, madam?' he reached out.

Phyllis recoiled slightly. 'No, no thank you. I can manage quite well.'

Why give someone sixpence to do something when one was more than capable of doing it oneself?

'Very well, madam,' said the porter, with another attempt at a salute before setting off across the concourse to find a more amenable customer.

At approximately the same time as Phyllis was getting on the Central Line Underground at Holland Park, a taxi turned up a side street, having just passed the British Library in St Pancras.

'I do hope you're not taking me around the houses,' said the woman in the back as she craned her neck to see where he was taking her.

'Beg your pardon, lady?' said the cabby.

'I said, why do we seem to be going the long way round?' Veronica East leaned forward and shouted past the glass partition that separated her from the driver.

He smiled a little to himself. 'There's a burst water main after the bombing last night in the Clerkenwell Road, so unless you want to get out and swim to the station, I'd say that this was the best route.'

Veronica decided to ignore the man, which was the way she dealt with anyone – or anything – who didn't behave as she wished them to. She bent down and very slowly slid her hands up her legs, straightening her silk stockings whilst looking up to see if the driver was taking a peek in his rear-view mirror at her. He wasn't. *What's the matter, old duck, don't fancy eyeing up a bit of shapely leg?* she thought. Of course, had she caught him peeking she would have given him a very large piece of her mind. Opening her vanity case, she retrieved from it a small compact mirror and her bright red lipstick. As she did so, a totter's horse and cart came out of a side road at full gallop with the totter hanging onto the reins for dear life as the horse bolted, having been spooked by something. The cabby hit his brakes as hard as he could, shooting Veronica forward, depositing her in the well between the backseat and the driver's partition.

'You all right, lady?' asked the cabby as he climbed out and opened the back door. He refrained as best he could from smirking as he looked at her in a heap on the floor with various items of make-up and false eyelashes strewn all over the place.

'Do I look all right, you damned fool?' she yelled, scrabbling about, trying to stop one of her lipsticks rolling out of the door. 'Get that, for God's sake; are you completely useless?'

He shook his head and decided that the best way to handle

customers like her was to let it lie; he had the upper hand when it came to the time for her to pay the fare.

'Sorry about that, lady,' he said. He could feel her cringe when he said "lady", which only added to his enjoyment. 'Totter's horse came out right in front of me.' He gathered up a few items, which she snatched from him.

'Why did you need to apply your breaks so hard?' she asked haughtily as she pulled herself back up onto the seat.

'I had no choice; I'd have killed the horse if I hadn't.' He handed her a false eyelash.

'It's only a bloody horse,' she snapped, taking the eyelash delicately from him, not wishing to touch the ghastly man. Who knew what diseases he carried about on him? She'd have to clean it thoroughly before wearing it again.

The cabby shook his head. *It takes all sorts,* he thought. If he hadn't needed the fare he'd have told her to sling her hook, but the fact was that fares weren't easy to come by these days, what with all the more well-off deciding to clear out of London away from the bombs. Unfortunately there were still a few stuck-up bitches like this one around, and their money was as good as anyone's.

They continued on their journey and were just about to pull up at Liverpool Street Station when a city gent ran out in front of them. 'Here, watch it,' called the cabby, hitting his brakes hard once more. Veronica held onto the strap to save a repeat performance. 'Five bob, lady.'

'You can have three and sixpence; I'm not paying for the time held up with that horse,' Veronica stated, firmly.

The cabby smiled; he'd knocked on the meter a couple of times without her seeing, so he was still a shilling up.

On cue, the station porter appeared at the curbside just as Veronica got out. Without saying a word – or, indeed, looking at him – she pointed to the two suitcases on the front stand of the taxi. The cabby's and the porter's eyes met and they both shook their heads.

'You won't be getting a cup of tea out of that one,' the cabby mumbled out of the side of his mouth.

The porter nodded.

Eric Cornwall had, over the years, learned to hide his limp by adjusting the weight onto his left leg in order that the right one wouldn't drag so much. This took effort on his part and when he was tired or, as now, carrying a heavy suitcase, he found it difficult to disguise.

Getting off the bus opposite the station, he waited for the road to clear of vehicles before attempting to cross. As he stood on the edge of the pavement, he noticed a very striking boy on the other side; he could swear that the boy had been looking at him, eyeing him up and down surreptitiously. Eric was a dab hand at noticing such things. *Well, you had to be, dear,* he'd thought many times, *otherwise you'd never meet anybody, would you? Pretty, but far too young,* he told himself. *Jailbait.* But then again, everything was jailbait in his world; he was just lucky that the police had never caught him. Still, no harm in window shopping was there? A rather formal city gent stopped on the pavement next to him as he waited to cross. Feeling naughty, Eric half-turned and gave the old boy a cheeky wink.

'You should be thoroughly horsewhipped, sir,' snapped the man, flustered, quickly taking the chance to cross the road, waving his umbrella angrily and nearly getting himself run over by a taxi, which was pulling up at the station. Eric couldn't resist letting out a laugh.

That would be Edgar, thought Penny Rose, *dear sweet, eager Edgar.* That happy, cheery knock, if knocks on doors could be cheery. She knew she shouldn't use him like this; she knew letting him take her to the station in his motorcar was cruel of her, that she was leading him on. He was so desperately in love with her. And

Penny? Oh, she liked him an awful lot, but he was a puppy dog; someone to play with; a mass of unruly hair and absolutely no dress sense. He had money, which was a bonus – an allowance from his father while he worked his way through five years of medical studies at the University College Hospital – but he wasn't Penny's type. Far too young, even though she was only twenty-five; she preferred a more mature man. She had one in mind but he'd dropped her, just like that. No, she mustn't think about it. Edgar was well-off and he had a sports car and Penny rather liked being driven down country lanes in the summer, her hair blowing in the wind. She just wished it wasn't dear Edgar driving her. *Stop it,* she scolded herself, *there's no point harbouring on about what might have been.* Edgar; dear, silly, not very bright Edgar. Goodness knows what sort of doctor he'll make; a rich one, that was for sure.

'Penny, old girl, are you there?' Edgar's voice came from the hallway. 'I've come to take you to the station. Are you ready?'

She opened the door and he stopped to look at her; 'You look damned ravishing,' he gushed.

'Don't be such a complete clod, Edgar,' she said, laughing at him. Why did he never seem to mind her laughing at him? Poor Edgar. She looked a mess and she knew it, in her old overcoat with a battered cloche hat pushed down on her head, a cheap cardboard suitcase and a vanity case on the floor beside her. 'I look like a bag lady and well you know it,' she scolded.

'I'd thought you'd gone off without me; taken a cab or got some other lucky bounder to take you.' Yes, he used words like "bounder" and "cad".

'Now you're just being an idiot,' she said, touching his cheek with her gloved hand. 'I promised you that you'd be my chauffer and so you shall. I hope you've got a peaked cap so you can look the part?'

Arthur and Connie Desmond travelled the Underground to Liverpool Street from Ruislip, a straightforward journey on the Metropolitan Line. Connie attempted to have a conversation about what lay ahead – the plays, the parts, the places they would visit – but Arthur sat with his newspaper open in front of him, ignoring her, for the entire journey.

From the Underground station he strode onto the pavement with just a small suitcase in his hand while Connie, fully laden with the large suitcase and a holdall over her shoulder, struggled up the steps, eventually stopping to put them on the ground for a moment in order to rest. Oblivious, Arthur spotted a rather attractive young woman ahead, who, having got out of a rather smart sports car, was making her way towards the station's main entrance. Leaping forward, he grabbed hold of the door's brass handle and opened one of them for her, tipping his hat. Penny Rose nodded and smiled; Arthur smiled back and followed her with his eyes, concentrating on her shapely legs. The smart young man who was following on with her luggage gave him what he thought was a threatening look; Arthur ignored it. Connie, watching from a distance, did her best not to get upset and, picking up the luggage, struggled on.

Through the station's tea room window, Hugh Munro pointed towards the man coming through the doors; Zelda Munro, his wife of many years, looked up, tut-tutted, and continued knitting, whilst occasionally sipping her tea. Not him, surely? And then they noticed poor Connie fighting her way through the station doors.

'I'd help her, but with my old ticker...' said Hugh, tapping where he thought his heart was.

Zelda smiled. Dear Hugh, he had always been a dreadful hypochondriac. She remembered when they were children together back on the Isle of Wight; whenever he caught the slightest cold he would be convinced that it was tuberculosis and that the men from the sanatorium were bound to turn up and take him away and put him into isolation for a year or more – unless he died, of course. Dear Hugh, yes, he'd had a little scare with his heart but nothing that a little rest wouldn't cure, the doctor had said. But Hugh wasn't convinced; he was sure that the slightest exertion would mean he was about to take his final bow.

'You stay there, dear,' said Zelda, putting away her knitting, 'I'll do it.'

'Coo-wee, Connie,' she called as she came out of the tearoom, waving her gloves in the air. They had known each other on the touring circuit for many years.

Hugh called over to the waitress for the bill and, taking out his purse, counted out the correct amount plus an extra thruppence as a tip for the girl. She thanked him and bobbed a curtsy.

'Connie… Connie dear!' Zelda called across the concourse. Connie Desmond stopped and looked about her.

'Connie, dear, it's Zelda. Don't go another step, I'll help you with your luggage, we have a trolley.'

Connie waved and put down her burden and waited for her old friend to join her.

'So, Randolph has got you and Arthur on board,' said Zelda, kissing her on the cheek.'

'Oh yes. Here we go again, so to speak,' Connie laughed and kissed her back. 'Henry didn't say you were on this one.'

'I'm afraid that Henry is getting very forgetful in his old age, and of course, he no longer has my Aunt Katherine to keep him in check.'

'An odd couple, if you'll forgive me,' said Connie, remembering Zelda's widowed aunt who had, shamelessly, allowed a man a good ten years younger than herself into her house – and indeed, into her bed – whilst setting up in business; oh, and not any old business, but a theatrical agency of all things. Connie remembered her as a beautiful but formidable figure in their agent's office.

'Aunt Kate was scandalous and that's a fact, but if it hadn't been for her, neither Hugh nor myself would even have thought of being in the business,' said Zelda, waving at the porter and pointing to the suitcases. They both laughed.

'Would you kindly put these cases on the trolley with ours, Mister and Missus Munro?' she asked as he came over.

'Certainly, madam,' he said, tipping his hat and making a mental note on how much tip he should get from this one.

'I say, would you mind not staring at my fiancé in that manner?' Edgar, red-faced, glared at Arthur as he passed.

Arthur ignored him and kept an eye on the shapely backside making its way across the concourse. He noticed his wife talking to Zelda Munro and saw that tedious husband of hers coming out of the tea room. *Oh God, not those two*, he thought. *The perfect couple. Bloody dreadful actors; so wooden. And he's more of an old woman than she is.*

'Where are the suitcases?' he asked as he wandered over.

'Zelda, very kindly, has put them put on their trolley,' said Connie.

'Honestly, darling, if they were too heavy for you, why didn't you say so?'

He smiled his most sincerest of smiles. 'She insisted on carrying both and wouldn't let me near them. Always wants to do everything herself, bless her.'

The Munros forced smiles and wondered how anyone could stand there and be such a barefaced liar.

'Well, well,' said Hugh, to break the silence, 'just like old times, eh? Only you'll find me a bit slower since my little problem.' His tapped his chest.

'Yes, I'd heard that you'd not been well, Hugh,' said Connie kindly.

'Heart,' Hugh replied, as if it was some sort of badge of honour, 'I can't do as much as I did, of course, and I can't have

Zelda lugging everything about, hence the porter. It pains me to throw away money but needs must, eh, old girl?' He nudged Zelda.

'It's only a few pennies and it keeps others in work,' she said.

'Quite the socialist, my wife,' said Hugh, knowing that neither of them would vote for Mister Attlee, even if he were the only politician in parliament.

'Have either of you any idea where we're going?' asked Arthur, lighting a cigarette.

Hugh moved away, coughing rather pointedly.

'Randolph hasn't said, he's been very secretive about it all,' said Zelda, getting herself between Hugh and Arthur's cigarette smoke. 'He just said to meet under the station clock at twelve o'clock and he'd be there.'

'Well, he isn't,' said Arthur, looking over.

Zelda looked at the watch on her wrist. 'Well, it's not quite twelve.'

Hugh laughed.

'What are you laughing at, dear?' she asked, puzzled.

'You, silly. There you were looking over at the station clock and then you go to the trouble of looking at your wristwatch to find out the time.' He laughed again.

'Oh yes, so I did. What a silly.'

Connie looked at them and then, realising, began to join in.

They're all such bores, thought Arthur as he started to make his way over to the clock, having noticed the pretty young girl standing on her own.

3

All Aboard

'Why can't they be on ruddy time?' said Randolph, looking at his pocket watch. It was just coming up to a quarter to twelve.

'Only fifteen minutes late, so far, guvnor,' said Sam, cheerfully, 'they'll be here in a minute.'

'I don't want them here in a minute, Sam, I want them here now. Half the stuff should be packed in the goods wagon already.'

'Well, they're not and that's all there is to it,' said Sam philosophically.

Randolph looked at the young lad. Eighteen years old but with a head on his shoulders of one twice his age.

'What would I do without your optimism, Sam? If only Hester could see you now, she'd be as pleased as punch,' he said, squeezing his son's arm.

'Leave this to us young chaps,' Sam said with a cheeky wink, 'You go and round up the children… sorry, I mean the actors.'

Randolph laughed and started to make his way along the platform.

'Oh, and Sam,' he stopped and turned back, 'when the lorry arrives, make sure you put the flattage on first, then the furniture, followed by the props and costume skips.'

'And what order did you think I was going to put them on,

guvnor, seeing as I've lost count of how many times I've done this?'

'Good point, old chap, good point,' roared Randolph, smiling and nodding his head.

As they spoke, two large Dawson and Son's lorries pulled into the loading area near to the train's large goods wagon. On previous occasions Randolph would have tried to squeeze everything onto one small wagon and risked damaging the scenery, but as Sir Peregrine had said that Whitehall would be footing the bill, he had thrown caution to the wind and ordered a large one.

'Here they come,' yelled Sam above the din of trains pulling in and pulling out.

Randolph made his way to the concourse, checking his coat pocket as he went to make sure he had all the tickets.

'Oh, and Sam,' he turned again, 'make sure the scenery's stacked properly; we don't want to find a pile of firewood at the other end.'

But Sam was already making his way to the goods van and out of earshot. 'Good morning, gents,' he said, addressing the railway workers whose job it was to load everything, 'before we start, let me state that what might look like a lot of old timber and badly painted canvas and some large, rickety baskets is, in fact, a treasure trove of magic, which needs to be treated as if it's the Crown Jewels from the Tower of London itself.'

The workers stopped and looked at him. They dealt with his kind all the time, and for all the talk of treasure and Crown Jewels, they treated everything in the same way, no matter what.

'We know our job, mate, so we don't needs no lessons in loading our wagons from the like of you,' said the foreman, turning to his fellow workers and shaking his head; a gesture they returned alongside a few tuts and *oh blimey*s and a 'Who does he think he is?'

The foreman then turned to the first lorry driver and his mate.

'Right,' he said, 'you two chuck it out onto the trolleys and we'll chuck it into the wagons. Look lively, this train is due out in twenty minutes.'

Sam shook his head and did his best fielding everything to stop the whole lot ending up in a heap on the ground.

Looking up the platform, Randolph saw Phyllis Campbell-Bennett coming towards him. He'd been dreading this moment, even though they went back a very long way.

'My dear Phyllis,' he said, kissing her on the cheek and stepping back to take her in, 'as beautiful and elegant as ever, if I may say so.'

'Enough of that nonsense,' she replied, not unkindly. 'I'm not taken in by all your flattery and pretty words, Randolph Laine, so you can stop that flummery before you start.'

Randolph held out his hands in mock surprise as another train rumbled, steamed and whistled into the station.

'So, dear, whatever have you got us into now?' she asked, not expecting a direct answer and not getting one.

'Phyllis, all I can say is that we'll all have a jolly time, I promise. Besides, I couldn't dream of doing this without you by my side, as you well know.' Randolph gave her a look that she had seen many times before. He could always get round her even though she did her best to stop him.

'Now, more to the point, how are you and the boy? I thought you both took the funeral very well, although it couldn't have been easy. Dear Hester, such a fighter to the last.'

Randolph nodded. 'Well, I think going on this little tour will help us through. We can never forget her, but she wouldn't want us to sit at home wallowing in grief. Apart from that, we can't afford to.'

'Dear Sam must miss her terribly,' she said, looking over to where the boy was in his element organising everything.

'Yes. He idolised her,' said Randolph.

'Well, he's a wonderful boy and I know she was very proud of him. You both did a marvellous job.'

'It's all down to Hester and the boy, they did it between themselves; I just stood back and let them get on with it,' said Randolph.

'Rather like you're doing now, by the looks of it, letting him do all the donkey work,' chuckled Phyllis.

'Well, I'm far too old for such things and besides, he's much more patient than I am with people like that,' he replied, turning to watch Sam gently remonstrating with the workmen. 'Now, shall we go and round up the troops?'

'So where is it we're going, dear?' she asked as he put his arm through hers.

'A tour of the east coast.'

'The east coast?'

'Yes,' said Randolph in the most matter-of-fact way he could. 'Norfolk, Suffolk.'

'I know where the east coast is, Randolph, but dare one ask why, bearing in mind the current situation the country is facing?'

'Because that's where Whitehall, who are paying for all this, has decreed.'

'Couldn't they have sent us to the other side of the country, Wales or somewhere?'

Randolph sighed and informed her that the area she had just mentioned was being flooded with members of the Old Vic Company.

'So the posh lot get the safe dates and we poor populists become target practice for the Luftwaffe.' Phyllis pursed her lips, cocked her head to one side and peered at him.

'Now, Phyllis, I'm sure the Luftwaffe don't actually drop their bombs on Norfolk itself, but in the North Sea.'

'From what I hear, their aim has been somewhat suspect of late and they have razed a few coastal towns to the ground.'

'Now, now, Phyllis, I'm sure that's an over-exaggeration.'

Phyllis shook her head and they walked on down the platform, Randolph taking another look at his pocket watch. Ten to twelve. Trains continued to clatter into the station, guards continued to blow their whistles and the engines answered in another key. The noise echoed around the vast cathedral roof.

Eric Cornwall was standing under the departure board when he saw Randolph approaching. He waved and smiled. Randolph raised his hat in acknowledgement.

'Oh my word, it can't be?' Eric exclaimed loudly when he saw the elegant elderly woman walking with him. Well, it certainly looked like her as they approached. 'It just can't be, I shall be in heaven if it is.'

A few passers-by looked around at the voice, some of them showing displeasure at such a display and others just amused. Eric was oblivious to them. Phyllis, however, was not, and looked askance at the young man.

'Do I know you?' she asked with a slight cut in her voice.

'Miss Campbell-Bennett,' Eric gushed, 'I saw you as Amanda in *Private Lives* at Richmond, when I was a boy.'

'You're not much more now,' she retorted, looking him up and down and reserving judgement.

'I so loved you in that. I so, so wanted to be you, in all those divine frocks and getting to kiss Miles Montgomery.'

A few more heads turned; a few more heads were shaken. Phyllis had come across many boys like him in her career.

'Dear Miles, poor soul. He didn't get back from France, I hear,' she said sadly.

Eric put a hand to his mouth, 'Oh, foot firmly placed in it. I'd no idea.'

'No,' said Phyllis, pursing her lips.

Randolph stepped forward and took Eric's hand,

'Welcome, dear boy,' he said quickly, to melt the ice a little.

'Phyllis, my dear, this is our new juvenile lead, Eric Cornwall.'

'Really?' She wasn't at all sure about this one. 'And why aren't you in uniform, may I ask?'

'Not suitable for military service. Nearly two years flat on my back.' He winked at her and pouted a little. 'And not for the reasons you're thinking. Polio – I'm a martyr to it.' He lifted his right trouser leg and exposed the withered limb and the built-up shoe beneath.

Phyllis looked at his leg and then looked up to his face.

'Well, I'm sorry. It seems that now I'm the one who has put their foot in it, so to speak,' she said, nodding her head as a mea culpa.

'Oh, don't worry,' Eric adjusted his trousers, 'every cloud and all that. Let's face it, do I look like someone cut out to go running about with a gun in my hand?' He laughed a little at himself. 'Anyway, if I'd been fit, I wouldn't have the chance of appearing on stage with the marvellous Phyllis Campbell-Bennett, would I?'

Phyllis gave him a raised eyebrow. Her raised eyebrow was known throughout the business. 'You won't get around me with a lot of old flannel like that, young man,' she said.

'Ooh, I don't know. It's worth a try,' Eric replied quickly.

Phyllis was immediately on her guard with this young man. Although she was used to this kind of behaviour, as he felt no need to conceal it himself. Homosexuality was against the law, but it was, tacitly, accepted within theatrical circles and 'West End Wendy's were not lacking in number; how many leading men were there feigning interest in, or even marrying, their leading ladies for the sake of public decency? But things were different in the provinces. Overt behaviour of this kind was more liable to be noticed and the law more stringently applied; plus bullyboys seemed to be able to smell out the Eric Cornwalls of this world. Phyllis could foresee trouble.

Meanwhile the rest of the Company were making their way

over to the station clock; all except Veronica, of course, who wasn't going to "make her entrance" with all the others. She stayed sitting on one of the benches, looking into her compact mirror, applying fresh lipstick and a little rouge to her cheeks. Satisfied that there wasn't any more damage, she put the make-up back in her bag and looked around her. It was then that she saw Phyllis Campbell-Bennett in the distance. *Oh God,* she thought, her heart sinking, *not her. What have I let myself in for? Randolph didn't say anything about... but he wouldn't, of course. And what if he had? You'd have still taken the job.* Acting jobs were bloody hard to come by with all of this war nonsense and, although she was decked in fine clothes and silk stockings with a confident – some would say arrogant – air about herself, she still needed the money – sugar daddies were hard to come by at her age.

'Oh well,' she said to herself, getting up and starting to walk towards the fray, 'let battle commence.'

Arthur stubbed out his cigarette, took a discreet swig of whisky from his hip flask and called over to the others, 'Randolph's coming; he's got the hideous Campbell-Bennett woman with him,' a comment that he really couldn't care less whether she heard or not, 'Make sure you genuflect and curtsey to the queen.'

Hugh shook his head at the man's rudeness. He liked Phyllis; she could be a bit grand at times, but she was good at what she did and had earned his respect.

'Well, I'm pleased that Phyllis is with us,' said Zelda, backing up her husband. 'At least we have a member of the Company who's disciplined.'

Arthur knew where the barb was aimed and decided to ignore the silly bitch.

Veronica East, having packed her vanity case, slowly rose from the bench and started to make her way towards Randolph and 'her ladyship'.

Eric's eyes locked onto her:

'Oh my dear, who's that tottering along on those heels?' he said, while she was still a little way off.

Phyllis turned to look then, taking a deep breath, peered straight at Randolph, who had taken out his pocket watch and was studying it as if for the first time. He knew what was coming and had been dreading it. He stiffened slightly to take the impact.

'Oh, Randolph, how could you?' Phyllis's face was like thunder and her eyes burnt into him.

'I forgot.'

'What?'

'Well, I didn't forget; I didn't think, then it was too late.'

Eric was standing with his mouth open. 'Oh my dear, isn't that Veronica East?' he said eventually.

'Unfortunately,' replied Phyllis through gritted teeth.

'She was Sybil to your Amanda at Richmond,' said Eric.

'You have no need to remind me.'

'But didn't she have a—'

Phyllis cut him off: 'If you want us to be friends on this tour, young man, I suggest you refrain from finishing that sentence.'

'My dear, I do hope you'll play nicely,' said Randolph, patting her hand.

'Randolph, as far as that creature is concerned, I shall make no promises. I'm at a loss that you could do this to me; I thought we were old friends.'

'We are, dear girl. I thought it would be all right now that Anthony and she had… I shan't go on.'

'I wouldn't if I were you.'

Phyllis closed her eyes tightly and attempted to think positive thoughts; opening them again and seeing the others in the distance, she waved over at them with forced jollity.

'I see you have Connie with us, which is lovely, although why you need to employ that appalling drunk of a husband, is beyond me,' she said out of the side of her mouth, still waving with a rictus grin all over her face.

Randolph blew his cheeks out. They weren't even on the train yet and it had started. It was his own fault, he knew that. Sam had warned him but he'd ignored it.

Veronica East was halfway down the concourse when disaster struck; one moment she was confidently sashaying towards them and the next, she had tilted to one side and fallen to her knees as one of her extensively high heels caught in a crack in the floor. The others froze and Phyllis bit her lip. After a moment's silence, Veronica let out a yell.

'For God's sake, don't all stand there gawping, help me up.'

A porter ran over to her and, grabbing her under the armpits, started to lift her:

'I'm not a sack of potatoes, for heaven's sake,' she complained, as he got her to her feet.

The porter lifted his cap and nodded, then walked off. *It takes all sorts,* he thought, as he grabbed his trolley and went about his business.

A wicker skip tipped onto its side and various costumes fell to the ground.

'Careful, gentlemen, careful. Not so fast,' said Sam.

'Do you want this lot on the train before it pulls out or still sitting on the platform?' enquired one of the Dawson drivers as he threw another skip from the back of his lorry, this time actually getting it to land onto the flatbed trolley. Sam had heard all this stuff many times over the years, but he found it best to smile and not get into an argument, which usually just ended up with nothing at all getting done.

'Carry on, gentlemen,' he said with a smile. 'Keep up the good work. Nearly done. All's well that ends well.'

'It's all right for you, mate,' said the other driver, 'you're just standing there with your hands in your pockets.'

'Not through choice, I can assure you,' Sam replied. It was true; no one could accuse him of laziness. The fact was that if he'd even so much as touched any of the items, they would have demanded to see his union card, and as he didn't belong to a union of any description they would have stopped work, there and then; bosses would have been called; words would have been said, and undertakings given that such a heinous crime would never happen again – oh, dear me, no. By this time, the train would be halfway to its destination and the scenery etcetera would be in a pile on the platform.

'Thank you, gentlemen, you're doing a grand job and no mistake,' said Sam, smiling as they looked askance at him and wondering whether to take offence at his words or not.

Unaware of the goings on at the goods wagon, the company of actors started to load themselves onto the train and shuffle down the corridor to look for the reserved compartments.

RESERVED – LAINE THEATRE COY
(LONDON – HALESTON)

read the sheet of paper stuck to the window of one of them.

'Here we are,' said Arthur, barging forward, throwing his small suitcase onto the luggage rack above and settling himself down in the window seat, facing the engine.

'We're not all going to fit,' said Penny, looking around at the others struggling along the carriage's narrow corridor with all their suitcases and bags.

'Well, I'm not moving,' said Arthur, determined that he was going to be comfortable on the journey and damn the others.

Veronica peered over at him. 'Well, there's no point in you getting comfortable, I need to change my stockings. You men will have to wait outside,' she said firmly. It was a command.

'Can't you do that in the WC?' asked Hugh innocently.

She snorted, 'Don't be absurd.'

Arthur shook his head, 'Well, I'm not standing outside in the corridor. I'm going to have five minutes' kip,' he said, and closed his eyes tightly to make the point.

Phyllis looked on from the corridor. *What a shame that the woman only fell onto the platform and not off it, preferably under a locomotive,* she thought. *No, Phyllis, for the sake of Randolph, one must keep one's council – for now, at least.*

Penny found herself jammed in the doorway by Connie's suitcases, with Hugh and Zelda pushing from the back.

'This is silly. How are we all supposed to fit in here?' she said, attempting to wriggle free.

Hugh, as ever, tried to work things out logically. 'Well, as far as I can see there's room for eight, at a push,' he said.

'Don't be so bloody ridiculous,' said Veronica, getting even more agitated. She was sure she could feel blood trickling down her leg and the thought of walking around in torn silk stockings was too much.

'Surely Randolph's booked two compartments? Check the next one,' she commanded Hugh. 'I can't move either way.'

Hugh did as he was told and looked into the next compartment. It had no reserved notice on the window and was full with two young couples and three very boisterous children.

'Not that one,' he said, over Zelda's head.

'What about the other side? Take a look on the other side,' ordered Veronica.

'There isn't one, only the WC.'

'Oh, wonderful,' said Veronica, 'not only will we be packed in here like sardines, we'll have the entire carriage going past to use the lavatory. Heaven knows what the smell will be like by the time we get to wherever it is we're going.'

'Ah, all settling in?' said Randolph cheerily as he climbed aboard.

Phyllis threw him a look and raised the famous eyebrow.

'I'd hardly say "settling". We have a slight problem with the seating arrangements; there aren't enough.'

Randolph breathed in through his teeth. 'Yes, well, I tried to get a second compartment reserved but there was no more room at the inn.' He poked his head into the compartment. 'Still, you all seem to be fitting in. Sam's staying up near the goods van so we won't have him to worry about.'

Looking on but not wishing to get involved in all the pointless bickering, Eric decided to make off down the length of the train to explore. *You never know,* he thought, *there might be a lonely soldier or sailor who needs cheering up.*

With everyone on board and right on time, the guard blew his whistle. The train whistled back and then, with a rattle and a jolt of its couplings, the engine slowly started to pull them out of the station.

Sam found it best to keep away from the actors for a while, to let them settle themselves in and get the pecking order sorted out between them, so he sat quite happily by the side of the goods wagon, reading a copy of *Oliver Twist*.

The train pulled itself through the last of the London suburbs and out towards Essex, and then up-country into the Suffolk countryside, chugging away happily whilst jostling its passengers from side to side as it rode over the points.

Having explored all the carriages down to the engine without finding a suitable young man to strike up a conversation with, Eric decided to make his way back to the others, bouncing off the sides of the corridors as he went. As he entered the carriage, he was brought up short by the sight of all the male members of the Company, along with Penny Rose, standing in the corridor outside the reserved compartment, which now had the blinds drawn down.

'What's going on?' he asked.

'We've all been banished,' said Penny. 'Well, the men have. Miss East is showing a bit of leg.'

In the compartment, Veronica rolled down the torn stocking and threw it angrily in the air. Without thinking, Connie caught it and, plunging her hand inside, felt the warm silk. She studied the damage with an expert's eyes. Zelda, meanwhile, retrieved her First Aid bag, which she took everywhere with her as Hugh was forever cutting or hurting himself and in constant need of a plaster or a bandage. Taking out a wad of cotton wool and a small bottle of iodine, she put the bag to one side.

'It's not a very big hole, Veronica,' Connie said, studying the stocking. 'It would be a shame to throw away a good silk stocking. I could always stop it running with a little varnish and a stitch.'

'You don't honestly think that I'm going to walk around with a gaping hole in my stocking? I'd look like a tart,' snapped Veronica.

Phyllis, who had got out her knitting, stifled a laugh and did a quick knit one, purl one to stop herself.

'Throw them away; I have others,' Veronica said, waving at it imperiously.

Zelda poured a drop of iodine onto the cotton wool and reached for Veronica's leg, only to have it pulled away.

'Veronica, dear, I'm trying to apply some iodine on that graze; I can't do it if you won't hold your leg still.'

'I'd love to be able to have some silk stockings,' said Connie, still examining the damaged one. 'Wherever did you get them?'

'I have friends,' replied Veronica tartly.

Phyllis held back another laugh and click-clacked away at her knitting, whilst Zelda gently lifted Veronica's leg once more.

'I'm sure I'll be able to find a cobbler to fix this heel back on,' said Connie, picking up the damaged shoe. 'It's a clean break.'

'Now sit still, Veronica, and I'll clean this up. They're not deep cuts, by the looks of it, just a few grazes,' said Zelda, inching slowly towards the first one with her cotton wool.

Veronica looked away and gritted her teeth.

'Will you just stop bloody talking and damn well get on with it,' she snapped.

Phyllis glanced up and tutted to herself.

Zelda held her council and gently pressed the soaked cotton wool onto a graze. Veronica's leg shot out as if it had received an electric shock.

'Jesus Christ!' she yelled.

Connie winced at the blasphemy but thought it best to let it go; there was no point in making things worse.

'What did you press so hard for? Christ, that stings like hell.' Another wince from Connie, but still she held her tongue.

'That's the iodine doing its job,' Zelda replied calmly.

'Are you bloody sure you know what you're doing?'

Phyllis looked. 'Oh, don't be so dramatic, Veronica. She's not sawing your leg off.'

The two of them exchanged glances. This was not going to end well, Phyllis was sure of it.

In the corridor, having heard the shouting, Hugh tried to sneak a look between the window frame and the edge of the blind.

'My Zelda is doing her stuff,' he said.

Arthur really couldn't care less, apart from the fact that he wanted to get himself sat down by the window to go to sleep. The rocking and rattling of the train, as well as the two large whiskies he'd had before leaving the house and the nips he'd been taking from his hip flask, were making him tired and even more irritable than usual – along with a slight twinge and stabbing pain at the top of his chest that he put down to acid stomach.

'There's nothing my wife can't do,' Hugh continued proudly, turning to Randolph. 'She nursed me through my heart attack. I wouldn't be here without her.'

Arthur took out his cigarette case and leaned against the window next to Penny, eyeing her up and down without a great deal of subtlety. He offered her a cigarette. She took it without saying anything. He flicked his lighter and, as if to steady his hand against the rocking of the train, he helped hold her cigarette in place as he lit it. Penny pulled away slightly.

Idly, Eric was attempting to look through the other side of the blind: 'She must have been very beautiful when she was young,' he remarked.

Hugh and Randolph looked over towards him and Eric shrugged. 'I love beautiful women; I just don't want to climb into bed with them.' He gave a little smile and then leant against the side of the train.

Arthur snorted and nudged Hugh to one side to take a look through the gap. 'Very shapely legs for her age,' he said, blowing cigarette smoke out of the side of his mouth and straight into Hugh's face.

'I say, Arthur, would you mind smoking somewhere else?' Hugh coughed a little more dramatically than was required to make his point.

Arthur ignored him.

'I think I should point out that this carriage is "No Smoking",' Hugh continued, pointing to the sticker on the carriage window.

Penny threw her cigarette butt out of the window and turned to Randolph. 'So where are we going, or is it still a secret?' she asked.

'Haleston.'

'Haleston? And where in God's name is Haleston?'

'On the east coast,' he answered. 'It used to have two theatres, but the one on the pier can't be used for obvious reasons and the other's been closed for years. It'll need a bit of a clean-up.'

'And are we expected to be cleaners as well as actors?' Arthur asked.

'Sorry, old boy,' said Hugh, quickly, 'but I'm going to have to back off heavy duties – the old ticker, you know. Need to take it easy and rest up, you understand?'

Randolph nodded, 'Yes, yes, you don't have to worry, old chap,' he said, tapping Hugh on the arm. 'It'll be a bit rough and ready to start with, I expect, but we'll muddle through, I've no doubt. The company spirit and all that.' Randolph looked around and wanted to believe that such a thing existed, which he was beginning to doubt.

'And this is it?' asked Eric.

'What?'

'The Company. This is the entire Company?'

'Nearly. There's one more but he's driving himself up,' Randolph explained.

'So there's someone with a motor?' Arthur's ears pricked up. Maybe he would be able to borrow it and see the sights, impress one or two of the local ladies.

'Yes.' Randolph nodded.

'And who might it be? Who do we know that can afford a car?' asked Hugh.

Penny was lighting another cigarette. She paused and looked over to Randolph. 'Who is it, Randolph?' Her tone was guarded and he could feel a chill.

'Teddy Shaw.'

Penny choked on the smoke. 'Teddy Shaw? You bastard.'

Randolph looked at her, confused. Now what?

Teddy Shaw had set out early in order to be able to enjoy the drive and not be in a rush. Even though his car was an open top sports model, capable of doing ninety miles an hour, Teddy wasn't interested in speed; apart from anything else, his petrol ration wouldn't allow it. Relaxed, he drove with one hand on the steering wheel and his arm on the door, with the wind blowing through his lightly Brilliantine'd hair. Dressed in shirt and slacks with a silk cravat round his throat, he was the perfect match for the car. With his matinee idol looks, he could easily be mistaken for Michael Wilding or Hugh Williams, the two British film stars of the time.

As he drove down the straight road alongside the railway line that led into Haleston, he could see and hear the locomotive passing him. A new theatre company was about to hit town. Smiling to himself, he realised that he was quite looking forward to getting back on the boards again; work had been a trifle thin on the ground recently. He was aware that his acting career hadn't panned out as he was promised, but that was partly his own fault. He had refused to play the game. So, a few weeks in the back of beyond wasn't the West End, but what did it matter? A stage was a stage wherever it was, and the public had a right to be entertained wherever they were, and that's what he loved about the business – hearing an audience laugh or gasp in horror; the sound of their applause was what kept him going. His chronic migraines may have stopped him from fighting Jerry, but he could still do his bit by entertaining Joe Public.

As the train started to pull into Haleston Station, there was the usual scramble to rescue bags and suitcases.

'No need to panic,' said Randolph in his fatherly way over the top of the ensuing chaos, 'the train terminates here.'

It made no difference; everyone apart from Penny was up on their feet, dragging cases off the luggage racks and banging into each other as the train rattled into the station.

'There's no point in sitting there, Penny,' said Phyllis, as she noticed that the girl had planted herself next to the window and was staring out of it. Her lips were tightly closed and her eyes glazed over with just the hint of tears. 'The train isn't going on, you know. As soon as the locomotive has attached itself to the other end, it'll be straight off, back to London.'

'Which is where I'm going,' Penny replied through her teeth without shifting her glare.

'Well, that's up to you, of course,' said Phyllis, picking up her suitcase and moving towards the narrow corridor as the train came to a shuddering stop. 'But in my day, one honoured one's contract, no matter what.'

'Haleston Halt, Haleston Halt,' shouted the station master over the sound of steam being let out of the side of the engine. 'All change, please, all change!'

The doors were flung open and the Company started to alight. Arthur, with just his small suitcase, barged his way through onto the platform.

'Don't push, old boy,' grumbled Hugh, 'I can't rush; have to take things slowly.'

But Arthur was past him before he could finish. Making his way along the platform, he took a swift slug from his hip flask and lit a cigarette.

At the same time, Penny pushed herself past Phyllis and Randolph as they stepped onto the platform.

'What's the matter with her?' said Randolph.

There was the roar of a car engine as Teddy turned into the forecourt of the station, spraying stones from under the tyres and coming to a halt.

'He is,' Phyllis replied, looking over at Teddy as he stood up in the car and called out, cheerily.

'Ill met by moonlight, fair Titania.' It was then he saw Penny. 'Oh, hell.' It was the first time he'd seen her since… Their eyes met and then Penny stormed off, ostensibly looking around for a taxi.

Phyllis looked on from a distance. 'He has forsworn her bed and company,' she muttered, Titania's reposte to Oberon.

'Is that right?' asked Randolph.

'I paraphrase the bard,' said Phyllis, over her shoulder.

'Can you give me any clues?' asked Randolph.

'All will be revealed in due course, no doubt.' Phyllis smiled.

'Why is it that I'm the last to know about everything?' bemoaned Randolph, shaking his head before quickly regaining his thoughts and noticing that the Company were scattering themselves to the four winds. Attempting to bring some order to the proceedings, he clapped his hands over the top of the sound of clanging as the railway men started to uncouple the engine from the carriages. He moved away from the train and tried again.

'Right, come on now, everyone. I think it best that we go straight to the theatre and get everything in, as soon as Sam has got it unloaded this end.' He looked about him to see if anyone was listening. They weren't. His eyes locked onto Connie and he continued, 'Ladies, if you'd be good enough to help Connie with the costumes, and gentlemen – yes, gentlemen, the props and scenery.'

Arthur wandered off into the platform lavatory as an excuse not to acknowledge Randolph's call to arms, and to have another swig from his flask and relieve himself.

Hugh looked concerned and, turning to Randolph, pointed to his chest and shook his head.

Randolph sighed. 'Sam, get the scenery on to one of the lorries and props and costumes on the other.'

Sam looked about him. Parked on the forecourt was just the one flatbed lorry with the legend "Taylor and Sons" on the sideboards.

'There's only the one, guvnor,' Sam called back.

'One?' Randolph looked around for the driver. 'Where's the other lorry? Has it broken down?'

The lorry driver took a pull on his roll-up and spat out a gobbit of phlegm.

'No, it's not broken down,' he answered eventually in a thick Norfolk drawl.

'Well, where is it?'

'I've no idea,' the driver replied, winking at his mate, who had just got out of the cab, also rolling up a cigarette and, following suit, spitting out some phlegm, before adding a sniff for good measure.

'Why ever not?' asked Randolph.

'Well, the thing is,' the driver paused and, lifting off his cap, scratched his head, 'we've only got the one lorry and this is it.'

'But Taylor said he could supply two,' snapped Randolph as he approached.

The driver and his mate exchanged another look; nodded to each other and then, in unison, turned back to Randolph.

'When did you speak to him, morning or afternoon?' asked the mate.

Randolph shook his head. 'Last Tuesday afternoon, if I recall.'

'Ah, well, that explains it,' said the driver.

'That explains it,' echoed the mate, and they looked at each other again and nodded once more.

'Explains what?'

'Why, he thinks he has two lorries when he only has the one.'

'Dear God, man, whatever are you talking about?'

'Our Mister Taylor likes to take a drink at The Bell at lunchtime, and that drink has the effect on him of seeing double, don't it, George?'

George, the mate, nodded. 'When he's had a bit of a drink he thinks he's got two lorries.'

'And when he's had a basin full, he sees so many of 'em, he thinks he's ruddy Pickford's!' And at that, the two of them stamped their feet and roared with laughter.

Sam looked over at them both. 'Blimey, we've been lumbered with Nervo and Knox.'

Randolph was in no mood for levity.

'I've not got time for all this. Sam, get the furniture, costumes and props on first, and you'll have to come back for the scenery.'

'Right then,' said Sam, as he looked about him for any members of the Company to lend a hand. 'Now, don't all rush at once or you'll have me over.' But for all of his attempts at humour, only Connie and Zelda stepped forward. 'That's the spirit, ladies; you're putting the men to shame. Come on, gentlemen, where's your musketeer spirit – all for one and one for all?'

Eric turned to Arthur and asked where Randolph had arranged for them to stay as he hadn't organised any digs.

'I expect he's sorted out some cheap deal with a lot of old seaside landladies,' Arthur replied, in his usual sceptical manner. He lit yet another cigarette. 'They're all a lot of lonely old souls – well, most of them.' He blew out some smoke. 'You never know, your luck might be in.'

Eric gave him a look.

'On the other hand, there might be the unmarried son hanging onto mummy's apron strings.' Arthur laughed and wandered off.

'Randolph tells me he's been able to book a local hotel at a very reasonable rate, with breakfast thrown in, so we should consider ourselves very lucky,' Phyllis stated, having overheard the conversation.

'That sounds fair.'

'It probably won't be up to the standards of the Savoy, but beggars can't be choosers.'

'I hope the rooms aren't damp,' Hugh butted in, 'or the sheets. I can't sleep in damp sheets; I'll get a chill.'

'I'm sure they won't be damp, Hugh,' Zelda reassured him. 'You mustn't worry.'

Arthur smiled and couldn't help winding up the silly old hypochondriac. 'The walls will no doubt be covered in mildew,' he stated, pulling on his cigarette. 'We're by the North Sea; with all that cold weather coming over from the Russian steppes, it stands to reason, everything will be soaked.'

Hugh turned to his wife with even more of a worried expression on his face than usual. She patted his hand and looked daggers in Arthur's direction. *Poor Connie,* she thought, not for the first time.

'Are we really staying in an hotel?' Connie piped up, hoping to lighten the mood a trifle. 'I've not stayed in an hotel since I was a little girl; we used to go down to Broadstairs and stay in The Royal Albion, which over looked the sea – it was so pretty. The waiters wore white jackets and black trousers with silk seams and the waitresses wore smart black skirts with starched aprons and they brought your breakfast to your room, if you asked for it, on large silver trays. Of course, we went down for our breakfast because Daddy said room service wasn't worth the extra money and it was much better to have one's meal in the dining room.' Connie's mind was back there. 'The crockery was fine white china,' she continued, 'and the napkins and tablecloths were starched and pressed to within an inch of their lives. And chamber maids came up to make the beds and tidy up even though Mummy made us make our beds ourselves and leave the room as we'd like to find it. And then there was a string quartet…'

Arthur, who couldn't bear his wife wittering on, turned to her sharply. 'There won't be any waiters in jackets, white or otherwise, nor any chamber maids, you ridiculous woman. There's a bloody war on, in case you haven't noticed.' He strode off. Zelda squeezed Connie's arm and gave her a reassuring smile. Connie patted her hand in appreciation.

From his car, Teddy looked on in amusement. He knew that the Penny problem would have to be tackled at some point but, for the moment, he was amusing himself by watching the usual clashing of egos, alongside all the unfulfilled dreams of those in front of him.

'Anyone want a lift? Room for a little one!' he shouted above the sounds of the locomotive being winched round on the large turntable at the end of the line, ready to puff its way up to the far end of the carriages for its return journey to London.

'Don't you have any taxis in this godforsaken place?' Penny Rose yelled, at the top of her voice, rather undiplomatically, to no one in particular.

The lorry driver looked across at her as he lifted a battered wing chair onto the back.

'You can have a lift with us, Miss,' he said. 'You can sit up front between George and me, but you'll have to watch out for the gear stick.' Whereupon he and George almost collapsed with laughter.

Sam, who was carrying the battered chaise longue with Eric, joined in. 'You can jump up on the back and stretch out on this chaise, if you like, Miss Rose, just like Cleopatra.'

But Penny was in no mood for jokes at her expense. The sight of Teddy Shaw had shaken her; her feelings towards him confounded and confused her. She hated him, or that's what she told herself, but at the same time she couldn't refrain from stealing a glance back over at him. There he was, standing by the side of his sports car, looking so smart and handsome with those bright blue eyes, those eyes that had bewitched her the first time she saw them. She stamped her foot and looked away, wiping an unwanted tear from her eye.

'Miss Campbell-Bennett, might I offer you a lift in my small, but nevertheless comfortable, sports car?' Teddy asked, respectfully.

'No, thank you, Teddy, dear.' Phyllis shook her head. 'I'm far too old to clamber in and out of sports cars. I shall walk, if it's all the same to you; it will do me the world of good to step it out and breathe in the salt sea air.'

'As you wish, dear lady,' Teddy replied, with a friendly bow. They had trodden the boards together on many occasions and never a cross word had passed between them.

'I shall see you all at the theatre,' Phyllis called out as she picked up her cases and started on her journey.

'Do you know where it is?' Randolph called after her.

'Not a clue, but I shall no doubt bump into it sooner or later, I'm sure.' And with that she strode off down the road, as if she knew the place like the back of her hand.

Before Phyllis had disappeared, Veronica crossed the forecourt and climbed into the passenger seat of the motor. Teddy looked at her and Veronica looked back.

'What?' she humphed. 'Do we really need to go through the "After you, Claude, no, after you, Cecil" routine? It's not ITMA.'

'I rather like ITMA on the wireless; that Tommy Handley makes me laugh.' Sam cut in as he carried a prop basket over to the lorry.

Veronica ignored him and looked into the car's rear-view mirror to check that her teeth had no lipstick on them.

'It's being so cheerful that keeps me going,' said Zelda with a wink to Connie as they took in the look on Veronica's face. The quote from the show's character, Mona Lott, seemed apposite and both Connie and Zelda laughed and shook their heads.

'I go; I come back,' shouted Sam to Teddy over the top of Veronica's head as he passed them again, keeping up with the catchphrases.

Veronica refused to crack her face. 'Are we going?' she asked tartly, unamused at the banter and cursing herself for mentioning the silly programme in the first place.

'I'm sorry, I didn't catch your name?' said Teddy with just a hint of irony, holding out his hand. 'I'm Teddy Shaw.' He knew perfectly well who she was and was as surprised as Phyllis at seeing her. He was aware of all the horrendous details and on present behaviour, had decided that he no more liked her than Phyllis did.

Arthur returned from the far end of the platform.

'Haven't you arranged taxis, Randolph?' he asked, without a hint of irony.

'No Arthur, I haven't, but if you'd spent less time moaning and a little more time helping, then perhaps we'd be able to sort something out.'

Phyllis made her way down the promenade, taking in the sights, sounds and smells of the seaside town. She was glad to get away from the others for a while, especially that woman. *No, Phyllis, stay calm. You're a professional, you've worked with many people that you couldn't bear the sight of but you put all that aside and ploughed on regardless – the show must go on and all that folderol.* However, that East woman was something else entirely and Phyllis could feel her heart palpitating madly as she thought about her, so she sat herself down on a bench in one of the many shelters that ran along the prom, looking out to sea. As the wind blew, the tide lapped in and out and Phyllis could hear the pebbles that made up the upper part of the beach shifting backwards and forwards. Along its length, thick iron stakes were criss-crossed at intervals as far as the eye could see, both ways, with barbed wire coiled between them as defences against the enemy landings. To the right of her, the pier reached out into the North Sea, its rusted metal supports holding up the wooden boardwalk down to the old Pier Theatre at the far end, boarded up now, of course, and looking very sorry for itself. A large gap of about fifteen feet had been made in the pier's structure, where the army had removed the boards to create a defensive "moat" in order that the enemy couldn't breach it. Beneath the gap, the sea roared in and out around its rusting superstructure, and the only way across the void was by means of a temporary bridge about two feet wide, which could be lifted up at the first sign of the invasion that most people expected to be at any moment.

As she sat looking out and listening to the sound of the waves accompanied by the seagulls' cries overhead, Phyllis mused on how many times she'd played places like this; many times, many, many times. She had a vague memory that she may have played here but couldn't recall what in. Perhaps it was just her memory playing tricks with her. These seaside towns, with their late Victorian or Edwardian architecture, merged into one after a while; perhaps not Brighton or Blackpool, but they were the exceptions that proved the rule.

She stared out to sea and pondered. It had been a strange old career. She'd never been in the front rank of the business even though she'd performed in the West End a few times in her younger days, but never in the lead. Good parts, mind, calling for solid performances. *Unfussy,* she mused, *and… solid.*

She stretched her neck out a little to look around her and let her mind wander onto this new Company. She knew Randolph, of course; they had walked out together back in the early days. She thought him so handsome then and was broken-hearted when, foolishly, she introduced Hester Simmons, her dressing room companion, to him at a party. Randolph was smitten the moment he clapped eyes on her. Eighteen years old and the prettiest girl he'd ever seen. Phyllis remembered looking at the two of them chatting away and looking into each other's eyes. She remembered how she ran off in floods of tears and cried herself to sleep and insisted that the theatre management change her dressing room. They refused. Had it not been for Hester being so… well, Hester… Phyllis may never have spoken to either of them again. For one so young, Hester was so grown up and sensitive to the moods of others; the note she left on Phyllis's dressing room bench was so heartfelt and caring, along with the flowers that accompanied it; it broke her resolve and they fell into each other's arms and sobbed uncontrollably, becoming the firmest of friends. She missed Hester. It was so cruel that one so kind and generous should have been stolen from her husband and her friends long before her death; that her mind should close down as it did, leaving just the outer shell, and those eyes that were sparkling and so full of life, should become blank and unseeing. Poor Randolph having to watch his beloved wife fading away with no memory of him or dear Sam, the boy she had saved from destitution.

This was, however, the same Randolph, Phyllis now reminded herself, that could be so completely unthinking as to employ Veronica East, knowing what she'd done to her, how she had… but she didn't want to think about it. She sighed. What was done was done and she would just have to make the best of it. *Bite your tongue, Phyllis, dear.* One honours one's contracts, she had told that silly Rose girl. And that was another thing – Randolph really had put the cat amongst the pigeons casting her and Teddy Shaw; although, to be fair, perhaps he wasn't aware of the history there. Dear Teddy, such a sweet young man. Well, not so young now but still disgustingly handsome, real leading man material. It was such a shame that he hadn't slept with the right people; hadn't slept with anyone for that matter, from what he'd told her, strictly entre nous.

As for the two married couples, she shook her head and looked up at some seagulls as a dollop of white droppings hit the glass awning above her. How apt, she thought, when thinking of Arthur Desmond, one of the most odious men she had ever met and on a few occasions had the misfortune to share a stage with. He was a complete ham; a lazy actor who failed to 'study' his lines and was constantly drying on stage and expecting others to get him out of a jam; a stage manager's nightmare. Poor Connie, having to put up with the appalling way he treated her – lording it about and flirting with any woman who looked his way. And a drunkard; thinking that hip flask of his was unseen. The only reason he worked at all was because of Connie's genius with a needle and thread; how she made even the most dreadful tat look good was nothing short of miraculous, as Phyllis had tried to tell her many times. But, poor dear, nothing could shake the idea from Connie's mind that she was the lowest of the low in the Company's pecking order. And as for her acting, Phyllis couldn't believe her eyes when she saw her in small parts; she was a natural, head and shoulders above her dreadful husband, although, admittedly, that wouldn't have been difficult.

Hugh and Zelda Munro, what could be said about them? Solid second-raters who kept going despite everything. Hugh's hypochondria could get a little irritating but Zelda's never-ending good humour and quiet nursing of her husband was endearing. She found both Zelda and Connie pleasant enough company when around the theatre although she preferred to spend the days on her own.

The young man, Eric Cornwall, would need watching – that one could get himself into a lot of trouble if he wasn't careful and even after this fleeting acquaintance, she had the distinct feeling that he wouldn't be. *Oh, really Phyllis, you can't nanny them all.*

Having got her breath, she stood up and brushed herself down before getting on the move again. As she made her way further along the promenade, she could hear what sounded like a bunch of primary school children playing. Turning, she saw where the noise was coming from – the Taylor's lorry, full to the gunnels with all the Company's furniture, props and costumes, making its way along the road towards her. Sprawled in the back amongst everything were the remaining members of the Laine Theatre Company, laughing and jeering as, behind them, Teddy was attempting to overtake them in his sports car. Penny Rose sat on the chaise longue looking out towards the sea and refusing to join in. Her reluctance was only topped by Veronica East's, who sat upright and stony-faced in the passenger seat of the car whilst Teddy beeped his horn continually before changing down a gear, flooring the accelerator and roaring past the lorry and off down the road, leaving the others in his wake.

Dear me, thought Phyllis, with a shake of her head, *this doesn't bode well.*

4

The Regent Theatre

Arriving at the theatre, the Company looked up at the exterior. The façade, it had to be said, was a little plain.

'I'm told that they've left the key under a brick by the stage door,' said Randolph to no one in particular as they made their way down the narrow alley that ran by the side of the building.

'There don't seem to be any dock doors to get the scenery in,' said Sam, having had a look around the back.

Randolph sucked his teeth and shook his head a little. 'Oh well, old chap, we'll just have to get everything in through the stage door for now and then see if we can open up the front for the big stuff.'

'Righto, guvnor,' replied Sam with a smile. 'You're the guvnor, guvnor.' With a wink he was off back to the lorry to manage operations.

'Right, everybody,' said Randolph, the genial general, 'all hands to the pumps and we'll get this stored inside in no time.'

Arthur, in time-honoured fashion, lit a cigarette and wandered off, while Hugh, also true to form, wittered on about not being able to carry anything heavy and, as expected, Zelda patted his hand to calm him.

Having found the key, Randolph unlocked the door.

Sam grabbed the heavy sofa off the lorry with George, the

driver's mate, and they made their way down the alley, closely followed by Teddy plus Hugh and Zelda with the chaise longue.

'We'll dump everything on stage for now and sort it all out when we're done,' called out Sam, squeezing himself and the sofa through the door.

Putting his end down, he peered into the gloom, looking for the entrance to the wings.

'Ain't there a light for this corridor?' asked George, peering into the darkness.

'You have a feel about on the wall for a switch, old chum,' said Sam, cheerfully, 'while I try and get some light on the stage.'

He pushed open a pair of double doors and looked through into the wings.

'Come on, what's the hold up?' asked Hugh, impatiently. 'This thing is damned heavy.'

Zelda and Teddy exchanged glances; Zelda had all the weight at her end and Teddy at the other, and Hugh stood in the middle with his hands underneath carrying a great deal of air.

'What's the problem, Sam?' asked Randolph, poking his head round the stage door and trying not to fall over a wardrobe skip, which someone had just dumped on the ground when all had come to a halt.

'There are no working lights on,' Sam called back.

'Isn't there a ghost light?' asked Hugh.

'No such luck.'

'What's a ghost light?' asked Eric, half in and half out of the stage door with a prop skip.

Arthur groaned. 'How long have you been working in the theatre?'

Eric shrugged his shoulders. 'Well, obviously not as long as you, dear. It was a simple question.'

Phyllis, as ever, came to the rescue. 'The ghost light is a light bulb, usually on a lighting stand, which is left on in the middle of the stage when the theatre goes "dark" or closed down for a while.

It's a sort of good luck charm, to tell everybody that the theatre will be back to life soon,' she said kindly.

'Oh, how sweet,' said Eric.

'Only they probably haven't heard of such things in this part of the country,' retorted Arthur.

'Not a good omen,' said Hugh, mopping his brow and sitting himself down on the chaise, which was now on the floor, while they waited for Sam to switch on a light in the wings.

To pass the time, Teddy lifted the lid of the old upright piano that sat abandoned in the corridor and started to pick out a snatch of a melody. The instrument was dreadfully out of tune and certain notes just clonked when he pressed the keys but, getting into his stride, he launched into a rendition of a Mozart piano sonata, which he played with as much gusto as he could muster – more in the vein of Scott Joplin than Arthur Rubinstein.

Sam peered into the darkness and delved into his pocket, bringing out some matches. He struck one. In the distance he could just make out a cat ladder that led up to a lighting perch about eight feet above the stage level, which he guessed would have the main light switches. Striking another match, he slowly made his way towards the ladder and had just put a foot on the bottom rung when a gruff voice came out of the darkness.

'You can't go up there.'

Sam jumped back and looked to see where the voice came from. Out of the darkness he thought he could just make out some sort of figure ahead of him, then a small shaft of light hit him full in the face.

'You can't go up there,' the voice repeated as a torch played on Sam.

He shielded his eyes. 'Hello, Sam Laine, stage manager for the Laine Theatre Company.'

'You can't go up there,' said the voice once more, like a stuck record.

'We're just waiting to bring our stuff in,' said Sam. 'May I ask who you are?'

'Tuppence,' said the voice, not lowering the torch.

'Tuppence?' said Sam.

'Tuppence,' repeated the voice.

'Is that your name?' asked Sam gently.

'Tuppence.'

'I see,' said Sam, not seeing anything in reality. 'Do you have another name? I'm Sam; what's yours?'

'Tuppence.'

'Yes, and a first name?'

'Mister Tuppence.'

'Mister Tuppence?'

'Mister Tuppence.'

'Well,' said Sam, realising that this wasn't getting him anywhere, 'it's very nice to meet you, Mister Tuppence.' Sam held out his hand; the gesture wasn't reciprocated.

'What in God's name is going on?' asked Veronica as she pushed her head round the stage door.

'Sam's trying to get some lights on,' said Hugh. 'There isn't a ghost light, for some reason.'

'Are we going to stand about here all bloody afternoon?' Arthur chimed in.

Teddy, still tickling the ivories, chirped up with a bit of Shakespeare, as he often did at times like these. 'How poor are they that have not patience! What wound did ever heal but by degrees?'

'*Othello*,' chimed in Hugh.

'Indeed,' laughed Teddy, and with that he continued with the sonata on the piano.

'Do we really need to be bombarded with Shakespeare?' Arthur could never remember quotes so got angry and disparaging of others who could. He wanted a drink and his hip flask was empty.

'And I hope that isn't bloody German music,' he snapped. 'The last thing I need is ruddy Jerry music.'

'Mozart, born in Austria,' replied Teddy, bringing the music to a crescendo.

'Well, at least that's something,' Arthur said back.

'The same as Hitler,' said Teddy, stopping and slamming down the piano lid.

Randolph placed his head around the corner and peered into the wings. A light was juddering up the wall as someone was climbing some sort of ladder.

'Sam, old chap, is that you? Have you found the light switch?'

'Mister Tuppence is just doing it now,' said Sam.

'Who did you say?'

'Mister Tuppence, guvnor.'

'Who's Mister Tuppence?'

The working light above the stage came on to bathe it in a rather dull, flat light.

'He is,' replied Sam, pointing up at the lighting perch.

Randolph looked up at a strange-looking man. 'Oh, right,' he said and then, rather unwisely, called up to him another piece of Shakespeare's *Othello*. 'Put out the light and then put out the light.'

The theatre was immediately plunged into darkness.

'No, no, Mister Tuppence,' said Randolph, waving his hand about.

Sam called up to him, 'Put the lights on again, Mister Tuppence, please. Lights on.'

'You'm wanted them off,' said Mister Tuppence in his rather strange lazy Norfolk accent.

'On, please, if you would be so kind,' Randolph called up.

There was a heavy sigh from above and then a clunk as the working light came on again.

After much lifting, cursing and swearing, skips, props and the furniture were eventually dumped higgledy-piggledy all over the stage. Claiming utter exhaustion, the Company collapsed onto the various items of soft furnishings.

'I really shouldn't have been asked to carry that table in,' said Hugh. 'I've a pain in my chest, I can feel it.'

Zelda dutifully rooted about in her bag and brought out the bottle of pills she had standing by for just such occasions. 'Take these, dear,' she said, 'and I'll get some water. Don't worry yourself, it'll just make it worse.'

Teddy walked out to the front of the stage and looked into the auditorium, which consisted of just a stalls level; the seating gently tiered with no circle or boxes. He turned to call up to the perch, 'Excuse me, Mister…?'

'Tuppence,' said Sam as he walked about the wings, getting a feel for the space.

'Yes, Mister Tuppence, I wonder if you'd be good enough to put the house lights on.'

Up on his perch, Mister Tuppence stopped polishing the handles of the dimmer controls on the large lighting board in front of him and turned to look over the rail to the stage.

'No one out there,' he said, and went back to his cleaning.

Teddy held up his hand and called up again. 'Yes, that's true, but you see, I like to be able to look out there, to take a look at it. Actors like to do things like that; we're funny that way.'

Without a word, Mister Tuppence hung his cleaning cloth over one of the dimmer handles and, searching out the correct dimmer control, grabbed hold of the handle and slowly raised it. The house lights came up in the auditorium.

They all took it in. The theatre was rather plain and had no architectural features as such.

'Well, it's no Matcham, that's for certain,' said Hugh.

'What was that?' asked Eric.

Hugh looked at him, rather disgusted. 'Frank Matcham, probably the finest theatrical architect that has ever lived.'

Eric gave him a blank look.

'The Hackney Empire,' said Zelda.

'The Palladium,' said Hugh.

'The Coliseum,' Phyllis piped up.

'The King's, Glasgow,' said Zelda.

'And Southsea,' Hugh chimed in.

'The Grand, Blackpool,' Zelda rhapsodized. 'Such a beautiful theatre.'

'Every one a masterpiece,' Hugh said, determined to have the last word on the matter.

'What's grand? What are you all talking about?' asked Veronica, walking back on stage having had a look in the wings and only catching the last few sentences.

'Hugh was saying that this theatre isn't a Matcham,' Zelda explained.

Veronica snorted. 'A Matcham? Dear God, look at it, it's more like a matchbox.' She lit a cigarette whilst snorting at her own joke.

It was true. It boasted no circle or boxes, no delicate alabaster plasterwork with gold relief; just a tiered lower stalls consisting of, Teddy guessed, around three hundred seats, if that, surrounded by plain plaster walls painted a dull off-white that was peeling in the corners.

'All the world's a stage and all men and women merely players...' Teddy suddenly let rip with Jacquie's speech from *As You Like It*, revelling in the cliché.

As he spoke he wandered from side to side of the stage, listening to his voice coming back at him off the back and side walls. He was just doing what every actor should do when arriving at a new theatre – checking the acoustics to see how much voice was needed to get across to the audience; there was no point in over using it if you didn't need to, and the public didn't want you to shout at them. 'They have their exits and their entrances,' he continued, 'and one man in his time plays many parts.' He stopped.

'Quite good,' said Phyllis, who'd been listening, 'A bit flat and dull when you were stage left, Teddy; we'll have to remember that.'

'At least it didn't die completely and fall on the floor when it hit the walls,' Hugh chimed in.

'The place is bloody empty,' Arthur couldn't help chipping in. 'It's probably like a wet dish cloth when the great unwashed are out there.'

Teddy shook his head, 'That's what I've always loved about you, Arthur, your unadorned optimism.'

'Well,' said Veronica, getting up and starting to look around, 'I'd say this place is a dump.'

'You'd prefer the Coliseum, perhaps, or the Theatre Royal in Drury Lane, I suppose?' said Phyllis, heavy with irony. 'The fact that neither of those illustrious theatres would have you anywhere near their hallowed stages…' She left the sentence hanging in the air and sat herself down again.

Connie was on her knees, feeling the front curtains.

'I'm going to have to get my needle and cotton out on these tabs,' she said, referring to them by the name theatre people called them. 'They're a bit worn through, but never mind, I'll soon have these as good as new.'

Forever the optimist, thought Zelda, as she looked over at her old friend.

'Not even proper tabs,' said Arthur from the other side, looking up above the stage. 'Not flown; there's no grid. This is more like a ruddy village hall than a theatre.'

The others ignored him. There was no point in trying to argue with the man as nothing would please him; he'd find fault with the Royal Opera House.

'Does anyone know what plays we're meant to be doing?' asked Hugh, rather clumsily changing the subject.

Randolph tapped his nose. 'All will be revealed in good time,' he said. Veronica grunted and Penny shook her head.

'Why all the damned secrecy?' Penny asked, not unreasonably.

'Careless talk costs lives,' replied Randolph, his tongue firmly in his cheek.

'We're talking about some bloody dreadful plays, not Churchill's invasion plans.' Penny was not in the mood for levity.

'I think you'll find, Penny, that those 'bloody dreadful plays' are going to be paying your rent and putting food in your mouth for a while,' said Phyllis crossly.

'Oh, I don't think Mister Churchill has any invasion plans,' said Connie, having only heard a part of the conversation and taking things a little too literally.

'What?' Penny snapped, wondering what the silly old dear was going on about.

'Well, after the evacuation from Dunkirk, surely it will be Hitler invading, if anything. Not that I'd want that, of course,' Connie tried to explain.

'Just let him try,' said Hugh patriotically, 'Our boys will soon beat them back.'

Arthur leant against the proscenium arch and pulled on yet another cigarette. 'Some hope,' he sneered. 'If Hitler decides to invade then we're all done for.' He couldn't bear all this patriotic nonsense. 'Once Jerry is here it won't be long before we're all marched into a field and shot.'

'Charming,' said Teddy, wandering off aimlessly in order to get away from all the negativity.

'Now, let's not have any of that kind of talk.' Randolph turned to the assembled Company and waved his hands in the hope of calming things down. 'Our job is to cheer the public up, not depress them. Let's hear no more of Hitler invading these islands in this theatre, if you please.'

Arthur shook his head. 'You may have your head stuck in the sand, Randolph, but we won't be singing *God Save the King* after every performance, more like *Deutschland Über Alles*.'

'We've got your scenery here,' said a voice from the wings. 'Where do you want it?'

'Thank God,' exclaimed Randolph. Whether he was referring to the scenery arriving or the excuse to change the subject, even he wasn't sure. 'Well, you'll have to bring it through the front doors,' he answered. 'Mister Tuppence, are the front doors of the theatre open?'

'No,' came the reply, after what seemed to be an age.

'Well, do you have the key?'

Mister Tuppence calmly folded his cleaning cloth and hung it over the large brass wheel at the end of the board. Without a word, he slowly climbed down the cat ladder onto the stage, and then down the steps to the auditorium, and walking very slowly, he made his way towards the front of the theatre while the Company looked on.

'Thank you, thank you!' Randolph called after him, to no response.

Sam appeared. 'Scenery's here, guvnor.'

'Yes, Mister Tuppence is opening the front doors, I hope.'

'Righto.'

'Arthur, give them a hand, would you?' said Randolph, wishing he hadn't as soon as the words left his mouth.

'I thought I was hired as an actor, not a damned navvy,' Arthur stated without moving.

'I'd help out, of course,' Hugh chimed in, 'only…'

'Yes, yes, we know,' said Arthur, putting him down.

'Don't you worry, Hugh, old chap, you just sit down. We'll cope, I'm sure.' Randolph wished he was back in his house in Fulham with a glass of whisky in his hand and a well-thumbed copy of *David Copperfield* opened on his lap.

Arthur threw out a "dear God" and wandered off.

'Randolph, dear,' said Connie, 'do I have a room for the wardrobe?'

'Yes,' replied Randolph, glad to be moving onto something more useful. 'There's a lovely large room at the far end of the corridor, I'm told. No stairs, you'll be glad to hear.'

No stairs, thought Connie, *such bliss.* Just about every theatre in the country had the wardrobe room right at the top of the building, up endless sets of narrow concrete stairs. She never could understand why they never thought of putting it on the same level as the stage – it would have made much more sense.

'Oh, how wonderful,' she exclaimed loudly. 'In that case, do I have a volunteer to help me move the costumes from here?'

No one moved, as expected.

'I couldn't possibly,' said Veronica, suddenly reaching down to rub her leg, 'I need to stay seated.' She sat down. 'My leg is playing up, dreadfully. I may even need to rest it completely tomorrow.' She attempted to throw Randolph her sweetest look.

Teddy raised his eyes to heaven.

'No need to worry, Veronica, we'll be reading through the play tomorrow morning,' Randolph said with his most sincere look. 'You'll be able to do that sitting down, dear.' *Bloody woman, why was I so stupid as to cast her? I really must be losing my marbles.*

Phyllis looked on and marvelled at the woman's performance; the wincing, with just a hint of a whimper, poor soul. *Worthy of an award,* she thought, turning away.

Patting Hugh's hand, Zelda pushed herself up off the sofa. 'Here, Connie, dear, let me help you.' She brushed past Veronica's leg as she made her way over.

'Why the damned wardrobe things couldn't have been put straight into the room is beyond me,' Veronica added to get in the last word, checking her face in her compact mirror for no reason. 'It would have saved all this nonsense.'

Teddy looked on from a distance. Whatever happened to the company spirit? The camaraderie of a group of players touring the country, like Priestley's *Good Companions,* a book that he'd read many times and would love to stage: Randolph as Jess Oakroyd; himself as Inigo Jollifant; Miss Trant, well, Phyllis of course; and Penny as Susie Dean. The Dinky Doo's; this lot were turning out to be The Dinky Don'ts.

'Well, this place has certainly seen better days,' he said, bringing himself out of his reverie and leaning against the front of the stage.

Penny did her best not to look at him; she lay back on the chaise and took a long and rather affected pull on her cigarette.

'This awful dust will have to be got rid of,' Veronica chipped in, whilst powdering her nose and sending scented powder into the air. 'It'll play havoc with my vocal chords.'

'And do you think we could ban cigarettes on stage, unless they're needed for business?' Hugh commented as the smoke from Penny's cigarette wafted by him. He could swear they all did it on purpose.

Penny opened one eye and blew a perfect smoke ring in defiance.

Hugh coughed rather too loudly and made great play of clearing his throat.

Trying not to show his despair, Randolph clapped his hands and assured everybody that they'd soon have the place ship-shape and Bristol fashion.

'I just hope it isn't holed below the water line,' thought Phyllis, idly.

'*Then tis time to do't, hell is murky,*' quoted Teddy, climbing back on stage while committing the cardinal sin of quoting from Macbeth in a theatre out of context.

Hugh took a sharp intake of breath as Phyllis turned on Teddy angrily. 'Not the Scottish play, Teddy; you know better than that.'

Teddy did, indeed, know better, but it had come out before he realised it. 'Go outside immediately, turn round three times, spit and then swear,' said Phyllis, in perfect seriousness.

Both Veronica and Penny exchanged glances and sniggered. Hugh put his head in his hands, imagining that the entire enterprise was now doomed.

Randolph sank into the armchair, deciding that he hated the lot of them.

Teddy, looking only the slightest bit sheepish, started to make his way towards the stage door. '*Bid me farewell and let me hear thee going,*' he said, taking a sweeping Elizabethan bow as he left.

Eric looked about him, waiting for someone to do something:

'*The rest is silence,*' he quoted to break it. 'Is there a broom?' he asked, eventually. 'Has anybody got a broom? I'm a dab hand with a broom.' *Well,* he thought, *sweeping up would be better than just sitting about.*

Veronica rose from her seat and started to make her way into the auditorium, passing Eric as she did so.

'A proper little housewife, aren't we,' she said, with a sneer. 'I'm sure that the stage manager could rustle up a feather duster for you.'

Eric looked at her as she swanned by him and his joy at meeting her at the railway station started to evaporate. *It could fast become a competition to see who could out-bitch whom,* he thought.

'Put a pinny on me, dear, and I'm anybody's,' he called after her.

Phyllis stared across at him. 'I think, young man, you should be a little more careful about your behaviour. The theatre, of course, is one thing, and your personal life is none of my business,' she said quietly, 'but this isn't London and the locals won't be used to people like you, to put it mildly.'

Eric turned and smiled at her. 'Don't you worry about me, Missus CB,' he said rather cheekily.

Phyllis snapped back. 'And I think that it's about time you learned some manners and respect,' she said sternly. 'My name is Miss Phyllis Campbell-Bennett, and I've been treading the boards since well before you were born. You have permission to call me Phyllis, if you learn some manners; otherwise it will be Miss Campbell-Bennett. But never,' and she waved her finger towards him, 'never – I say, never – CB. I am not Cochran and you, for all your effeminate ways, are not Dougie Byng,' she said, referring to the theatrical producer of the time Charles (CB) Cochran and one of his many star performers, Douglas Byng, who somehow got away with a persona onstage that if he were caught out in the street behaving in the same way, would be thrown into prison. Eric raised an eyebrow, smiled and wandered off to find a broom.

Hugh had been following the exchanges and was on Phyllis's side regarding the boy's behaviour; no good could come of it. Not that he was against it. Well, having been in the business since he was sixteen, he'd come across it enough times, and if Zelda hadn't been with him, he was sure he'd have been "given the eye" by many a fellow actor.

'Do we have any stage management, Randolph?' he asked.

'There's only Sam at the moment, but I've asked for a card to be put up in one of the shops for a local volunteer.'

'I'm sure there'll be some poor stage-struck child out there somewhere, wouldn't you say, Hugh?' Phyllis said with a smile.

'I'm afraid there usually is, Phyllis; yes, I'm afraid so,' he replied, remembering how he and Zelda were "discovered" as children, all those years ago.

And they were both right.

Molly Baxter had seen the Company arrive from her bedroom window above the café her parents ran, just across the street from the front of the theatre. She had the card in her hand and had been waiting for the right moment. Her mother suggested that it would probably be best if she waited a while so they could get settled in; they didn't need an over-excited young girl dancing about them making a nuisance of herself when they'd just arrived, did they? Her words were said with love; she wanted her only child to be happy again. They had both been plunged into such enormous sadness after receiving the news of her father's ship being lost with all hands. For the first time in three months, Jane Baxter could see a glimmer of light coming back into her daughter's eyes. And she had no wish to knock her back.

Running downstairs, Molly popped her head round the door of the kitchen, where her mother and aunt were preparing the ingredients for the next day's luncheon menu. Molly stood with an eager look on her face and when her mother nodded and gave her a huge smile, her heart leapt and she ran out of the door and across the road.

In the alley by the stage door, Teddy was going through a ritual. He knew it was all stuff and nonsense, of course, but if he didn't go through the motions and something dreadful happened on stage then he'd never forgive himself and Phyllis would never let him forget it, which was even worse. He closed his eyes tight and turned around three times, very slowly, making sure he didn't spin himself into the wall – one, two, three, the required amount. With his eyes still closed, he brought up a gobbit of spit and spat it onto the ground close by and then, not too loudly, proceeded to swear. 'Bugger,' he said, and then, throwing caution to the wind, he let it all out in full force, thinking about the Penny situation as he did so. 'Bugger, bugger, bugger.'

On opening his eyes he jumped back, as standing only a few feet away was a young girl of around fifteen or sixteen, with a look of mild shock and amazement.

'I'm so sorry,' said Teddy, trying to gain his equilibrium. 'I hope I didn't—'

She interrupted him. 'Are you one of the theatre people?' she asked.

Teddy laughed. 'Yes, yes. How did you guess?'

Tilting her head to one side, she asked what he was doing; she thought it seemed rather odd.

'Yes, it is rather odd, you're right there,' he replied with a smile. 'All a bit silly, really.'

'Then why do you do it?'

'Superstition,' replied Teddy. 'The theatre is full of superstitious nonsense. I'm sorry if I offended you.'

Molly seemed to ignore the apology and held out the card. 'I've come about this advertisement I saw in Claxton's window,' she said.

'Claxton's?'

'Mister Claxton, the newsagent, next to Mister White, the chemist,' she said, quite innocently.

'Oh, the Mister Claxton next to Mister White's,' Teddy answered with a smile. He looked at the card. '*Volunteer required for theatrical work*,' he read. '*Assistant Stage Manager wanted. Enquire Mister Randolph Laine, esquire, Producer, The Laine Theatre Company c/o Regent Theatre.*' Teddy looked up at the girl. She seemed a little young but was obviously brave enough to put herself forward; yes, a good requirement for an assistant stage manager.

'So, are you an assistant stage manager?' he asked, not unkindly.

'I don't know,' Molly answered honestly.

Teddy put on a serious face, which in reality wasn't that serious at all. 'I see. I take it from this that you'd like to be an assistant stage manager, even though you don't know what one of those is; is that right?'

'I think so,' Molly answered.

'Right,' said Teddy in response. 'So can I take it that as you don't know what one is, you don't know what it is you'll be asked to do.'

Molly shook her head and looked at her shoes. She could feel the hope that she'd nurtured since seeing the card ebbing away. 'No,' she said softly.

Teddy's heart was breaking for her. He placed his hand under her chin and lifted it, and bent down so he could look her in the eyes. He could see the tears welling up and feel her body starting to shake.

'Well, first of all, I think I should tell you that, in my professional opinion, you look to me exactly like an assistant stage manager.' His voice was calm and kind.

Molly, in her despair, didn't take in what he said. Teddy let her have time to work it out. Very slowly, he could see her eyes brighten a little and a slight look of confusion crossed her face as the realisation of his words sank in.

'Do you really think so?' she asked falteringly.

'Believe me, I've worked with many assistant stage managers in the last... no, I'm not going to tell you how many years, but a lot – and in all those years I've never seen such a perfect fit for the job as you.'

Molly couldn't believe her ears; she was so amazed that she forgot to breathe and the "thank you" that came out was almost inaudible.

'I tell you what, why don't I give you a quick lesson in what the job is and then we can go and see the boss?'

Molly's face brightened. 'Would you like a cup of tea at the same time? My mum runs the café across the street,' she said.

'Do you know, that is a perfect idea.' Teddy laughed. 'You see, you're doing it already.'

Molly looked blank.

'The best way for an ASM to get an actor to do what you want him to do,' Teddy explained, 'is to offer him a cup of tea. Would there be a halfpenny bun going as well, do you think?' At which they both laughed and made their way over to the café.

Back inside the theatre, slowly but surely the scenery was unloaded from the lorry. Sam and Arthur came down the aisle carrying the last of the stage weights and braces.

'These things weigh a bloody ton,' said Arthur, who was struggling along with one weight in his hand.

'Twenty-eight pounds apiece, to be exact,' said Sam, who was happily carrying two.

'If I get a hernia...' Arthur stopped and dumped the weight onto the floor, dropping it a few inches from the ground so as not to trap his fingers, which he had already done once and was determined not to repeat. 'That's as far as I'm taking that.' The twinge in the top of his chest had returned briefly.

Sam shook his head and stepped over the abandoned weight and continued down the stalls towards the stage.

'Where is everybody?' asked Arthur, seeing that the stage was deserted.

'I can hear voices in the corridor,' said Sam as he put his weights down against the back wall. 'They're taking a look at the dressing rooms by the sounds of it.'

Which was indeed what they were doing when Sam and Arthur made their way to the dressing room corridor.

'Well, that can't be helped, I'm afraid,' they could hear Randolph saying, his voice a little strained.

Veronica was pacing up and down, 'I really think it too much that I should have to share,' she stated loudly, opening various doors, looking in and then slamming them shut.

Randolph tried again. 'There are only two rooms we can use, as I've said before. Boys in this one,' he opened a door to reveal a long room with dressing room mirrors, which could take all the men at a pinch, 'and this one,' he turned and opened a door next to it, 'for the ladies. Or the other way round if you prefer; they're both roughly the same size.'

'Small,' said Penny archly before walking off.

Arthur shook his head. He had done his bit, as far as he was concerned, and was in no mood for hanging about the theatre any longer.

'Randolph, do we really need to do this now? I'm dying for a drink.' The hip flask in his pocket was in desperate need of a refill.

'More to the point,' chipped in Hugh, 'we haven't booked into the digs yet and I'm in need of a bit of a lie down.'

Randolph did his best to hold his temper. He'd had some difficult companies in his time, but this bunch were trying his patience already and it was only the first day.

'Yes, all in good time,' he said, close to snapping, 'and it's an hotel, not digs, Hugh. We just need to get this sorted out tonight; I don't really want to waste time tomorrow morning going through it all; we'll need to get on with rehearsals, otherwise we'll run out of time.'

Veronica made her way further along the corridor, determined not to give up. She opened a door at the end and looked in; the room was tiny but it contained a small table and a mirror on the wall and was obviously the star's dressing room, if such a small theatre could be said to have had any stars performing there.

'This one,' she said, suddenly. The others turned. Randolph physically wilted, realising that he was now in a very difficult political position. He walked down the corridor and looked into the room. It was the one he'd been told about and had kept up his sleeve.

'Well, the thing is Veronica,' he stated quietly, 'as Phyllis is, I think you'll agree, the senior and most experienced member of our little Company, I thought—' But his thought was interrupted. Veronica knew exactly what his thought was; she'd known it as soon as she had seen the room and she was determined to nip this thought of his in the bud, *tout suite*.

'Nonsense,' she proclaimed loudly, making sure that everyone would hear her. 'Phyllis is a team player, aren't you, Phyllis?' She was staring Phyllis in the eye. 'She'd hate not being with the other ladies. She likes nothing better than a good old gossip while putting on her slap. Don't you, dear?'

Phyllis's face stayed resolute. She was not going to let the bitch get to her; she was determined to hold her fire for now until she was certain that she could get a bullet into the woman's heart.

'How right you are, Veronica,' she said. 'There is nothing I like more than a natter over a cup of tea; so much more pleasant than sitting by oneself playing patience.' They exchanged looks. 'Please take the room, I have no need of it – but thank you for the thought, Randolph. As ever, the perfect gentleman.'

Dear Phyllis, a complete professional and good friend, thought Randolph.

Teddy Shaw popped his head around the corner and took in the sight before him. *Time to break all this up,* he thought, having heard the tail end of the conversation.

'There they are,' he stated a little over loudly but succeeding in pulling the attention away from the two women. He turned to Molly to give her a final bit of advice. 'Just remember what I told you and everything will be tickety-boo.'

Molly nodded and took a deep breath. Teddy had given her all the information she needed for the job, including not being scared of Randolph; he was a pussycat and not a tiger, he had said, so he wouldn't bite.

'Ah, Randolph.' Teddy put his arm round Molly and they marched confidently down the corridor. The Company looked the girl up and down. Penny turned away, not wanting to look at either of them.

'I wondered where you were, Teddy. I've been explaining about the dressing rooms.' Randolph, as ever, was in his own little world and it took him a moment to register the young girl.

'This is Miss Molly Baxter and she would like to become our Assistant Stage Manager.' Teddy gently pushed her forward and placed his hands on her shoulders to hold her steady should she start to shake, as before.

Randolph, glad that the subject of dressing rooms had been

superseded by something less onerous, put on his serious theatre producer's face (or what he thought was one) and looked at Miss Molly Baxter.

'Well,' he said, just for something to say until he could think of anything else. 'So tell me, Miss Baxter, you want to be our ASM, do you?'

She nodded. 'Yes.'

Teddy had told her that "assistant stage manager" was a bit of a mouthful so people tended to refer to them as ASMs.

'And have you ever been an ASM before?' Randolph continued in a kindly but ever so slightly serious tone.

'No, sir,' said Molly in the smallest voice that anybody had ever heard – or in this case, not heard.

'What was that?' asked Randolph, holding his hand up to his ear and cupping it.

Teddy leant down to her. 'You'll have to speak up a bit, Molly,' he said. 'ASMs sometimes have to shout very loudly to get over the din of actors chattering all the time.' The last few words were said very pointedly towards the others in an attempt to try to make them have some common decency and not mutter and make the poor girl even more nervous than she was already.

'Well?' said Randolph, to prompt her to answer again.

'No, sir,' she said in a firmer and louder voice.

Randolph then asked her if she knew what an ASM did.

Having gone through just about everything that could be gone into while drinking a mug of tea and munching on a halfpenny bun, she felt confident in answering while it was fresh in her mind. Teddy squeezed her shoulders and she, taking a deep breath, launched into her speech.

'The job is to set the properties… the props, for the actors on stage or in the…' The word was on the tip of her tongue but… something like birds…

'Wings,' Teddy said out of the side of his mouth.

'Yes, wings,' she said, kicking herself and then losing track of what she was meant to say next. Oh, yes. 'Take charge of the prompt book and make sure that everybody knows their words, make the tea and do just about everything else backstage.' She let out a long breath and could feel her face burning.

Randolph smiled at her and then turned to the Company. Connie, Zelda and Eric clapped enthusiastically. Hugh just wanted to have a lie down and Arthur leant against the dressing room door, hoping that all this nonsense would be over soon so he could get to the pub.

'Jolly good,' said Randolph, 'that sounds about everything, I'd say. Now, what about your age?'

'Sixteen, sir,' she said.

'And you said that I was too young,' said Penny into Teddy's ear as she pushed past the lot of them. Teddy wanted to answer back but knew that this wasn't the time or the place.

'Well, Miss Molly Baxter, do you think that your mother and father would approve of you wanting this position?'

Molly's head dropped and she could feel the tears in her eyes, not from fear but the thought of her late father welling up within her.

'Daddy's ship was lost with all hands back in January,' she said, her bottom lip quivering, 'but Mummy…' She couldn't finish the sentence.

'I've met Molly's mother – she runs the café over the road and she thinks that this would be a good thing for her to try,' said Teddy softly.

'Oh, poor dear,' said Connie, wanting to give the girl a big hug.

'I'm so sorry, Molly, I didn't wish to upset you,' said Randolph, a little at a loss. 'Well, in that case, there's nothing else to be said except, on behalf of the entire Laine Theatre Company, to welcome you as our newly appointed Assistant Stage Manager.'

Connie, Zelda and Eric applauded again, Hugh muttered a "well done", Veronica was just glad it was all agreed, and Arthur weighed up in his mind how this little innocent might come in useful.

'How marvellous to have such a lovely young lady in the Company,' said Phyllis, coming forward and shaking the rather bemused Molly by the hand.

'This is Missus Campbell-Bennett, Molly,' said Randolph. 'She is the most experienced member of our Company and should be treated with great respect,' he continued a little pompously, with a little dig in the direction of Veronica.

'Nonsense,' said Phyllis. 'You must call me Phyllis, and I will call you Molly, and we will be great friends, I'm sure.' Phyllis stroked Molly's face and smiled.

'Is that it? Can we all be let out of school now?' Arthur said pointedly. 'Well, whether we are or not, I'm off for a drink.'

'I really think we should check into the hotel first,' said Randolph. 'It's on the front. It might even have a licensed bar.'

'As long as it has dry sheets, I'll be happy,' Hugh chimed in.

5

The Cliff Hotel

The Cliff Hotel sat high up, as the name suggested, almost directly opposite the pier below. It was a large imposing building, which loomed over the landscape. There were two ways to reach it from the promenade below, either by way of the steep concrete steps that zig-zagged their way up the face of the cliff itself, or by the more gentle but round-about narrow road that wound lazily up to it. Whichever way you took, you would eventually notice that its red brick façade was visibly crumbling in places, and the window frames and the timber around the front doors gave away the fact that the damp and salty sea air had eaten into the fabric of the wood, which was only being held together by large amounts of paint, although even this was now peeling away to expose the precariously rotting timbers.

'It's as big as The Savoy,' said Connie excitedly, her childhood memories once more coming to the surface as they all stood back looking up at it, having taken the more genteel route.

'The rooms will be freezing cold,' Arthur piped up in his usual cheery manner. 'You can see the windows aren't sealed properly; there's damned great gaps. The north wind will blow a gale around the place.'

'The guttering doesn't look too good, either,' Hugh joined in, looking up at a broken down pipe. 'I expect the slates on the roof have slipped as well; that will let the rain in.'

Randolph wanted to strangle the both of them but held his temper. *For God's sake,* he thought, *it is a ruddy hotel, bed and breakfast, being paid for by Whitehall.* Although he wasn't sure that Whitehall was aware of that, but that was down to good old Perry, not him.

'Come on, now,' he beckoned them all, 'let's get inside and then we can unpack and relax for the evening. A busy day tomorrow.'

They entered the reception area, which was vast but almost totally devoid of furniture, with no relaxing armchairs around the large fireplace. The fireplace itself had no fire burning in it and looked as if it hadn't for many a long year; a large sheet of boarding had been propped up over the grate, most likely in order to stop the wind howling down the chimney and into the hotel itself. From the chill in the air, one could safely assume that the ploy hadn't worked. Veronica shivered rather over dramatically while Hugh mumbled on to anyone within earshot that he could definitely feel the damp in the air, which didn't bode well.

'Well, it's hardly a hive of activity,' said Phyllis as she looked around at the peeling wallpaper in the top corners of the room.

'Is there a bell or something?' said Arthur, poking around. *How can an hotel reception not have a damned bell?* he thought. 'Is there anybody here, for Christ's sake?' he called out.

Connie flinched at her husband's blasphemy but she knew better than to say anything.

After a moment, a door could be heard closing somewhere up on the landing, and then the creak of floorboards, footsteps and the banging of a walking stick. From along the landing a large woman, looking rather dishevelled, stopped to look over the banister rail.

'Who is it?' she called.

'Ah, good afternoon,' replied Randolph, straining to look up at her. 'Missus Goddard?'

'Miss Goddard,' bellowed the woman.

'Do forgive me, Miss Goddard. My name is Randolph Laine and these good people are the members of my theatrical company. I believe that you are expecting us.'

'Humph,' humphed Miss Goddard, rather sternly. 'I was expecting you this morning. Were you the man on the telephone I spoke to last week?

'Yes,' said Randolph, 'but I don't recall saying when exactly—' He wasn't given time to finish.

'Twelve o'clock, I stated. Twelve o'clock is when new guests are to book in. I would have said that quite clearly – I always do as matter of form, so's not to have any confusion.' She looked down on them both physically and mentally. 'Luncheon is served at twelve-thirty; I would have said that, I always do. There's no one about in the afternoon; we don't have the staff for the place to be open all day with guests just wandering in willy-nilly. I would have said that, I always do. You'll be given your own key for the front door, which is kept locked from ten o'clock, straight after breakfast – I would have told you that as well. I'm up at six o'clock every morning so that breakfast can be served by seven-thirty. I need to rest in the afternoon. I would have said that, I always do.'

They stood whilst she made her way down the stairs, having shot off her monologue without taking a breath. She was a largish woman with rather fat ankles.

'Yes, well. I sympathise, completely,' replied Randolph.

'Yes, he always does,' said Sam, cheekily.

'But we're here now,' said Teddy.

'Yes, I can see that you're here now,' she said as she arrived at the bottom of the stairs. 'I've got eyes in my head. But how was I to know that you were coming at all? I've not received the deposit on the rooms; I would have told you there was a deposit on the rooms, I always do.'

Randolph's heart sank. Perry had promised that he would get Miss Finch to sort all this out.

'Well, I'm sure it's on its way,' he floundered.

'That's alright for you to say, but how do I know it's on its way? How will I know that I'm going to be paid for all these rooms and breakfasts? I've my bills to pay, you know.'

'Madam, as I explained to you on the telephone, the bill for our accommodation is to be paid by His Majesty's Government. Sir Peregrine Worsley himself assured me of the fact.'

'And who's Sir Whatshisname when he's at home?' People with titles didn't impress her; that was for sure.

'Madam, Sir Peregrine is a senior member of the British Civil Service and has the ear of many within Mister Churchill's government. I'm certain that the money will be on its way to you very shortly. The Chancellor of the Exchequer and the Treasury, as I'm sure you'll understand, are a little busy financing the war effort at present.'

'Well, all I can say is, if they don't get their finger out and pay me what I'm due, you'll all be sleeping on benches on the promenade and fighting the seagulls for any scrap of dropped food.'

'Are there many people staying here at the moment?' asked Hugh, wondering what sort of room they would be given. He hoped it wasn't on the top floor; he didn't want to have to climb too many stairs every day with his heart being…

She cut across his thoughts. 'Look for yourself. As you can see, the hotel is full to the rafters,' she said, her voice overflowing with irony.

'Were there many in for luncheon today?' Connie asked, remembering the hotel dining room from her childhood, abuzz with chatter and the clatter of knives and forks on china plates.

'Luncheon,' the woman spat out the word. 'There were as

many people for luncheon as there are staying here.' And with that, she placed herself behind the reception desk, opened the guests' signing in book and slapped a pencil down on top of it.

'Well, as you're all here you might as well sign in, and then I'll show you up to your rooms.'

'I'd be very grateful if my wife and I can have a room on the first floor,' said Hugh, signing in.

'Married couples are all put on the first floor,' said the woman, matter-of-factly.

'What do you mean?' Veronica sniffed.

'I would have thought that was obvious,' said the woman.

'Not to me,' replied Veronica firmly.

The woman looked down as Phyllis signed the book.

'You can sign in for both of you, you know,' said the woman, looking from her to Randolph.

'Why ever should I wish to sign in for this gentleman?' Phyllis asked, confused.

'Aren't you a married couple, then?' The woman looked at the both of them.

'Well, we are, but not to each other,' replied Randolph, then he laughed.

The woman did not.

'You can rest assured that I won't be having any of that in this hotel.'

'No, I'm sure you won't, Missus…?' said Sam.

'Miss. It's Miss Goddard; there is no Mister Goddard and never will be.'

'I'm not surprised,' said Eric, looking askance at her.

The others held back their sniggers.

Miss Goddard stared at him. She took an instant dislike. The feeling was mutual.

'Married couples on the first floor, single ladies on the second and single gentlemen on the third,' said the woman.

'Is there by any chance a bar in this puritanical establishment?' asked Arthur sarcastically.

The woman looked at him with as much distain as she could muster, and that was a great deal. 'I do not allow alcohol to be consumed on these premises at any time, either in the public rooms or guest rooms, and should I discover any then the culprit will be told to leave immediately.'

'Dear God,' Arthur mumbled, tapping his pocket to make sure that his hip flask was safely tucked away.

6

First Rehearsal

Apart from Teddy, who had come down early and was already out and about, the only person missing from breakfast the next morning was Veronica, which came as no surprise to anyone. The evening before, she had stated very loudly that she would not be down by nine o'clock. She had no intention of getting up before eight-thirty at the earliest, and then she would need time to apply her make-up before making an appearance. Connie had rather foolishly suggested that perhaps she could put her make-up on after breakfast, then there would be no problem.

'Don't be ridiculous,' Veronica snorted in return. 'You may wish to parade yourself naked in public, but some of us have our reputations to think of.'

Phyllis raised an eyebrow and wondered whether it was a little late for her to worry about damaging her reputation.

'I wonder…' said Hugh as the young waitress set down his plate of fried egg, bacon and mashed fried potatoes. 'I wonder,' he repeated, 'whether it would be possible to have another egg and not the bacon?'

The girl shook her head. 'I'm sorry, sir,' she said in her thin voice, which was barely audible, 'the rules are only one egg per guest allowed, owing to the chickens.'

'What about the chickens?' asked Hugh.

'Missus says the farmer told her that they've stopped laying on account of the bombs,' the girl replied.

Connie looked up. 'Bombs? But surely there aren't any bombs here, are there?'

The girl looked at her and nodded. 'Oh yes, madam. There have been lots of bombs. Mostly in the sea, mind, but the Germans bombed Faraday Avenue just two weeks ago. Luckily it fell in the park, but it killed Mister Paterson as he was taking his dog for a walk.'

Arthur looked over to Randolph.

'Oh, marvellous,' he said. 'We escape the bombs in London only for them to have a go at us here.'

'I'm sure it doesn't happen that often, does it, girl?' Randolph smiled at her, willing her to agree with him.

'Sometimes the German planes fire at us with their machine guns as they dive. They fired on people down Church Street a month or so ago; luckily no one was shot but Missus Turner was badly cut by the glass shattering in the chemist's window, and it was the second time he'd had to replace it.'

They all exchanged glances and tucked into their breakfasts, trying not to think too much about bombs and German aircraft strafing them as they walked to work.

Connie looked around at the cooked breakfasts arriving, nursing her piece of toast.

'I didn't know we could have a fried breakfast,' she said, to change the subject. 'I thought, what with the rationing…'

'I told you that you could, but as usual, you didn't listen. You heard me order it,' Arthur cut across her, and then pointedly dipped a piece of bacon in the egg yolk and ate it.

'But what about the rationing? Isn't that breaking the rationing?' she asked.

'There's no rationing in restaurants and hotels,' said Arthur, putting another piece of bacon in his mouth and swilling it down with his tea. 'Everybody knows that.'

'I didn't,' said Eric.

'Within reason, that is,' Randolph clarified. 'Some things aren't available, of course.'

Connie nodded but really was still rather confused as to why she couldn't go to the butcher's and buy as much bacon as she wished, but hotels could.

At exactly nine thirty, Veronica East walked into the dining room, sat down at a table and lifted her fingers to summon the young waitress, who was in the middle of clearing the empty plates and putting them on the sideboard by the kitchen door.

Veronica waved her hand in the air again. 'Waitress,' she said and followed it up with, 'Girl.'

'Yes, Miss,' said the girl as she came over.

'I'd like two poached eggs on some toast, and please make sure that the egg white is cooked and the yolks aren't hard.'

'I'm sorry, Miss, but breakfast is over,' said the girl a little sheepishly.

'Nonsense, it's not half past nine yet.' Veronica snapped back.

'I'm afraid that it's nearly twenty-five minutes to ten,' said the girl, pointing towards the large grandfather clock in the corner, which had seen better days.

Veronica lifted her arm and tapped it. 'This is one of the finest Swiss watches, purchased in Mayfair, and it clearly states that it is only nine twenty-eight.' Interestingly, Veronica didn't actually show the girl the watch, so she had no time to see if what was being said was correct; in fact, she didn't actually see a watch at all, only the haughty woman tapping the cuff of her blouse.

Thinking it best to leave it there, the girl wandered off to the kitchen announcing that she would see what could be done and dreading the fact that Miss Goddard would no doubt shout at her.

'Well, hurry along, girl, I haven't got all day.'

Phyllis placed her napkin on the table and rose from her seat. 'Really, Veronica, why must you always be such a bitch?' she said, passing her table before marching out, not waiting for an answer.

'Come on, old chap,' said Randolph to Sam, wishing to get as far away as he could. 'We need to get that theatre open and ready for business.'

'Righto, guvnor,' replied Sam, biting into his last piece of toast and getting to his feet. 'No time to lose.'

'Don't be late, Veronica,' Randolph called as they both hot-footed it out of the dining room.

She ignored them.

Getting the lights on in the theatre was not plain sailing with Mister Tuppence in charge. The place was plunged into darkness, just as they had found it the day before. Groping their way along the darkened corridor and into the wings, Sam and Randolph looked up at the lighting perch, where the shadowy figure of Mister Tuppence was bent over a large fuse box and was, by the light of a torch, pulling out one enormous fuse after another, examining it closely, cleaning it methodically, and then replacing it.

'Mister Tuppence,' Randolph called up.

Having inspected, cleaned down and replaced another fuse, Mister Tuppence slowly turned and looked in their general direction, although, disconcertingly, not at them.

'I wonder if it would be possible to have some sort of working lights on the stage, and perhaps the house lights?'

'No.' He turned back to his fuse box and pulled out another of the huge fuses.

'No?' said Randolph to the man's back. 'Could you explain to me why not?'

Once again Mister Tuppence inspected, cleaned and then replaced another fuse before returning it into its housing, 'There's no electric.' He continued with his work.

Randolph tried to stay calm. 'But why is there no electric?' he asked.

'Turned off,' said Tuppence, matter-of-factly.

'Why is it turned off?'

'Turned it off.'

Randolph looked at Sam in despair. 'What's he talking about, Sam?'

'I think he's saying that he has turned it off.'

'And will he be turning it back on again?' Randolph asked Sam, who then called up to Mister Tuppence.

'Will you be turning it back on again, Mister Tuppence?'

'Yes.'

'When?'

'When I'm done.'

'And when will you be done?'

'When job's finished.'

Getting nowhere, Randolph gave up. 'Jolly good. Well, let's hope that it's finished soon, shall we?'

Mister Tuppence didn't answer but there was a distinct "hmm". Randolph shook his head.

After another few more minutes had elapsed with the both of them standing in the pitch black, there was suddenly a loud *clunk* followed by a couple of clicks, and the stage working light and the houselights bathed the building in a dim glow.

'*And God said, let there be light: and there was light. And God saw the light, and it was good; and God divided the light from the darkness,*' said Randolph, looking up to the heavens.

At ten o'clock, the members of the Company started to drift in, in the way that actors have done throughout the ages – wandering in in dribs and drabs, with an air of not really knowing what they are actually doing there or, indeed, if they are in the right place anyway. And when they have arrived and taken their coats off, there is always the ritual of just needing to make a cup of tea, of going to the lavatory and trying to remember where they have put their play script before realising that they've left it on the dressing table back at the hotel and castigating the stage manager for not having any spare copies – or pencils.

'Now, come on, Molly Malone – while that lot are getting themselves sorted out we need to rearrange the chairs and stuff so they all have a place to park their BTMs for the read-through of the play.'

Molly nodded but looked a little confused. 'Sam, my name is Molly Baxter, not Molly Malone.'

Sam laughed. 'That may indeed be so,' he said as he pointed towards the other end of the chaise longue in order that she would help him move it. 'But you'll always be Molly Malone to me. Think of it as your stage name.'

'Sam!' The call came from Randolph, who had been sitting dozing in the front row of the stalls; it was only hearing Sam and Molly talking that had roused him. 'I thought everybody would be here by now. Where are they all?' He banged the front of the stage in frustration.

'They're all sorting out their dressing rooms, guvnor.'

'But we did that yesterday, Sam,' Randolph fumed.

'Come on, guvnor, you know actors. Until they've made their space a little home from home they're good for nothing,' Sam chided.

Randolph groaned, sat himself down again and closed his eyes.

Along the corridor it was a hive of activity.

'Whose bed is that?' asked Veronica, pointing to a small, low camp bed in the far corner of the men's dressing room.

Teddy looked up, having laid a small towel on his area of make-up bench and placed his hairbrush, comb and make-up tin tidily on the top of it.

'It's mine. Why?' he said.

Veronica sniffed. 'Why on earth do you need a bed in your dressing room?'

'Why do you think, Veronica? To have a lie down if I need to. Is there a law against it?'

Veronica turned away and nearly bumped into Arthur, who had just arrived having snuck into the café and scrounged a cup of tea from Molly's mother.

'Do you really need to smoke in here?' asked Hugh as Arthur wandered in blowing out the smoke from his cigarette.

'I'm sorry if it's upsetting you, old chap, but it is a free country; well, it is at the moment, so I might as well take advantage while I can.'

Down the corridor, Veronica could be heard calling for "that little ASM girl" and making off towards the stage area.

Coming the other way, Connie was carrying some flowers in a jam jar, which Veronica nearly knocked out of her hand as she stormed by.

'I've bought some flowers,' said Connie, stopping in the doorway to the men's dressing room.

'How sweet of you, Connie,' said Teddy, smiling at her through his make-up mirror.

She smiled back and stepped into the room to place them on the bench, only for her husband to push her away with a scowl.

'Don't put the damned things there, for God's sake,' he bellowed, 'they're in the way. What did you bring them for? There's not enough room in here as it is.'

Connie floundered and her bottom lip started to quiver. *Why does he have to belittle me at any opportunity?* she thought. She hovered with the jam jar.

Teddy stood and took it from her, 'I'll sort them out, my darling,' he said.

He is such a lovely man, thought Connie. *It is such a shame that he hasn't found the right girl. I would have had him like a shot.* She blushed at the thought and left the room as quickly as she could, all of a fluster.

'You really are a prize shit to that girl,' Teddy spat out as he passed behind Arthur. 'I've no idea why she stays with you.'

Arthur pulled on his cigarette and then threw the stub onto the floor and ground it out with his shoe. 'Listen, old boy,' he answered with a sneer, 'I think you and I would get on a lot better if you kept your nose out of my marriage.'

Clap! Clap! came down the corridor. 'Come on, ladies and gentlemen, let's be having you,' Sam called, clapping his hands again, 'Chop, chop, fidy, fidy!'

Slowly the Company got to their feet or looked at themselves in the mirror, as if they were going out on stage to perform in front of a packed house as opposed to starting a read-through of a play in front of an empty auditorium.

Veronica, meanwhile, had stormed into the wings and accosted Molly. 'There you are, girl. I need a cushion for my dressing room chair.'

Molly nervously answered that she didn't think they had any spare cushions as they were all needed on the stage.

'Nonsense,' said Veronica, grabbing one of the cushions off the sofa. 'I'll use this one. Though I don't know why I have had to get it myself. It's part of your job to make sure that the artistes have everything they need. You'd better learn that quickly or you'll be out that stage door in no time.'

Molly, having been warned about such behaviour by Sam, grabbed hold of the other end of the cushion. 'I'm sorry, Miss East, but this belongs onstage.'

But Veronica was not to be beaten by some slip of a provincial girl. 'Not anymore, it doesn't, and I shall make sure that your insolence is reported to Mister Laine,' she spat out, pure venom, and she walked off hugging the cushion to her breast as Connie was coming the other way.

'We've been called,' she said to Veronica innocently as she pushed past her, ignoring her completely. 'Has she been beastly to you?' Connie could see the look on Molly's face and the tears in her eyes.

'Why does she have to be so rude?' asked Molly, the tears falling now and soaking her cheeks.

Connie put her arms around her and comforted her. 'We're not all like Veronica, Molly, dear. You'll get to know the good ones from the bad.' Connie took out her handkerchief and wiped the girl's eyes.

In the stalls, Randolph was dozing again, tut-tutting and mumbling to himself. He couldn't abide tardiness. He'd had it drilled into him when he first started working with Horley Wilkins, who ran the theatre company where Randolph, on his first day, was five minutes late. The memory bubbled back up into Randolph's semi-conscious mind. He had tried to explain that the tram had derailed on the Edgware Road and that he'd had to get off and run the length of Oxford Street and the Charing Cross Road, but Horley Wilkins was not interested; he had brought out his pocket watch. *Six and a half minutes late, Mister Laine; six and a half minutes that we will never be able to retrieve, Mister Laine; six and a half minutes that are forever lost to us.*

'But the tram...' Randolph remembered stuttering.

'Ah, the tram; yes, the tram,' Horley Wilkins had repeated, his voice quivering and sounding more like a Dickensian character by the second. 'An inanimate object, an object that has no soul or sense of time. A tram that, when it comes down to it, is a contraption consisting of metal, timber and other materials set upon wheels.' Randolph smiled in his sleep as he remembered Wilkins, who was now in his stride, crafting his speech. 'A tram which, by its very nature, cannot be tardy. The driver, on the other hand, or the conductor let us not forget the conductor, the giver of tickets – yes, yes, they can indeed be tardy, for they are human, but the tram itself, Mister Laine, is not human, it is a tram and therefore, of itself, can never be late. You, on the other hand, are human and can be late and are indeed late.'

Randolph remembered his heart sinking, but Horley Wilkins' heart had risen and he was now in his pulpit dressed in surplus and dog collar in Randolph's dream. 'You must show forethought, Mister Laine, and not arrive at the tram stop and catch the tram that will get you here, at your place of work, just on time. No! Nor must you think that the tram before will be sufficient to your needs. No! The tram in which you will travel will be the one before that or the one before the one before that, for you must remember that, as you start on this journey into the theatre, unlike the tram driver or the tram conductor – who, no doubt, were drinking ale in the London taverns the night before and who are merely humans –you, Mister Laine, have been chosen for a noble profession. Therefore you are a god and must rise above the world.' Horley Wilkins' gaze was up into the heavens, or at least the peeling roof of the rehearsal room above the Salisbury Tavern in St Martin's Lane. He looked down at Randolph, perhaps thinking that his oratory may have gone a little too far. 'In short, Mister Laine, catch an earlier tram in the future or you will be out on your ear, God or no God.'

Randolph woke with a start and jumped to his feet.

'Come on now,' he called out, pulling himself back into the Regent Theatre, with Horley Wilkins long ago taken to perform in front of the real God, 'this really isn't good enough; you know how much I hate tardiness.' He waved his hands about, pointing towards the chairs, sofas etcetera strewn about the stage. 'Sit yourselves down, anywhere for the moment; I might move you around later.'

'Can't we just get on, for God's sake?' Veronica exclaimed, seemingly completely oblivious to the fact that her wandering onto stage ten minutes late was one of the main reasons why they hadn't.

Molly watched from the wings, attempting to understand what was happening around her. They all seemed to be acting like schoolchildren. Phyllis sat in the most comfortable armchair, which Teddy had been guarding for her, fending off Arthur who had his eye on it.

'Now, Randolph,' Phyllis said, as if chairing a meeting and calling on the first speaker, 'perhaps you'd be kind enough to put us out of our misery and inform us what play we will be starting off with?'

Randolph coughed and cleared his throat; he'd not been looking forward to the reception he was sure he was going to get, but he had no choice.

'I wonder what it is,' said Connie, turning to Zelda. They were like two schoolgirls in a playground.

'Well, it won't be Hamlet, that's for certain,' said Penny.

'Coward, I expect,' Hugh offered, bringing up his imaginary cigarette in its holder to his lips and blowing out imaginary smoke. 'We'll all have to walk around like this and talk in, terribly, terribly clipped voices,' he said in a terribly, terribly clipped voice.

Randolph opened a suitcase and placed it on one of the seats in the stalls. 'Molly, hand these around will you please, dear,' he said, bringing out some thin cardboard folders. 'I've written the names on the front. Sam, give her a hand, if you would?'

They split the folders between them and passed them to the Company. '*Charley's Aunt*?' said Phyllis as she opened her folder.

'Really?' said Connie. 'What fun; lots of lovely frocks to spruce up.'

'You can't be bloody serious?' said Arthur.

'*Charley's Aunt*? How can we be doing *Charley's Aunt* for heaven's sake?' said Penny, looking around at the male Company members. 'It's about university undergraduates and their girlfriends.'

'For once, Penny, I fear I agree with you,' said Phyllis, shaking her head.

'What do you mean?' said Veronica, putting her hand up to tighten the skin around her throat.

Phyllis looked at her. 'Well, dear, most of us are hardly in the first flush of youth.'

'What on earth made you choose this old turkey?' chimed in Arthur.

Randolph held his hands up. 'I know, I know,' he said. 'I'm afraid I had no choice in the matter. It was the only way I could get the money. We only need to play it for the first couple of weeks or so and then we can move onto something more suitable to our average age.'

Veronica shook her head. 'Average age? What nonsense. I can't see the problem, myself.'

Phyllis raised her eyebrows, 'And which part are you playing?'

'It says Kitty,' Veronica answered. 'That's perfectly within my range.'

'If memory serves, Kitty is around nineteen years old; it's been a long time since you saw that number.'

'Meaning?'

'Nothing, dear.'

Randolph's instinct was to cut in before any more was said, but Phyllis was in her stride and even though she knew she would be able to get some stronger punches in later on in the tour, these little jabs were all valuable to weaken her opponent.

'I'm sure a good coating of Five and Nine will cover the wrinkles,' she stated, referring to the greasepaint numbers that were used as facial make-up, 'and help hide a multitude of sins.' She smiled before changing the subject. 'I take it that I am to be cast to type with the part of Donna Lucia?' she said, not having opened her copy of the play yet.

'Wait a minute,' said Penny, flicking through the pages of the script. 'I don't have the whole play here; it's just got Amy's lines in it.'

Arthur thumbed through his copy. 'These are ruddy cue copies,' he snapped. 'Why have we got cue copies?'

Randolph, as well as dreading telling them about the play, was also nervous at their reaction to not being given full copies of the plays, with only their character's lines and the cue line from another character before it.

'Yes, I know, I know,' said Randolph resignedly, 'but I couldn't afford to get full copies of the play so I had these cue copies made up.'

There were general mumbles from the Company.

Arthur stood up and waved his folder in the air, rather like Mister Chamberlain with his piece of paper in nineteen thirty-nine. 'I really don't think that I can rehearse if I don't have the entire play to refer to.' He looked around for someone to back him up. Penny, even though she hated to think she could agree with anything that Arthur Desmond said, had to on this occasion, and said so.

Teddy shook his head and smiled at her righteous indignation.

'And what's so funny, Mister Shaw?' she said, spitting out his surname, which made Teddy smile even more.

'Get off your high horse, Penny; we all know this play backwards. I don't know about you, but I must have done it four or five times; I've played just about every part except yours and Phyllis's.'

Randolph decided that enough was enough and made his way up the steps from the auditorium onto the stage. 'Can we all just calm down. Our little ASM, er…' In the moment he had quite forgotten her name.

'Molly,' prompted Sam.

'Yes, I know her name, Sam,' Randolph snapped back – something he didn't often do and which Sam took little notice of when he did. 'Yes, Molly here has a full copy of the play, which she'll be using as a prompt copy in the corner,' he said, referring to the area where Molly would be sitting at the side of the stage, cueing any lighting changes. And of course, as director, I have a full copy. So, Act One.'

Randolph opened his copy of the play and started to read out the opening stage directions. '*Set in JACK's ground-floor rooms at Oxford University, England, in the late eighteen hundreds. JACK* – that's you, Sam – *has an unlit pipe in his mouth, and is sat at his writing desk trying to compose a letter. He takes the letter and rips it up.*'

'*I can't. I can't get into the vein,*' read Sam, in character.

Molly sat on her stool in the prompt corner and Mister Tuppence looked on from his lighting perch as he continued to clean and polish all the equipment, shaking his head every so often. Molly tried to follow the play with her finger as the others read but she found the whole thing very confusing. From what she could gather, the play took place in the rooms and garden of Oxford University, of which she'd seen old photographs; all she knew was that it was a very old place with lots of large buildings.

At a break for tea they all trooped over the road to the café and Molly's mother served up tea and biscuits.

'I'm not sure I understand it,' said Molly.

'Well, first of all it's a lot of old fluff,' said Sam.

'Fluff?' said Molly.

'A lot of old tosh,' Sam said, as if this made any more sense. It didn't. 'You see, the play's a farce, where a lot of posh people do daft things for reasons better known to the writer of the play.'

'But why is Mister Desmond going to have to be dressed up as a woman?' Molly asked. Even though she'd heard the first act, where this is all explained, she still didn't understand.

'Blimey,' said Sam good-naturedly, 'you want it chapter and verse, don't you?'

'I want to understand it,' she said, and then had a drink of her tea.

'Right,' said Sam, 'I'll take you through the whole play.' And he did. He explained that two young men, Jack – which was the part he was playing – and Charley, who Eric Cornwall was playing, are in love with two girls, Amy and Kitty – Miss Rose and Miss East, only they're not allowed to see the girls without Charley's aunt,

Donna Lucia being there – Sam pointed at Phyllis – as in those days, it wasn't the done thing in society for a young girl to meet a boy without a chaperone.

'What's a chaperone?' asked Molly.

'Well,' answered Sam, 'it's usually a very sour-faced old lady.' Phyllis, overhearing, put on a sour face, which made Molly laugh.

'Why do the girls need to have a chaperone? Aren't they allowed out on their own?'

'They were to make sure that the boys didn't have any ideas,' said Phyllis. Molly frowned; she didn't understand what ideas they might have.

'That's because you are a very well brought up young girl and obviously haven't been with any boys who have had ideas,' Phyllis replied, tapping Molly's hand.

'You mean like kissing?' she said, blushing slightly.

'Or something worse,' Arthur butted in with a rather unpleasant laugh as he passed to take his teacup for a refill.

Phyllis shook her head. 'Exactly like kissing,' she said.

Molly had never been kissed. Both her parents had kissed her goodnight, of course, and her mother still did, but not lover-like kissing. She thought about her father's kisses a lot; he would wrap his arms around her and pick her up and kiss her on the cheek as he spun her round.

'So, what's this to do with Mister Desmond wearing ladies' clothes?' she asked, as if to change the subject.

'That's to do with the fact that at the last minute, they hear that my character – Donna Lucia, Charley's aunt – isn't coming, and so they need someone to take her place so they can meet up with the girls without getting into trouble.'

Molly smiled and nodded her head, still not quite sure she'd got it.

'Of course, when my character does arrive,' Phyllis continued, 'it will all become clear to you, I'm sure.'

Molly wasn't so sure it would.

Back in the theatre, while the Company read the two remaining acts of the play, Molly decided to write out a list of who was who in the play in order to help her work everything out. She did so in her best handwriting:

```
BRASSET (MANSERVANT) — MISTER LAINE
DONNA LUCIA (REAL AUNT) — MISSUS CAMPBELL-BENNETT
KITTY (IN LOVE WITH JACK) — MISS EAST
AMY (IN LOVE WITH CHARLEY) — MISS ROSE
JACK (IN LOVE WITH KITTY) — SAM
CHARLEY (IN LOVE WITH AMY) — MISTER CORNWALL
LORD FANCOURT BABBERLEY (BABS AND DRESSED AS CHARLEY'S
    AUNT) — MISTER DESMOND
SIR FRANCIS CHESNEY (JACK'S FATHER, I THINK) — MISTER SHAW
SPETTIGUE (A VILLAIN?) — MISTER MUNRO
ELA DELAHAY (COMPANION TO DONNA LUCIA) — MISSUS MUNRO
MISSUS DESMOND (WARDROBE MISTRESS. NOT IN PLAY THOUGH)
```

She read it back, hoping that she had got it all right. Looking up, she noticed a nail in the wall above her little desk and pushed the sheet of paper through it so the list would be in front of her all the time.

Looking around her little domain, she felt quite important. Sam had told her that the prompt corner was her space and no one else's. She'd never had her own place where no one else was allowed before. She'd let Sam sit there if he wanted; he was above her in the pecking order as the Stage Manager, and she was his assistant. She'd let Mister Laine and Miss Campbell-Bennett as well, out of respect, but not anyone else. Actually, she'd let Mister Shaw as he was nice and he was the one who helped her get the job, and he had insisted that she call him by his Christian name, Teddy. She'd never been allowed to call – or even thought of calling – an adult by their Christian name before; it felt a little strange and grown up.

7

Billy Pryce

When Private William Colin Pryce left his parents' home on the outskirts of Peterborough that Monday afternoon he had no idea where he was going, although his orders said that he was meant to be reporting back for duty at Aldershot Barracks by seventeen hundred hours that day. His mother wanted to go to Peterborough Station with him to see him off but Billy knew that it would just upset the both of them, and he didn't like to see his mother cry in public. Billy had seen her cry many times, usually at the hands of his father, Freddie Pryce.

He tried to put on a brave face, but they both knew that he was in no fit state to return to active service. He was never suited for a life in the services even in peace time, let alone during the carnage that he'd seen over in France. Every night as he tried to sleep, he would replay it in his head – the images of wading into the sea and being pulled onto a small boat while German fighter pilots strafed the beaches, cutting down the British soldiers just feet away from relative safety; the lad who had been talking nineteen to the dozen to him out of fear as they waded out and who suddenly fell silent – the next time he saw the lad was when his body floated backwards behind him, his face just a bloodied mass of skin and bone where the bullets had hit him; how he threw up in the sea as another jerry plane strafed the water in front of him. Had he not stopped for that second to look for his talkative friend, he too would have been floating lifeless in the Channel.

Walking down the street, Billy Pryce turned and waved back to his mother, not knowing if he'd ever see her again. He made a determined effort to smile and then turned away and marched off around the corner and out of sight. He was in a daze; he had no idea what to do or where to go. Would he just get on the train south as he was ordered to or would he run? Run where? His head was a mass of confusion. He had no idea who he was or what he was doing anymore.

When he arrived at Peterborough Station, he stopped and sat down on a bench and took out his travel warrant. He stared at it. The destination was pre-designated, as nearly all of them were; the army didn't want its soldiers diving up and down the country for gratis; there'd be no telling what they'd get up to – they needed to keep an eye on them. They were trusted enough to be shot at, said one of Billy's mates, but not trusted enough not to do a runner. Was that what he was about to do, a runner? How could he? The only clothes he had were his army uniform; it hadn't even crossed his mind to pack some civilian clothes.

He looked down at the piece of paper again. Aldershot, it said. Aldershot Barracks, that's where he was told to report when his leave was up, and then where? Back to France? No, they wouldn't do that, would they? The Germans were all over the place. They'd be all along the coast now, standing on the cliffs with their binoculars, looking over the Channel towards the English coastline; eyeing up the white cliffs of Dover, working out the best place to invade. No. He stopped himself. Hitler knew exactly where he wanted to invade; he'd have it all worked out, just as he'd worked out invading Poland and up into Norway and then France. Yes, he thought, Hitler had a plan and the invasion of Britain was next, and they were being sent to the south coast to try to hold it off. Some chance. The British boys were beaten, a mess. "A disorganised rabble", his sergeant had called them, before copping it himself. It was only a matter of time. They could all see that the officers hadn't a clue and the whole thing was a shambles. What did Churchill think he was doing? They were lambs to the slaughter, just like the last time. Cannon fodder. He folded the travel warrant, put it back in the top pocket of his tunic and took in some deep breaths. Where would he go?

One thing he was certain of: he wasn't going to Aldershot. He'd had enough and he needed to run. He'd spent every night of his leave lying in bed trying to work out what would happen if he went AWOL, absent without leave, if he deserted. How long would it be before they caught up with him? *Don't think about it. You just need to get away; you can't go back, Billy.* It was as if he was talking about someone else; he felt separated from himself. He'd felt like that for a while as they'd retreated, knowing the Germans were just behind them – he didn't feel attached. He was watching himself from a distance.

'Hello, soldier.' The voice was close and he looked up to see a uniform. Luckily, it only belonged to a member of the railway station staff. 'Where are you off to, then? Going back to get the buggers?' The station master was friendly. 'I wish I could join you, lad,' he said, 'but I'm too old and my eyesight's not as good as it was so I wouldn't be much use; I wouldn't be able to see Jerry well enough to get a potshot.'

Billy nodded and attempted a smile, then, seemingly out of nowhere, he asked when the train to Haleston would be. Haleston – what had made him ask that?

'They sending you to Haleston, are they?' said the station master. 'Your regiment up there, are they?'

'What?' Why had he said Haleston?

'Oh sorry, of course you can't say, can you? What am I thinking? Careless talk costs lives, eh?' Billy had no idea about anything anymore. 'You're in luck, lad, there's one due in ten minutes. Here, show us your pass and I'll see you onto the platform.'

Billy's heart nearly stopped. 'I haven't got my travel pass,' he said, trying to sound convincing. 'I must have lost it somewhere.' He patted his top tunic pocket, where the offending warrant for Aldershot was neatly folded. 'I'll have to buy a ticket.'

The railway man looked at him hard and then gave him a wink. 'You wait there, lad.' He limped off into the station and called over to his pal in the ticket office. Within a couple of minutes he was back with a small piece of card in his hand.

'Here you are, son,' he said, 'One second-class ticket to Haleston-on-Sea, on the house. I would have got you a first-class if I could have swung it but I'd cop it if the bosses found out.'

Billy thanked him and felt dreadfully guilty.

'It's the least we can do., what with you boys risking everything to keep Hitler away.' He raised his hat and scratched his head. 'Well, you'd best be on your way, lad. Platform three's the one you want. It's the stopping train, I'm afraid, so it'll take you a while to get there. Hope it don't make you late; don't want them putting you on a charge, do we?' He laughed. Billy forced another smile and with a mumbled "thank you", he threw his kit bag on his shoulder and made his way to the platform, turning around at the foot of the bridge to nod towards the railwayman, who saluted him rather badly, forcing Billy to salute smartly back before making his way up and over to platform three.

As he stood there waiting, he had no idea how he was going to live. He'd not be able to use his ration book, would he? He hadn't a clue. It was all so… He was lost in his thoughts, all of which made no sense.

A train whistle brought him back to the here and now. It was the London train, the one he should have been about to get on. As it got closer he felt a shiver go through him. You've got the travel warrant, Billy, he told himself, if you got a shift on you could get back to the correct platform and jump on it. He looked at the footbridge and then back along the line as the train puffed ever closer. He leant down to pick up his kit bag, but as he did so he caught sight of the ticket collector walking onto the platform opposite. The man waved at him. Billy was caught. What should he do? The London train rolled into platform one and came to a halt. A blast of smoke came from its engine and the coaches rattled as the train stopped, the sounds echoing and pounding through his head. He could still make it; it was sure to be a while before it left, he thought. But for all his thinking, he didn't move; he was riveted to the spot and within no time, he heard the blast of the guard's whistle and a counter blast from the train's, and slowly the engine started to move forward. He just stood and stared. There was no going back. Whatever happened now, that was it. He heard another blast of an engine's whistle and, looking after the departing train, saw the Haleston train on the other line, passing it.

As he stood on the platform, he realised why Haleston-on-Sea had come into his mind; it was where he went for a week's holiday with his mother every year when he was small. A week away from his father, away from the arguments and hatred. Haleston-on-Sea was of course a place of safety, a sanctuary; that's why it had come into his head like that. A place of calm.

As the train pulled in, he looked through the windows as they passed. He could see that a lot of the compartments were empty. If he could just sit down on his own for a while to gather his thoughts… He pulled open the door and stepped into the carriage, and made his way along the narrow corridor. He slid back the door of an empty compartment and threw his kit bag down on the seat, then slid the door closed again and pulled down the green canvas blinds on the inside windows, hoping that it would put others off from entering. Flopping himself down in the corner near the outer window, he waited for the train to start to pull out and continue on its journey towards the east coast.

What was he going to do when he got to Haleston? He had no idea. He weighed up whether he could afford a couple of nights in a seafront bed and breakfast house. Would any be open? Would it be safe? The old landladies, he remembered, could be nosey old busybodies and dreadful gossips. What would he tell them when they asked why a young soldier was wanting to stay? What would he tell anybody? Nothing had been worked out. He'd be caught in no time and… No, he didn't want to think about it. *Close your eyes and go to sleep, Billy,* he told himself. *Rest; something will come to you.*

Outside, the landscape changed to the black, flat Fenlands with long straight drainage ditches as far as he could see. Eventually the line started to follow the coast and out of the window the sea glinted in the afternoon sun. He closed his eyes and, folding his arms, sank into the seat and started to doze.

8

Molly and Arthur's Skirt

After having lunch at the café, where Jane Baxter had cooked them a tasty corned beef and vegetable pie, they all trooped back at two o'clock in order to get the play 'on its feet'.

'What does that mean, Sam?' asked Molly as he came into the wings.

'It means to start to move the actors about the stage so they know where to stand without bumping into each other,' he answered.

'So what do I have to do?' Molly asked.

'Not much at the moment, apart from watching and taking it all in. We'll have our scripts today so you won't have to worry about prompting us,' Sam replied.

'Prompting?' Molly felt dreadfully out of her depth.

'That's when we've forgotten our words. You'll have the play in front of you here in your corner and when one of us forgets the next line, you'll call it out,' Sam explained.

'But how will I know that you've forgotten the line?'

'Well, it'll either go very quiet for a while and everybody on stage will look blankly at each other, or one of us will shout out "Line!" very loudly or "Yes!", and will probably be very cross and go into some ridiculous excuse about someone coughing, which put them off, or the line before not being given properly or something like that.' Sam laughed as Molly looked blankly at him. 'Don't worry, we won't get to that until tomorrow, so you can sit down in the stalls if you like and watch it from there – it'll give you a better idea as to what's going on.'

Which is what Molly duly did.

All seemed to be going well to start with, Molly thought. Sam and Eric were on the stage, and every so often Randolph came on as the old retainer, Brasset. Then they all left and Arthur Desmond came on and started to steal champagne bottles – or that's what she read in the script in front of her.

'Sorry to stop,' said Arthur, having gone to the cupboard and opened it, 'but where are the props? The bottles? Don't we have any rehearsal props? Where's the ASM girl?'

Molly looked up in horror. What had she forgotten? Nobody had told her about rehearsal props – she didn't even know what they were.

Sam leapt in to the rescue. 'We haven't had a chance to get any bottles yet, Arthur. You'll have to mime the business for now.'

'Can't you get any bottles? Is it that difficult to get a few ruddy bottles?' Arthur cursed.

'Arthur, dear chap,' Randolph said as he stood at the side of the stage, 'we're all still on the book; you won't be able to juggle props and read at the same time. I'm sure Molly will have bottles and other things when we've all got the books out of our hands, won't you, dear?' He turned to Molly, who had gone bright red and wasn't sure what to do. She could feel tears welling up.

'Molly and I will be doing a prop run tomorrow. We've got it all sorted out,' said Sam quickly, 'so not to worry.' He turned, winked at Molly and smiled.

Arthur Desmond snorted. 'It's not easy doing comedy business without the props to rehearse with,' he stated, in order to get the last word in. 'And a bag to put them in,' he added to top the complaint off.

'Yes, yes,' said Randolph, 'perfectly understand. Bottles and a bag, yes, I'm sure that stage management has made a note. Good. Now shall we go back to your entrance, Arthur?'

They did, and Arthur made great play of taking invisible bottles out of the cupboard and putting them into an invisible bag.

LORD FANCOURT (Arthur) *But I've given my word.*

JACK (Sam) *What are you playing?*

LORD FANCOURT (Arthur) *A lady; an old lady; and I've never acted in my life before, and I'm going to try on the things before those fellows come.*

CHARLEY (Eric) *You can try them on here. Where are they?*

LORD FANCOURT (Arthur) *In my rooms, in a box on the bed. Rattle, rattle.*

JACK (Sam) *Fetch them, Brassett, quick!*

LORD FANCOURT. *No, I'll fetch them with my little bag. Rattle, rattle.*

(JACK and CHARLEY intercept him; they struggle to get the bag.)

LORD FANCOURT (Arthur) *Rattle, rattle.*

Eric suddenly stopped acting. 'Do you think you could stop saying rattle, rattle?'

'It says here that the bottles are rattling in the bag. So I'm rattling the invisible bottles in the invisible bag,' Arthur stated without a hint of irony.

'It's very off-putting, wouldn't you say, Randolph?' Eric replied, turning to the director.

Randolph just wished they could get on with it.

'Arthur, I think we can just assume that the bag is rattling for now.'

'As you wish, but I don't know how we're supposed to react to the rattling if there isn't any.'

The others looked on from their seats in the auditorium and shook their heads; they wouldn't even finish the first act before opening night at this rate.

They continued.

JACK (Sam) *Well, what is it?*

CHARLEY (Eric) *Read that. (Hands letter.)*

JACK (Sam) *'Important business, don't expect me for a few days. Lucia d'Alvadorez.' No!!!*

'For goodness' sake, Connie, what are you doing?' It was Arthur, behind the scenery.

CHARLEY (Eric) *She's not coming!*

JACK (Sam) *But she must! Go—wire—telegraph.*

'Hold still, Arthur, dear. It will help with your...' Connie could also be heard.

'Help with my what, for God's sake? Leave me alone, can't you?' Eric reacted to the noise but tried to continue.

CHARLEY (Eric) *No use. There's no time.*

JACK (Sam) *But hang it! The girls won't remain without a chaperone. What are we to do?*

'Stop fussing around me, woman,' Arthur yelled. Again, Eric tried to keep going.

CHARLEY (Eric) *(Looking through window.) Here they are! They're coming!*

JACK (Sam) *What on earth are we to do?*

'Do we need all this noise, Randolph?' Eric called out, throwing his script down on the side table in frustration.

At which point, Arthur Desmond stomped on stage with Connie trotting up behind him with a long calico underskirt in her hands, trying to tie it round her retreating husband's waist.

'But it will help you move like a woman.'

'I have no desire to wear a bloody skirt while I'm rehearsing, Connie,' he spat as he turned to Randolph. 'For God's sake, Randolph, get this bloody woman away from me.'

Randolph closed his eyes and hoped that when he opened them again he would find it was just a nightmare.

'Randolph!' Arthur bellowed. 'Did you hear me?'

Randolph had indeed heard him, only too clearly, and opening his eyes, he sighed:

'Arthur, old boy, what can I do? I mean, she is your wife. I really can't get involved in your domestic squabbles.'

Nice try, thought Phyllis from her seat in the stalls where she was dozing, *but he won't get away with that.*

'This is not a domestic squabble – the bloody stupid woman wants me to wear this thing,' he turned to the underskirt and ripped it from Connie's hand and threw it across the stage.

Teddy picked it up and started to dust it down, holding it up to his own waist.

'Well, you are playing *Charley's Aunt*,' he said, laughing and twirling his body with it.

Molly laughed as well, which received a very black look from Arthur. Molly blushed and sank in her seat.

'It's not a laughing matter,' he reported, 'and I'll thank you, Teddy, not to stick your nose into my business. Concentrate on your own performance, such as it is.'

'Connie, dear, why do you want Arthur to wear this skirt? It does look a little tatty?' asked Randolph to try and defuse the situation.

'It's not the proper skirt, Randolph, it's just an old underskirt,' Connie explained.

'Yes, I see,' said Randolph, not really seeing at all. He was just desperate to get on with the rehearsal.

Connie took the skirt from Teddy and tried again. 'Arthur, dear, it will help you during rehearsals to walk like a woman.'

Arthur exploded again. 'And why would I want to walk like a bloody woman?'

'Because you're playing one, dear.' Connie whimpered back.

'No, I'm not, I'm playing a man who dresses up as a woman. The man is not a woman,' he sniped back.

'Oh, for Christ's sake, can't we just get on?' said Veronica wearily, waiting to make her entrance with Penny and looking to Randolph to put an end to this torture.

'Agreed,' said Penny. 'If we don't start we'll never be ready for the first performance… which is when, exactly, Randolph?'

Randolph took a deep breath. 'Seven days' time; we open next Tuesday.'

'Well, let's get on with it then,' Penny replied.

From her place in the auditorium, Molly wondered if it was always going to be like this.

Hugh put his hand up. 'Connie is right. I wore a skirt in rehearsals the last time I played your part, and it did help.'

'Well, I'm not you, thank God,' replied Arthur, taking out a cigarette and lighting it. Blowing out the smoke, he walked as far away from his wife and the offending article of clothing as he could, and sat.

Randolph wondered why he bothered. They were all as bad as each other. 'Right, well, as we've stopped I think we should run through it all from the beginning again.' Randolph really couldn't cope with hearing any more about skirts. 'Connie, dear, we won't bother with the skirt until we're all off the book, but thank you – yes, you were quite right to bring it up.'

Veronica gave Randolph one of her looks. 'So, you're going back?'

'Yes. I'm so sorry, ladies, I know you were there waiting for your entrances but we will continue next time, I promise.' Randolph clapped his hands. 'Right Sam, set from the beginning, if you would.'

'All set, guvnor,' Sam called out, 'and raring to go.'

'Good, good.' And off they went.

Not wishing to suffer it all again, Phyllis decided to take Connie back to her wardrobe room and help her to finish unpacking everything.

'Oh, you don't need to do that, Phyllis,' said Connie, although she was secretly pleased to have some company. 'You should rest, or perhaps learn your lines.'

'Learn my lines?' Phyllis laughed. 'I hate to think how many times I've done this play. At least twice as Amy and once as Kitty, and this will be my third Donna Lucia. I know the part better than the playwright. Besides,' she continued, as they were passing Veronica, 'there's nothing I like more than a good old gossip, is there, dear?'

Veronica chose to ignore her and walked off towards her little dressing room, out of the way from the others for a while.

Phyllis and Connie both shared a schoolgirl giggle and wandered up the corridor, chatting.

'I was only trying to be helpful,' said Connie, with a worried look on her face. 'I do hope that Randolph isn't too cross with me.'

'Whatever makes you think that Randolph is cross with you?'

'About the skirt.'

'I don't think you'll find that Randolph is at all cross with you. Don't fret yourself over that.'

'Oh, I do hope not.'

Molly was watching Sam from the stalls, hoping that she wasn't making it too obvious, the thought of which made her blush. He was friendly and nice and kind, and he explained everything to her without getting in the slightest bit cross when she said or did something silly. *Yes*, she thought, as she watched him acting on the stage, *he's really... I do like him.*

From the stage, Sam could see the distant figure of Molly sitting in the auditorium. He wondered, as he strutted about the stage, what she was thinking. *Why am I wondering that?* he thought.

*

When he woke, Billy's head felt heavy. He looked around and was glad to see that he was still alone in the compartment. Out of the window, the sea was stretching out towards the horizon. Beach huts; beach huts suddenly came into his mind. Why on earth had beach huts jumped into his head? He could bunk down in one, that's why. He had his army blanket and great coat to wrap himself up in and his kit bag for a pillow. He'd slept in less comfortable places and at least he'd be out of sight and not have to spend what little money he had on somewhere to sleep. He could use it for a meal or two and perhaps a half of beer until he'd worked out what to do.

The train pulled into Haleston Station around mid-afternoon. Throwing his bag on his shoulder, he walked out of the station without being stopped by anybody. As he made his way along the seafront, he mused how strange it was to see it so empty. He recalled the hustle and bustle of the crowds alighting from the train all those years before. Dads calling out to the rest of the family to "stick close by, now; we don't want you getting lost and spending your holiday with another family, do we?" There were no crowds on the seafront to merge into; no sound of a hurdy-gurdy off in the distance playing happy sing-along tunes; no Punch and Judy on the beach or Pierrot shows; no great swathes of holiday-makers gaily making their way along the prom or sitting in rows of deck chairs and sunning themselves on the beach. Just him. *Of course it is just me,* he thought. *A soldier standing out like a sore thumb.* He wondered whether he should have dived off into the back streets but it was too late now. Why didn't he think of packing some civvies in his bag? Because he hadn't thought; he had been incapable of thought, that's why. Everything was jumbled up in his head and nothing was thought through and now it was too late – he'd committed himself and there was no turning back. He cursed and felt the tears stinging his eyes, or was that the the salty sea spray carried on the wind?

He sat on a sheltered bench and looked at the pier; his favourite place where, as a child, he'd discovered a perfect hidey-hole below it, which nobody knew about, where he could just sit with his feet over the side, the waves lapping over them when the tide was right. Would it still be there? He studied the gate at the head of the pier, now all chained and padlocked with barbed wire coiled either side. Walking up to it, he pushed at the gate; it moved. Whoever had locked up had not wrapped the chain around enough times to stop it from opening a little, and when he pushed at it there was a large enough gap for someone to squeeze through if they didn't mind negotiating the barbed wire that was placed loosely around it. That could be moved aside without much trouble. He peered through the gate and noticed the gap made by the Royal Engineers along with the narrow swing bridge. Past that, at the end, the Pier Theatre, where every year they would go to see the summer variety shows with their singers, dancing girls, comics, magicians and ventriloquists, whose grotesque dummies gave him nightmares. The shows, which alternated nightly, were full of colour and gaiety. The theatre was all boarded up now, with the strings of light fittings, which were always festooned across the front, empty of their painted bulbs and swinging loosely in the stiff breeze that was coming off the North Sea. He thought about pushing through the gate to take a closer look but decided that it could wait until he didn't have his kit bag, and just in case someone was looking – the last thing he needed was a local bobby or one of the lace curtain-twitching landladies to see him.

He watched the waves coming in and out just as they had at Dunkirk, only the beach here was covered in barriers and barbed wire in the vain attempt to keep the enemy out. Stopping at the stone steps that led down to the hard standing where the faded beach huts stood in a line going off into the distance, he looked up and down the prom; no one was in sight. He turned to look at the windows of the boarding houses opposite; not a lace curtain was twitching, as far as he could see. Making his way down the steps, he proceeded to walk along the line of huts. They were all padlocked. He pulled on a couple of the locks but they stayed firmly shut. Further and further down the beach he went, until he saw what looked like the door on one of the huts not firmly closed. He examined it closer and, sure enough, the hasp was hanging off its screws and the padlock, although closed, was hanging down. The door opened freely when he pulled it. He looked around again; the coast was clear. He opened the door and dived in, pulling the door tightly closed behind him. It was dark and damp inside and smelt of stale saltwater. He'd slept in a lot worse over the past year, and at least there wasn't any danger of being shot at by a sniper. He knelt down and felt the floor. The floorboards were caked in sand, which was to be expected, along with some small stones that he brushed to the side with his hand. He leaned his kit bag against a wall. This would do for now; it was out of the way and he couldn't think why anyone would want to come down there nosing about. The Home Guard perhaps, but he'd take that risk.

Sitting down with his back against the wall, he felt tired, confused and afraid. He was hungry, even though his mother had cooked a good fry-up before he left, using up all her rations. He pulled his water bottle out of the bag and, loosening the top, took a swig. *Not too much*, he thought. Perhaps he could get a beer in a quiet little pub later; sit in the corner and hope that the locals weren't too nosey and no other soldiers were about. He had no idea if there was a barracks up here; he supposed there must be one around somewhere along the coast. That was another thing he'd not thought through.

Exhausted, he let his head fall back against the wall and felt the tears stinging his eyes. His life was over. He had no idea who or what he was anymore; a coward in his father's eyes, and now the army's. They'd be after him at some point. If only he knew where to run.

*

Thankfully, by six o'clock Randolph had plotted the Company through the first act. As most of them had performed the play before, there wasn't much discussion to be had as to the whys and wherefores of the play – not that this old chestnut, as Hugh had called it, required much explaining. Even Eric, who had never seen the play, wasn't having any difficulty with his part. Of course there was always Arthur, who seemed to sulk his way through the afternoon, but that was to be expected of the man. Randolph wished he could have given the part to Sam, who would have had a lot of fun with it and played it perfectly, but he knew that casting his son in the lead would have caused even more ructions. *Oh, well, he thought, just plough through it and then try to fine tune it the best I can.* Which in all honesty, as he was well aware, wouldn't be by much in some circumstances.

'Thank you, ladies and gentlemen, a good day's work,' he called out, clapping his hands and trying to sound as if he meant it. 'Time for refreshment, I think. So, has anyone found out where the best pub is around here?'

Before anybody else could answer, Molly's voice cut in. 'The Cockleshell, in Hope Street, just around the corner. My dad said that it had the best beer.'

The others turned and looked at her and her face started to burn again. Teddy Shaw, as ever, came to the rescue,

'Aha,' he said loudly to the others, pointing towards her, 'I knew this girl had the makings of a first-class Assistant Stage Manager.'

Molly smiled and then blushed even more. Perhaps she shouldn't have said anything; perhaps it wasn't her place.

Sam winked at her. 'Quite right, Teddy, that's exactly what's needed from a good ASM – knowing where to get a smashing cup of tea, and knowing where the pub with the best beer is.'

'Well done, old girl, you've come up trumps,' said Teddy.

Molly was pleased with the compliments but they made her blush even more.

Even before this exchange had finished, Arthur Desmond was already out of the stage door and on his way to The Cockleshell, without any other prompting.

Molly was too young to go into a pub and even though she knew Mister Stirling, the landlord, and he wouldn't have minded, she thought it best to go straight home. So, saying her goodnights, she crossed the road back to the café. After having a wash and brushing her hair, she offered to help in the kitchen. It had been an odd day, she thought, and the Company were all rather odd as well. She didn't like Mister Desmond or Miss East very much. Miss Rose wasn't the friendliest, even though she was nearer her age, but the others all seemed very nice, especially Mister Shaw and, of course, Sam.

9

THE COCKLESHELL

The Cockleshell was what one would think of when imagining a public house in an English seaside town: low-ceilinged and timber-framed with fishing nets and other paraphernalia that could easily have just been brought in from the morning's fishing and left to dry while the trawlermen warmed themselves by the open fire and supped at their ale. Along one side of the main bar were three small booths that sat four, with a table in the middle to put your beer on while you played a game of cribbage or dominoes. The Cockleshell was, then, a local pub for local people, fishermen and farmers who worked the land and sea thereabouts.

In the far corner, hidden away in one of the booths, Private William Colin Pryce sat nursing a half pint of beer. His head was lost in his thoughts as members of the Laine Theatre Company trouped into the main bar with the confidence that actors seem to have when in a group – still performing and putting on a show.

Randolph introduced himself to the landlord, who he took to be the Mister Stirling that Molly had spoken of.

'We will be in town for the next few weeks, dear sir,' said Randolph in full Actor-Manager mode, 'and we hope to frequent your establishment throughout our stay, if that is satisfactory to you?'

John Stirling had learned his trade as a publican in London's West End and had come across many like Randolph and his band of strolling players, so was on top of the situation straight away.

'Well, sir,' he said good-naturedly, 'if you place your money down on the counter I'll consider it a pleasure to serve whatever you require, if I have it in stock.'

'Splendid,' said Randolph.

'Only I feel that I should make it clear, so's not to have any future confusion – and I say this without meaning anything by it, mind – that this premises is strictly "No Credit".' Saying this, he pointed over his shoulder to the sign, which spelt out those very words. 'Now, if that's clear,' the landlord continued, 'what can I get you to drink?'

Taking out his wallet with a flourish, Randolph assured him that credit would not be necessary and, having surreptitiously checked how much money he had to hand a little earlier, turned to the Company to inform them that the first round was on him. He had enough to see him through a few days until Sir Peregrine's money came through, which, he reasoned, should be any time now. Arthur, on the other hand, having eyed up the "No Credit" sign, started to put a strategy together to get round that little problem. He'd have to charm the landlord into giving him a little leeway.

The pub was almost empty. Two women, probably in their early thirties, were sitting at a table at the far end of the bar, chatting and looking over at the newcomers and giggling amongst themselves; and two young lads, large muscular boys, were leaning on the bar trying to chat up the barmaid whilst keeping an eye on the strangers, and not for the same reasons as the young women. Both lads had downed a fair amount of beers after a hard day's work milking the cows, digging ditches and banging in fence posts on the nearby farm, so the beer wasn't touching the sides as it went down.

In the far booth, Billy kept his head down and supped his drink slowly to make it last. He didn't want any questions aimed at him – "You're not a local boy. Where's your regiment?" and the like. The two farming boys looked over towards him once or twice and nudged each other. He hoped that they weren't trouble; he'd heard stories of young lads who hadn't joined up picking on lone soldiers for sport, probably to show that they were men too. Suddenly, however, all his thoughts were shattered when the old upright piano in the corner of the bar burst into life.

Teddy ran his fingers up and down the keys with a flourish and then, looking up at Sam, went into the musical introduction of a ditty that Sam had taught him.

'When stepping out in Drury Lane,' Teddy sang as Sam gave a laugh,

*'The young girls came to watch us,
With me all dressed
In all me best
They like to take a look, thus...'*

Sam took up his place next to the piano, as he'd done many times before. This wasn't just any old Cockney ditty, to Sam it was – he told anybody who asked – the song that saved his life; the song and dance routine a scruffy street urchin did in front of a "fine lady" to earn a penny, but which did much more than that. It earned him a new life and without it, he was certain, he would either be in a pauper's grave or languishing in a prison cell. It was the song that broke Hester's heart and made her determined to save the boy.

'With Joe, me pal,' Sam joined in, his heart swelling, as it always did when he sang it. Teddy joined in.

*'The London gals
Would swoon at two such handsome fellers
They'd never seen the likes before
A brace of cockney swells as*

*We'd saunter down the lane
As cocky as could be
Our silk top hats
And patent shoes
Our grins from ear to ear
What did we have to lose?
The Ladies, they would swoon
As we swung our canes aloft
Oh to be in London town
When you're a grand young toff.'*

The others looked on; even Billy lifted his head and a sad smile appeared on his face. The two farm lads pretended to ignore it while the two young women took in the piano player and the young lad who, after the last verse, had gone into a soft shoe shuffle. This brought a cheer from Connie and Zelda, and Hugh swayed his head from side to side with the music. Phyllis clapped along as Eric, who had never seen this routine before, looked on. Arthur, on the other hand, wandered over to the bar to see if he could chat up the barmaid while the others weren't paying attention to him. Penny and Veronica decided that they weren't in the mood for any of this and sat themselves in a corner booth and sipped at their drinks.

'Trust him to be the life and soul of the ruddy party,' said Penny between clenched teeth.

Veronica raised her eyebrows; she really must get to the bottom of Penny's feud with Teddy Shaw. Sex was bound to be at the root of it, and that always raised her curiosity.

'What's he done to upset you, dear?' she asked.

Penny picked up her drink. 'I don't want to talk about it.'

Veronica wasn't going to be fobbed off with that; more digging would be required. Downing her drink in one go, Penny made her way to the bar to order another.

'Such a talented lad, your Sam, and so kind,' said Phyllis, turning to Randolph.

'Hester adored him,' he answered, even though they had had this conversation many times before. 'She was very proud of him.'

At the bar, Arthur's wandering eye had landed on the two women, and while the others were concentrating on the entertainment he nonchalantly looked across to them both and mouthed 'Drinkies?' along with a little gesture with his hand. Never ones to pass up the opportunity, they looked at each other and nodded. He bowed his head slightly and then turned to get the barmaid's attention,

'A pint of bitter, if I may,' he said to her as she polished the glasses. 'And what are these ladies drinking?'

She couldn't resist a wry smile. *Not ones to refuse a free drink from a bloke, those two,* she thought, as she put the polished glass on the shelf and wandered over to him, *and this bloke looks gullible enough to fall for putting his hand in his pocket on a promise. Silly bugger.*

'Mine's a gin and lemonade,' the plainer one called over.

'Mine's the same,' said the prettier one, the one that Arthur was aiming to do his finest work with, given half a chance – although the other would suffice, if it came to it.

The barmaid nodded and as she did the honours, she wondered what the women's husbands would say if they caught this Jack the lad buying their wives drinks. Still, they were probably out at another pub getting drunk and sniffing the barmaid's skirts there, so deserved what they got.

Arthur brought out his silver cigarette case and his ivory inlaid silver lighter and offered the women a cigarette. He flicked the lighter and held its flame up to the cigarettes, first to the plainer; and then, bringing up his free hand, he placed it on the prettier one's hand as she held the cigarette to her mouth. The barmaid shook her head and went back to her glass polishing.

Over by the piano, Teddy's fingers raced over the keyboard while Sam's dance routine went into overdrive, with wings, scissor kicks and pirouettes. Most members of the Company cheered, the usual suspects chose to ignore it all, and the local boys decided that they didn't like these interlopers in their pub, disturbing the peace.

''Ere, mate,' shouted the taller lad to Sam. 'Why ain't you in uniform?'

His chum chipped in. 'You shouldn't be dancing, boy, you should be fighting.'

'That's enough of that, lads,' the landlord called over to the boys, waving his hand. 'It's nice to have a bit of entertainment, I'd say.'

Over at the table, Connie stood up and clapped along as Sam's dancing got more and more frenetic.

'Do we need that bloody noise?' the taller lad called out over it all.

'We came in for a quiet drink,' the second chimed in to make sure he got his say. 'We've been working out in the fields all day. We just want some peace and quiet.'

Phyllis craned her neck round. 'What's the matter with those two young men?' she asked Randolph.

'Young people who can't take their drink,' he replied.

As he said this, the older and taller lad put down his beer glass, swaggered over and menacingly stood in front of Sam. Undeterred, Sam continued with his routine, facing the boy off. He was born in one of the roughest areas of London and wasn't going to be bullied by this lad, even though he did look like he could flatten him with one punch. Teddy kept bashing away at the piano keys as the others looked on to see what was going to happen next. The smaller lad slid over towards the piano, then BANG! The lid was slammed down. Luckily Teddy had cottoned on a split second before and moved his hands out of the way just in time.

'What the hell?' he shouted as he stood up from the piano. The room went silent, with Sam stopping mid-routine.

'That's better,' said the taller lad, staring Sam in the face. Randolph was on his feet and storming over to the boy.

'What on earth do you think you're doing?' he asked, full of indignation.

'All right, all right,' said the landlord, coming round from the jump.

The smaller lad swaggered over to Randolph. 'We come in here for a nice quiet drink, old man; we're regulars, like, and this is our local,' he said, pushing Randolph in the chest, which made Sam step forward, only to have Teddy grab his arm to make sure he didn't do anything silly.

'We don't want none of you 'furinners' coming here from London, taking over, do we, landlord?' said the smaller lad with a sneer.

'I think it's time you boys went home,' John Stirling replied.

'What? Us? We're nowhere near finished yet, John,' said the taller lad, picking up his beer and taking a sup.

Arthur, who had been standing far enough off, was determined not to get involved but, feeling the eyes of the two women on him, he was unsure how best to react. His instinct was to steer well clear of trouble, if he could, but he didn't want to look a coward in front of the pretty one.

'Haven't you two had enough?' he said, trying to sound confident and strong.

The small lad sauntered over to him and put his face up close. Arthur heard the two women draw in their breath, which strangely pleased him and stopped him from backing off sharpish.

'If I want a drink, I don't need a pansy like you to give me no permission,' the lad said, his spit hitting Arthur in the face, which made him turn sideways. He brought his handkerchief out to wipe the spittle from it. Thankfully, the boy just sneered and then walked away. Arthur gave his back a brave look, as if to say "Try that again" but hoping against hope that he wouldn't.

From the booth, Billy slowly got to his feet and attempted to make his way to the door unnoticed. The taller boy was eying up Eric, who, in turn, was staring at the scene like a rabbit caught in the headlights.

'What are you staring at?' said the lad.

Eric tried not to show how terrified he was. Physical violence was something that appalled him.

'I'm not staring,' he said, eventually.

'Why ain't you in uniform?' said the lad. 'Why ain't you in uniform like this soldier boy, here?' He pointed towards Billy, who froze, heart pounding.

The tall lad crossed over to him and put his arm round his shoulder as if they were best pals.

'Now, this bloke is a proper man,' he said, pulling Billy into him a little. The young soldier wanted to escape but hadn't the courage to pull away. The boy stank of beer and manure. 'You're not like this lot here, are you, mate? Actors, ain't they, landlord? Pansy boys, I'd say.' Billy winced. He'd heard those words so many times coming out of his father's mouth and now, in the place where he'd hoped to be safe, there they were again.

'Not like you 'ere,' the boy said again, with another squeeze of Billy's shoulder. 'Just back from France, are you, mate?' Billy didn't answer; he didn't need to, the lad did all the talking for him. 'Just back from Dunkirk, this boy is. Seen fighting, this boy.'

'Not like you pansies,' his friend chirped in.

Sam could take no more. 'All right, so why aren't you brave lads in uniform then?' he asked, stepping forward.

"Cos we work on the land, boy. On the farm. Real work; man's work, that is.' He looked over towards Eric again. 'But then a bunch of girls like you wouldn't understand that, would you?'

Phyllis, thinking that she was doing the right and proper thing, rose up and beckoned Eric to sit with her,

'Don't get involved, Eric. Come and sit down here.'

'That's right,' taunted the tall boy, 'you go and sit with your old grandma.'

'You, young man,' said Phyllis, rising up with fire in her eyes, 'are in need of a jolly good horse whipping.' Old grandma, indeed. She sat.

The lad turned back to Sam. 'We're reserved occupations, see. Farmers. Someone's got to grow the food and feed the pigs and milk the cows. But I tell yer, if we were called up, we'd go off and fight Jerry.' He turned back to Billy, who was trapped. 'This boy's been fighting Jerry, ain't yer, mate?'

Billy winced and began to shake.

'Why don't you leave the chap alone?' said Sam.

'I ain't harming him,' said the tall boy coldly. 'Why would I harm him? He's been fighting.'

Sam couldn't contain himself any longer; the little street fighter took him over.

'Think you like fighting, do you?'

Teddy made a move towards him. 'Sam, I'd leave it.'

The boy looked at them both.

'What's your problem, piano man? Don't want to damage your nice little hands?'

But before the boy had finished speaking, Teddy had landed a forceful jab in the boy's stomach, sweetly followed by an uppercut to his chin, which sent him staggering backwards on his heels. The others looked on in surprise as the other lad grabbed hold of Teddy and tried to wrestle him to the ground, only to be pulled off by Sam, who picked him up by the seat of his trousers and threw him across the room, where he landed with his head under the table where Connie, Zelda, Hugh and Phyllis were sitting. As he tried to stand, Phyllis stuck her heels into his back while Zelda gave him a sharp kick in the stomach.

Throughout this, Arthur stood outside the fray, "shielding" the two young women from harm, while Billy sidled towards the door before making his escape. Eric watched him go and, following, moved towards the door, only to be held up by the landlord appearing with a large Alsatian dog, which was pulling strongly at its leash. Eric stepped back to let the animal pass.

'Right, you two,' said John Stirling, tugging the dog back, 'out of here now.'

The taller lad was getting back to his feet and was about to grab Teddy's leg when he saw the dog snarling a few inches away from him. He shuffled back on his backside to get out of the way.

'We didn't start it, John,' he said.

'Out now or I'll set him on you, and don't think I won't.' John Stirling was no fool. He had acquired a fresh bunch of drinkers for a few weeks and he wasn't going to let these two farm boys get in the way of his profit margin. 'Furriners' they may be, but these 'furriners' had money to spend. The local lads may be banned for a couple of weeks but they'd be allowed back in when this lot had gone on their way.

Meanwhile, Eric quickly made his way to the door and out into the street. In the darkness he could just see the young soldier in the half moonlight, hurrying along the promenade on the other side of the road.

Stopping, he wondered why he was following the soldier. There was something about him, something he wanted to know more about, but he had no idea what that was or why. He could see the sadness in the lad's face. This wasn't something that usually bothered him – he was far too selfish to care about other people problems; that is, until tonight. Eric was brought back to the here and now when the pub door opened behind him and the two lads staggered out. Quickly, he threw himself into a darkened doorway. It was about the only time that he was grateful for the blackout. He held his breath as the farm boys stumbled past, drunkenly cursing the world, too drunk to notice the soldier on the far side diving down the steps as quickly as he could.

Inside the bar, the landlord pulled the dog back behind the bar and through the cellar door.

'I'm most terribly sorry,' said Randolph, coming over towards the bar.

'Yes, sorry about that,' said Teddy, nursing his hand. 'I'm not sure what came over me.'

The landlord held up his hand. 'They're farm boys,' he said. 'They've a lot of brawn but not a lot of brain, those two.'

Connie looked around her. 'Where's the soldier gone?' she asked no one in particular.

'I saw him leave when the fighting started; I'm sure he's seen more fighting in his young life to want to witness any more,' said Phyllis.

'Poor boy,' said Connie, 'he only looked about sixteen. A child; far too young to be a soldier, surely?'

Arthur stepped forward now there was no danger of getting a fist in his face.

'Well, somebody's got to save us from Hitler,' he said pompously.

'And it isn't going to be you, that's for certain,' said Phyllis.

Deciding to ignore her, he started to go back towards the two women, but they'd decided that they'd seen enough for one night and muttered that they'd best get home. Being left without female company, Arthur turned and gave a big smile to the barmaid, who in turn walked away and continued polishing the glasses.

'Well, I'm off up the apples and pears,' said Randolph, having had enough for one day, 'and if I may, I humbly suggest that you all do the same. I don't want you all staying here boozing all night and getting into any more fights.' He let out a hollow laugh. 'There's lots to do tomorrow and I would like to have all of you there, so to speak, not just your mortal remains.'

'Yes, well, I'm certainly ready for my bed,' said Phyllis, getting to her feet.

'We'll just finish off our drinks and then we'll be joining you,' said Zelda.

'Actually, I could do with another,' said Hugh, 'seeing as most of mine landed on the floor when Sam threw chummy boy at us.'

'And me,' said Connie, looking across at her husband, who turned away from her immediately.

'I'll get you one, Connie,' said Hugh, having seen Arthur's response. *What a dreadful man,* he thought.

10

Eric and Billy and Connie

Eric made his way across the road and looked down over the rails and onto the beach huts, but he could see very little as the moon disappeared behind a cloud before reappearing. It was a half moon that reflected in the water as he hobbled down the stone steps. He could just make out the barbed wire defences on the beach as he made his way along the concrete pathway by the sea wall, but the young soldier was nowhere to be seen. Eric stopped by the first hut. He looked at the door and noticed the padlock. He slowly started to make his way along the line, touching each lock and hasp as he went. The soldier was here somewhere. He continued, trying the locks until a hasp dropped when he touched it. Putting his ear to the door, he could hear rustling, like a large rat in the rafters, cornered and trying to find a way out. Eric stood still and held his breath for a moment, hoping to catch any other sound… sobbing, not loudly, but it was there all right; the soldier was in there, crying.

'Hello,' he whispered softly through the door. The noise stopped. 'It's all right, I won't hurt you.' The body inside moved. 'I won't hurt you. The others have gone. I just want to make sure that you're all right, that's all. I won't hurt you.'

There was no answer. Eric gently pulled the door towards him and peered in. In the corner was the dim outline of the soldier, sitting huddled, his knees up into his chest, his arms wrapped tightly round his body.

'I'm Eric.' He stepped in a little further.

The soldier cowered into the corner even more.

'I won't hurt you. I promise. I've just come to make sure you're all right. I promise you, it's just me. It's just me.'

Billy looked up at him.

'This place stinks,' said Eric, sniffing the air and turning his nose up. 'You can't stay in here, dear, it smells worse than a lavatory.'

The soldier shuffled and drew his legs in tighter; his head buried further into his tunic.

'Come and sit outside, get some air. Have a little chat, if you like.' Eric stepped back outside a little, hoping that the boy would follow. He didn't.

'Suit yourself.' Eric turned away, leaving the door open, and sat himself on the sea wall, his legs dangling over the side, staring out to sea.

After a few minutes, Eric could hear movement behind him that mingled with the sound of the waves on the beach below. He didn't turn round or say anything; he even surprised himself by not making some comment. The soldier eventually sat down next to him. Neither spoke. Eric could hear that the boy's breathing was short and out of the corner of his eye he could see his entire body shaking.

'What do you want?' asked Billy, turning to face the fresh-faced lad at his side.

'Nothing,' replied Eric. 'You looked like a frightened rabbit, that's all, so I thought…' He stopped. He didn't really know what he'd thought.

Billy turned back and looked out to sea once more. 'I suppose you want to know about the war. I suppose you want to hear about how heroic we were.'

Eric shook his head. 'No, it's not that, I...'

'Looks calm, doesn't it?' Billy said before Eric could finish. 'Imagine that beach full of soldiers, thousands and thousands of them. Imagine soldiers being marched up and down by the Sergeant Major, barking orders. Can you see them? They're out there.' He pointed to where the imaginary soldiers were marching in ranks along the beach. 'Quick march; right turn; left wheel; marching on the spot, march; halt! All for what? Why were they marching us up and down that beach? Up and down, up and down, going nowhere.'

Eric sensed that the soldier wasn't talking to him but more to himself.

'To stop us from thinking about what we'd been through. The long march back to the sea, with the Germans on our tails, knocking us out at will by the hour. Chasing us into the sea to drown like rats. To stop us thinking about the slaughter that we could do nothing to end.' He glanced across at Eric and then back out to sea. It sounded calm and they both could hear the tide lapping gently over the pebbles.

'They shot the horses in the head. All those beautiful animals. They pulled heavy guns and all our stores. Slaughtered. *No room for horses in the boats and we don't want Jerry to have them, do we, lads?*'

Eric wondered whether he should respond, but then thought it best just to listen.

'Boats – what boats?' Billy continued with an ironic laugh. 'We couldn't see any boats. Thousands and thousands of men and boys huddled up on a strange beach in France, waiting for them to advance on us; and we'd have nowhere to go except into the sea. Drowned rats,' he repeated.

He sat in silence again, staring out towards the invisible horizon. Eric shivered, from the cold or from the visions being conjured from the boy's words. Perhaps both.

'The aircraft came. We could hear them in the distance. Heinkels or Messerschmitts or Stukas – some of the boys thought they could tell by the sound of the engines. I couldn't care what type they were, I just knew that they were making their way towards us, and we had nowhere to hide. Time just stopped and we all looked up into the sky to spot them, then they'd be there – very low, fast, diving, their bullets strafing us. We either ran or threw ourselves into the sand, but there was no escape apart from luck. Some of the bullets ripped through the bodies, almost cutting them in half.'

The tears were falling now, dripping down the boy's cheeks. His lip was quivering. There was silence except for the sea and a few seagulls screeching overhead.

Eric looked over as Billy's head dropped into his chest. Putting his arm out, he went to put it round the boy's shoulders, but before he could the lad was on his feet and heading back to the beach hut.

'I can't go back, you see. They want us back. What for? We can't go back to France; the Germans have got that. They'll be standing on that beach now, looking across the sea towards us. It'll look just like this now,' he said, looking across the defences, 'all barbed wire just in case we're daft enough to try to come back, but it's only a matter of time before they cross the Channel and come for us. And the army will be on the coast waiting to fight them. They want me to be there waiting to fight them. We don't stand a chance.' He stood silent for a moment then said, 'I can't go back.'

Eric couldn't even start to imagine what he'd been through. The thought of men trying to kill each other was beyond him. How could you willingly go through all that knowing that you could end up dead, and for what? He'd experienced bombs falling on London, but up until now none had come his way, and he'd like it to stay that way.

'You won't go to the police, will you?' Billy turned and looked earnestly at him.

'Why would I?'

'I'm a deserter, that's why.'

'I won't go to the police.'

'If they find out where I am, they'll come and get me.'

'Won't they know to come here anyway; won't they come to your house?'

Billy gave half a laugh. 'I don't live here.'

Eric didn't understand.

'We used to come here on our holidays, Mum and me. We used to stay at a guest house.' He leant back to see if he could see it above the huts. He couldn't. 'Just over there, somewhere on the prom. Missus Potter. I thought about staying there tonight but I couldn't risk it.'

'Why not?'

'Because she is a nosy old busybody. She'd put two and two together. She'd gossip. They could shoot me if they find me.' He stared back out to sea. 'I can't risk anything; I shouldn't have been in the pub in this,' he tugged at his uniform, 'standing out like a sore thumb.'

'So where are you going to go?' Eric asked.

'Who knows? I'll kip down in there for a couple of nights then try to work something out,' he said matter-of-factly.

'But there's no bed,' said Eric.

'I'll sleep on the floor.'

'You can't do that.' Eric had never had to sleep rough in his life so had no idea what it would be like, other than uncomfortable and that he'd hate it. 'There's a bed in the theatre,' he said suddenly, remembering Teddy's camp bed. 'It's only a fold-up one. You could sleep on that tonight.'

Billy looked at him. Why was this boy being so kind? The last couple of years, he'd been around soldiers who taunted him, called him names. One or two of them had even tried to push themselves onto him when they were alone but he never gave in to their advances and ended up getting a series of beatings, which the officers turned a blind eye to. Some of the officers were just as bad but he had managed to fend them off as well. He had no one to turn to and now this young man, who he had never met before, was offering to help him. It was so unusual in his life and he felt a little wary of it.

'I've been thinking about how we can get you out of that uniform and into some civilian clothes,' said Eric, turning on the dim forty-watt light bulb in the corridor, having groped about in the dark for the stage door key under the stone and pushed the blackout in the doorway out of the way. 'Do you have a name, by the way?'

'Billy,' he mumbled, not knowing whether he should reveal anything.

'Well, Billy, look sharp. We haven't got all night.' Eric took him by the hand and led him towards the wardrobe room.

Men's suits and women's skirts and tops hung up on a couple of clothes rails. It wasn't the norm for a company back then to have so many costumes as actors were usually told to supply their own, but Randolph, having been an actor and producer since "God was a boy", had pilfered the odd suit or skirt along the way. Having Connie in charge of wardrobe helped as she wasn't averse to asking kindly ladies of means, who liked to go to the theatre, for any cast-offs they may have; thereby many a widow had passed on their late husband's wardrobe to them while it was still warm. There were one or two pieces that could quite easily have come from Savile Row and graced many an illustrious gathering such as Ascot or the benches of one of the two Houses of Parliament – but, having been thrown into various wardrobe skips on a Saturday night after the last performance and stored in damp cellars for months on end, everything was now a little moth-eaten. Patches covered tears or holes in the material that had been eaten away or worn thin. There wasn't a gent's suit jacket that didn't have reinforcement on the well-worn elbows. Any attempt at keeping the costumes clean was only partially successful, with collars and cuffs still showing dark marks from greasepaint, hair cream and sweat. No matter – all the clothes could be used whenever the play was set; whether the Victorian era or the nineteen-thirties, the audience wouldn't know the difference after Connie had weaved her magic on them.

Billy stared at this array of costumes.

'We'll find you something, dear,' Eric stated as he looked along the rails, pulling off an item and putting it against Billy, then stepping back to look before shaking his head and trying another. 'It's all right, your secrets are safe with me; all of them.' He winked and then lifted off a lady's skirt and was about to offer it up, then thought better of it.

Billy stood in a bit of a daze and let Eric lead.

'Not your colour,' he giggled. Billy found himself blushing and couldn't help a smile forming. A man's suit was produced.

'Exceedingly dull, dear, but probably more in keeping with the surroundings, wouldn't you say?' He held it up. 'Near enough the right size, give or take. Try it on.'

Billy hesitated.

'Listen, we can get you all kitted out in civvies and tomorrow you can be on your way if you want.' Eric put the suit back up to him. 'Well, come on dear, we haven't got all night.'

Billy shuddered, hesitating before starting to unbutton his tunic. Blushing, he slipped behind the clothes rail. Eric laughed.

'It's all right, there's no need to hide; I've seen it all before and I won't jump on you if that's what you're worried about.'

Eric pondered while Billy continued to undress amongst the plethora of costumes. He wasn't sure that he fancied the soldier boy. He didn't really go for the quiet type; he preferred a man more in keeping with the taller lad in the pub, with a bit of meat on him, although this did have a tendency to get him into trouble if he misread the signals. He'd had to make a run for it on numerous occasions.

Billy undid his belt and started to get himself out of his army trousers. 'Well,' said Eric, teasing, 'there you are down to your underpants and we've only just met,' and he winked at the boy, who blushed again.

Back in The Cockleshell, Connie had decided that she really wasn't in the mood to listen to her husband's drunken chatter or be the subject of his verbal abuse that night. He had decided that he wanted to spend the evening drowning his sorrows, no matter what Randolph had said. He just had the barmaid for female company even though it was obvious to everybody, except Arthur, that she wasn't in the least bit interested, but he was well on his way to being oblivious to other people's feelings. Zelda and Hugh eventually decided that enough was enough, which meant that Connie had to make up her mind whether to stay until Arthur had had enough or go back to the hotel without him and wait until he staggered in an hour or so later, intent on starting an argument just for the sake of it. Neither idea appealed to her greatly, so she came to the conclusion that it would be safer, perhaps, to stay out of his way and pop back to the theatre. There were lots of alterations to be getting on with and she could always get forty winks in her armchair. Anything would be better than getting into a drunken argument. The ridiculous thing was that if she were sleeping, or pretending to be, when he got back to their room, he'd purposely wake her in order to chastise her for some reason or another, but if she wasn't there, it wouldn't cross his mind that something could have happened to her and he'd fall into bed without a second thought.

Negotiating the blackout, she made her way down the narrow alleyway and fumbled about in the dark trying to find the key. She lifted the stone but couldn't find it. *What a bother,* she thought.

She really wasn't in the mood to go back to the hotel now. She looked at the door; it wasn't fully closed. She hesitated a moment, wondering whether she should fetch someone. It could be thieves, but what if it was just one of the Company? Actors were always hanging about theatres at all hours; after all, it was their second home, and their dressing rooms were their little places of refuge. She gently pulled the door open and the blackout curtain hanging inside moved in the breeze, revealing the dim light from the corridor. She pulled the door closed, not wanting the air raid warden shouting at her to "put that light out" – not that she'd seen any air raid wardens in the town, or any soldiers for that matter, apart from the young lad in the pub. She hovered in the doorway, wondering what the best thing to do would be. Enter and hope not to get beaten on the head by a burglar, or go back to the hotel and get verbally abused by her drunken husband? She entered, closing the door behind her as fast as she could, and stood with her back against it, hidden from anyone who may be lurking, behind the blackout curtain. She cocked her ear for any sounds of footsteps. Nothing. Very slowly she popped her head round the material and peered down the length of the corridor. Nobody.

'Hello,' she called in her little, nervous, high-pitched voice. 'Hello, is there anybody there?'

In the wardrobe room, Eric and Billy froze. The young soldier was standing in his underpants and Eric was taking the suit trousers off the hanger.

'Hello,' called Connie again, as she ventured out from behind the curtain. 'Mister Tuppence? Mister Tuppence, dear,' she made her way in, 'is that you?'

'It's the dizzy old Desmond woman,' said Eric. Billy stayed rooted to the ground. 'We'll have to hide you. We don't want her coming in here and seeing you in your undies, do we? Whatever would she think?' He looked around and his eyes fell on the large wardrobe skip. Apart from a couple of old blankets, it was empty.

'Right, dear,' he whispered, pointing at the skip, 'you should fit in that if you scrunch yourself up.'

Billy shook his head, but Eric wasn't waiting about and grabbed him, pulling him towards it. 'Come on, no time to linger; you get in while I hold her up.' Eric started towards the door before turning as he was about to open it. 'Get in, you silly cat,' he hissed, and he pulled the door closed behind him, peered round the corner and saw Connie coming towards him.

'Hello, Connie,' he said, making her jump out of her skin. 'What are you doing here at this time of night?'

'Oh, Eric,' she twittered, tapping her heart and giving a little nervous giggle. 'It's you. I thought I was going to be accosted by burglars.'

'Sorry dear, just me, I'm afraid, but I could go and look for some nice burly men if you'd prefer.'

'Oh no, Eric. That's all right.' She took a couple of deep breaths. 'Ooh, that's better. Now, whatever are you doing here at this time of night?'

'Couldn't sleep, dear, so thought I'd pop along and get used to the place. You know, make it feel like home and all that rot.' He smiled and tried to make it all sound convincing. 'What about you, when it comes to it?' he continued, leaning against the wall, his body firmly blocking the way.

'I thought I'd get on with a bit of sewing,' she answered and made as if to pass.

'Actually, I was just going to make a nice cuppa – Shaw has a kettle in the dressing room. Would you like one?' he said, playing for time.

'Oh no, I'm all right at the moment, thank you.' She tried again to get past.

Eric knew he couldn't keep trying to hold her up so stood aside and hoped he could figure out a way of getting Billy out of the wardrobe without her seeing him.

'Are you going to be long, Connie dear?' he asked as nonchalantly as he could.

'Oh, I expect I shall spend the night here,' she answered, tottering off towards the wardrobe door. 'I can get a lot done when it's quiet.'

Eric sucked in his breath. Connie opened the door and went in.

As she got inside, the skip basket moved a little and a creak came from its wicker structure. Connie looked up at it.

'Oh,' she said.

Eric quickly made his way over and promptly sat on it. 'What?' he said guiltily.

'That,' said Connie. 'It moved.'

'That's me sitting on it. Look.' Eric shifted his backside on the top, which made the skip wobble and creak some more.

Connie was confused. He wasn't sitting on it when she saw it move the first time, she was sure of it, but as she dug into her bag and retrieved her spectacles, she decided to think no more of it. She tottered over to the little table, which had her box of needles and threads on the top, and started to look through them.

Eric blew out his cheeks and tried to think of a way of getting her out of the room again; the soldier boy would never last the night cooped up in the skip, that was for sure.

'Do you really think it's a good idea being here all alone at night?' he asked eventually. 'I'd never forgive myself if something happened to you.'

'Whatever could happen to me?' she asked, looking over the top of her spectacles.

Eric shrugged. 'Oh, I don't know. Someone could walk in; after all, the stage door's unlocked. What about those two rough boys in the pub? They could have worked out that we were from the theatre and decide to break in and get their revenge on us. They could set fire to the place or something,' he continued, hamming it up rather too much to sound convincing.

'Do you think so?' she asked.

'You can't be too careful. What if the Germans dropped a bomb on the place? I'd never forgive myself for leaving you here,' he continued, getting off the skip and crossing over to her. 'I think you should go back to the hotel now. I'm sure you'll have plenty of time for all this during rehearsals. I could always help if you need it; I'm a dab hand with the needle and thread.' He placed his hand on her shoulder and was about to coax her up and out of the door when the skip creaked again.

'There it is again,' she said, peering at it. 'It moved again.'

'Rats or mice, I expect.'

'It must be a very large one,' Connie answered, approaching it.

'Don't open it, dear. Rats can be very dangerous; they jump up and go for your eyes, I've heard.'

Connie either didn't hear him or chose to ignore his warnings. She lifted the lid an inch or two and peered in. 'There's a body in there; it's a body!' she screamed, jumping back and recoiling in horror, as the lid lifted slowly and Billy uncoiled himself, attempting to stand.

'It's not what you think,' said Eric quickly, as she looked the half-naked boy up and down.

'What's he doing in there? What have you done? What's he doing in there?'

Eric attempted to calm her but she would have none of it.

'Oh my word, it's the soldier in the pub,' she said as he started to climb out of the skip and look around for his uniform.

'Please Connie, let me explain.'

Eric waved his hands at her as the boy struggled to put on his uniform trousers and mumbled, 'Sorry, so sorry.'

'I know what it might look like, Connie dear, but it isn't; nothing was…' Eric paused a moment, trying to find the right words, 'going on.'

She sat herself down by her little table and shook her head a few times. 'It doesn't matter, Eric. I'm not...' She stopped. What was she? 'No, it's none of my business. It was just a bit of a shock, that's all, dear.'

Billy was shaking like a leaf trying to button his flies.

'Don't panic, dear, we'll sort it out,' Eric said to pacify him, as Connie wiped her mouth with her handkerchief.

'Now then,' she said, suddenly pulling herself together. 'Eric's right, there's no need to be frightened of me. I've been in the theatre for many years and I think I've seen most things in my time. This was a little novel and out of the blue, I must admit, but no harm done.' She had become quite calm now and smiled at the soldier as he stood staring at her. She may be calm but he wasn't.

'Now, perhaps it would be a good idea if I knew your name,' she continued calmly. 'I'm Connie.'

Billy kept staring and wondered whether he should make a run for it. What if she should tell the police?

'It's all right,' she continued, as if reading his mind, 'I won't tell anybody. It's our little secret.' She gave him a friendly smile.

'Billy,' he answered after a moment.

She looked kindly. 'Again, dear? I'm a little deaf.'

'Billy,' he said a little louder. 'Billy Pryce.

'Billy Pryce, there,' she said, satisfied. 'Well, I'm Connie Desmond and I don't bite.' She gave a little laugh. 'Now, why don't you sit down, Billy Pryce, and tell Connie what this is all about. Just between us.'

There was something about this woman that Billy felt comfortable with. Yes, she reminded him of his mother. There was kindness in her eyes that shone out at him. He relaxed a little.

'Well, Connie dear...' Eric said, sitting on the arm of the armchair.

Connie held up her hand. 'No, Eric, I was talking to Billy. Let him speak for himself. Yes, I think that would be for the best, don't you think?'

Eric was stopped in his tracks. His instinct to gossip and be at the forefront of a conversation was very strong. He loved telling a good juicy story that he could embellish with a biting comment here and there to spice it up a little, but in view of what Connie said he just raised his eyebrows and pursed his lips a little.

'Eric, dear, why don't you go off and make us all that nice pot of tea you were talking about earlier while Billy and I have a little chat?' It wasn't really a question.

For the next couple of hours, Billy told them both of the horrors that he had witnessed in France; how the Germans, with almost super-human force, had blasted their way through France and how the Brits had been forced to retreat towards the coast before they were cut off. There had been rumour, he told them, that soldiers in Belgium had been caught with no way out and were slaughtered.

They listened intently but couldn't imagine the horror.

Taking a breath, Billy came round to his family. Talking about it was very cathartic. His father, his drunken temper and how he would sooner see his son blown to pieces by an enemy bomb than be caught and tried as a deserter. He had no idea whether deserters could still be shot but that didn't stop the nightmares – the vision of his father with a rifle, pointing it towards him.

'No, surely not,' said Connie, looking up from her sewing. 'I can't imagine that your father would really do such a thing,' she said.

'He would,' said Billy coldly.

She tut-tutted and shook her head whilst still sewing away. 'So now that you've run off, what will you do? Where will you go?'

He shook his head,

'I don't know. I haven't thought about it. I couldn't.' Tears started to creep down his cheeks and he broke down and started to shake uncontrollably again.

Eric sat on the sidelines. For someone who usually loved a bit of drama, he felt very subdued. For the first time in his life, he could feel real emotion instead of a concocted façade. It was all rather alien and he had no idea how to deal with it. Connie, on the other hand, had no such problems and, putting down her sewing, she took Billy in her arms and hugged him tightly, making soothing noises and stroking his hair. He clung to her as he trembled in her arms and all the tears inside him rushed out and engulfed him in raw emotion.

'Eric, dear,' said Connie above the sobs, 'I think we should find somewhere for this young man to have a lie down and get some sleep.'

'I'd already thought of that,' said Eric, pleased to be the centre of attention again, even though he knew that he wasn't. 'Teddy Shaw's got his camp bed in our room.'

'Oh yes, good,' Connie said. 'Well, in that case bring the blankets that are in the skips and make up the bed for him.'

Eric wasn't very good at taking orders but, despite himself, he collected the blankets as Connie picked up a couple of cushions and gave them to him to use as pillows.

'We'll have to get him up before Teddy arrives in the morning,' Eric stated as they settled Billy into bed a few minutes later.

'I'll be here to see to that,' said Connie as she gently closed the door of the dressing room. 'Now, I suggest you get back to the hotel or you'll be in no fit state for rehearsals tomorrow and Randolph will be very grumpy with you.'

A wealth of new and strange sensations filled Eric's head as he made his way back to the hotel, which confounded him. He couldn't stop thinking about Billy Pryce, this soldier boy who he'd only met a few hours before. He'd often cursed his disability; all those years lying on his back and not being able to walk when his polio was at its worst. The frustration and anger that welled up in him at not being able to get about and be like other boys, alongside knowing that he wasn't like other boys in other ways too – he had no name for it and these things weren't spoken about. He was different.

Connie sat herself down in the old armchair, taking up the shirt she'd been working on. Reloading her needle with some thread, she turned the shirt inside out to get to the collar, which was fraying badly. As she sewed, she thought of what that poor young man had been through. Just a boy, put through such horrors – and such a sensitive lad, she could see that. It was late now, nearly two in the morning. As she continued with her sewing and lost herself in her thoughts, the boy's life made her think of her own life. It often went through her mind what it would have been like if Arthur Desmond hadn't turned up when he did and she had not fallen for his surface charm. She loved her job looking after and mending all the costumes for the various companies. Yes they were a little down-at-heel ventures on the whole, hardly Number 1 or Number 2 tours performing in the great theatrical cathedrals that adorned every large town or city in the country, but no matter. The costumes had seen better days, but that was part of the fun. "Make do and mend" was her motto and she was very good at it. She enjoyed the odd occasion when she was asked to perform as well, but she was only really in her element with a needle and some thread in hand, when she was free to make, as best she could, as many silk purses out of sows' ears as she was allowed. It stopped her from dwelling on the way Arthur treated her. Oh, she knew that she made excuses for his appalling behaviour towards her, but his life had been a disappointment, poor dear, he hadn't achieved what he thought was the recognition that he was convinced he was worthy of and was bitter about it; his behaviour towards her was just him lashing out in frustration, that's all. Did she still love him? She knew it was foolish and destructive and that the others felt sorry for her, and there were times over the past year or so of the war that she had hoped that he'd be called up and that one day she'd receive the telegram telling her that he'd gone missing in battle, so she could remember her husband as she'd have liked him to be and would be able to tell people, in the future, what a marvellous husband she had once had – an ideal husband. But it wasn't to be. Even though he liked to think of himself as ten years younger, he was too old to be called up; something he was grateful for, but that at the same time made him too old to be the Lothario he thought himself to be.

All these thoughts were going through Connie's head as she replaced the collar, while her eyelids started to get heavier and heavier until they closed completely and she dozed off with the needle half in and half out of the material.

11

Teddy Takes Charge and Phyllis Explodes

Teddy Shaw liked to get up and out as early as possible in the morning – straight out of bed as soon as he awoke and a little nap in the afternoon, for half an hour. It was the only way he could get through the day and keep the intense migraines that had plagued him his entire life at bay.

He was the first down for breakfast at eight and then took himself off for a brisk walk along the seafront to breathe in the fresh salty air, which seemed to keep his head clear.

As he stepped out along the prom, he used the time to think. How could he make his peace with Penny Rose? She was never out of his thoughts, yet he'd hurt her badly. Why in God's name couldn't he tell her the truth? Because he was ashamed, that's why. Ashamed? Was that the right word? Embarrassed. Extremely handsome Teddy Shaw; one of those men, that other men dream of being; "the blighter gets even more devilishly handsome as he gets older." But would they envy him so if they knew his secret? Would they want to be him then? He doubted it. The best thing Teddy could do was try to ignore it – play at being good old Teddy, the life and soul of the party. That's why he'd walked out on her; he couldn't bring himself to tell her the truth. Why? Perhaps she'd laugh at him, mock him and throw him out, telling all her friends that he was a fraud, a fake: "The thing is, Celia, for all those matinee idol looks, Teddy Shaw can't… you know. Who'd have believed it?" Now Randolph, with his classic lack of thought, had thrown him and Penny together again, and seeing her after all this time had made all the feelings he had for her come rushing back. He knew that he had no choice; if he wanted her back then he would have to take the risk, when the time was right. If only he knew when the right time would be.

He stopped and looked out to sea. A few deep breaths to clear his head, then he'd make his way to the theatre and take a look at his lines.

He was surprised to find the stage door unlocked. The light was on in the corridor. It was still only eight thirty so no one, as far as he was aware, should have been there apart from Mister Tuppence, and it seemed that he tended to come in through the front. Passing the piano, Teddy decided to flush out anybody by running his fingers up and down the keys and playing a few chords, fortissimo.

Billy Pryce's and Connie Desmond's eyes opened as if linked together. *What was that?* they both thought, as one. It took a moment for Billy to remember where he was and then, in a blind panic, he pulled back the blankets from the bed. Connie, having been fast asleep in the armchair with needle and thread in the shirt collar, let it drop to the floor as she got to her feet as quickly as she could.

'Come out, come out, wherever you are,' chanted Teddy, before singing as loud as he could, *The sun has got his hat on, hip, hip, hooray, The sun has got his hat on and he's coming out to play*, before closing the piano lid and making his way along the corridor. Opening the dressing room door, he was surprised to find a young man struggling to get to his feet from the camp bed.

'Hello, hello, hello,' Teddy said, quite calmly. 'Who's been sleeping in my bed?'

Billy tried to untangle himself but his foot caught in a tear in the blanket and he fell onto his knees.

'Hold on, old chap,' said Teddy. 'No need to panic. Stay calm. I don't bite.'

Connie came out of the wardrobe room and made her way along the corridor as she heard Teddy's voice.

'Ah, Connie,' he said, as she rushed into the room, 'is this young man anything to do with you?'

Connie nodded her head. 'Yes, I suppose he is, Teddy, yes,' she twittered. 'I'm so sorry, I'm afraid I took the liberty—'

Teddy held up his hand for her to stop.

'My dear Connie, you of all people have no need to apologise. I'm sure you have a perfectly good reason.'

'Well,' she started, 'it's all rather complicated…' and she proceeded to tell him everything, while he filled the kettle and lit the primus stove under it. Billy settled back on the camp bed, not knowing what was going to happen next.

Eric woke heavily. He wasn't good at getting out of bed at the best of times and felt he needed his full eight hours' sleep. It took a moment or two for him to get his bearings and suddenly remember the events of the night before. The soldier, he thought, and looked at his wristwatch. Nine fifteen. He staggered out of bed and splashed his face before quickly making his way downstairs. He looked in the breakfast room, hoping to see Teddy Shaw munching away happily at his toast.

'Has anyone seen Teddy?' he asked from the doorway.

'He's long gone,' said Hugh. 'An early bird, that one; he never hangs about in the morning. He'll be at the theatre by now.' Hugh bit into his slice of toast.

'Arthur, did Connie come back?'

'Why?' asked Arthur in an uninterested tone.

'I saw her at the theatre after the fight and I just wondered, that's all.'

'She's probably still there, then.' The others looked over at him. His lack of interest in his wife's whereabouts still came as a surprise to them. Zelda shook her head.

'Oh really, Arthur,' she said. 'Connie could be lying in the gutter having been robbed or something, for all you care.'

'She isn't in the gutter, Zelda,' he snapped. 'She'll be sewing a tatty piece of material that is masquerading as a costume. She prefers the wardrobe to the bedroom, any day or night.'

Eric hadn't hung around for this last exchange; he was out of the door and making his way down the road, hoping against hope that Connie had got Billy up and out of the way before Teddy found him.

The dressing room was empty and the camp bed no longer in the corner. 'Hello, old chap,' came a voice from behind him. 'If you're looking for your soldier friend, Connie and I have set him up under the stage, out of the way of prying eyes.'

Eric spun round to be greeted by Teddy's smiling face.

'Perhaps it would be a good idea, now you're here, to pop over to the café and see if you can cadge some breakfast from Missus Baxter for him; he looks half starved, poor chap.' Teddy dug out some money from his pocket and handed it over to him. 'Here's a couple of bob, that should cover it.'

Slowly, the rest of the Company started to wander in, as usual in dribs and drabs.

Arthur, who – even though he was a heavy drinker and should have been used to it by now – was nursing a hangover from hell and his mouth tasted like a farmyard. It was the rum. After the others had gone, the landlord had gone down to his cellar and brought up some that, he said, had been aging nicely in an oak cask about half a mile out to sea, along with its brothers and sisters. Smugglers' rum, dark and mellow on the tongue; nectar that made you want to have some more, which had a delayed punch to it that could knock you sideways when you weren't looking.

The sea air, which many said was good for clearing the head, was having no effect on him whatsoever, and every step brought a dull thud behind his eyes. He looked at his watch. Nine fifty; ten minutes until he'd be needed in rehearsals. No rush, he reasoned, as Randolph was starting with the beginning of Act Two and he wasn't on straight away; there was time to go over to the café and grab a mug of tea.

Randolph was pacing the stage, as ever, impatient to start. Eric was using the delay to try to force Charley's lines into his brain; he'd got the first act in but he'd not looked at his script at all since the end of rehearsals the day before and he was playing catch-up, fully aware that Sam and a few of the others had their entire parts firmly embedded in their heads. He had the choice of either keeping hold of his script or struggling through and asking for a prompt from the girl.

Molly was also staring at the play as she sat on her tall stool in the prompt corner, waiting for them to start. Sam had explained that Randolph was adamant that he wanted them all "off the book" today. Most of them had done it before, at one time or another, so there was no excuse not to know their words. He'd warned her that they'd be calling out for their lines all day and it was her job to keep her finger on the script and jump in with the next line when it was called for.

'Shout it out nice and loud,' Sam had said. 'There's one thing an actor can't stand – a stage manager who whispers the lines, even during the play.'

'But I can't shout it out if there's an audience there; they'd all hear it,' said Molly, unsure.

'No they won't; they never do. Don't ask me why but, for some reason, the public very rarely hear a prompt.'

'Don't they?' said Molly. 'Why not?'

'Because you don't exist, see.'

Molly frowned.

'I know you're sitting in the corner, the actors know, but the audience don't; why should they? The first thing to learn is that stage managers don't exist, but without them the show probably wouldn't go on.' He laughed but Molly was even more confused. 'Not to worry,' he said. 'You'll soon learn and understand all this stuff. It's a strange old game and no mistake.'

Molly was still trying to get her head around all this when she noticed Arthur coming through the doors into the wings. In his hand he held a mug of tea, and one of the first things Sam had taught her was "no food or drink allowed on the stage, except when used in the action of the play – no excuses; no exceptions."

'No drinks on stage, sorry,' she said, turning as he came down the wings, sipping from the mug.

'What?' Arthur scowled.

'You're not allowed tea on the stage, Mister Desmond.'

He was in no mood to be told what he could or could not do on the stage by this silly slip of a girl, who'd only stepped in a theatre for the first time two days beforehand. Even with a gallon of tannin inside him, his head was still thumping.

'Expert after a couple of days, are you?' he asked with a sneer.

Molly pointed to the handwritten sign that she had pinned up on the wall. 'I've put a sign up; Sam said I should. It says—'

Arthur stopped her abruptly. 'I can read what it says.' He knew he was in the wrong but he was damned if he was going to be told. He looked at her for the first time; she was a pretty little thing. Perhaps a bit of charm wouldn't go amiss.

'Listen, old thing,' he laughed. 'Why can't we just overlook me having this cuppa, just this once, eh?'

'Sorry, it's against the rules, as you well know, Arthur.' This was from Sam as he walked into the wings, having overheard. 'You've been in the game long enough to know the rules, and we don't want any drinks being spilt over the set, do we?'

'What bloody set?' Arthur snapped, taken off guard. 'There is no set. The stage is bloody empty.'

Sam was not to be moved; he could sense the others craning their necks from the stage. 'Start as you mean to go on,' Sam pontificated.

Randolph sighed. He was anxious to get started and not have another argument, which was bound to get out of hand.

'Come on now, Arthur, it's past ten and you should know by now that I hate lateness. We can't start until you're ready.'

'I'm not on for the first ten pages, Randolph,' he said defiantly. 'If you'd started at ten, by the time I arrived, if I hadn't have got stopped by little Miss Bossy-boots here, I'd be ready for my entrance.' He pointed over at Molly like a schoolboy who has been caught out cheating. Molly's chin started to tremble but then she remembered what Connie had said about some actors being bullies and ASMs being easy prey, so she took a very deep breath, told herself not to be a silly, and opened her copy of the play.

Arthur drank down his tea and then banged it down on the desk next to her. 'Take this back to your mother, girl.'

However, Sam picked it straight up again and, grabbing hold of Arthur's hand, pushed the mug into it. 'Rule number two, stage managers aren't actors' skivvies. Take it back yourself.'

'Oh, for God's sake, can't we just damned well get on? We'll never finish this bloody awful play at this rate!' Veronica stamped her foot with impatience.

'Yes, let's just move on, shall we, and continue with Act Two. So, now the settings have changed from Jack's rooms to the garden outside. I'm hoping that the act change and the setting of the garden furniture etcetera won't take too long, but I'll leave that in Sam's more-than-capable hands to work out. We can only have one interval and we don't want to lose the audience by keeping them twiddling their thumbs for too long, Sam, so I was hoping that we can all muck in with the change.'

Right on cue, Hugh piped up. 'I just need to say that I'd love to help but with my old ticker—'

Randolph held up his hand. 'No, no, of course not, Hugh, perfectly understood. Any volunteers?' He looked about him as Arthur sidled onto the stage.

'Well, don't look at me,' he barked, his head feeling like it was stuffed full of cotton wool. 'I'm wearing a bloody skirt so won't be able to do anything.' And with this, he dumped himself into the armchair.

'I'm sure I could do a bit of furniture moving, if that helps,' Teddy, as ever, volunteered.

Penny blew out her cheeks and shook her head again; always the gallant, the blue-eyed boy. If only they knew.

'Yes, well, jolly good, thank you Teddy. I could move a few things myself. We'll work something out. Yes. Now, where were we?'

'Sunning ourselves in the garden, guvnor,' said Sam cheekily to lighten the mood a fraction.

'Good. Yes, in the garden, thank you Sam. Now, there'll be an archway here, I think – is that right, Sam?'

Sam nodded. 'And two pathways leading off, here and here.' Sam pointed. 'They'll be marked out by little borders of plants – if I can find any, that is.'

'Good. And the outside walls of the building will be the flattage turned round as they're double sided, isn't that right, Sam?'

'On the nose, guvnor. We'll spin them round and by magic of the theatre, within seconds the inside will become the outside. Molly and I will have it all done and dusted in the blink of an eye, won't we, Molly Malone?'

Molly nodded eagerly and marvelled at Sam's confidence, without really understanding what he meant.

And with that, they started from the beginning of Act Two.

BRASSETT (Randolph) *Well, we're sailing along. He makes a wonderful lady does his Lordship and not a doubt about it. A bit* *singular to look at, perhaps, but then look at some of your old ladies! Nobody'd believe 'em possible, and he don't seem a bit worse to look at than two or three I could mention holding very 'igh positions, too. Both the old gents have got their eye on her. Lor'! If only they knew. I fancy Sir Francis is favourite, although old Spettigue fancies himself. (Chuckles.) Well, College gents'll do anything!*

With his head thumping as it was, Arthur couldn't remember a single word – not that he'd made a serious attempt to learn them – and he'd left his cue copy at the hotel. Suddenly Molly could feel someone behind her.

'Sorry, old girl, but I need to take a shoofty at the words,' he said, leaning over her, looking down and flicking over the pages of her prompt copy until he found his part. Molly turned her face sideways as the stale smell of cigarette smoke and alcohol wafted up her nose. She wasn't sure what to do but she knew that she had to keep up with the actors on stage in case they needed a prompt.

'I need to follow the words, Mister Desmond,' she whispered, trying to turn back the pages and find where they were in the script without breathing in too much.

'I won't be a bloody minute,' he snapped back, pressing himself hard against her back and trying to see the words, which were barely illuminated by the dim desk light.

'But they might need me to prompt them,' Molly said, trying to flick the pages back yet again.

'Oh, shut up, girl.' Arthur pushed her away and thumbed the pages roughly, tearing a corner of one of them in his fury. Molly could feel his arms pressing and brushing the front of her cardigan. She attempted to move back a little but he was around her, pinning her to the stool as he leaned over.

'Line!' came a shout from the stage. 'Line!' Sam's voice rang out as Molly looked around in panic. Arthur jumped back and sauntered up the wings.

'Sorry, sorry,' Molly flicked frantically through the pages.

Sam strode over to her. 'It's all right. I know the line now; it just slipped me mind.' He gave her a wink. 'Don't worry, I'm keeping an eye on that one,' and he nodded towards Arthur's receding back. Coming back onto the stage, he apologised to the others.

'I'll take it from my exit line, then,' said Randolph. 'Molly dear, we're going from Brasset's line, "Oh beg pardon, sir."' They picked up the scene and carried on.

Under the stage, Billy Pryce lay on the camp bed and listened to the voices as they filtered down through the floorboards, along with the shower of dust as they paced about the stage above him.

JACK (Sam) *Oh yes, she's come. Go on, Charley, introduce your aunt.*

CHARLEY (Eric) *Donna Lucia d'Alvadorez, Sir Francis Chesney, Jack's father.*

LORD FANCOURT – as Aunt (Arthur) *How do you do, Sir Francis?*

SIR FRANCIS (Teddy) *How do you do?*

LORD FANCOURT – as Aunt (Arthur) *I'm Charley's aunt from Brazil. Where the nuts come from.*

Billy always laughed at that line when he heard it: 'I'm Charley's Aunt from Brazil, where the nuts come from,' he mimicked as he paced about as best he could beneath them. He tried to imagine who was who from the faces he'd seen in the pub. The older man must be Teddy, who had given him his camp bed. Then there were the two younger voices. He listened and eventually could make out which was Eric, even though he didn't sound the same as when he spoke to him, and the other must have been the boy who sang and danced. The play sounded a bit silly.

CHARLEY *Yes, what is it?*

JACK *My dad's getting himself a rattling good spanking brandy and soda.*

CHARLEY *Brandy and soda? What for?*

JACK *To propose to Babbs, that's all!*

CHARLEY *I knew something awful would come of this. We shall be found out and disgraced. How could you let it go on?*

JACK *Well, don't blame me. It was the fault of your muddle-headed aunt not knowing her own mind and leaving us in the lurch. I could strangle her.*

Billy started to doze, with the words from above starting to sink, unbidden, into his brain.

'I'm Charlie's aunt from Brazil, where….'

Although she felt a bit shaky, Molly tried not to let it upset her. She didn't understand why Mister Desmond wanted to lean over her like that; he was just a very rude man and the alcohol smell and cigarette smoke had made her feel quite ill. She told herself to just concentrate on what was happening on the stage and not think about it, so she watched and listened while Randolph put the actors in the right places. Sam promised that he would teach her all the mysteries of the stage, or as many as he could, but there was so much to learn. She'd heard the actors refer to 'stepping on the green'; what on earth did that mean? Why were the sides of the stage called wings? What did "break a leg" mean? And upstaging?

She found out about the last one soon enough when a fine example of the art came to the fore that afternoon. It started in a fairly civilised manner early on when Phyllis, Veronica, Penny and Arthur were all on stage rehearsing the third act. Veronica nonchalantly made her way to the back of the stage as Phyllis was talking to her, in character, which meant that Phyllis had to turn her back towards the auditorium.

'Veronica, darling,' Phyllis said, through gritted teeth, 'I'm sure you sat on the chaise at the same time as you said that line when we did that before. It was so much tidier.'

'Which line, darling?' Veronica replied through her immaculately white teeth. 'Randolph, dear, which line is Phyllis referring to?'

He scrambled about in his script. 'Ah, yes, the line...'

'"Oh do tell us, Missus Beverley-Smythe,"' Molly's voice sang out perfectly from her prompt corner. Having heard the word "line", she was in like a whippet.

'Yes, yes, thank you, girl,' Veronica sneered at her.

'Thank you Molly,' Randolph repeated, but a great deal kinder. 'Yes, you sit on the *"Oh do tell"* and then Penny, you sit on your next line. That's right, I think.'

Phyllis raised an eyebrow and attempted not to look too smug. 'Let's go from... Molly dear, where's best to go from?'

Molly stuck her head back in her script trying to focus on a line, any line. '*"How rude to interrupt like that"*,' she said quickly, not knowing if it was the right place or not.

'Thank you, dear,' said Phyllis, kindly, 'a perfect place, and the line is so wonderfully apt, don't you think?' She looked around at the others and smiled.

'Let battle commence,' added Teddy quietly in Hugh's ear.

'I fear we could be here all afternoon on this scene,' Hugh whispered back with a heavy sigh.

In her corner, Molly could feel the tension mounting. Knowing that this could escalate very quickly, Randolph toyed with the idea of finishing rehearsals early, but he knew that he couldn't afford to waste time. He went through what had to be achieved: They had to finish the first blocking of the moves that afternoon or they would never catch up. Besides which, he'd asked Sam to stay after rehearsals with Molly to put up the scenery for Act One, so he could rehearse on it the next morning and hopefully get together with Mr Tuppence to talk about the lighting and then...

And then it happened; the top came off Phyllis's pressure cooker and the words spewed from her like lava. 'For heaven's sake, Veronica, will you stop fiddling about inside that bag during my speech,' she fumed, crossing the stage and ripping the offending article out of her adversary's lap and throwing it into the stalls, missing Randolph by a couple of inches.

'*"This bodes some strange eruption to our state"*,' said Teddy, quoting Shakespeare's Horatio.

'And may the best man win,' Sam replied with a laugh.

Veronica rose imperiously and smiled the smuggest smile ever seen; she had achieved her aim. 'Really, Phyllis, I fear for you, dear.' Her patronising tone cut through to everybody.

The women were face to face.

Molly poked her head round from the corner, wondering whether she should go and gather up all the items that had been scattered about by the flying handbag.

'You are the most evil and hideous woman I have ever had the misfortune to meet in my life.' Phyllis spat the words into Veronica's face and a spray of spittle could be seen in the air and landing in her eyes.

'*"A hit, a very palpable hit"*,' Teddy mumbled to himself. Sam turned away and stifled a laugh.

Veronica did not move, save for plucking out a small handkerchief that she kept tucked up her sleeve and gently wiping her face. She was enjoying this and wasn't prepared to let the moment go.

Randolph, having been struck by the odd lipstick and eyeliner pencil, sighed and started up the steps, as Teddy moved in and put his hand gently on Phyllis's shoulder.

'Why don't you have a sit down for a moment, Phyllis,' he said in her ear, 'and calm yourself down.'

She wanted to scratch the woman's eyes out but knew deep down that she wasn't really an eye scratcher; she normally hated the sight of two women cat fighting.

'Thank you, Teddy,' she said, turning towards him and patting his hand. 'I'm perfectly calm now.' She took in a very deep breath and turned to Randolph. 'I'm most so dreadfully sorry; I hope you will forgive me?'

Randolph nodded. 'Perhaps we should call it a day,' he said quietly.

'Nonsense,' she snapped, straightening herself up. 'There are only two or three pages left, so let us carry on regardless.'

'Why do they hate each other so much?' Molly whispered to Sam as they scrambled about on the floor between the seats, collecting the handbag and its erstwhile contents.

'It's been going on for years,' Sam whispered back. 'I'll tell you another time.'

'We found all we could, Miss East,' said Molly as she handed the bag back to her. She actually wanted to say that the horrible woman should be made to find everything herself, but Sam had informed her that the Stage Manager's job wasn't to pour more fuel on the fire but attempt to put it out.

Molly paused and waited. She recalled her late father saying to her once, when she had forgotten her manners, 'I believe the words *"Thank you"* are the ones you're searching for.' She so wanted to say this to Miss East as she snatched the bag back from her, but Sam's words came into her head – "Your job is to put out the fire" – so she just turned and walked back towards her little corner.

'Thank you, my dear,' said Phyllis pointedly as Molly passed her. She smiled at her. She was a nice lady; Miss East must really have done something very bad for Miss Campbell-Bennett to get so cross.

Under the stage, Billy had risen from the bed and stood listening to everything that was going on above.

He could almost hear Randolph's relief as Arthur said the curtain line.

LORD FANCOURT *And I relinquish all claims to being Charley's aunt.*

Randolph clapped his hands and thanked them for "all your hard work", thanking God that it was all over until tomorrow. 'Ten o'clock tomorrow morning – Act One from the tippety-top and in the set, if Sam and Molly can use their Herculean efforts to put up it tonight. I'm sure it would be appreciated if some of you would be willing to lend a hand; not obligatory.' He turned to Hugh. 'Not you, Hugh, of course; goes without saying.'

Arthur had already walked off, winking at Molly as he went by her and lighting a cigarette.

'Aren't you going to help, Arthur?' Connie asked, as he walked past her.

'I'm a bloody actor, woman. I've been an actor for twenty-five years; I do not put up scenery.' He'd done more than enough helping already, in his mind, and he wasn't going to do any more. Without a moment's guilt, he made his way along to The Cockleshell for a hair of the dog or two.

Teddy raised his hand and reiterated that he was willing to give a hand.

'Oh, you would, wouldn't you? Butter wouldn't melt in your mouth,' said Penny, sneering at him.

Teddy span round and took hold of her arm.

'Penny, we need to talk,' he said as quietly as possible. She pulled away.

'Don't you damn well touch me,' she hissed. 'I need a drink.' And she walked off, not looking back. Teddy's urge was to follow her but he was stopped as Zelda sidled over to him.

'None of my business, of course, but I'd leave it for a while, perhaps. She's still getting used to you being here; it's all a bit of a shock.' Zelda gave him a knowing smile.

What the hell does she know? he thought. *Does every bugger know everything about my life?* He felt rather peeved, to say the least.

'You know this business,' she said, as if reading his mind. 'It's a proper old gossip shop.' She tapped him on the arm and turned to her husband, 'Come on, Hugh, if you're not going to do any manual work, you can take me for a stroll along the prom,' she said.

'Right then,' said Sam. 'The sooner we can get this up, the sooner we can throw a pint down our necks.'

'Good show,' Teddy replied, forcing himself to get back his full bonhomie.

'Right you are, Molly Malone, pin back your lug holes as this is your first lesson in how to put up scenery.'

'Tell me all you know, Sam,' she said, stepping up confidently.

'That's my girl,' he answered. 'Now, this funny old thing here is called a flat or flattage – don't ask me why, it just is – and it's made from timber and canvas. Now then, flat is a piece of scenery, used to represent a wall usually. A series of flats can be joined together to make a run, where each flat is supported by being tied together by a sash line and held up by a brace, in this case a French brace – now, don't go asking me why it's called that because I haven't a clue. Anyway, it's this triangular frame hinged on the back here, and you balance a heavy stage weight or two on the bottom to hold it firm.'

12

Phyllis and Randolph Have a Moment Together

Phyllis left the theatre at a pace. She was more than angry; she was incandescent with rage, not only at that dreadful woman but at herself for losing her temper in that way. She had promised herself as they set out from London that she wouldn't rise to any provocation, that she'd ride out this particular storm calmly and professionally. She had failed miserably, and was furious with herself.

'Phyllis.' The voice came from a distance but was unmistakably Randolph's. He strode towards her, stick swinging, along the promenade. 'Listen, old girl, this is all my fault. I'm sorry.' He stopped, arriving at her side. 'I didn't forget; I didn't think. I put the Company together too quickly. Sam told me I was making a rod for my own back when I told him what I'd done. I booked her without… well, I asked her and when she agreed I hoped that it would be all right. Don't ask me why I hoped that, but I couldn't think of anybody else, so I did it.' He waffled on a little more before Phyllis held up her gloved hand.

'Oh, do be quiet, Randolph. What's done is done; I'd sooner you didn't harp on about it. I've come out here to allow the whole sorry business to be blown out to sea to make land fall in Norway or Sweden, or wherever it is over there.' She waved her hand out towards the sea. 'Now, you're welcome to walk with me, if you wish, but I don't want to hear another word on the subject, do you hear?'

He heard.

They started to walk along the promenade. The seagulls were screeching overhead and the waves lapped gently over the pebbles on the beach below.

'Have you heard from Anthony recently?' asked Randolph.

She didn't answer for a while.

'I had a letter a few weeks ago,' she said, after they'd gone a little further. 'He told me that he'd been busy making a few films for the studio – RKO, MGM or the other one, Twentieth Century Fox – one of them, I can't remember which, but it makes no difference, I'm sure they're all the same, churning out ridiculously silly moving pictures.' She stopped a moment and looked out to sea. 'One, he tells me, was with a singing cowboy. Why on earth would you have an English actor in a Western? Don't they have enough American ones over there?' She shook her head without taking her eyes off the sea. A seagull screamed overhead as if agreeing with her. 'Still, he did write that he has landed a part in a film which has Lawrence Olivier in it. He says that he has no lines but has been promised a very nice close-up.' She turned to Randolph, who could see the tears forming in her eyes – or was that the salty sea air?

'Does that count as acting, Randolph?' She dived into her bag, pulled out her handkerchief and dabbed the water away as best she could. 'I shall never forgive that woman for taking him away from me, turning my only child against me just out of spite, and then making a fool out of him when she'd finished having her fun.' She blew her nose, put the handkerchief back into her bag and squeezed the clasps shut with a click. 'Ashamed, he jumps on a boat to the other side of the world to try his luck in Hollywood, thinking he's another David Niven; as if one's not enough. He tells me that he has been registered with the Central Casting Actors Agency as "Anglo Saxon type, number two thousand and forty-one". I ask you!' She sniffed. 'Oh, Randolph, if only he'd have just come home to me, I would have forgiven him everything.' She paused a moment, thinking it through. 'But he was always a coward; even as a child he took the mildest rebuke to heart.'

The tears, and they were most definitely tears this time, began to fall and she slumped down onto one of the sheltered benches. Randolph sat himself next to her and gently took her hand. She was miles away; she was with her son, scrabbling around to find work on a new continent, and then her thoughts went back to the past.

She was back in the theatre, the time when she had bullied the producer into giving the juvenile lead to her son even though she knew he wasn't up to it – but he was handsome, like his father, which made up for a lot. Of course, it wasn't the first time that she had come across Veronica East; there was that dreadful tour of the Coward play that young Eric had seen them in, but she hadn't realised how much of a snake the woman was until the next tour when she watched her making moves on Anthony. In Phyllis's eyes, Veronica was no more than a fading beauty with little talent, trying to hold onto her youth by having a young man on her arm. She warned Anthony to stay clear but he was young and dazzled by this older, experienced, attractive woman wanting him; it appealed to his ego. Being her only child, he had been attached to his mother's apron strings all his life. Not academically bright, he'd become rather wayward, which was the reason Phyllis wanted him with her – so she could keep an eye on him. Oh, how that had backfired on her! During rehearsals, Veronica's behaviour on stage had grated; she was tardy in her time-keeping, regularly turning up late and failing to have the good manners to apologise; she treated the poor hard-working stage manager as if he was dirt and then expected him to be her lackey; and, worst of all, she was an exponent in the art of upstaging a fellow performer and getting away with it by using her sex to flatter and fawn over the producer (even the ones who, through their own sexual proclivities, would have had no interest in her) – she had them all wrapped around her dainty little finger.

She tried to get Anthony to see sense, but the more she did, the more Veronica turned on the charm. She was a "femme fatale" and Anthony was her prey. By the end of the tour, mother and son weren't speaking. Veronica made a point of booking small self-contained apartments free of any snooping theatrical landladies who had ears like bats and eyes like hawks, waiting to catch out any errant squeaking of floorboards as male members of the Company went in search of female companionship. In the end Veronica and Anthony were sharing an apartment, albeit in separate rooms – or at least, the apartments contained two bedrooms; whether one of them was ever used was a subject of intense gossip amongst the rest of the Company.

Randolph waited patiently as all these thoughts flickered through Phyllis's head.

'Will he come back from America, do you think?'

She shook her head, 'Oh, I've absolutely no idea. No, I have no idea.' She looked out towards the sea again, shaking her head from side to side. 'When she'd had enough of him, she discarded him, threw him out just as I warned him she would. She'd done what she'd set out to do; made herself the dominant woman in his life, over me, and then tossed him out into the cold night knowing that he'd be too much of a coward to tell me, to face me.' Phyllis shook her head. 'He sent me a cable from a steam ship from halfway across the Atlantic Ocean. Did I tell you that?'

Randolph nodded; he knew the whole sordid story.

Her eyes began to sting and tears began to roll down her cheeks again, which she dabbed once more. 'The Yanks like the Brits in Hollywood, he told me years before – Charlie Chaplin, Stan Laurel,

Leslie Howard, Charles Laughton, David Niven, and of course, Olivier. He'd list the lot and dream of the day when his name might join this illustrious pantheon.' She sniffed and snorted in distain. 'He couldn't face me, Randolph. He couldn't bring himself to come home to me. I told him, time and time again, that he'd be welcomed when he decided it was time. But no, he decided to throw in his lot with singing cowboys and goodness knows who else.'

Randolph kissed her on the forehead. 'This is my fault, old girl, what a silly arse I am.'

'Yes, Randolph dear, you really are a silly arse, aren't you?' They both laughed and he pulled her towards him and they sat together for a moment with just the sea and the gulls as background music.

'I shall talk to her in the morning. I'd pay her off and send her on her way, rejoicing, if I could afford it; sadly the money hasn't arrived from London yet. Not that I can think of anybody else who would do it instead.'

'Leave it be, my dear, leave it be,' Phyllis waved her hand again. 'The more attention you give her the worse she gets. Something deep down inside her loves to make other people unhappy. Perhaps she's unhappy herself; who knows what may have happened in her past that has made her like this. There's always a reason why people are like they are, don't you think?'

Randolph nodded.

'No, I shall just have to grin and bear it.' She let go of Randolph's hand, slapped her legs and got up from the bench. 'I'm getting a little chilly; a nice cup of tea back at the hotel, I think, and a little nap before dinner.'

Randolph stood and offered to join her for that tea, and then he thought that he needed to take a look at "the old dicky-birds".

'The words don't stay in my head as easily as they used to,' he stated. Phyllis nodded and agreed that she too had to work harder to remember her words these days. Putting her arm through his, they continued down the promenade like Darby and Joan.

13

A Lesson in Stagecraft and Petty Pilfering

Back at the theatre, Sam had taken Molly through the finer points of putting up scenery, from 'running flats' from one side of the stage to the other, cleating them together with sash rope by whipping the sash over the top cleat – which was way out of reach and was like trying to lasso cattle, something he'd seen in a few Tom Mix Western films – and then weaving the sash down the length of the flat around and over the cleats, then tying them off tightly so there would be no gap between the two flats to form a wall. After a few false starts, Molly was soon lassoing the sash over the top cleats as if she'd been doing it all her life.

'A natural,' Sam called her, which made her blush but feel good at the same time.

They swung out the French braces on the back of the flats and balanced a couple of stage weights on each of them, and in no time at all, the Act One set, representing Jack Chesney's Oxford rooms, was standing on its own with all the furniture in place. With much thanks all round to Teddy and Molly, Sam called it a day. Molly went back across the road to the café, with lots of different emotions but also brimming with the anticipation of telling her mother everything about her day, only missing out the bit about

Mister Desmond being so nasty, as there was no point in worrying her.

Having visited Billy under the stage, Eric informed him that he had had an idea of how to get him some food and was about to see if he could put the plan into action. His thoughts were on the kitchen at the hotel. There was bound to be something in there lying about; if only he could think of a way of getting in there without the awful Miss Goddard seeing him.

He approached the back of the hotel where he thought there might be an open window or the back door left unlocked. However, he was brought up short when he noticed a woman wrapped in a coat with a head scarf covering most of her face coming round the corner. She was clutching a loosely wrapped newspaper parcel, which she hastily stuffed under her coat, and looking around guiltily. Nipping behind the wall, Eric watched her pass. When the woman was out of sight he popped his head round the corner and noticed another woman, all wrapped up and obviously not wanting to be recognised, coming from the other direction. As she arrived at the kitchen's back door, it opened and she was greeted by Miss Goddard. Eric jumped back, before slowly peering round the wall and watching the manageress avariciously holding out her hand, Scrooge-like, as the woman fumbled about in her handbag for her purse whilst being chivvied on. Once money had changed hands, Goddard handed over a newspaper parcel, just like the previous one, and the woman retraced her steps and disappeared. *So the old girl is selling on her rations, she must be,* he thought. Hotels and restaurants weren't under the same strict rationing system, and although they couldn't get hold of everything, they were allowed far more than the average household – just as he had heard the others talking about the other morning at breakfast. The devious old bag.

Making his way round to the front, he waited outside the hotel's main doors and pondered on what he should do next, not realising that the perfect opportunity was about to present itself to him on a plate. Old Mother Goddard appeared from the dining room and waddled over to the stairs. She stopped and rubbed her leg. *Gout,* thought Eric with a snigger, *probably too much port wine. The old girl is a secret tippler for all her talk of the demon drink!* He watched through the glass door as she slowly made her way up the stairs, puffing and panting. Eric craned his head to watch her disappear along the landing and up the narrow stairs to her own suite of rooms.

Quietly unlocking the door and pushing it open, he entered the reception and craned his neck to check that the old girl had gone. Then he quickly made his way into the dining room. Stopping a moment and listening out for her return, he reasoned he had around five minutes to have a sneak around. He looked through the little window in the kitchen door. The coast was clear. He pushed at the door. Entering, he could see another couple of wrapped parcels on the long scrubbed table in the centre, ready for the next lot of customers. Next to them lay open a small black notebook. He took a quick glance, turning a couple of pages. Written in a neat hand were the names of her customers, with amounts and prices set out as only a proficient bookkeeper could: Missus Riley – ham, 4 slices, sixpence; Missus Oakely – 4 rashers bacon, 2 eggs, 2 sausages, one shilling and threepence.

Looking around the room, he noticed that a door with a small wire mesh window in it was slightly ajar. There was no doubt that she intended to come back, so he knew he'd have to put a shift on. Once inside the walk-in larder he saw rows of mesh-covered plates on the deep shelves that lined the walls, containing fresh fruit, various joints of meats – including ham, beef and pork – and cheese, a large yellow block of it. On the other shelves were vegetables and tins of pressed ham, Bully beef and fruit cocktail. He grabbed a couple of the tins of pressed meats and tinned fruit and put them in his pocket. Taking a large knife out of a drawer, he slowly lifted the cover from the block of cheese and cut off a large chunk, then wiped the knife with his handkerchief and placed it back in the drawer and returned the cheese to the shelf. *That is enough,* he thought, *don't push it.* Coming back into the kitchen, he paused. A noise. Just the wind rattling the window panes. Eventually he found himself back in the dining room with his pockets bulging with his ill-gotten gains. Popping his head round the door to check that the coast was clear, he hobbled across the reception and out of the hotel just as Miss Goddard started making her way down the small stairs from her rooms.

'I've haven't got anything to open the tins,' Eric explained, having presented Billy with the fare. The young soldier leapt into action, bringing out a sturdy-looking army knife and piercing a tin in a few places. Moving the blade around, he eventually peeled back the lid to expose the sliced peaches inside and offered it to Eric.

'No, it's all yours,' Eric said, feeling rather pleased with himself for having done something for someone apart from himself.

Billy attacked the contents and finished it off by drinking down the juice. 'My throat's as dry as a desert,' he said as he guzzled down the juice. 'Is there any chance that we can get out tonight? I need some air and I want to show you something,' he asked as he wiped his lips on his sleeve.

'I've got to work and learn my lines tonight, otherwise old Laine will have my guts for garters, but tomorrow we could. How does that sound?'

Disappointed but understanding, Billy agreed and lay back down on his bed. Pulling the blankets over himself, he fell into a deep sleep.

14

Randolph Makes a Telephone Call

Hidden away from the air raids, deep under the streets of Whitehall, there was the steady sound of buzzing and the chatter of women's voices. Along the walls of a cavernous and depressingly gloomy room lit by a series of light bulbs hanging from the arched ceiling, which burned dully under large green metal lamp shades, rows of telephone operators were busy fielding calls to and from various civil service departments. This was, in fact, the most important telephone exchange in the country. With Bakelite headsets over their ears with a strange, horn-shaped mouthpiece sticking out of them, the operators connected incoming or outgoing calls by inserting a series of jack plugs into a bank of patch panels in front of them.

Buzz, buzz…

'Good morning, how may I help you?… Putting you through now… I'm sorry, caller, but I'm getting no answer from that office. Please call back later.'

Buzz, buzz…

'Good morning, how…? Putting you… Please try later.'

Buzz, buzz…

'Good morning…'

About a third of the way along the furthest wall from the door, in the darkest part of the room, Ruby Butterworth was getting a little flustered. She had only been in the job for a few days. She had only applied for the post in order to get out from under her mother's feet, having been nagged by both of her parents that she should do something useful for the war effort.

Perhaps one of the callers would be someone important – not Mister Churchill, obviously, that would be silly, but the Minister for War perhaps? The calls never stopped coming in from minor civil servants. Having been stuck at her post for three hours already, Ruby was desperate to visit the young ladies' room; she kept feeling sick and was scared stiff that she might be pregnant. She'd only met the soldier boy a couple of times. Alfred, he had said his name was.

'Call me Alfie.' He'd given her the wink as they were both buying tickets at the local cinema to see *Goodbye Mister Chips*. She told him that she thought that Robert Donat was very handsome, and Greer Garson so pretty.

'Not as pretty as you though,' he'd said quickly, as if he had had the reply rehearsed and waiting to be used. Ruby had blushed and then he smiled, and she was smitten, there and then. They sat together in the stalls and he attempted to put his arms around her. She shivered at his touch – no boy had ever done that before – and she liked the feeling.

The next evening they went for a drink together at a nice little pub just off Brixton Hill, and it was having left there, as they were walking down a quiet little side street near her parents' flat in New Park Road, that he gave her the old sob story about nearly being killed in France and having no way of knowing if he'd get through the war, and how he didn't want to die without knowing what it was like to 'be with a girl'.

She had fallen for it and now it seemed she'd paid the price.

She knew that if she asked to be relieved before her allotted break, her supervisor – a woman who, she was certain, no man would want to impregnate – would scowl at her all day and make her life more of a misery than it was already.

'Good morning, how may I help you?' she said as her board buzzed at her again and she flicked down the switch.

'Good morning to you,' said the man at the other end. Randolph was standing in a public call box outside the chemist's in Haleston high street. 'Would you be good enough to put me through to Sir Peregrine Worsley's office, please?'

'Which department is that?' asked Ruby as she started to flick through the index cards affixed to the bench in front of her, just as the other operators did whenever calls came in. (Ruby noticed that some of the old hands seemed to have all the different civil servants' names and numbers in their heads without having to look them up.)

'Yes. The Council for the Encouragement of Music and Arts. CEMA, I believe it might be under. C-E-M-A.'

'One moment, please, sir.' Ruby flicked through to the Cs. She could feel the eyes of her supervisor burning into her neck from across the room. She tried to quicken up. 'CEMA, CEMA, CEMA,' she muttered to herself.

'What was that?' enquired Randolph on the other end.

'Just give me one moment, sir.'

'Yes, yes. Don't hurry yourself, my dear.'

He sounds a nice man, she thought. *I wish they were all like him.*

Inside the telephone box, Randolph drummed his fingers and wished the girl would get on with it; he only had two pennies left and he was loathed to waste them.

'Yes, I've found it. Putting you through now,' she said with a smile in her voice, plugging the jack plug into the correct socket to connect to Sir Peregrine's office. In her headphones she could hear the gentle purring of the phone at the other end down the thin copper telephone line, which ran up under the great Whitehall thoroughfare, along the Strand and into Kingsway. Ruby marvelled at how easy it was to contact people nowadays, although she had no idea how it was achieved. There was no answer. She waited a little longer. She could feel the presence of the supervisor directly behind her now – she could see one of her flat, highly polished brogue shoes and a rather fat ankle out of the corner of her eye.

'What is the problem, girl?' came a manly voice from just behind her.

'No answer, Miss Nugent,' she said, gulping.

'Then tell the caller there is no answer and take another call. Can't you see the light flashing in front of you? It might be someone important who wishes to speak to the Prime Minister. Chop, chop.' She clapped her hands, sharply.

Ruby meekly flicked down the switch. 'I'm sorry, caller, but there's no answer from that office.'

'Ah, I see. Right,' said Randolph at the other end, pushing in another penny to continue the call. 'Well, would you be kind enough to pass on a message? Is that possible?'

She wished it was possible as she liked helping people, but she knew that there would be no way of being able to.

Ruby could almost feel the heat coming from her supervisor's nostrils. 'I'm sorry, sir, but I'm not at liberty to take messages. May I suggest that you try later?'

'Yes, yes, of course, but thank you all the same, my dear,' replied Randolph, cursing that he'd wasted his second penny.

'Thank you, sir, I hope you have a pleasant day.' She knew she'd regret saying that as soon as it came out of her mouth, but her mother always taught her to display good manners at all times. She thought that Alfred, her soldier boy, had had good manners – that is, until he ran off like a whippet having had his way. She quickly flicked another switch to take a new call before the dragon behind her could say anything.

Randolph Makes a Telephone Call

'Good morning, how may I help you?'

The person on the other end wasn't someone wishing to speak to the Prime Minister.

15

Onwards and Upwards

Rehearsals continued at their normal pace, as did the constant bickering. From below, Billy could hear the same voice shouting "Line!" or "Yes?" every few minutes, which was followed by Molly shouting it out at the top of her voice. He heard the old man ask, 'Arthur, dear, have you even attempted to learn the part?'

The question was answered by a female voice. 'I think he's waiting for divine intervention, aren't you, Arthur dear?'

'Yes, thank you, Veronica,' the old man cut in, 'Let's not have yet another set to, please.'

It wasn't long before Billy had heard the words so often that he was convinced that he knew them better than this Arthur did, and on the odd occasion, he felt like shouting them through the floor before the girl did.

'How's our young friend?' Teddy asked Eric as they were leaving the stage after rehearsals on the Thursday evening.

'He wants to get out for some air tonight.'

Teddy wasn't surprised. 'Good idea.'

'But what if he's seen?' Eric asked.

'Disguise him, old boy,' Teddy answered. 'There's enough costumes and make-up around here; he could be your old grandfather taking a stroll down the prom, prom, prom, with his favourite grandson.' Teddy went into doddery old man acting and laughed. 'You can use one of my moustaches, as long as you don't lose it.'

It was an idea.

Connie clapped her hands excitedly when it was put to her and agreed on the spot to help out, and an hour after rehearsals had finished, young Billy Pryce had become aged Walter Warbottle in an ill-fitting three-piece suit, cream shirt and spotted bow tie, with Randolph's character wig spirit-gummed onto his head along with one of Teddy's moustaches, and finished off with a battered old trilby hat on his head.

'Now you look like a really doddery old man, you'll need to learn to walk like one,' Eric stated, standing back and taking in the sight in front of him. At which point, Connie magically produced a walking stick and Eric proceeded to give Billy his first acting lesson.

Before long, Eric and Walter were tottering off down the prom, arm in arm, trying to stop each other from giggling uncontrollably. Billy hadn't been this happy since he and his mother had ambled down the very same promenade amongst the other holiday-makers, licking at their ice cream cones and trying to stop the melting chocolate from dribbling down their chins.

This evening the seafront was empty apart from one other aged couple who came towards them and to whom Walter courteously doffed his hat, which broke them both up to such an extent that they had to dive into one of the covered shelters in order to stop being seen doubled up with laughter. The late evening sunlight beamed down on them and the sea was calm with seagulls gliding overhead. Yes, all in all, a perfect evening for a stroll along the prom, prom, prom.

'*As the brass band plays, tiddly, om, pom, pom,*' they sang and danced as they went along.

Passing the entrance to the pier, Billy stopped. The little ice cream stalls, which vied for trade in happier times, were boarded up now and stood forlornly either side of the tall iron gates. Around the gates was a necklace of loosely coiled barbed wire. Before Eric realised it, Billy had started to pull a coil of wire back from the gate, revealing a gap. He signalled to Eric and bent down and very carefully squeezed through. Eric looked around in panic.

'What are you doing?' he asked, half attempting to pull him back.

'Quick, squeeze yourself through.'

'What?'

'Come on, I want to show you something.' Billy beckoned him anxiously. Eric didn't like adventures.

'You'll be seen. Doddery old men don't crawl through barbed wire.'

'Quickly.'

Gingerly, Eric started to manoeuvre his way through.

'Some kids must have broken through and put it back so they could play on the pier whenever they want,' said Billy. 'So there's no hope that it will hold the Germans up if they land on the pier the other way.'

He took Eric by the hand and the two of them started to make their way along the boardwalk.

'Be careful, some of the boards may be loose,' said Billy as they rattled ominously under foot. Eric's instinct was to go straight back onto proper terra firma, but the young soldier pulled him along until they came to the gap where the entire section had been broken away.

'The army have pulled up the boards to stop the Germans – or that's the idea, at least – but they've put this narrow bridge in so people can get across,' he said, walking on a flimsy-looking structure that comprised three boards joined together, hinged on the land side and with chains going up to a wooden frame. 'If the invasion happens, they pull it up on these chains, like a drawbridge,' Billy explained.

Eric looked down to the sea below. His legs started to turn to jelly and his head swam. He stepped back quickly with the one thought of getting off there as quickly as possible.

Meanwhile, Billy had made his way across the bridge and turned to call back for Eric to follow.

'If you think I'm stepping foot on that…' Eric stopped. His stomach turned and he stifled a nervous belch.

'It's perfectly safe, just don't look down,' said Billy with even more confidence.

'You must think I'm doolally tap,' Eric answered firmly.

'But I want to show you something,' Billy said to his new friend, almost pleading, coming back over to him and putting his hand out. With his heart in his throat, Eric ever so slowly took Billy's hand and shuffled forward towards the bridge.

'Don't let me go,' he said, his voice shaking as he tried to stop his legs buckling from under him.

'Now grab my waist like a train and just walk across as if you're walking down the street. Don't stop and just look at the back of my head.'

They started across. Billy placed one foot in front of another at a quick march and, before they knew it, the both of them were sitting on a covered bench on the other side of the pier with Eric shaking but safe.

After letting his friend get his breath, Billy peered out from the shelter to make sure that the coast was clear.

'Come on.' And off they went down the pier.

'Don't run, Billy.'

'But we don't want to be seen.'

'But I can't run; it hurts my legs.'

Billy stopped and looked at him.

'Polio, dear. Five years in bed, flat on my back. My leg muscles aren't that strong,' Eric explained.

'Sorry, I didn't know.'

'Doesn't matter. Anyway, what's so special about what you're going to show me?' Eric asked, changing the subject.

'You'll see,' Billy took him by the hand again and set off past the Pier Theatre. With its boarded windows and peeling stucco façade, the old place looked like it would crumble into the sea at any moment and behind it was a decked area of about ten-foot before some railings and the North Sea going off into the horizon.

'Is this it?' Eric asked.

'I used to come here when I was a small, all on my own while my mother was dozing in a deck chair on the beach,' Billy explained. 'All along here were the old boys fishing, their rods leaning on the railings, smoking their pipes and gazing out to sea, waiting for a fish to bite.'

Eric wasn't sure why he was being told this.

'They'd let me stand and watch them. Then, one day, this old chap came along with all his gear, only he didn't set down his things by the railings, he suddenly bent down and...' Billy bent down as he relayed his story, 'lifted this brass ring and pulled up this trap door.' And so saying, he eased the trap open, revealing a hole about two feet square. He dropped the door back on its hinges. Below, Eric could see a rusted cat ladder, covered in seaweed and slime, which led down to a platform about eight or nine feet below.

'It's a landing stage for the fishermen so they could tie up their boats out here instead of having to heave them onto the beach if they were just coming in for a short time – that's what this old boy told me anyway – and then he started to climb down so he could do his fishing away from the others.' Billy crouched down and placed his feet on the ladder.

'You won't catch me going down there.' Eric was adamant.

'It's safe,' Billy assured him. 'Come on, I didn't let you fall into the sea back there, did I? Just come down after me and take it slowly; some of the rungs will be slippery, so just one foot at a time and hang on tightly. Don't worry – I'll catch you.'

Still Eric hung back.

'I did the same when the old boy said I could join him,' Billy recalled as he started to climb down. 'He helped me down and then he brought out a length of rope and tied it round my waist, through the belt loops on my shorts, and the other end on the bottom rung of this ladder, with just enough slack so I could stand beside him and watch him fish and not fall in. "We don't want you being washed overboard by a big wave now, do we?" he said. "What would your mother say?"'

Eric listened but was far from convinced.

'Do you have any rope to tie me off?' he asked, calling down through the hole.

'No, you'll have to hang on, but the sea's calm today, like a mill pond, so there won't be any big waves to wash you away,' Billy answered.

Eventually and very gingerly, Eric started to climb down the ladder. The rungs were covered with seaweed, making it impossible to get a firm footing, but Billy grabbed hold of his ankles and guided him down. He could feel a tingling in his legs and once or twice he froze, unable to move up or down until he felt an arm round his waist as Billy helped him onto the platform.

Sitting on the edge, Billy wrapped his legs either side of a rail support so he couldn't fall forward. Below, reaching down into the sea, was another cat ladder, even more rusted and caked in even more seaweed. Sheepishly, Eric sat a little further back, not wanting to get too near the edge. The boards were wet, green with vegetation and as slippery as an ice rink.

'This became my secret place. I'd come here every day if I could and sit next to the fisherman, or if he wasn't here, just sit alone, gazing out across the sea.'

'I can think of a more comfortable secret place myself,' Eric said a little snootily.

Billy looked back at his new friend, who was fidgeting about trying to find a dry spot but to no avail.

'It's very damp,' he said.

But Billy had turned back and was staring out to sea again. 'I would hide here. No one else could see me; or that's what I thought. I could just sit and dream. Be myself. Nobody knew I was here.'

Eric looked at Billy's profile, then, ever so slowly, he manoeuvred himself and sat beside him. Billy half turned and smiled. Very gently, Eric kissed him on the cheek as tears fell from the boy's eyes. He gently wiped them away as Billy turned and put his arms around him.

Back at the theatre, they lay on the camp bed together, giggling as they attempted not to roll off or tip it over, but mostly they just lay in each other's arms in the darkness below the stage.

That night, after Eric had left, Billy looked up at the boards above him. All was quiet now; there was no bickering or shouts of "line". It was almost too quiet. Unable to sleep, he pushed himself from the bed and stumbled up the rickety stairs, and in the darkness groped his way along the corridor and into the wings. Feeling about along the wall, he made his way down to the prompt corner and felt about for a light switch. Molly's desk lamp came to life, giving out its shaded blue glow. He peered out onto the stage and angled the lamp in order that some light spilt across it. Pushing his way out past the proscenium arch onto the stage, he crossed to the centre. He turned out front and, after a moment or two, started to quote the curtain line from the play.

'*Oh no, never again, I give you my word. I'll give you the clothes if you like, I've done with them. Miss Delahay has consented to think me over as a husband, and in future I resign to Sir Francis Chesney, all claims to Charley's Aunt.*' And then he proceeded to take a long low bow as the audience, in his imagination, applauded wildly.

Eric unlocked the front door of the hotel. The grandfather clock ticked in the reception area. He stood a moment and wondered whether he should risk pilfering any more supplies. It was late and there didn't seem to be anyone about; it was worth a try. He turned the dining room door handle. The door opened and he entered. Crossing to the kitchen door, he tried it. What luck; the door creaked open and he started to cross towards the larder.

'So it's you, is it?' Miss Goddard stood with a stick in her hand, which she lifted with menace.

He stopped, his hand on the larder door. He turned to her.

Miss Goddard was controlling and meticulous with her housekeeping; She ruled the hotel and any misdemeanours from the staff were jumped on with ferocity. Every tin of peaches, pears or Bully beef was counted daily; every block of cheese measured; every cold cut of meat examined minutely; everything noted down in her book, and the entire staff knew it. It would be a fool who tried to pull the wool over the old girl's eyes. What they didn't know was that her little book was a pack of lies. The numbers written down were not the same as those counted in front of them; they were all manipulated in order that she had leeway for her nefarious black market operations.

'I knew I shouldn't have agreed to have theatricals in my establishment,' she said, menacingly. 'You're nothing but a bunch of rogues and thieves, and that's a fact.' She looked him up and down. 'So now I've caught you. I knew I would catch the culprit in the act if I waited here long enough.' Eric imagined her sitting there all night if needed. 'What have you got to say for yourself?'

Eric didn't say anything; he just looked straight at her. Her, with that supercilious face on her, thinking she'd got him cornered, but she could think again. He slowly walked towards her and stood on the other side of the large table and let his face fall into a wide grin.

'Well?' she said, her eyes popping out of her head. He could swear he saw steam coming out of the old dragon's nostrils. 'What's the matter? Cat got your tongue?' she continued.

Eric very slowly lifted a hand and looked at his fingernails and then, flick, he snapped his hand open and turned it towards her with the gesture of the cat showing its claws.

'Meow,' he said and he hissed at her, his teeth fang-like.

'I see,' she said, slightly taken aback but determined not to show it, 'cheeky young scamp we've got here, haven't we?'

Eric meowed again. Another hiss.

'Well, you won't be so cheeky when I get the constabulary onto you. Then we'll have you and your friends onto the street before you can whistle. What have you got to say to that?'

Eric turned, walked back towards the larder and brazenly walked in. Retrieving a knife from the drawer, he slowly turned back to her and brandished it ever so slightly towards her, making her jump back. He smiled and took the mesh cover off the block of cheese and cut himself a chunk before turning back to her and placing the cheese in his mouth, making great play of enjoying every bit.

The dragon's face was on fire.

'Why, you young…' She raised her stick and made a step towards him.

'That's right,' said Eric, as he cut off another piece of cheese, 'you come at me with your stick, then the police can lock you up for assault and battery… as well as black marketeering.'

She stopped in her tracks.

'What do you mean? What are you talking about?'

'Oh, you know exactly what I mean, dear. All those nice ladies waiting at your back door so you can hand over some little newspaper parcels in exchange for a few bob.'

'How dare you accuse me of such a wicked thing?' she said, attempting to brazen it out. 'I've lived in this town all my life and I've never been so insulted.'

'Really? You do surprise me, an old harridan like you.' Eric was starting to enjoy himself. 'Well, what are you waiting for?' he said. 'I thought you were off to find a local policeman?'

She was between the devil and the deep blue sea and she knew it. What had he seen?

'How dare you accuse me of such things?' she repeated. 'Where's your proof?'

Eric looked at her. He had no proof apart from what he'd seen with his own eyes.

'I'm certain that the local housewives; Missus Ryley and…' he tried to recall the other name in her little black book, '…and Missus Oakley, is it? We've got good memories, us "theatricals". It's one of the tricks of the trade.'

Miss Goddard stood frozen to the spot.

'Well,' he continued, now fully in his element, 'I'm sure they won't be too happy when an inspector from the Ministry of Food comes a-knocking on their front doors. I hear those johnnies are even more ruthless than old Adolf, and they don't take too kindly on those cheating on their rations.' And with that, he lopped off another chunk of cheese and popped it into his mouth before walking past her and out of the kitchen, through reception and out onto the forecourt, where he was violently sick. The undigested cheese looked back up at him and he started laughing. Turning back, he could see the old girl watching him through the window. He bowed towards her, showed her his claws once more, and with a silent "meow", hobbled off down the road to the seafront.

16

Teddy and Penny and Arthur

The words were still failing to get into Arthur's head, which probably had a lot to do with the fact that he stayed in The Cockleshell all evening instead of sitting down quietly and learning them. He could usually be found, therefore, leaning over Molly at her prompt desk, his hand either resting on her shoulder or, unseen from the stage, on the top of her leg, whenever he was waiting for his next entrance.

Molly did her best to keep him at bay when she saw him coming down the wings towards her but pulling away from his clutches wasn't easy. She knew that Sam was looking out for her but, she reasoned, he had enough to think about without worrying about her and she didn't want him to get into an argument with Mister Desmond and for it to cause more bad feeling – the air was thick enough as it was between Miss Campbell-Bennett and Miss East – so she thought she should just have to grin and bear it.

Penny Rose, on the other hand, was not in any mood to grin and bear Teddy Shaw's presence. Every time she saw him, every time she heard his voice, her feelings became a mass of confusion. She didn't know what to think; she didn't know what to feel. Part of her wanted to punish him and make him suffer and…

'Penny?' It was Randolph. 'What?'

'Your line, I think, dear.'

Penny attempted to pull herself back to the present.

'Molly, dear, Miss Rose's line?'

Molly put her finger on it and was about to say it when Penny cut in.

'I know it. I don't need the line. Sorry, I was miles away.' Teddy was looking over at her. 'I'm sorry, Randolph, I've a bit of a throat. Will you excuse me a moment? I need to get a glass of water.'

'Yes, yes.' He needed a break himself. 'Why don't we all take five minutes?'

Teddy dived across the wings and along the corridor and then hovered outside the ladies' dressing room.

'Penny.'

She marched past him, looking down to the floor. He grabbed her arm, which she shook off; he let her go without a struggle.

'Penny, please, can't we just talk about this?'

'There's nothing to talk about.'

'Penny, please,' he pleaded, and went to grab her arm again.

'Don't touch me; don't try and touch me.' She spat it out and her eyes were on fire.

'Penny, why won't you let me explain? We could go somewhere quiet, drive off to a country pub and talk things through. Grant me that.'

'How jolly romantic,' she sneered back. 'A lovely country pub; logs on the fire and comfy armchairs.' She stared at him. 'Go to hell, Mister Shaw.' And she stormed off.

Randolph stopped at the top of the corridor to let her pass. He looked back towards Teddy, who had closed his eyes in frustration.

'Teddy, old chap,' Randolph called down to him, 'after rehearsals, I think it's about time I bought your drink, don't you?'

'I was thinking of going off for a drive, actually,' Teddy said on the spur of the moment.

'Ah, right,' said Randolph. 'Understood. I don't mean to pry, sorry.'

'But since you're buying,' Teddy replied, not wishing to be rude, 'it would be churlish of me to turn down a Scotch or two, so why not?' Teddy slapped him on the back and they went back on stage.

Randolph clapped his hands to get the Company's attention and give them what he hoped they would take as good news. 'Sorry, yes, before I forget; we won't be rehearsing on Saturday as I need to sort out the lighting states with Mister Tuppence, but I'm afraid Sunday will be a full day at the coal face, after church – that is, for those of us who need divine intervention.'

'Oh, it's far too late for any of that; I'm sure God gave up on all of us years ago,' Veronica smirked, giving Penny a look as she saw her drying her eyes.

'Speak for yourself, Veronica,' Phyllis countered. 'I, for one, will be paying a visit to the local church; I hear it's quite charming. I shall make some time to pray for your soul, dear.'

Veronica snorted and sidled over to Penny, who was standing with her arms tightly folded across her chest, staring off into the wings.

'You need a little drink, darling,' she said, placing her arm around the younger woman's shoulder.

Another tear started to roll down her cheek.

'Don't let a man destroy you, darling. Fight back. Auntie Veronica's a dab hand at that. She'll show you how.'

In The Cockleshell, Sam was at the piano, quietly playing any melody that came into his head. Hugh and Zelda were sitting at what they thought of as their table. Veronica was working overtime to become Penny's bosom pal as they sat at another table drinking as if the place was about to run out of gin. Arthur was standing in the corner, quietly chatting up the prettier of the two women from the first evening; her friend was nowhere to be seen. He was completely safe from Connie's prying eyes – not that he cared what she thought – as she had gone back to the hotel with a migraine after too much sewing, or that was her excuse. In reality she just wanted to get a few hours of uninterrupted sleep before being subjected to a night of Arthur's inebriated snoring.

Arthur's eyes were on Teddy Shaw; he had a plan now that Randolph had let slip that they weren't working on Saturday afternoon. As soon as Teddy walked over to the bar on his own, Arthur winked at his new female companion and shuffled across to him.

'Teddy, old chap, just the man,' he said sotto voce, 'what'll you have?'

Teddy was on his guard immediately. Arthur Desmond only bought a drink if he wanted something in return. He was as opaque as a newly cleaned window.

'I'm in the chair, old chap; just getting one in for Randolph and Phyllis actually. What would you like?' Teddy replied, in an attempt not to allow Arthur the upper hand.

Desmond came in a little closer. 'No, I'm alright, old chum,' he answered quietly.

"Chum", thought Teddy. *This must be the devil of a large favour he's angling for.*

'I'm… with company, if you know what I mean?' Desmond winked. *All men together; while the cat's away; you know the score, old chap.*

Teddy knew the score all right. He'd been keeping half an eye on the nasty, lecherous toad all evening, with his arms around that slut at the end of the bar, putting his hand on her backside when he thought no one was looking. Poor Connie.

'I have a little favour to ask, actually.'

'Oh really?' Teddy replied innocently.

'Yes. You see, the thing is, man-to-man, I was wondering if I could…' He looked back at the woman and gave her a wink. 'Well, the thing is, I wondered,' he repeated, 'whether you could see yourself to letting me have a little borrow of that motor of yours on the Saturday afternoon, if of course you weren't thinking of using it yourself?' The unsaid words were "if you're not thinking of using it for the same reason I want to use it", but he didn't need to say it.

Teddy wanted to punch this apology of a man in the eye. How did this slug think that he could be party to allowing him to cheat on Connie, one of the sweetest people he'd ever met?

'Well, well,' said Teddy, leading him on and returning a wink, 'you are a sly one, Arthur. Whatever would Connie say?' Teddy nudged him playfully.

Good boy, thought Arthur.

'Oh, don't worry about her; she's in a world of her own. My little female friend and I, well, we thought that it would be rather fun if we could have an afternoon away from the others.'

'Your little female friend?' asked Teddy teasingly, raising an eyebrow; all chaps together etcetera.

'Yes,' replied Arthur, laughing a short, caddish laugh.

Teddy looked over Arthur's shoulder and watched as his "little female friend" downed yet another large gin and looked in great danger of going "arse over tip" off her bar stool at any moment.

'I'll fill her up,' Arthur continued. 'The car, I mean.' And he laughed the most disgusting laugh, before being pulled up short by a loud crash as the lady in question fell face first onto the bar before sliding, in a very unladylike manner, onto the floor, making everybody turn to see her in a heap and out cold. Sam struck up a dramatic flourish on the piano and got up to see what he could do to help.

'I'd leave her where she is,' said John Stirling, the landlord, half-jokingly. 'She does it so often, I've been thinking about putting a mattress and a couple of blankets down there for her.' He then looked across at Arthur. 'What would you like me to do, sir, call the local taxi service to take her home, or will I get the boy to run down to the Nelson Arms and fetch her husband instead?'

Arthur's face dropped like a stone while the others stifled their laughs.

'Call the taxi,' Arthur answered through his teeth, taking out half a crown and slipping it over the bar. He had no desire to meet the woman's husband, that was certain.

'That should cover it,' said the landlord, taking the coin knowing full well that Charlie, the local cabbie, only charged a shilling to take her home normally.

Arthur bit the inside of his cheek in frustration.

After the woman had been dragged from the pub, the evening progressed quietly enough. Phyllis and the Munros finished their drinks and took themselves off to find some fish and chips before having an early night.

Veronica East wasn't going anywhere and continued feeding Penny Rose large gins and whispering poison into her ear. It didn't take much to get Penny drunk and after three large ones, she was well on her way. Veronica was determined to get the story out of Penny that evening.

'I've noticed that that dreadful woman has been quietly getting young Penelope inebriated and luring her into her confidence. Silly girl,' said Phyllis to Zelda, as they walked along one of the cobbled alleyways that led up to the High Street. 'A very dangerous thing to do.'

Zelda nodded. 'I'm afraid Penny strikes me as very naïve. I've noticed that she obviously has a thing for Teddy Shaw.'

'Really?' said Hugh. 'I hadn't.'

'That's because you don't have a woman's intuition,' replied his wife with a smile.

'You mean I'm not a nosey parker,' said Hugh. 'Teddy's far too old for her; I mean, she's only a child.'

'Twenty-six, I'm told,' replied Phyllis.

'And Shaw must be forty or near enough, surely,' Hugh retorted.

'And there, my dear Hugh, is the crux of the problem.' Phyllis nodded. 'Or that's what he's told her; not that it's the full story.'

'So what is?'

'My lips, I'm afraid, are sealed.'

'Oh really, Phyllis,' snorted Hugh, 'you're an old tease.'

'That may well be true, but at least I won't be using the information to hurt anybody,' she replied. 'I just hope that Penny's lips stay as sealed as mine in front of the East woman.'

The Munros nodded.

'I really don't want to talk about it,' said Penny trying to keep her eyes from going out of focus.

'Oh come, darling, get it off your chest. There's no point in letting it all fester. I'm going to get us both another drink and you can tell Veronica all about it; I'm a very good listener.'

She certainly was a good listener; information was power and any good bit of gossip could be stored and used later to her advantage. This was how she operated.

Making her way to the bar, Veronica nodded sweetly towards Teddy, who was standing with Sam over by the piano. Teddy acknowledged her, returning the gesture and wondering what she was up to; he knew that she wasn't to be trusted, that was for certain. If only he could get closer to overhear their conversation, but he knew it would be pointless.

Veronica returned to the table and put the gins down. 'Well, darling, tell me all.'

Penny took a sip of her drink.

'There's really nothing to tell,' she answered, looking over Veronica's shoulder towards Teddy.

'Oh, don't be a tease, darling; I bought you a nice little drink in anticipation of juicy gossip; you have to tell me now, those are the rules.'

Penny Rose took another look over towards Teddy. He'd

broken her heart, she was sure of it and he'd ruined her life before it had hardly begun. Suddenly her anger, frustration – something – got the better of her:

'He's a bastard, a self-serving egotistical bastard.' She was staring straight at him as she said it.

'That's the stuff, darling, get it off your chest. Tell Veronica what he's done to you.' She was going to keep digging until she got to the bottom of the whole sordid business; at least, she hoped it was sordid – there would be so much more fun to be had if it was. 'He didn't leave you... How shall we say? With a little...' She looked knowingly at Penny's belly.

Penny laughed and laughed again. 'Pregnant, you mean?'

'Well?'

'Not a chance; never came near me.'

'Really?' said Veronica. 'Do go on.'

Penny took another drink. 'There's nothing more to tell.' She had been back in her flat, sitting with him on the sofa, wanting him more than anything else in the world. 'He just stood up, put on his coat and left; not a word,' she mumbled, staring into her glass. 'Then he had the nerve to send a letter to say that he thought I was too young and that I mustn't be silly, as it was for the best that the whole thing should be forgotten about.'

'Well, it sounds to me, darling, that you were barking up the wrong tree all along,' Veronica said as she leaned in to hear her better. 'Some men, of course, aren't sure what they are, but it sounds to me that Teddy Shaw is a friend of the Cornwall boy.'

'No, I know he's not like that,' said Penny, shaking her head, the tears yet again falling down her cheeks. 'I'm sure of it.'

'Well, in that case, what you need, darling,' she stated, 'is a bit of revenge therapy.'

Penny took a sip of her gin and the alcohol started to kick in even more mercilessly.

'What do you mean by revenge therapy?'

'Make him jealous, dear,' Veronica said, casually.

Penny snorted. 'Jealous? Who the hell around here can I make him jealous with? Not the boy?' She was looking over at Sam, who was still tinkering about on the piano. 'What is he, nineteen?'

'No, not him.' Veronica glanced across at Arthur Desmond, who, having lost his little friend, was looking a little lost and getting drunker by the minute.

'You can't mean him?' scoffed Penny, cottoning on.

'You don't have to do anything, darling; God forbid. Just lead him on in front of Shaw; that'll get the both of them going. They might indulge in a little fisticuffs. Bloody noses all round. What fun. Serve them both right.'

Ridiculous, Penny was telling herself, *that's just ridiculous,* but the drink seemed to be overriding her common sense. It was all becoming a bit of a blur.

'Teach him a lesson; rub his nose in it,' Veronica was going in for the kill, determined to put the cat among the pigeons. *One stone and three birds,* thought Veronica, mixing her metaphors in her head.

Penny, had she been sober, would have stopped the conversation there and then; however, Veronica East was a mistress at mind games and Penny, despite herself, was falling under her spell.

'What about that silly old wife of his?' The words just came out of her but she wasn't sure how or why.

'Her?' Veronica had nothing but contempt for the woman – a silly, wittering waste of space. Useful, she supposed, if one needed a dress altered or some such, but nothing else. She despised women like Connie Desmond. 'Serves her right for being so dreadfully dull.' She turned to Penny and they both started to laugh.

'I couldn't, not with him; he's so sleazy. What if he tried to kiss me?' she said with a shiver.

'You'll just have to duck out of it, darling. I'm sure it wouldn't be the first time you've had a frog puckering its lips at you.'

Penny's mind went back to Edgar, dear sweet eager Edgar. Not a frog – no, that would be too cruel – but no Prince Charming either. And despite herself, she laughed, her befuddled brain coming around to the idea, as she looked again over at Teddy, partly wishing to lay in his arms and partly wishing to hurt him so much, just as, she reasoned, he had hurt her.

'Can you imagine the atmosphere in rehearsals tomorrow? What fun, darling.' For Veronica, this was all too delicious to contemplate. Just one more little nudge should do it.

'Arthur, darling,' she called across the bar. 'Penny just mentioned to me that she thought you looked dreadfully lonely over there now your little friend has gone. She can't bear to see you sitting there all alone, can you, darling?' She turned to Penny, who took another sip of gin. 'Come over and join us girls.' She beckoned him seductively with her finger, knowing that he was in no fit state to refuse – and of course, he was too self-obsessed to realise that he was being set up. 'Sit between us, darling. You can be the meat in our sandwich. You'd like that, wouldn't you, darling?'

In his state, Arthur thought he was in heaven, not realising that he was, in fact, entering the gates of hell.

Over by the piano, Teddy was pondering the situation. He knew Veronica couldn't stand Arthur Desmond and positively loathed a pretty little twenty-seven-year-old girl like Penny normally; she would be far too much of a threat.

'What's she up to, Sam?'

'They all look a trifle worse for wear to me,' said Sam, looking over the top of the piano, still playing.

'The East woman is as sober as a judge. She's up to something. I wouldn't trust her an inch.'

'She looks sloshed,' Sam commented.

'Play acting, and not very well at that,' Teddy replied, not taking his eyes off her.

Two more drinks and Veronica would have them where she wanted them.

Arthur moved closer to Penny and made great play of whispering in her ear, and Veronica laughed heartily to complete the impression of bonhomie. Over the next half an hour, Arthur was coaxed into buying another couple of rounds, which Penny had difficulty finishing. She could hardly focus, but at the same time could hear herself giggling like a little girl. Veronica smiled inwardly as she could see that the time was right to put the next part of her plan into action.

'Time to go, don't you think, my darlings?' she said, standing up a little too soberly before realising that she should, perhaps, play the lush a little. 'Oops,' she said with a laugh as she staggered, rather over-dramatically, and knocked against the chair next to her.

Arthur, for all the booze inside him, was busily working out his next move: how to lure Penny into his lair. He held out his hand to help her up. The effects of far too much gin made Penny sway. The bottom half of her body seemingly wanted to do the opposite of the top half.

Veronica put her arm through Arthur's while he put his other arm around Penny's waist as they started to make their way over to the door.

As she passed, Veronica gave Teddy a wink.

'Penny, why don't I walk you back to the hotel?' Teddy whispered as she came level with him.

She snorted contemptuously and staggered backwards a step. 'Oh, you've had your chance, Teddy Shaw,' she slurred.

Her eyes, he could see, were completely dead.

He moved forward to pull her away but Arthur pushed him back. Sam grabbed Teddy by the arm to restrain him.

'I say, old chap, why don't you mind your own business?' Desmond sprayed out foul-smelling spittle as he spoke. 'You've had your chance. I'm looking after the little ladies now.' He chuckled and turned a drunken smile towards Penny, who was trying to keep herself upright.

Teddy started to lunge forward but Sam had him in a tight grip.

'They're doing it to upset you, Teddy,' Sam stated, holding him, now the voice of reason. 'Don't rise to it. It'll just make them worse.'

As soon as they hit the fresh sea air, Penny's head began to swim and her legs felt like jelly. The only thing keeping her upright and moving forward was Arthur Desmond's vice-like grip round her waist. She wasn't sure where she was anymore and the voices next to her were distant.

'Well, isn't that just like me,' said Veronica, as they were climbing the hill towards the hotel. 'I think I've left my room key on the table in the pub. You two go on and I'll just pop back and get it.'

It took a moment for the words to sink in and by the time Penny had realised what she had said, Veronica was already striding away from them, with a malignant self-satisfied look all over her face.

'I've got you, old girl,' Penny heard Arthur saying in her ear. He lit a cigarette, one-handedly so as not to let her go, blowing smoke out of the side of his mouth before coughing violently. The smoke made Penny feel even more nauseous as it wafted across her face; her head swam even more.

Attempting to unlock the hotel's front door, Arthur's grip on her loosened slightly and she tried to wriggle free, but Desmond wasn't going to let his prey go that easily. He pushed the door open with his foot and regained a firm hold, and rather violently pulled her across the lobby and towards the stairs. She wanted to scream but the only noise that came from her was more of a whimper.

Step by step, they made their way up the stairs. Penny could hardly move her legs as Arthur coaxed her first up one flight and then up the second.

Unseen, Veronica had made her way up the hill behind them and now stood by the front door, watching the fun. It was all going to plan most beautifully.

Unsteadily and unfocused, Penny fumbled and dug about in her bag for her room key. Having found it, there was no way that she would be able to find the lock.

'Why don't I unlock the door for you?' said Arthur, attempting to take the key from her.

Instinct told her to keep a tight hold of it.

'Don't be an old silly,' Arthur retorted rather forcefully, trying to grab the key out of her hand again. 'I just want to see you safely into your room, then we can have a little drink. I got the landlord to fill up my hip flask for a nightcap. I thought you'd like a little nightcap. We could both have a little nightcap.' He swayed backwards, his eyes closing for a brief moment.

From somewhere, Penny's survival instinct kicked in and she knew that she had to get into her room alone. Keeping a tight hold of the key, she placed a finger on the keyhole to locate it so she could insert the key and turn it. She could feel Desmond pressing back against her and, although her head was a fuddled mess, she seemed to realise instinctively the danger she was in, so she did her best to shield the door from him as she slid in the key and turned it slowly.

'Come on, old girl, let me help.' He pushed his body even harder against her as she went to turn the handle and open the door.

'I'm all right,' she heard herself say, 'I'm here now. Thank... thank you, I'm all right, I'm all right.' And then, out of the blue, she suddenly backed herself into him, catching him unbalanced and making him stumble against the opposite wall. Quickly she pushed open the door and threw herself in, and turned to close it just as Arthur placed his foot between the door and the frame.

'Come on, play the game, no teasing; Arthur hates to be teased,' he hissed, angrily.

But common sense was breaking through the alcoholic haze and she kicked his shin. In the moment that he reacted to the pain, she pushed him backwards across the hallway and slammed the door closed. Pushing herself against the door and trying to hold it shut, Penny attempted to put the key in the door to lock it, as Desmond threw himself against it, snarling in anger.

'You'll pay for that, you bitch.'

Thankfully, she just managed to turn the key in the lock before the full force of his body could push it open. Desmond fell back from the door, cursing loudly.

Making sure that the door was fast, Penny staggered over to the small wash basin and was immediately sick into it.

Veronica East walked casually up the stairs with a huge smile playing across her face.

'Well, Arthur, dear,' she said as she passed him, 'it just doesn't seem to be your evening.' She unlocked her own door and entered her room.

'Bitch!' Arthur shouted at her before kicking Penny's door in frustration. 'You're both bitches!'

Veronica locked her door from the inside, a grin travelling from ear to ear.

17

Penny and Teddy

The next morning, Randolph checked with Miss Goddard whether any post had come for him, only to be told that there was nothing.

'Ah,' he said, as she stared at him.

'And,' she said haughtily, 'I have still yet to receive any payment for your lodgings. I hope I shan't have to wait much longer.'

'Yes, I'm sorry about that,' replied Randolph, attempting to sound confident, 'but I promise you the money will arrive shortly.'

Ma Goddard sniffed. 'This hotel doesn't run on air and promises. If I don't have payment by tomorrow, you'll be having to find alternative accommodation.'

Randolph took out his pocket watch and looked at it as she spoke. Nine o'clock. *Perry should just about be getting into his office about now*, he thought.

'And I shall expect recompense. That watch of yours will do for a start,' she called out, as he hurried out of the front door.

Randolph made his way along the high street, his stick clicking on the pavement as he marched along as confidently as he could. Inside he didn't feel in the least bit confident. Perry had promised that he had everything in place when he called him just before leaving London and said he was not to worry, "old chap". Popping into the local newsagents, Randolph asked the young girl behind the counter whether she would kindly change the threepenny piece he had in his pocket into three penny coins. He glanced at the headlines as he waited for the girl to open the till. "LONDON WILL FIGHT STREET BY STREET" ran one; "FLYING BOMBS KILL 2,752 – INJURE 8,000 – VERY HIGH TOLL IN LONDON" was a more horrifying one.

Thank God we're not there, he thought, as the girl handed over the pennies.

He opened the door to the telephone box and, having placed one of the coins into the slot provided, dialled the number that would put him through to the Whitehall telephone exchange. *I hope none of those flying bombs landed on 123 Kingsway*, he mused as he waited for an answer. On hearing the pip, pip, pips through the telephone receiver, he pressed button A and hoped for the best.

'I'm sorry, caller, but there is no answer from that number. Please try again later.'

Randolph slammed the telephone back onto its cradle. Well, at least the operator hadn't made him waste a second penny.

'Damn,' he cursed rather too loudly as he exited the telephone box, causing a little old lady to tut as she went by. Randolph lifted his hat a trifle in way of apology but she was already crossing the road away from him.

'I've got a message for Mister Laine,' said a young lad, wandering onto the stage and holding out a piece of paper. Phyllis recognised him as an errand boy she had seen a few times at the hotel. Randolph took the note and began to read, sitting down heavily in the armchair as he took the information in. *Dear God in heaven, this is all I need.*

'What is it, Randolph?' asked Phyllis as he handed the paper over to her.

'Well, don't keep it to yourself, darling. What does it say?' queried Veronica in her most cynical voice.

Phyllis looked up and stared straight her.

'This is your doing, isn't it? I've watched you cosying up to that poor girl since the start,' Phyllis hissed. 'You are the most despicable creature I have ever had the misfortune of—'

'I've really no idea who or what you're talking about,' Veronica replied, feigned innocence written all over her face.

'What is it, old girl?' Hugh asked Phyllis, genuinely concerned.

'It's from Penny; she has decided that she can no longer be a part of this company and is going back to London on the first available train,' said Randolph wearily.

'Oh no, what's happened?' asked Zelda.

'Ask Lady M over there,' Phyllis answered, coming as close to mentioning the Scottish play as she dare.

Veronica lit a cigarette and turned to look out of the French windows, as if viewing some beautiful landscape and not a piece of rather badly painted canvas three feet away, and blew out the cigarette smoke with as much elegant disdain as she could possibly muster.

Teddy took the note from Phyllis and scanned it before looking down to Arthur, who was lounging in the third row of the stalls, his feet up on the back of the seat in front, casually smoking and looking into space.

'If you've hurt her, Desmond, I'll swing for you.'

'What, dear boy? Who are we talking about?'

Teddy's instinct was to take hold of the man and pummel him but Phyllis's voice brought him round.

'For heaven's sake, Teddy, don't waste your time on him. Go and find her before it's too late.'

Nodding and giving her a peck on the cheek, Teddy Shaw rushed from the stage, out of the stage door and down the alleyway.

Connie, who had been watching everything from the wings, shook her head and made her way back to her wardrobe room to bury herself in her sewing. It was her only refuge.

Teddy ran along the cobbled back lanes and into the high street, trying to work out which way would be best as a shortcut to the station. Overhead the seagulls screamed and whirled about the rooftops. All his worst fears from the evening before swirled about his head. The bitch East and that cad Desmond; he'd put nothing past either of them. He cursed himself for letting Sam stop him from intervening.

Heart pounding, he ran across the station forecourt and through the deserted ticket office. He stopped. She was there, sitting on a platform bench, her suitcases on the ground and a vanity case on her lap, clutched tightly to her. Her head was dropped and a gloved hand covered her face. Her shoulders heaved as she sobbed.

He approached slowly and stood looking down at her. He was afraid that if he spoke she would lash out at him or run off, so he would say nothing until offered the chance – if it came.

She could feel his presence; she recognised his aftershave. She adored the smell of him. She daren't look up.

'I hoped it would be you,' she said, taking her hand from her face and lifting her head slightly but not looking at him. 'I thought the Campbell-Bennett woman might feel it was her duty.'

'May I sit?'

She nodded. He sat next to her, not touching her; just far enough away to be… to be what?

'Before you ask, I've been thinking about last night. I don't want to talk about last night. I can't get it out of my head. Please don't ask me about it.' She turned to face him, her eyes red from a night of tears. 'I can't stay. I should have gone straight back when Randolph told me you were coming. I wanted to; I don't know what stopped me.'

Teddy held his council. This was not the time to be witty or clever, to chastise or to plead forgiveness. It was a time to just let her talk it out.

'But I couldn't. Despite myself, I wanted to see you. I wanted the chance to ignore you, to shout at you, to hurt you so badly. I wanted to...' A cry came from deep within her, like a wounded animal.

Teddy held off. He so desperately wanted to comfort her.

'But I couldn't, when it came to it. I was just play acting, pretending to ignore you, to shout at you, to hate you. It was all a sham. Inside I wanted you so much. So very much. I still want you. Seeing you, more than ever.' She turned to him once more. 'Why, when you hurt me so deeply, when you threw me aside? When I offered myself to you. I was desperate for it to be you. I so wanted you to be the first. I still do, I still do.' Another heartfelt cry came up and her whole body crumbled into him.

Teddy froze. *"I so wanted you to be the first. I still do, I still do."* The words hit him in the stomach. Could he tell her his secret? Would she understand? Could he risk it?

'And I wanted you to be the first too.' The words were out of his mouth. 'I still do.'

She turned slowly and looked at him, trying to understand what he had just said.

'Don't mock me, please don't mock me.' The words nearly stuck in his throat.

Penny shook her head. 'Why ever would I mock you?'

'"Suave, debonair Teddy Shaw. Those matinee idol looks. He'll make the ladies' heads turn",' he said, slowly, remembering how the theatre impresarios had sold him when he first started out. '"They'll be lining up outside the stage door every night; you'll be able to take your pick, lucky chap."' He smiled. 'Only I didn't, I couldn't; I was too bloody shy. And the older I've got, the more difficult to...'

But he didn't finish the sentence as Penny's lips pressed against his, stroking his face with her gloved hand.

Teddy's heart swelled and he took Penny in his arms and

kissed her with more passion than he knew he ever possessed.

They sat on the bench in each other's arms. Neither wanted to move away from the other. Eventually, Penny lifted her head and looked up at him. She saw the tears streaming down his face and reaching up, she wiped them with her thumb, and then took his head in her hands and kissed him.

'What shall I do?' she asked. 'I've made such a fool of myself. What do I do, Teddy? Help me, Teddy.'

'Don't let them win, that's the first thing. Show that dreadful woman that she hasn't won. Show Desmond that you're not frightened of him. Believe me, they'll both pay for what they've done. I'm here to protect you, darling girl.' He kissed her again and, standing, held out his hand. Taking it, she stood, collected her luggage and nodded.

The sun had gone behind the clouds, closing out the blue sky as they made their way down the side of the hotel. Penny clung onto Teddy's arm as they walked along. She had no idea how she would be able to face the Company. Everything was bound to be common knowledge – at least up to a point, although Arthur Desmond wasn't ever going to admit his actions, that was for sure.

Entering the hotel, Teddy spotted the young lad who had delivered the note and, giving him thruppence, asked him to return to the theatre and tell Mister Laine that they were dropping off Miss Rose's luggage and that they would return soon.

'But not too soon,' said Penny.

JACK *Babbs – your aunt!*

CHARLEY *Babbs! (Turning upon JACK.))My aunt!*

JACK *It's the only one you've got, so you'll have to make the best of her.*

LORD FANCOURT *(In the wings.) I say – look here.*

(He enters, dressed in a tatty rehearsal skirt with hat, etc.) How's this?

JACK *Splendid! (Knocking at the door.)*

LORD FANCOURT *(Looking at door.) Who's that? (He makes to exit.)*

JACK *(Seizing him by shoulders.) The girls.*

> 'Line!'
> 'The girls,' said Molly loudly from her corner.
> 'Dear Lord, Arthur,' Randolph cut in from his seat in the stalls. 'All you had to do was repeat what Sam has just said.'
> 'I know, I know. I just had a blank, that's all,' Arthur snapped back. 'There's no need to make a song and dance about it.' In truth, his mind was elsewhere. It was on the night before. Humiliation did not sit well with him. 'Give me the line again, Sam.'

JACK *(Seizing him by shoulders.) The girls.*

LORD FANCOURT *(Looking at JACK). The girls?*

JACK *Charley's aunt can't come.*

LORD FANCOURT *Can't she? I'll go and take these things off.*

(JACK and CHARLEY grab him.)

> 'Do you really need to grab my arm so hard?' Arthur complained, turning on Sam.

'If you insist on standing so far away from me, I can't get hold of you to pull you back gently,' Sam replied, stopping himself from wanting to throw the odious man bodily into the stalls.

Randolph stood. 'Yes, Sam, not so hard, old chap. Take half a step closer to Arthur when you say "the girls", if you would. And Arthur, turn yourself towards Sam a bit at the same time. That should do it.' *Diplomacy, compromise,* he thought, *the director's standby.*

JACK *No. They won't stop otherwise.*

LORD FANCOURT *Won't stop! What do you mean?*

JACK *You must be Charley's aunt!*

LORD FANCOURT *(In dismay.) Me? No!*

Under the stage, Billy listened intently and mouthed all the lines to himself; by now he just about knew everyone's parts. Connie constantly visited and brought him mugs of tea and various bits of food that she'd squirrelled away from the café. Apart from the lack of sunlight and fresh air, he was quite comfortable in his little subterranean hidey-hole.

Rehearsals had been moving along even slower than usual – *If that is possible,* Randolph thought disconsolately – owing to the fact that Mister Tuppence kept plunging the theatre into darkness in order for him to put up some lights out the front; and because the wiring had a lot to answer for, he refused to plug the lamps into the mains without having thrown the switch first to make sure there was no electricity going into them while he fiddled with them ten feet up a ladder.

Asked if he could wait until they finished rehearsing, Mister Tuppence mumbled that working at the theatre wasn't the only thing he did, you know, and this was the only time he had and if they didn't like it they could perform their play in the darkness and he'd leave them to it.

Randolph, knowing when he was beaten, decided to give the Company an extended tea break and told them that they would reconvene after Mister Tuppence had gone off to do whatever it was he had to do for the rest of the day.

'We'll stagger through the first act straight after that.' he said wearily. 'Molly, dear, perhaps you'd pop over to the café with a shipping order.' Molly stood, frozen.

'He means make a list of who wants what to drink so your mum can get all the teas, coffees and buns ready for us, so she's not having to rush,' whispered Sam helpfully.

'Right,' she said, picking up her little notebook and pencil.

'What about Teddy's and Penny's lines?' asked Hugh, turning to what was left of the Company.

'Well, let's hope that they're back by the time we get to them, otherwise we'll just have to get Molly to read them in,' Randolph replied, having received the message from the boy.

Hearing this, Molly felt a thousand butterflies fluttering away in her stomach and her face starting to burn.

'I'll wash, you dry,' said Sam, as he brought out the tray of dirty crockery to the café's kitchen.

'Are you trying to take over my kitchen, young man?' Jane Baxter replied as she followed him with the pile of dirty plates. He was such a nice boy, she thought. Putting down the plates on the side, she thought now might be the best time to tackle him on a subject she'd been thinking about.

'I don't mean to be rude, Sam, and please don't take offence, but...' she started to say.

'It's all right, Mrs B, I know what you're about to ask me,' he said, putting the tray on the draining board and starting to put the cups and saucers in the sink. 'Why ain't I in uniform like those other brave boys?'

Jane Baxter nodded. 'I don't mean to pry.'

'You ain't prying, Missus B, it's a fair question. In reality, I think that the War Office, or whoever it is in charge of this stuff, may have lost me papers.'

'How can they have done that?' she asked.

'It's a long story but… well, you see, the thing is, I've not always been Sam Laine; that only happened after the guvnor and the missus took me in. My real mum… well, let's just say she had a bit of a drink problem and, as they say, when a lady has a bit of a problem with the demon drink, she also tends to have a bit of a man problem to go with it. Not to put too fine a point on it, when a lady's a little inebriated she gets less fussy about what type of bloke she hangs around with, and how many.'

At this, Jane Baxter blushed; she was a Norfolk girl, born and bred – in fact she'd never been out of the county – and although not an ardent churchgoer, she tried to live her life according to the scriptures.

'I'm sorry, Sam, I didn't know.'

'Bless you, Mrs B, why should you? That's how life is. We don't choose our parents.' Sam winked as he plunged his hands into the hot water and started rinsing the crockery.

'So I take it then that you had brothers and sisters?' she said, a little hesitantly.

'Three brothers and four sisters. There were eight of us in all.'

She gasped.

Sam laughed. 'Yes, my old mum got about a bit and no mistake.'

Jane Baxter had never heard the like.

'So what name were you born with?'

'I was Leonard – well, Lenny – Corbett, after the man that my ma thought was my dad. He was a bottom of the bill comic on the London variety circuit, who worked under the professional name of – would you believe? – Inky Page. Thank Gawd it wasn't his real name is all I can say. Anyway, Ma had a thing about theatricals, especially comic turns; she'd do anything if a man made her laugh.'

She couldn't believe her ears.

'Sorry Missus B, I didn't mean to embarrass you, but that's the way it is. So, there being the eight of us filling up the house, I used to take myself down the road to get out from under her feet, and having learned a little ditty from the old boy who begged for coppers outside the local boozer, I'd do a little song and dance routine for anybody willing to throw a penny into my hat, and that's where the missus saw me and took pity.' Sam placed another cup and saucer onto the draining board. 'Anyway, after a while, Ma was shipped off to the asylum, the booze having rotted her mind and sent her completely doolally tap. Us lot were taken off to an orphanage and it was from there that the guvnor and the missus caught up with me and took me in as their own. If it wasn't for them, I'd have been in prison more like, or rotting in a pauper's grave.'

Turning away, Jane Baxter produced a handkerchief from up her cardigan sleeve and attempted to wipe the tears from her eyes without Sam seeing.

'So when they brought me back to their beautiful large house, I knew that my life had changed for good. So with a new life, I thought I needed a new name, and as the guvnor had just been reading me stories about Mr Pickwick and his meeting up with the boot boy, Samuel Weller, and me taking to the character in an instant, I decided that Sam would be a good name for me. Anyway, to make this long story short, even though we changed my name through the official channels at Somerset House and all that, somewhere along the line it seems that it's got lost in all them corridors and I expect the authorities are still searching about for Leonard Corbett to call up. Don't think for a moment that I'm trying to dodge the war – I'm more than happy to do my bit, but what with the missus falling so ill and then leaving us, and the guvnor being lost without her, I felt I needed to stay and help him get this little enterprise on the road. When we wrap this lot up, I'm sure I shall quick march myself down to the recruiting office.'

As Jane Baxter took the tray of newly washed cups and saucers back into the café to put on the shelf, she shook her head. What a sheltered life she had led. She knew nothing of poverty – or alcohol, for that matter, never having had more than a glass of fortified wine at Christmas. Poor Sam, the boy had been through so much.

Returning after a half-hour break and having spent another penny in yet another abortive attempt to speak to his old school friend – *"I'm sorry, caller, but I'm getting no answer from that number. Please call again later."* – Randolph trudged back to the theatre whilst praying to Apollo and Dionysus that they could make some progress with the play before it all collapsed around his ears.

'Please keep going if you can,' he said as firmly as he could from the front of the stage. 'Don't stop and please, please, pick up your cues, so I can get a feel of how it's shaping up. All this stop-starting really is most debilitating.'

'Shaping up,' said Arthur, still full of tea and bun. 'It'll be the same mess as it always is.'

'Well, it wouldn't be such a mess if certain members of the Company had learned their lines,' said Hugh. 'Poor Molly seems to be saying more of the words than certain people on the stage – no names, no pack drill.'

'I think it would be best if you just concentrated on your own performance. It strikes me as being one of the dullest I've ever seen,' Arthur Desmond retorted, stifling a yawn, and wanting nothing more than to have forty winks in the stalls.

'Don't you think it best if we stopped all this continuous bickering and got on with what we're here for? A bit of decorum would not go amiss,' snapped Phyllis.

Veronica made a snorting noise. 'Fat chance of any decorum in this Company,' she scoffed.

'Veronica, perhaps it would be for the best if you kept that mouth of yours firmly shut, except to say the words the playwright has given you,' Phyllis fought back.

Teddy and Penny made their way along the hotel landing hand in hand. Teddy's thoughts now were of a new beginning; a whole new life that, he hoped, stretched ahead of them both together. Picking Penny up in his arms, he kissed her, as he had kissed her so many times in the past hour, before carrying her down the stairs, singing a little ditty quietly to himself as he went – *"Upstairs, downstairs, in my lady's chamber."*

He whisked her across the lobby and through the front doors, whereupon he kissed her once more.

'What was that you were humming?' she asked as he spun her round in his arms.

"Nothing, nothing at all,' he stated, stopping and giving her a peck on the nose.

'Oh,' she said with a giggle as he gently put her down onto the pavement, 'I thought you were going to carry me back to the theatre.'

He took her face in his hands and kissed her once more, before suddenly pulling away.

'What is it?' she asked, as she saw his smile turn to a frown. 'Teddy?'

'Shush, listen a moment.' He leant his head back a little and looked up. 'Run!' Grabbing her hand, he pulled her towards the concrete steps that wound their way down the cliff face. There was a high-pitched whine, in the distance at first, but which became louder and more menacing as they both stumbled down the steps. Pushing her down and into the cliff face, he threw himself against her as an air-raid siren started to compete with the sound of the German

Stuka bomber coming in steeply, before climbing again and roaring over them. A cloud of dust filled the air as an almighty explosion drowned everything else out. Bricks and timber crashed onto the railings above before cascading down the cliff around them.

It was Hugh who heard the siren first, followed by the low rumble as the bomb hit its target. Everybody stopped in their tracks as the theatre shook and years of dirt and grime fell from the grid above the stage onto them.

'Right, everybody,' said Randolph firmly, clapping his hands and walking off the stage and into the corridor. 'Follow me.'

'Where the hell is he taking us?' asked Veronica, trying not to show the fear welling up inside her.

'I'm taking you under the stage,' said Randolph pointedly. 'We'll take cover there.'

Arthur sneered and lit a cigarette. 'Oh yes, I'm sure that having a few planks of wood over our heads is going to stop any Jerry bombs from killing us.'

'Oh shut up; if you're not going to say anything helpful, I suggest you just keep quiet,' said Phyllis. 'And put that damned cigarette out. We don't all wish to choke to death on your smoke.' As far as Phyllis was concerned, she would happily have left both Arthur Desmond and Veronica East to their fates.

'What are we going to do? They'll find Billy,' said Eric, sidling up to Connie.

'I'm afraid there's nothing we can do about that, dear,' she said kindly, 'but don't worry, we'll talk them round if there's any fuss.'

One by one, the Company made their way down the darkened stairway.

'Why are they bombing here?' asked Zelda.

'They're dumping their bombs so they don't have to go back to base with them. They'll be short of fuel so will need to lighten the load,' said Hugh.

'But where have they been?' asked Connie.

'They were trying to bomb the heart out of England, I have no doubt,' said Hugh rather profoundly, which confused Connie even more.

'He means the Midlands – Birmingham, Wolverhampton, Coventry – I expect,' said Phyllis.

'Lots of factories up there; munitions, I shouldn't wonder,' said Hugh.

'Steady, Hugh, careless talk costs lives,' said Randolph sternly.

'I don't think anybody's listening down here,' said Arthur, as he stumbled, fell down the stairs and tripped over the camp bed. 'What the hell's this? This is Shaw's bloody bed. What's it doing down here?'

'Hold up,' said Sam as he and Molly made their way after them. 'I've got some candles. Does anybody have a lighter or some matches? Arthur, you smoke – may we borrow your lighter, old chap?'

'I want it straight back,' Arthur said, handing his lighter over rather begrudgingly.

'Of course, of course,' Sam answered politely.

He and Molly began to light the candles and place them around the space. In the flickering candlelight they looked for places to sit as clouds of ancient dust showered them from above, bringing on a coughing fit from Hugh that he couldn't stop.

'It's no good,' he said, between seizures, 'I can't stay down here; I can't get my breath.' A great rasping noise came from his chest. Zelda put her arm around him and, taking one of the candles, she guided him back upstairs.

'Oh Zelda, do you think going up there is a good idea?' asked Connie, with genuine concern.

'If the bomb's got our name on it, darling,' she said, 'then so be it. If Hugh doesn't get some fresh air he will choke to death anyway.' And with that, she and Hugh made their way along the corridor towards the stage door.

Veronica, who had been looking around for a quiet corner away from everybody, attempted to brush the dust and dirt off a pile of old sacking when it moved slightly. Jumping back, she screamed, making the others jump as the sacking rose like a ghost. Randolph, taking the lead, stepped forward and pulled at it, dropping it to the floor to reveal Billy, covered in dust and dirt.

'Who in God's name are you?' Randolph barked.

The others turned as Eric went over to the apparition and started to brush him down.

'Careful, he might be dangerous,' said Arthur. 'He could be a Jerry spy.'

'Don't be silly,' said Connie, running her fingers through the boy's hair to clear the dust and soot. 'Billy wouldn't hurt a fly, would you, dear?'

'Billy? Billy?' said Arthur, aghast. 'Connie, do you know this boy?'

'Yes,' said Connie, rather confidently. 'We're friends, aren't we, Billy? He's helping me with the costumes.'

'What the devil do you mean?' snapped her husband.

She picked up a pair of trousers that lay on top of an old tea chest and held them up. 'He's been sewing the turn-ups in your trousers for me. I'm afraid they're a trifle dirty now. I shall have to put them in to soak.'

Arthur ripped the trousers from her and stared at them, and then, not knowing what else to do, threw them on the floor.

'Oh Arthur, you are impossible,' she snapped at him, picking them up and taking them over to the candlelight to examine them. 'Look, now you've torn them. Arthur, you really are most childish.'

Arthur stepped back. Connie had never snapped at him like that before and it threw him off guard for a moment.

'Perhaps I should explain,' said Eric, stepping forward.

'Are you in on this too?' snapped Arthur.

'He's a runaway from the army,' said Eric.

'So,' said Arthur, turning to the others and pointing, 'we're shielding a bloody deserter. Bloody marvellous. So now we'll all be shot for aiding and abetting.'

'Oh, don't be so ridiculous, Arthur,' said Phyllis, walking towards the boy and smiling at him. 'Nobody is going to be shot. Look at the lad. God alone knows what he's been through. Were you over in France, dear?'

Billy nodded.

Phyllis took his hand. 'And was it as bad as they say in the newspapers?' Billy didn't answer but just hung his head. 'You poor boy.'

'Well, I vote that when this raid has passed over, we take him to the nearest police station and hand him in,' muttered Veronica censoriously.

Phyllis span round to her. 'Well, I vote we clean him up and work out what the best thing to do for his safety is.'

Randolph thought that this was just another fly in the ointment that he really didn't need, but then he looked over to his beloved Sam, who he and Hester had saved so many years ago, and in an instant he knew that he couldn't abandon the boy.

Putting on a haughty woman's voice, Randolph addressed his son. '*Now, here you see David Copperfield, and the question I put to you, Mister Dick, is what shall I do with him?*'

'*What shall you do with him?*' said Sam, scratching his head and making a face like Stan Laurel. '*Oh! Do with him?*'

'*Yes,*' said Randolph, with a grave look and his forefinger held up. '*Come! I want some very sound advice.*'

'*Why, if I was you,*' said Sam, considering, and looking vacantly at Billy, '*I should... should wash him!*'

'*Janet, Mister Dick sets us right. Heat the bath.*'

Arthur turned to them both. 'What the blazes are you two talking about?'

Whenever there was a problem that couldn't be solved,

Randolph and Sam would turn to the great Charles Dickens for guidance, but for now Randolph couldn't be bothered to explain.

'No matter,' said Randolph with a sigh as the "all clear" sounded out in the distance.

Mister Tuppence ran along the street as fast as he could and down the side alley.

'Where are the others?' he asked breathlessly as he saw Zelda and Hugh by the stage door.

'What is it, Mister Tuppence?' Zelda was rather shocked as she had never heard him say an actual sentence before; his usual communication was done by grunts, mostly.

'The others, the others,' he said, waving his arms about, pulling open the door.

'They're shielding under the stage,' said Zelda.

'Are they all there?' he said, not stopping to hear the answer.

'Why, what's the matter?' said Zelda, following him.

'You heard the bombs, you heard the bombs.'

'Yes, of course.'

But Mister Tuppence did not answer.

'Are you all here? Are you all here?' he shouted as he saw the Company slowly making their way back to the stage.

'What is it, Mister Tuppence?' asked Phyllis.

'I heard that two of yer were at the hotel earlier,' he said.

'Yes, Mister Shaw and Miss Rose,' Randolph replied, rather formally.

'It's gone,' said Mister Tuppence.

'What is?' asked Randolph.

'The hotel, the hotel, it's gone.'

'Gone?'

'It got a direct hit. It's gone.'

Connie held her hand up to her mouth. Veronica turned around and stared at the man. Phyllis shook her head.

'Teddy! Oh no, Teddy!' she said, quickly pushing past him.

'Don't go out there, ma'am, there might be more of the buggers.'

But Phyllis was storming along the corridor. 'We've got to try to save them,' she called out.

'Come on, Arthur.' Connie beckoned towards her husband as he clambered up the stairs.

'Where are you going, woman?' he asked wearily, not moving an inch.

'We've got to try to find them. Dig them out with our bare hands.'

'Have you lost your senses? If they're under the rubble you'll never find them.'

'You stop and listen. You go along the surface of the rubble and then you stop and listen.' It was the boy. They all turned to him. 'It's one of the things you learn in training.'

Randolph looked at him. 'Would you come and help us?'

Billy nodded. 'Yes.'

Air-raid wardens and local policemen were sorting through the rubble when they arrived. Billy immediately climbed up and started to listen for any sounds.

'Here, what do you think you're doing?' said one of the policemen, standing guard.

Billy stopped and looked around at him. 'I'm trained in search and rescue.'

'Trained?'

'Army trained,' said Billy, as he turned back to the task in hand.

'Right,' said the policeman. 'That's alright then.'

'We think that Ma Goddard was in there, and the girl,' said one of the wardens to him, 'We think the boy may have gone home but nobody's heard.'

Billy started to move the shattered bricks gently to one side.

The rubble lay everywhere, but somehow the staircase stood, seemingly untouched, although the stairs went to nowhere as the landing had crashed to the ground along with most of the bedrooms. One bedroom stood, an island in the sea of rubble, with an iron bedstead, its head still against what was left of the wall, and a wardrobe on its side with the doors ripped from their hinges.

'Just about my entire life is somewhere in there,' said Veronica bitterly as she made to light a cigarette.

'Put that cigarette out,' shouted the warden at her. 'Can't you smell the gas, woman?'

Veronica snorted and walked over towards the cliff, stubbing out her cigarette as she went.

'Shh, I can hear something.'

It was Billy, his ear close to the rubble. He waved his hand for quiet and those around passed on the silent message.

'I can hear someone – someone moaning,' he said.

The other rescuers moved in and, one or two having patted Billy on the back, began to dig, with Sam diving in to do what he could. Arthur Desmond walked to what was left of the cliff railings and lit a cigarette.

'Is it Teddy, do you think?' said Connie to no one in particular. Phyllis took her arm and said that she hoped so.

'It might be the both of them. Could it be, do you think?' Connie squeezed Phyllis's arm.

'They're down here,' said Veronica after a moment, lighting a surreptitious cigarette and looking down over the mangled railings. She could make out the tops of their heads as they sat wrapped in each other's arms, Teddy's jacket over Penny's shoulders as she shook and sobbed from fear and relief.

'What?' queried Randolph, turning to her.

'Quiet!' It was Billy. Having stopped moving debris, he was trying to listen for signs of life.

Randolph held up his hand in apology as Phyllis came over to him and looked down. Trying to suppress her own tears, she started to make her way down the steps to the couple below. They both looked up at her.

'We're fine,' said Teddy, holding out his free hand to her. 'A bit shaken up, but no bones broken.'

Distraught with happiness, Phyllis bent down and wrapped her arms around the both of them, pulling them into her like a mother hen having found her chicks.

Slowly and carefully, the rescuers moved the bricks and timbers to one side by forming a chain. Every so often, Billy held up his hand and they stopped and he listened again.

'Hello,' he called down, 'can you hear me?'

A low whimpering noise came back; they could all hear it. Some rubble moved below them.

'Don't move; keep as still as you can. Just hold on, we're coming to get you. Just hold on,' Billy said, with as much confidence as he could muster, and they continued, brick by brick, until they could see her.

'It's Miss Goddard,' said one of the wardens, looking down and making out a figure.

They continued to dig her out, carefully moving the broken bricks and timber from around her. The policeman signalled to the ambulance men to bring up a stretcher and it wasn't long before she was freed from the wreckage and on her way to hospital.

'Well done, lad,' said the policeman. 'Good work, boy. Lovely job.' And he patted him firmly on the back. 'With this lot, are you?'

'Sort of,' Billy said quietly as he stepped back onto the pavement. Quickly, Eric came up to his side.

'Yes, he's with us,' he said, putting his arm around him and pulling him out of the way of too many questions.

'Funny old lot, them theatricals, if you ask me,' said one of the wardens to the copper.

'Right,' said the policeman, nodding his head. 'A good lad

though, for all that.' They watched the two young men walking off down the road together.

'So now what do we do?' asked Hugh. 'Any ideas where we can stay now?'

The policeman said that they could try the bed and breakfasts; failing that, the local village hall had a supply of army beds for this eventuality, along with some blankets. He wasn't sure that there'd be any room in the hall itself though.

'In that case, we could pitch our tent in the theatre,' said Randolph, aware that he had no money to pay for bed and breakfasts.

'You alright, Miss?' asked the policeman, as Phyllis and Teddy gently dusted the dirt and cement from Penny's dress as they came up the steps.

'Yes, I'm alright, thank you,' she said, straightening herself up and throwing a defiant look over to Veronica and Arthur, who were standing together a little way off. She cleared her throat. 'I'm quite alright, thank you.'

'I just thought that perhaps you might want to go for a check-up at the hospital. I'm sure the ambulance could take you,' the policeman offered kindly.

'Thank you,' she said, 'I'll be fine now.'

'Are you sure, darling?' Teddy asked.

Hearing the word 'darling', Veronica turned away.

'Look, I'm as fit as a flea,' Penny answered pointedly, putting on a brave face in front of Veronica and Arthur, who continued staring out to sea.

'I'll look after her,' Teddy assured the policeman, taking her by the hand and leading her past her tormentors.

Around an hour later, the company of players could be seen walking along the high street, clutching a camp bed and one or two blankets apiece.

'I say, Randolph.' It was Arthur. 'Would it be possible that the ghost could walk early this week?' he asked, using the time-honoured theatrical euphemism for getting paid.

Randolph sighed. 'I'm afraid not, old chap, not this week.'

'I really can't bear the thought of trying to sleep on one of these damned things for a night, let alone any longer.' Arthur juggled with the rolled-up camp bed under his arm. 'Only I thought, if you could see yourself to plonking some readies in my hand, I could try to find some digs.'

'There's a bit of a problem there, old chap. I'm afraid the money hasn't come through yet.' *And might never,* thought Randolph.

'Well, can't you ask your friend, Little Lord Fauntleroy, to sell one of the old master's that he has, no doubt, hanging on a wall of his stately home, in order to send you a few quid to tide us over?'

Randolph closed his eyes in despair for a moment. 'Peregrine is a Knight of the Realm and not—'

'Well, whatever the hell he is, tell him to pull his finger out and open his bloody wallet,' yelled Arthur, before charging off again, dropping his blanket on the ground and cursing roundly as it unrolled itself.

As they all trooped into the theatre, Molly ran across the road from the café to tell them that her mother had put together a good hot evening meal for all of them "on the house" and to come over when they were ready.

'Most grateful, most grateful,' Randolph muttered, 'Thank you, Molly, and please thank your mother. That would be most welcome.'

'So what do we do with the little deserter?' It was Veronica, as she plunged her fork into the stew and dumplings in front of her.

'I don't think that this is a conversation we should have in public,' Randolph stated sagely.

'It isn't public; there's only us here.'

'That's as maybe,' said Randolph, 'but—'

'So you don't want to discuss it, in other words. Well, I do. If you think I'm going to be held to account and whisked off to prison for that little soldier boy, then you can think again.'

'I agree,' said Arthur. 'I say we hand the little bugger in and be done with it.'

'You seem to have forgotten, all too quickly, that the "little soldier boy" may have saved someone's life today,' Zelda commented, totally disgusted by the way the conversation was going.

'And three cheers for that, I say,' said her husband, patting her hand.

'And I say that we should all calm down and not do anything for now.' Connie looked around the table for some sort of consensus, without a great deal of hope. Her courage seemed to be growing by the minute, much to her husband's annoyance.

'Well, you would,' he snapped at her, 'you've been hiding him for days.'

'Yes, I admit it. What will you do, Arthur, report me to the police as well? Is that what you want – your wife languishing in prison as well?'

Arthur cut into his dumpling. *There was always that*, he thought.

'We will do nothing at the moment,' said Phyllis calmly. 'If I may, I will have a little chat with him to see what's what.'

Veronica pushed her plate away. 'Have a little chat, and what good would that do? Unless you can get him to hand himself in. I don't want him anywhere near me.'

'I've an idea,' said Arthur. 'Teddy can drive him out to the country in his little car and drop him off somewhere; leave him to find his own way.'

Phyllis shook her head. How could this man be so callous? 'Where do you suggest he should take him, Arthur? Out onto the fens and drop him off by one of the drainage ditches? Perhaps he'll do the decent thing and drown himself, then he won't trouble you – or indeed you, Veronica – again.'

'I don't give a damn where he takes him as long as it's away from us,' Arthur spat out.

Connie looked at her husband in disgust; he really was the most hateful creature. 'Oh, how could you, Arthur?'

Arthur span round to her. 'Oh do stop whining, for God's sake, Connie,' he snapped, 'He's not your child; what's he got to do with you?' And with that riposte, he slammed down his knife and fork and made his way outside to get some air and, more importantly, to light another cigarette and take a swig from his hip flask. The others sat in silence. Zelda patted Connie's hand.

'Well, I'm in need of a drink,' said Sam, breaking the silence. 'I don't know about you lot but I might need a few tonight.' And, taking his plate up to the counter, he gave Jane Baxter one of his best smiles. 'Thanks for the grub, Missus B.'

'A pleasure, Sam,' she said kindly. 'Now, you must all come over for your breakfasts in the morning – you'll all need a good meal inside you before you start all your acting and the like.'

Randolph stood and brought out his wallet, which he sadly noted was getting more and more depleted.

'You're very kind, Missus Baxter,' he said. 'Now, how much do I owe you for all this?'

'You just keep your money, Mister Laine,' she said. 'If we can't help people out when needs must then we're not worth being placed on this earth.' She was looking through the window at that Mister Desmond smoking; she'd heard every word he'd said and, having put two and two together with what Molly had told her about the young deserter they'd found, she knew the score.

Randolph made an impressive show of wanting, most emphatically, to pay his way but, in the end, he placed his wallet firmly back in his jacket pocket, rather relieved.

'And Sam, here's something for that young lad I've heard about,' Jane said with a wink, handing over a covered plate of food. 'And make sure he comes over with you for breakfast; I'm sure he'll blend in.' She patted Sam's arm. She'd grown very fond of Sam Laine – and so, she was in no doubt, had her daughter.

'I'll drop this off and then come back and help you dry the dishes, Missus B,' Sam called after her as she collected the dirty plates.

'You'll do no such thing, young man; you've done more than your fair share for the day. You'll go to The Cockleshell and have your fill of beer, and no argument.'

'You're a treasure, Missus B,' he smiled, blowing her a kiss.

'And you're a smooth talker, Samuel. Now be off with you,' she laughed.

18

Sergeant Green

Sergeant Green was a career soldier, a lifer, like his father and grandfather before him. To look at him and to hear him speak, you could be fooled into thinking that he'd been born into the wrong era; he wouldn't have looked out of place back in the days of the Zulu War, wearing a scarlet tunic and pith helmet and marching through the veldt. Harry Green wasn't a shouter; he preferred a quieter approach to discipline. He was a tall, well-built man, whose voice came up from his lower chest, passed over his vocal chords and produced out of his mouth a brown, chocolatey but strangely forceful voice, which could carry across the parade ground or in the heat of battle and reach its intended target without sounding strained, and because of this, the men under his command seemed to respond easily to his orders. Even the officers had a genuine respect for him.

He didn't take his duties lightly, although he often despaired when faced with a lot of raw recruits who hadn't a clue how to fight, and officers who hadn't a clue how to command. It came as no surprise to him when, having been sent across to France in the first wave, the Germans were all over them like a rash and the lads were ready to turn tail as quickly as they could.

It seemed that no one had any idea how to stem the tide of the German infantry's advance; they seemed to keep coming at them, night and day, without stopping – great swathes of automatic gunfire, along with German hand grenades lobbed from every angle – with the result that many thousands of British troops were chopped down, never to rise again.

It was during one of these sorties that Green himself was blown off his feet by a grenade, which exploded in flight near him, spraying out streams of stones and window glass from the building he was sheltering behind. Fierce stabbing pains shot through his shoulder and legs, along with pin pricks of red-hot sensation on his face and hands as the explosion sent up a cloud of gravel, which lodged itself in his naked flesh. Before he knew it, he was being shipped back to England on one of the first boats out.

'Let me say first of all, Sergeant Green, that I know you to be a first-rate soldier and, between you and me, I wish I had more like you under my command. That's to go no further than these four walls, of course.' Colonel Thornton laughed a sort of officer-class bray; at the same time, he gave a conspiratorial wink. Green knew the Colonel to be a good man, but not one who had one iota of strategic military sense. But no matter; he meant well and did all he could for his men, and appreciated those under his command.

'Thank you, Sir,' said Green, 'Mum's the words, as ever, Sir.'

'Jolly good,' said the Colonel as he stared down at some paperwork on his desk.

'The MO tells me that you're very keen to get back in the saddle and return to full duties. Very commendable, Sergeant; just what I'd expect from you.'

Come on, come on, Green thought, as he stood with his hands behind his back, on the opposite side of the desk. *You know what you're going to do; what you're going to say. Stop the bloody theatricals.*

The Colonel cleared his throat, looked up and gave him a fatherly smile.

'I've been going through the MO's notes and it seems that your wounds are healing well, but he says you're still getting pains in your leg and your shoulder. Is that right?'

Green's heart sank. He could tell by all this flannel that his request was going to be refused. Bloody officer speak. *Let's all beat about the bush for a while. They must think we're all as thick as...*

'All in all,' the Colonel continued, turning another page and making it look as if he was reading it for the first time, 'yes, he thinks you're coming on very well, considering what you've been through. Jolly good show.'

Here it comes. 'However...' *There it is...* 'He feels that there is still some way to go before he can sign you off and put you back into the front line. The bone in your leg, he says, has mended, but he is concerned that the bone will still be too soft and doesn't think you should overdo it. I'm sure you understand that it's my duty to go along with the medicos on this.' He looked up at Green, who remained stony-faced and outwardly calm.

Bastards, he thought.

The Colonel sat back in his chair, relieved that he'd got the first bit over and that the fellow had taken it well – or at least, had given that impression, which was all that counted when all was said and done.

'Now, I know that this isn't what you wanted to hear; you want to get back out there, even after everything you've been through, which is highly commendable, as I say.'

Green just wanted him to say "dismiss", so he could about turn and march the hell out of there, but he knew the Colonel had some sort of speech prepared and he could do nothing but stand there and listen to it.

'Now, I realise that the last thing you want to do is sit on your backside all day so I've got a little idea, which, although it's not a perfect solution, I think you'll find is better than nothing. I hope you'll agree.'

What bloody choice do I have? he thought. 'Yes Sir, thank you Sir.' Green knew the form, it was ingrained in him; three generations of the army in his blood saw to that.

'Well, I'd hold on a moment until you've heard my idea, before any thanks are due. You may, of course, hate the idea.' He laughed the brayed laugh again.

Yes, of course I might. Probably will. But you'll hear no complaint from me and you bloody well know it, Sir! 'I'm sure I won't, Sir,' he said, again the response asked for and dutifully given by a professional soldier who knew the game. He had no choice but to play by the rules. Army rules.

The Colonel looked over to one side of his desk and retrieved another sheet of paper, and again took a moment or two to pass his eyes over it.

'It seems,' he started eventually, 'that one of our children has gone astray.' He looked up and smiled. Actually saying that a soldier hadn't returned from leave out loud, seemed like an insult to the regiment. Talking around it like a concerned father was, to his mind, a more tactful way of approaching the problem.

Green stood at ease and waited.

'Yes,' continued the Colonel, looking down again at what was obviously a report. 'Private William Pryce,' he articulated clearly, as if taking it all in for the first time, whereas in reality he had worried at this all morning, wondering how he'd handle it. It never looked good for an officer to have someone under his command run off; no, it didn't look that good at all. Best to get the lad back quickly and quietly if possible. That was when he thought of Green. The man was aching to get back into the thick of things and although this wasn't some battlefield, he knew his reputation well enough to think that he might be just the man for the job. Nothing heavy-handed, no shouting or bawling, no quick marching and running around the parade ground with a rifle over his head until he dropped, then throwing a bucket of rainwater over his head and getting him back on his feet to run around some more. No, no, no, thought the Colonel, he didn't want that. Just get the lad back for a few days in the glasshouse and then keep an eye on him. Green would be the perfect candidate. He was a gentleman soldier.

'I need you to have a ferret about and see if you can find this laddie, and get him back here as soon as you can without too much fuss; slowly, slowly, catchy monkey.' He looked up again. 'He's probably hanging onto his mother's apron strings. Yes, that'll be it, and I think, Harry, you're the man to prize him away and get him back here without too much trouble.'

Harry? First name, eh? Trying to be chummy. Don't suppose he'd like it if I called him Denis back. No, of course not. So being sent off to find a frightened rabbit and then hoppity-hopping it back to barracks, was he? Not Green's idea of soldiering, but he knew he had no say in the matter; an order is still an order, and when you take the King's shilling it buys him the right to get you to do as you're told.

'Very good, Sir,' he said, as they both knew he would.

'Good man,' replied the Colonel, sorting through more paperwork, which at the start of the proceedings was in a nice neat pile but had now spread itself all over the desk. 'Now, where is it? Ah, yes,' he pulled out a sheet of paper, 'the name and address of the parents etcetera, and you'll be issued with an open travel warrant and the relevant papers.'

So it had been arranged before he'd walked through the door.

'I believe the lad is a sensitive soul, if you get my meaning, but I'm sure he'll be in good hands. I trust you to bring him back to us unharmed, Harry. That'll be all.'

'Sir!' Sergeant Green came to attention, did an about turn and marched off towards the door and into the outer office, while the Colonel smiled and returned his attention to another pile of papers on his desk.

On the other side of the door, Green closed his eyes and took a deep breath. Corporal Dunning, the Colonel's secretary, smiled as he handed over the travel warrant and papers. Sergeant Green gave him a look and shook his head.

'Well, it'll be better than sitting on your arse in the mess all day, Sarge,' said Dunning.

'Well, you should know, Dunning, you've been sitting around on your arse since the day you first joined the army,' said Green, taking the documents and marching out into the corridor. In Green's mind, being an office wallah wasn't being a soldier.

Standing outside on the pavement and looking up at the windows, Sergeant Green wondered what was happening in there. Was there someone looking out of the window? Had he been spotted and the boy warned? Was he at this moment running through the back of the house and over the garden fence? No, he thought, no, his instinct told him all was calm, so he knocked on the front door and waited. There was silence inside. He knocked again and heard a loud voice from somewhere.

'Someone's knocking at the bloody door, don't you hear it?'

His shoulder was aching a bit after the train journey from Aldershot to Peterborough, so as he waited for the door to open, he stretched his arms back, trying to ease the muscles. Hearing footsteps in the hall and the door chain sliding back, he straightened himself. The door opened.

'Missus Pryce?' His voice was friendly, not intimidating.

'Yes?' said Billy's mother, looking at his uniform. *Oh my goodness*, she thought, and she started to shake and tears started to fall down from her eyes. 'Is it Billy? Has something happened to Billy?' She was beside herself.

'Now, now,' said Green softly, 'there's no need to upset yourself, Missus Pryce. Perhaps you'll allow me to come in; I just need a little chat with you.'

Agnes Pryce stood to one side and beckoned the sergeant into the hallway. 'Is your husband home?' he asked.

'Yes,' said Agnes, 'but he's sleeping at the moment.' She was hoping that he'd fallen back to sleep again after shouting at her. She didn't want to involve him, especially if the sergeant's visit was anything to do with Billy. 'I don't want to disturb him at the moment,' she whispered, looking back at the closed door to the living room. 'Perhaps we can talk in the kitchen, if that's convenient?'

'Wherever is best for you, ma'am,' said Green as politely as he could. *No point in rushing into things and panicking the woman,* he thought as he followed her into the back of the house. Without thinking, he pulled out one of the chairs from around the table and beckoned her to sit. Uncomplainingly, Agnes did so and he walked calmly round to the other side of the table and sat himself down. He looked at her face and smiled.

'Now, Missus Pryce, the last thing I wish to do is give you any worry,' he started, 'but I think it's best that I don't beat about the bush.'

Agnes put her handkerchief to her mouth and took a deep intake of breath.

'Can you tell me, ma'am – and I ask you to think carefully before you answer –'

What does he mean, think carefully? Think carefully about what? Agnes thought.

'Is your son William Pryce?'

'Yes.' It came out as more of a croak.

'Thank you,' said the Sergeant. 'And can you tell me, ma'am, is your son at home at the moment?'

Agnes didn't understand.

'No Sergeant, he's gone back to his barracks,' she answered, wringing her hands.

'I see,' he said, 'and when was that? When did he go back to his barracks?'

'Monday morning.' *It was Monday, wasn't it? What day was it now?* 'Yes, late Monday morning,' she repeated.

'You're sure of that now?' The voice was calm. 'Take your time.'

What did she need to take her time over? He went back on the Monday, last Monday.

'It was Monday,' she said again, almost in a whisper. 'Why, Sergeant? What's happened to him?'

'Don't fret yourself, ma'am. All in good time.' His voice was reassuring. 'So he left on Monday morning, and would I be right in thinking that you've not seen him since?'

'No, of course I haven't,' she said, wringing her hands. 'How could I?'

Throughout all this, Green had been keeping half an ear out for any noises upstairs; he'd heard nothing so far, and was rapidly coming to the conclusion that the boy wasn't there. 'When he left,' he continued, 'did he seem nervous? Scared perhaps? Not wishing to return to his regiment?'

She wanted to scream that of course he was scared, of course he was nervous! He'd been through hell. He never wanted to go back. She tried to find the words.

'He shouldn't have been sent out there, Sergeant. He's a very sensitive boy; it wasn't right.' She started to sob and took the handkerchief from her apron pocket.

'Please don't upset yourself, ma'am. I'm sure everything will sort itself out, but I have to inform you that your son failed to return to barracks on Monday evening as per his orders.'

'Then where is he?' she asked. 'Where is he?' she sobbed again as the kitchen door opened and Freddie Pryce stood in his collarless shirt with his trouser braces hanging down.

'What's this?' he growled.

Sergeant Green could smell the stench of beer on his breath from where he was sitting.

Agnes sobbed again.

'Mister Pryce?' said the Sergeant, standing up.

'The boy, is it?' said Pryce. 'Done a runner, has he?'

'What makes you ask that, Mister Pryce?'

'Because he's got no guts, that's why,' Pryce answered. 'It's all her fault, coddling him.'

Sergeant Green didn't take with deserters but he wasn't just going to stand there and hear any soldier maligned.

'It's my understanding, Mister Pryce, that your son saw a great deal of action over in France – as did I, sir, and if my experience is anything to go by, all the lads, including your son, displayed a great deal of courage.'

'So why are you here?' asked Pryce, failing to stifle a belch, the stench from which easily made its way over to Sergeant Green's nostrils.

'I'm afraid that your son hasn't returned to barracks, and I've been sent to guide him back safely, sir,' Green answered, in the kindest way he could find.

'Guide him back? Fat chance. I'd horse-whip the bugger and drag him back to face the firing squad.'

It took a lot to shake Harry Green, but hearing a father say that took him back a step or two.

'I'm sure you don't mean that, sir,' he said.

Pryce laughed. It was evil and nasty. 'Give me the gun and I'll do it myself.'

Green thought it best to change tack. 'So, I take it that the boy isn't here in the house?'

'If she's hiding him here, I'd kill the both of them,' spat Pryce again.

'Yes, I dare say you would, sir,' said the sergeant, looking over at the man's wife. Poor woman. Harry Green started feeling very sorry for the boy, if this is what he had to put up with for a father.

'Is there anyone else he could have gone to? Other members of the family who might have taken him in?'

'Irene, her sister,' said Pryce with a sneer. 'That's where he'll be. 146 Clarence Road; it's not far, you'll find him there.'

'No, Fred.' Missus Pryce looked up, still sobbing. 'She'd tell me if he was there.'

But Pryce ignored her, as he always did.

'She's as soft as that one,' he said, pointing at her unsteadily, leaning against the doorjamb. 'Thick as thieves, those two. Yes, he'll be in her spare room and she'll be feeding him up and fussing over him like a puppy.'

'She'd tell me, I say,' Agnes pleaded.

'Yes,' said Pryce again, as he started to turn out of the room, 'that's where you'll find the little bastard. You find him and stick him against the wall.'

Sergeant Green felt the need to leave the house as soon as he could. The man made him feel sick and he had to control the instinct to flatten him. It was obvious that the lad wasn't there so he took his leave, turning down the offer of a cup of tea, having made a note of the sister's address and pocketed a small photograph of the boy, which the mother had told him had been taken at school three or four years earlier. Looking at it, Green could see his fresh features. *Delicate,* he thought. *Sensitive eyes.* Harry Green noticed those sorts of things.

Setting off down the road, he thought about what the father had said. He had lost his father when he was only thirteen. He never came back from the trenches; he was slaughtered out there in the Belgian mud. His father, thought Green, was the polar opposite to Pryce's father; he was a kind man who knew that, when the time came, he had no choice but to do his duty for king and country. It was this that was instilled in his son and as soon as he was old enough to join up, he continued what his father and grandfather had done.

The boy wasn't at the aunt's house, he knew that in his gut. No, he'd scarpered. What he had to do now was figure out where he'd scarpered too. The railway station – yes, that would be his next port of call; the lad would have boarded a train to somewhere.

'Yes,' the ticket collector said. 'I remember the young soldier. Monday, if memory serves. Nice lad. He'd lost his travel warrant to… where was it?' He went over to the window of the booking office and had a chat with the booking clerk. 'Haleston, on the coast,' he said, coming back, 'end of the line. Yes, that's where he was going. He said his lot were stationed there. I gave him the ticket myself. Nothing wrong is there, Sergeant?'

'Are there any trains going that way today?' asked Green, not wishing to get drawn in.

'I'm afraid not, Sergeant. The last one was at midday. There's only the one a day from here.'

Green cursed under his breath.

'If you need to stay somewhere, there's the Railway Tavern over there. He does rooms. He keeps it clean although it can get a bit rowdy of an evening.'

Within half an hour, Sergeant Harry Green lay on a bed at the Railway. His leg was hurting like the blazes, his shoulder had stiffened and he had difficulty getting comfortable, but after a while he found himself dropping off into sleep. *No hurry, Harry,* he said to himself, *the little bugger won't get away from you.*

19

Camping Out

To say it was a strange night with all the Company in the theatre on their camp beds would be an understatement.

Veronica had put her bed, as best she could, in her little dressing room. The room was too small with her make-up bench and chair, and so the chair was unceremoniously thrown out of the room and across the corridor. *If I hadn't wasted so much money on last night's little enterprise with that stupid girl, I might have had enough to pay for some digs for the week*, she thought. *Damn these silly little people.*

Teddy wondered if he should set up his bed next to Penny's until Phyllis kindly offered to look after her, so he put up his bed with Sam in the men's dressing room whilst Phyllis put up hers next to Penny's in the women's.

Hugh and Zelda, who had never spent a night apart since their wedding, were determined not to be separated (well, Hugh was determined, which came to the same thing) so Zelda and Connie put up a little screen made up of the clothes rails and some blankets and partitioned off an area of the wardrobe. The Munros put their camp beds closely together to form a rather unstable double bed.

Connie knew that the last thing that Arthur would want was to be in the same room as her (and vice versa, to be honest) so it came as no surprise when he took himself off, cursing the cards he'd been dealt in life, and placed his bed in one of the stage wings, while Connie, relieved that she wouldn't be subjected to his bad breath and snoring for a few nights, was left to her own devices on the other side of the clothes rail from Hugh and Zelda.

Randolph decided that he might be more comfortable on the chaise longue onstage rather than a low camp bed, which he knew his back wouldn't be able to cope with.

And so all in all, in one way or another, they settled down for the night.

Penny lay awake thinking of all that had happened in the last twenty-four hours: the altercation with Arthur, the near-miss with the bomb, and how much she loved Teddy – even more now that they had made love. The tears that she now shed were ones of relief. Without prompting, Phyllis leant over and took her hand.

Teddy lay staring at the ceiling, thanking God or whatever for bringing Penny back to him.

Connie, in the wardrobe, was unable to get off to sleep as all she could hear was Hugh mumbling about everything to poor Zelda – the play, the soldier boy under the stage, the bomb, whether Teddy and Penny would stay together. Connie lay listening – there was no way that she could avoid it – wondering how Zelda put up with his continual chatter, not realising that Zelda had long ago worked out how to ignore Hugh, namely by slipping in and out of a doze and responding with an odd, sleep-induced grunt, which Hugh took to be her agreeing with him. He was really lucky, he thought, to have landed such an agreeable woman.

Arthur, having had too much to drink again in The Cockleshell, was snoring loudly and Randolph was forced to cover his ears with some cushions to try to muffle the noise. At times he was of the mind to take the said cushions and smother the horrid little man with them, which, he mused, would kill two birds with one stone. Poor Connie; she deserved much better.

Sam was thinking about Molly; her face kept popping up into his head. *You silly bugger, Samuel,* he told himself, *don't you go falling for the girl now. For a start, she wouldn't be interested in the likes of you. Also, when the run at the theatre is over, we'll be on the road to somewhere else and there is no way that Molly will be allowed to come along. Missus B is a good old stick but she wouldn't want her daughter gallivanting off with the likes of me. Blimey, what with everything I've told her about my past, she'd pull Molly away as quick as you like. So, fellow-me-lad,* he said to himself, *go to sleep and forget all about it.*

Over the road, in her little bedroom above the café, Molly had only one thought in her mind: how could she persuade her mother to allow her to go on the road with Mister Laine's Company? Molly knew her mother liked Sam – she loved the way that he would help clear the tables for her and help serve the lunches – but she wouldn't allow her to go off with him, would she? She knew that she was being silly. She loved her mother and now, with her father gone, she wouldn't want her to think that she wished to abandon her. No, whatever she imagined she felt for Sam, it was her job to stay and help out at the café.

Jane Baxter lay in her bed worrying about Molly's future. She had grown very fond of young Sam, and hearing about his childhood and how he was saved from poverty had made her even more fond of the lad. Call it motherly intuition, she could see that Molly was growing very fond of him. Molly was still very young but with this war, young men were going off and sometimes, like her husband, not coming back. A woman needed the companionship. Her Reg had been a good kind man and all she wished for was Molly to find someone half as good as her father, when the time came.

20

A Certain Lack of Funds

Sitting on her bentwood chair under the traffic of Whitehall, Ruby Butterworth had just come on for her shift, answering calls and putting people through to the country's civil servants. Her morning sickness was now becoming much more regular. What with that and the sleepless nights trying to work out how she could tell her parents of her plight, all she wanted to do was to curl up in a corner and die. She hoped that her supervisor would be Miss Davenport and not the ogre, Miss Nugent. Miss Davenport was younger and less severe, and didn't look at her as if she was some sort of criminal when she asked to take a toilet break. But there was to be no such luck. There she was, standing in the corner of the cavernous room, looking even more like a prison warder than ever; her brown brogues shining in the dim lights.

'Good morning, how may I help you?' said Ruby as she switched the switch on the exchange in front of her.

'Good morning. I wonder if you'd be good enough to put me through to Sir Peregrine Worsley's office, please?'

Ruby's heart jumped a little; it was that nice man from a few days before. She recognised his kindly voice.

'Oh, good morning,' she said into her headset as she flicked through the book of index cards on the desk in front of her. 'It's the council for the something of music and something, isn't it? You called the other day.'

For a moment Randolph was taken off guard, and then he remembered the girl who seemed very sweet but had made him use a second penny.

'Yes, yes, that's right,' he said, putting on a cheery voice even though he felt anything but cheery.

'One moment, I'm just looking for the number.' Ruby thumbed through the book. *That's funny,* she thought, as she arrived at the department heading and started to turn the cards to find Sir Peregrine. The card was no longer there; only a gap where it had been. The card had been removed. She looked through a few more cards to check in case it had been taken out and not put back in the correct place. No, it wasn't anywhere. She wasn't sure what to do. Should she call over Miss Nugent? No, she couldn't bear it.

'I'm so sorry sir, but we don't seem to have a number for that office.'

Randolph almost stopped breathing. 'Whatever do you mean?'

'I'm afraid that we have no card in our directory for Sir Peregrine Worsley.'

'But it was there the other day.'

'Yes, I know, sir, but it seems to have gone.'

'Well, what about his secretary, Miss Finch?'

'No, I'm afraid not – she would be on the same card, sir.'

Randolph froze at the other end. His entire world stopped. He thought he was about to have a heart attack and a strange strangled noise came from his throat.

'Hello, sir, are you alright?' said Ruby, having heard the noise loudly in her headset.

Randolph was silent.

'Sir?'

'What is it, girl?' It was Miss Nugent, who had come up onto Ruby's shoulder.

'I don't think the gentleman at the other end is very well, Miss Nugent,' replied Ruby, concerned.

'Whatever are you talking about, girl?' said Miss Nugent, pulling out Ruby's headset from the exchange and plugging hers in. 'Hello, are you there?' she said in her most forceful no-nonsense voice.

At the other end, Randolph had to pull the receiver away from his ear so as not to be deafened.

'Is there anyone there?' Miss Nugent bellowed again. 'Are you sick?'

But Randolph wasn't listening. His mind had gone numb and he fumbled about attempting to replace the receiver on its cradle.

'There's nobody there, you stupid girl,' said her supervisor, pulling out her headset. 'Whatever's the matter with you?'

Ruby was starting to breathe very heavily and she had gone quite cold. She knew she had to get to the toilet before it was too late, but she was unable to speak and Miss Nugent was standing, blocking her way.

'What the deuce is the matter with you, girl? Speak up.'

But Ruby could not speak up; instead she threw up. The contents of her stomach shot out of her mouth and onto the front of the supervisor's skirt. Unable to move, her eyes were fixed as her breakfast dribbled down Miss Nugent's legs and onto her shiny brown brogues.

One hundred and thirty miles away, as the crow flies, to the north east, Randolph Laine made his way along Haleston high street in a daze. Gone, disappeared, no card. Whatever could that mean? Dear God in heaven, now what could he do?

Back at the theatre, the overriding topic of conversation was whether Randolph should send Sam off to find out if any of the seaside landladies would be willing to put them up.

'Bloody good idea,' said Arthur. 'I hardly slept a wink last night on that damned bed.'

Molly heard the door open into the wings and saw Mister Laine stop in the doorway. She watched as he took a few deep breaths and mumbled to himself, 'Best foot forward.' Setting off, she noticed him stumble. She dived off her stool and ran over to him.

'Are you alright, Mister Laine?'

Randolph took a deep breath. 'Yes, thank you, Molly. A little out of puff, that's all. Bless you.' Taking another deep breath he strode onto the stage.

'Ah, Randolph, just the man. We've been talking as a Company and—' said Arthur immediately as he saw him.

But Randolph cut him off before he could go on, clapping his hands and striding confidently towards the front of the stage.

'Right, everybody. Beginners Act One, Scene One, from the top and no stopping. And no prompting, Molly. If they don't know their lines, then they are to busk their way out of it. So, positions please, chop, chop.'

Arthur stared at him for a moment and then, lighting a cigarette, walked off the stage towards the prompt corner.

'Is everything alright, Randolph?' asked Phyllis, sotto voce, as she made her way to the stalls to watch.

'Tickety-boo, old girl, tickety-boo,' said Randolph, forcing a weak smile.

'You can be the most dreadful actor at times, Randolph,' she answered, squeezing his arm as she passed.

*

Sergeant Green had got himself a nice corner seat by the window and before the engine had cleared the town's outskirts, he had started to doze, his sleep the night before having been constantly interrupted by drunken laughter and the heavy pounding of an out-of-tune piano alongside the locals' out-of-tune rendering of *It's a long way to Tipperary.* His entire body ached from his injuries and the fact that the bedsprings were sagging to such an extent that he could almost feel his backside hitting the floorboards every time he tried to turn over. He felt crocked – not that he would have told the MO that. *Fit as a fiddle, Sir, ready for anything.* Which he most certainly wasn't.

He could feel the spot near his collarbone where the shard of metal had buried itself. An inch to the left and he would have been a goner, but he tried not to think about that. He felt the shoulder stiffening and he dreaded falling asleep, knowing that it would be playing up like merry hell when he woke. And his leg? If he was on it too much he would feel a stabbing pain and the sensation like electricity shooting up it, and a heavy throbbing at the point where shrapnel had broken the fibula. He stretched his leg out to ease it and the pain shot up it. They'd wanted to keep it in plaster for longer but he'd talked them out of it; he didn't want his leg muscles to weaken any more than they had, but he knew that he was using it too much.

When he got to Haleston he'd find some digs and have a long hot bath. Yes, a good soak to ease the aches and pains and then a good feed up – fish and chips as he was going to be at the seaside, and a doorstep of bread and butter, plus a mug of good strong tea. Yes, that would set him up for the days ahead. No need to rush into anything; a few enquiries, nothing too pressing so's not to scare the natives. Be fatherly, be concerned about the lad, that sort of thing. Show them the photograph; tell them how worried his parents were about him (only half a lie – who wouldn't want to run away from the father?) As the CO said, he didn't need to go at it like a bull at a gate. He'd appointed the right man for the job, even though he did say so himself.

The boy was a nice-looking lad, had a sweet face, he thought. Yes, he could very well be one of his boys.

The train was quiet and he slept for most of the journey. It was a good thing that the train was terminating at Haleston as he could kip without fear of missing his stop; as it was, he was only half awake when the train pulled in.

*

'Molly, old girl.' Arthur was on her shoulder before she realised it. 'You heard the old boy. I need to take a look at the old dickie birds, before we start, just to refresh the grey matter.'

'But don't you have your own copy of your words, Mister Desmond?' she asked, shivering at the thought of him leaning over her again.

'No need for the formality, my dear, you can call me Arthur. We can't have all that "Mister Desmond" malarkey if we're going to be friends, now, can we?'

Molly had no wish to be Mister Desmond's friend. She just wanted him to go away.

'Come on, old girl, let's take a shoofty.' He exhaled more stale alcohol and cigarette smoke as he pressed himself against her, putting his hand initially on her shoulder before letting it slip down ever so slowly towards her breasts. She shifted on her stool and looked over to see if she could catch Sam's eye.

'Don't be a silly, Uncle Arthur isn't going to hurt you,' he said, catching the look. 'We're friends now, aren't we?' Pointedly, he removed his hand and placed it behind his back and used the other to thumb through the pages as he mumbled his lines to himself. Molly sat stock still and tried not to breathe.

'That's the ticket,' he said, patting her on the shoulder. 'All done and dusted.' He walked back up the wings, pulling on his cigarette and blowing out the smoke nonchalantly.

'Well, have you been able to get hold of your chum?' Phyllis asked Randolph as they tucked into their shepherd's pie in the café at lunchtime. She had steered him to a small table in the corner, away from the others.

'The thing is,' Randolph leant into her, 'he seems to have disappeared. And his office telephone number is no longer on the files, according to the silly girl at the exchange. I expect she was looking in the wrong place. I'll just have to try again later. I'm sure it's nothing, but until I can sort it out, I'm afraid that the ghost will not be strolling through our merry band of players.'

'Perhaps it will come through eventually,' Phyllis answered – "perhaps" being more the operative word than "eventually".

'The thing is, Randolph, I don't think I can risk sleeping on a camp bed again tonight, with my heart being as it is,' said Hugh, grabbing him as they walked back over to the theatre. 'Can't you send the boy out to sort out some digs?'

Randolph wasn't sure why sleeping on a camp bed in the theatre wardrobe would have any adverse effect on someone's heart, but he decided to let it pass.

'I'm glad you bought that up, old chap,' Randolph started, not being in the least bit glad, 'but the thing is, unfortunately, things are a little bit short in the money stakes at the moment.'

'But what about the money you had from London to pay for the hotel?' Arthur joined in. 'Let's face it, old Ma Goddard isn't going to need it where she is likely to be going to,' he stated in his usual insensitive way.

Randolph cleared his throat. 'The problem is that the money hasn't come through yet. You know what it's like dealing with Whitehall.'

'I have no idea what it's like dealing with Whitehall, thank God, as I've never had to deal with it,' Arthur retorted.

'I'm sure it will arrive next week and all will be well,' said Phyllis, butting in. 'But until then, if you wish to go off and find some digs for the rest of the time here, then you'll have to dig into your own pockets.'

'But old girl,' said Arthur, 'what if there's nothing left in said pockets apart from a handkerchief and some fluff?'

'I'm sure if you refrained from spending what you've got in The Cockleshell on the local floozy,' Phyllis countered, 'you might have a little left.'

Arthur walked away, pulling on his cigarette.

Somehow, Randolph managed to get them to knuckle down to rehearsals for the rest of the afternoon, but it wasn't easy. He really had to finish as the next day would consist of sorting out the lighting for the play with Mister Tuppence, and on Sunday they would need some form of technical rehearsal to make sure that Molly could write down all the lighting changes, such as there were, in the prompt copy, in order that she knew when to use the very basic cue light system on the wall in front of her to tell Mister Tuppence, who would be above her on his perch, when to change the lights from one 'state' (as Sam told her they were called) to the next. She would do this, Sam explained, by first switching on the red 'Standby' light (the other end of which was another red light up on the lighting perch in front of Mister Tuppence) and then the green 'Go' light switch next to the red one, to tell Mister Tuppence when to leap into action and push up or pull down the levers on the vast lighting contraption, either manually or with the aid of one of the large metal wheels on the end of it, which were attached by various chains and cogs to the levers to bring the lights up or down as required.

Phyllis, not being required for the first act, slipped out of the front of the theatre, off into the high street and over to the local bank, where she asked to see the manager as a matter of some urgency. Half an hour later, she placed some brown envelopes into her bag and toddled back to the theatre, and took up her seat at the back of the auditorium as if she hadn't moved, until it was time for her to step out onto the stage herself.

*

'Haleston Halt, Haleston Halt,' shouted the station master, 'this train terminates here, all change please, all change.'

Stretching the stiffness out of both his leg and shoulder, Sergeant Green picked up his kit bag and disembarked, trying to keep the pain from showing on his face as his leg gave from under him and he nearly fell onto the platform. He sucked in his breath to stop himself from yelping.

'Seen any soldiers around here?' he asked the station master as he took his ticket.

'Well, there's the barracks back in Yarmouth, I believe, but the soldiers don't come here, not since the engineers came to break up the pier and put the defences up on the beach.'

'Ah yes, of course,' said Green in as casual a manner as he could. 'So none of the lads come up here to take a bit of a holiday since returning from France?'

The station master shook his head. 'From what I hear, the boys saw enough of beaches and the sea over there to last them a lifetime.'

The sergeant nodded and said he'd vouch for that before wishing him a good morning and walking on. It was only after he had disappeared that the station master remembered the young soldier who came off the train a few days before. *Oh well,* he thought, *the sergeant was only making conversation and it's no business of mine.* And with that, he didn't give it another thought.

Not wanting to walk far, Green strolled along the prom. Looking up, he could see that part of the cliff face had fallen away, and stepping back towards the sea, he looked up and could see the bombed out ruins of a building above.

'Bloody Jerry came the other morning and did that, the buggers,' said an old boy who was passing by. 'The old Cliff Hotel, that was. Not anymore.'

'Any casualties?' Green asked.

'Old Ma Goddard. They got her out but she didn't last the night, from what I hear. And a young girl. They've not found her yet, as far as I know.'

'I'm sorry,' said Green.

'Oh well, that's war for you,' answered the old boy before doffing his cap and walking on.

Green watched him go and then continued, looking at the windows of the seaside boarding houses. Some looked closed up and unwelcoming but then he came across a brightly painted house with flowers in pots on the windowsills and a vacancy sign; he decided to try his luck. Missus Hart was just the ticket.

'Hart by name, and all heart by nature,' she said when he introduced himself. They agreed that he would stay for three nights. *Well*, he thought, *no point in rushing* – and when she told him that she had a lovely deep bath and plenty of hot water, the thought of a nice hot bath was too much to ignore.

'There are those who don't seem to appreciate our soldiers,' said Missus Hart, 'but nobody can say that of me. Don't worry about the three-inch rule with the bath water, neither; I'll turn a blind eye, if you will.'

Green noticed the way she was looking at him, and as she spoke she slid her hands down her skirt in order to straighten it out. He also couldn't help noticing that she had a pair of very shapely legs, something that became even more pronounced as she walked up the stairs in front of him with the room key in her hand.

'Here we are,' she said, opening the door, 'a nice room with a sea view and an armchair. And I'm told the bed is very comfortable; I've had no complaints about the bed, that's for sure.' She let out the faintest girly giggle.

Green took the key and thanked her.

'The bathroom's down the hall.' She pointed. 'And I could do a fry-up for you in the morning, about eight o'clock, how does that sound? I've got a bit of bacon left and an egg. There's a front door key with your room key, let yourself in, but don't worry about disturbing me, I like to sit up and have a read in the evening, or listen to the wireless with a glass of sherry.'

The sergeant thanked her and watched as she slid down the stairs. He smiled to himself. *Barking up the wrong tree there, dear lady*, he thought, *but I'll have to lock my door tonight*.

He threw his kit bag on the bed and stretched his neck; his whole body ached to blazes. He stared out of the window towards the sea. From his vantage point he could see the beach defences. *Beach defences, my eye, a bit of barbed wire will hardly stop the Germans in their tracks for long from what I've witnessed*. But then again, nothing seemed to stop them; they just kept coming in ranks, day and night, ploughing on through whatever was placed in their way while the British Expeditionary Forces backed off, along with the French infantrymen, to get away as far and as quickly as they could.

Off to one side of him was the pier, again covered in barbed wire, and he could see the large break in the boardwalk and the temporary swing bridge on the land side. *Dear God in his heaven*, he thought, *the bloody Jerrys would be over that without missing a step*. If Hitler decided to invade, there would be bugger-all to stop him and they'd all be doing funny salutes and eating dreadful white cabbage with pink sausages that the Krauts loved. *No thank you*, he thought, shaking his head as he hobbled down to the bathroom to have that good soak in the bath, making sure he'd locked the door before taking off his uniform. After all, it wouldn't do to have Missus Hart poking her head round and taking a peek at what she shouldn't.

*

'I wonder if I may have a word with the Company, before we all go off for the evening,' Phyllis engaged Randolph as he was about to call it a day.

'Go off?' It was Arthur, of course. 'And where are we going off too? Oh, yes, the pub, and then to toss and turn all night on a bloody uncomfortable camp bed.'

'Arthur,' Phyllis snapped at him. 'If you learnt to keep your council once in a while, you may hear something to your advantage.'

'Please continue, Phyllis,' said Teddy.

She opened her bag and produced the brown paper envelopes.

'Sam, dear, I wonder if you and Molly would be kind enough to hand these around. There are ones for you both, of course.'

Sam came forward and took the pile and handed a few to Molly.

'Inside each are five one-pound notes as a gift. For you all to be going on with until the bean counters in Whitehall pull their fingers out. This is from my personal bank account, but no matter about that.'

Sam hesitated – she couldn't afford to do this, surely – but Teddy was ahead of him.

'Phyllis, this is very kind of you,' he said as he was handed his envelope, 'but I, for one, can survive without depriving you of your hard-earned savings.'

'I would never say it was hard-earned, Teddy. A few pounds put away from when I was at my zenith.'

'Hard-earned savings, Phyllis, which are yours. I can only speak for myself, and others must do what they think, but with heartfelt thanks, I can't accept your generous gift.' And with that, Teddy pressed the envelope in her hand and kissed her on the cheek.

'I can't take your money, Missus Campbell-Bennett.' Molly's voice surprised everyone. With growing confidence, she stepped forward with her hand outstretched. 'My mum wouldn't hear of it and I'm sure dad wouldn't either if he were here. I love being part of this Company and don't need to be given money to work for you all.'

Teddy murmured a 'well done' as she came back past him, and this made Molly feel even better for the choice she had made.

Sam was next to come forward. 'I wouldn't dream of taking it, but bless you.'

Arthur Desmond could feel the gorge filling his throat; he could quite happily take it. The old bitch was rich, so why not?

'Arthur and I couldn't possibly take your money, Phyllis,' said Connie, as she held out her hand towards Arthur's envelope, 'could we, Arthur dear?' Arthur clenched his teeth as he handed the envelope begrudgingly to his wife, before storming offstage and around to The Cockleshell to drink himself to oblivion once more on a tab that he now had no way of paying off when the time came.

In the end, Phyllis had all the brown envelopes back in her bag, *Oh well,* she thought. 'Well, the least I can do is stand a round in the pub,' she said, a gesture that was gratefully accepted by all in a form of a compromise.

'Billy, dear,' said Phyllis. 'Will you join us for a drink?'

Billy hesitated.

'Come now, dear, you're part of the Company now, at least for a while.'

'Do you think that's wise?' asked Randolph.

'Well, the poor lad can't hide away in here for the rest of his life,' she replied.

'We need to be careful, Phyllis,' said Hugh, sidling up to her. 'If we're seen with a deserter, we could be in all sorts of trouble.'

'It's all right, Phyllis, we thought we'd take a walk and get some air, didn't we, Billy?' said Eric, having heard enough.

'Walk, dear?' asked Phyllis. 'Well, of course you're free to do what you wish.'

After a good soak, Sergeant Green wrapped a large towel around himself and, checking the coast was clear, padded down the landing and back into his room, turning the key. He felt fresher but he knew that if he didn't get a good night's sleep, he'd be good for nothing in the morning.

Crossing over to the window to close the curtains, he stood watching as a young lad and his grandfather took the early evening air, strolling along the prom towards the pier. Had he stayed watching, he would have been a little surprised at seeing the old man suddenly pull a coil of barbed wire out of the way, crawl through the gap and head off down the boardwalk. But he hadn't stayed; he'd pulled the curtains together and painfully put on his long johns in an attempt to keep his joints warm, and climbed into bed.

Teddy and Penny had sat themselves in the corner by the piano as Sam picked out a few melodies and with mock sincerity sang the words over his shoulder towards them.

> *Lovely to look at,*
> *Delightful to know and heaven to kiss.*
> *A combination like this,*
> *Is quite my most impossible scheme come true,*
> *Imagine finding a dream like you!*

'I've a good mind to go to the police myself.'

'Oh, Arthur.'

'Dear God, you're all so damned naïve. The boy's trying to integrate himself so you'll all shield him.' There was no sign of Arthur's little lady friend so, for once, he was sitting at a table with the others and not holding up the bar.

'He's frightened, Arthur,' said Connie, ignoring his jibe. 'He's been telling me all about what was happening over there. His friends were killed in front of him.'

'You always were a soft touch, Connie.' Arthur grunted back.

'Yes, it must have been absolutely ghastly, of course,' said Veronica flippantly, 'but I'm with Arthur. One of us should go to the police and tell them we have a deserter in our midst, and they can be responsible for him. I'm not be going to prison for aiding and abetting, I assure you.'

'Yes, so you've said before, Veronica,' said Zelda, who wasn't prepared to see the lad thrown to the wolves. 'How would you feel if you had a loved one over there being shot at?'

She wouldn't know, she's never had any loved ones, thought Phyllis, but she refrained from saying it out loud.

'I know how I felt when we thought that Hugh would have to join up in nineteen fourteen. It was only his weak heart that saved him; I could never see Hugh surviving the trenches with such a delicate temperament.'

Hugh sat drinking his beer, not sure how he should take that remark.

'May I remind you that through the efforts of that young man, a person was pulled from the rubble of the hotel yesterday,' Phyllis piped up.

'Does anybody know if she survived?' asked Hugh, turning round to the barman. 'Landlord, have you heard what happened to the lady from the hotel?'

'She died on her way to hospital, so I was told,' he replied, as ever polishing a beer glass. 'At least they found her. There's still no sign of the young girl though, poor dear. She's still buried somewhere under there, as far as I know.'

'How shocking,' said Phyllis, shaking her head.

'Oh, not the girl who brought our breakfasts?' said Connie tearfully. 'Oh, how dreadful. Her poor parents, what must they be going through?'

Unable to bear the women's wittering anymore, Arthur stood and took himself over to the stool at the end of the bar.

'Sam, do you think that just for one evening we could have a quiet drink without that jingle-jangle going on in the background?' he snapped across the bar.

'Oh, aren't you fond of a bit of Mister Coward, Arthur?' Sam replied teasingly as he started to sing the first refrain of *If love were all*.

I believe in doing what I can
In crying when I must
In laughing when I choose
Hey ho, if love were all...

Arthur cursed him under his breath. He cursed them all. He especially cursed Teddy Shaw and that silly girl, sitting there hand in hand like "love's young dream".

'Of course, we're breaking the rules,' said Eric, breaking off a piece of batter.

Having sat together looking out across the waters below at the end of the pier before the night set in, they were now back in the auditorium eating fish and chips brought with the half a crown that Phyllis had pressed into Eric's hand before leaving for the pub.

'What is?' asked Billy, feeling more human having been taken under the wing of most of the Company and feeling he was able to relax a little.

'This is – eating fish and chips.'

Billy laughed. 'Why, is it illegal to eat fish and chips? I thought they hadn't rationed fish and chips.'

'They haven't, thank goodness. But they're not allowed in the theatre. It's one of the golden rules; that and quoting from the Scottish play.'

'What's the Scottish play?' Billy frowned.

Eric laughed. 'I'm not allowed to say its name in here, otherwise I have to do a forfeit or this play would be doomed to failure; all nonsense, of course. Anyway, it's something to do with the smell. The smell of fish and the salt and vinegar supposedly wafts through from backstage into the auditorium and lingers. It's just silly nonsense, of course, like saying "Macbeth".' He stopped and thought about what he'd let slip and then started to laugh. 'Oh, who cares? It's only a word. Macbeth, Macbeth, Macbeth,' he shouted at the top of his voice, marching up and down the aisle. 'Is this a dagger I see before me? When shall we three meet again, in thunder, lightning or in the rain?'

'STOP!' The voice was itself full of thunder and rage and it filled the theatre. 'Stop that at once, you foolish child.' It was Phyllis, with forty odd years of projecting her voice to reach the gods. 'You ignorant child,' she continued, storming down the steps to the auditorium and, before Eric could do anything about it, grabbing hold of his ear and frog-marching him towards the stage door. 'You vile, ignorant boy; you foolish, foolish child,' she hissed in his ear. 'If I had my way, I'd horse-whip you.' She threw him down the steps into the alleyway – who knew she was so strong? 'Now close your eyes, turn round three times, swear and spit,' she barked. 'Do it, you stupid boy, do it.'

The venom in Phyllis's voice stung him, but before he had time to spit some poison back at her, she was off again.

'I've tried to help you, guide you, get you to grow up and stop behaving like a spoilt child, and this is what you do, how you repay me.' She shook her head. 'Isn't life difficult enough for you, already?' she asked. 'Do you think all your silly bravado will help you?' She took in a deep breath and calmed down a little. 'I hear that in Nazi Germany, they throw young men like you into prison to rot. Let us pray that Hitler is thwarted if he should decide to invade this island, otherwise…' She couldn't bring herself to continue. 'Now do as I told you,' she said, spinning her finger around. 'Round three times, spit and swear, while I get my breath.'

Reluctantly, Eric did as he was told.

'I know it may seem like a lot of theatrical superstition, but it's the only religion we have.'

'Bugger,' Eric said loudly, before sitting down on the step. 'Jolly good. That's better.'

Phyllis sat down next to him and took his hand in hers.

'Now, we need to talk. I can see that you and the boy are fond of each other, but there are some in this Company who want rid of him as soon as they can be, and if you're not careful they will call the authorities.' Phyllis tried to reason with him. 'We must do everything to stop that happening, which includes you growing up, smartish.' She tapped his hand and humphed. 'Now, that's enough from me. Go on, get back to your fish and chips and hope the smell has gone by the morning, or Randolph won't be as lenient on you.'

As he made his way back into the building, he wasn't sure how to react to any of this. Phyllis's outburst had rather taken the wind out of his sails and he started to feel a little ashamed of himself – it was an odd sensation, not one he could recall feeling before. He had built a protective wall around himself, which Phyllis had broken down within a few minutes, and he now stood exposed. He had no idea how to handle it.

Dear me, Phyllis thought as she watched him go. *I'm surrounded by a sea of emotional wreckage.*

21

Lighting and Mister Tuppence

It was Saturday morning and Randolph was sitting alone in the centre of the stalls. The place was as silent as the grave.

He closed his eyes a moment and thanked the Lord that, for one day at least, he didn't have to listen to the constant bickering of actors. He assumed that they were off doing what most actors did on their one day off: spending the day in the nearest pub (Arthur Desmond came immediately to mind); writing letters (Phyllis would be writing letters – she was an avid letter writer – no doubt one would be to her son in Hollywood); taking a motoring trip out into the countryside and, no doubt, finding a nice quiet pub and then having a lay down in a farmer's field after (that would be Teddy and Penny, doing just what he and Hester used to do in their first flush of love). The others? Hugh and Zelda, with Connie in tow, would be sitting on deck chairs on the prom, he expected, watching the tide coming in and out and dozing.

He opened his eyes, took out his pocket watch and peered at it. Eleven o'clock and still nothing done.

'Are you ready yet, Mister Tuppence?'

Silence.

'Mister Tuppence, are you on your lighting perch?'

Silence.

'Mister Tuppence, we really must get on.'

Mister Tuppence finally appeared carrying a tall wooden ladder, which he brought down the aisle and, pulling on the sash rope, extended until it got as high as a metal bracket that had been screwed into the wall. Having set up the ladder against the wall, Mister Tuppence retraced his steps and after a moment or two returned with a large lantern.

Randolph looked on with increasing bemusement.

'Are you sure you're hanging that lantern in the right place? It looks to me to be a long way from the stage area – I can't see that the light will be strong enough to light the actors from there,' said Randolph

'It can't go nowhere else,' said Mister Tuppence as he started to climb the ladder, lantern in hand.

'Why not?'

'Because this is where the bracket is for it.'

Randolph shook his head and sighed. It was going to be a very long, frustrating day.

'Jack Casey?' said Jane Baxter, when Randolph asked about Mister Tuppence whilst he was having lunch in the café, having achieved absolutely nothing the entire morning.

'Jack Casey?'

Molly's mother laughed. 'Mister Tuppence. You were asking about Mister Tuppence. That's not his real name; Jack Casey's the name his dear old parents gave him. Poor soul.'

'Then why…?'

'Oh, that came about because a few unkind locals went around saying that he was "tuppence short of a shilling" when he came back from the first war. Shell-shocked, they call it. It was very sad. Poor soul.'

'I see.'

'Before the war, Jack was the man you went to when you needed something mending or the electricity went off, as it did all the time; he could fix anything. Clever with his hands, they said.' Jane continued as she went about the café clearing and cleaning the tables, 'When he was called up he went into the Royal Engineers; building trenches, making tunnels for the troops to be able to get from one trench to the next, that sort of thing. Well, it was inevitable, when you think about it. One day, he was on the front line fixing a trench or something – I don't know what he was doing – but it received a direct. That's what they call it, I think. Jack and three others, shovels in hand, were digging away and clearing the poor devils who had been buried there previously and making it safe for the next lot of soldiers. I don't know how true this is, but one of the soldiers made some comment about it being all right where they were as lightning didn't strike twice in the same place, but he was wrong. A shell landed in the trench and all of them were blown sky high, not one of them in one piece apart from Jack, who, the way I heard it, just picked himself up out of the mud and, without a word, started to walk towards the enemy lines until an officer grabbed him and pulled him back. Poor man didn't utter a word for two years, they said.' She started collecting all the little salt and pepper pots onto a tray and placed it on the counter. 'When they discharged him from the hospital, he was sent out back into civilian life without so much as a thank you. When he came back here, he'd just shuffle about the town, mumbling and stuttering away to himself.'

'Oh dear, oh dear,' said Randolph as he drank down his tea, beginning to feel rather guilty for getting cross with the old boy earlier.

'The children used to follow him around chanting "Mister Tuppence, Mister Tuppence – got any change for a shilling, Mister Tuppence?" Children can be very cruel – cruel and unfeeling. He was called it so many times that in the end he started calling himself Mister Tuppence. Poor soul,' Jane Baxter repeated. 'That's when my Reg gave him a job. He would just stand and wait for Reg to ask him to do something, then he'd go off and do it. Then somebody at the council asked if anyone knew someone who could do some electrical or engineering jobs for them and we suggested Jack. By all accounts, he found the old lights and whatnot in the theatre, which were all rusted and such, and mended them.'

Having paid for his tea, Randolph put his hat on his head and tipped it to Missus Baxter, before making his way back down the side alley, reminding himself to try and not get cross with the old boy again.

It was another twenty minutes before Mister Tuppence came down the ladder and walked up the aisle and onto the stage. Randolph watched him, biting his tongue and hoping against hope that they might, just might, get started. Mister Tuppence climbed onto the stage and looked up, studying the lanterns that he had spent the entire morning putting up. Nodding, he made his way over to the wings and disappeared from Randolph's view. Having climbed the cat ladder to his perch then wiped his hands on his old bit of cloth, he shambled over to the railing and called down to Randolph to inform him that the lights were now in place and that he was now ready to start whenever Randolph was. Having conveyed his message, he stood by the large lighting board and awaited further instructions. It was now two thirty in the afternoon. Randolph shook his head, scratched it and sat down, trying to stay calm.

'House lights out, please,' said Randolph.

As the house lights juddered out, Randolph pulled out a little torch from his pocket that he kept solely for the job in hand, opened his copy of the play and turned to his notes.

'Right, Mister Tuppence,' said Randolph, 'I need a nice, soft lighting state that suggests an early summer evening.'

There was total silence for a moment and then a voice came from the darkness.

'So what is it you want? Full up, half up or off?

22

Dress Rehearsal

'Do you think they do anything down there?' asked Hugh, as he and Zelda lay next to each other for the third night in their camp beds after a day of lounging in deck chairs on the prom and eating yet more fish and chips.

'Whatever do you mean?' said Zelda as she tried to get off to sleep.

'Come on, old girl, do I need to spell it out?' replied Hugh. 'It's an awful thought.'

Zelda sighed and turned over with her back towards him. 'Go to sleep, Hugh. It's the dress rehearsal tomorrow and there's still a lot to do.'

'Well, we're ready; word perfect, both of us,' he said, 'which is more than can be said for some people.'

Zelda knew who he meant but as Connie was on the other side of the makeshift partition, she didn't want her hearing them gossiping about her husband.

Connie lay in her camp bed. She tried not to listen in on the others' conversation – she was taught that it was rude to 'earwig' – but she had no choice as the only thing that separated the talker from the listener, on this occasion, was a blanket and Arthur's *Charley's Aunt* black silk dress, his two black underskirts and long white bloomers, all of which she had diligently ironed and hung up on the costume rail, which was standing by the side of the bed.

'Go to sleep, Hugh, and do stop clucking on.'

Hugh, as ever, was quite hurt by that. Clucking on? He didn't cluck. 'I'm only saying what's what.' He really hadn't got the hint. 'The man is bloody drunk all the time, can't remember a word and smells of cigarettes.'

Zelda turned around quickly and hissed at him, 'Hugh, stop talking; walls have ears and these walls are very thin.' She pointed towards the blanketed partition.

'Well, don't blame me if he doesn't come in with his lines when he should, that's all I'm saying.'

'Why would anyone blame you?' Zelda answered, confused. 'Everyone knows what he's like. Now go to sleep.' She said the last three words slowly and pointedly before turning her back on him again.

There was a pause, then out of the darkness, 'Don't I get a good night kiss?' said a childishly thin voice.

'No,' replied the child's mother, not too unkindly, 'you don't deserve it; you've been very annoying.'

'Oh,' said the child, deflated. 'Right.' Hugh sighed dramatically and Zelda gently shook her head. She knew that in the end she was going to have to turn over so he could kiss her good night, just as he had done every night of their married lives, but she'd let him suffer a bit first. He'd huff and puff and make other little noises like a spoiled child. It was just a case of how long she could stand it.

Hugh duly huffed and puffed and turned on his side, and then turned onto his other side, which wasn't easy without the damned bed toppling over and spilling him onto the floor. He was sure he felt the legs leave the ground. He started clearing his throat and gave out a pathetic little coughing sound. Zelda decided that enough was enough and that she and poor Connie, a few feet away, needed to sleep.

'Come here, my little Hughie,' she said in her little girl voice.

Hugh allowed himself a little grin but didn't move. *She won't get round me that easily,* he thought, only they both knew that she would.

'Zelda wants a kiss good night,' she said.

'I'm not sure Zelda deserves it,' replied Hugh.

She wished they could just get on with it, but she also knew that the game had to be played to the very end or she'd never be allowed to sleep.

On the other side of the clothes rail, Connie took out her handkerchief and bit into it to mute the sound of her laughter.

'Please Hughie, don't tease Zelda.' She was good at sounding as if she enjoyed this little charade, but in reality, she had got extremely bored with it many years before. But if it pleased Hugh, and shut him up, then so be it.

'Well, only because you asked so nicely,' he said, turning over to face her.

On cue, Zelda turned and faced him; they kissed on the lips and smiled at each other.

'Good night,' she said.

'Sleep tight,' he answered.

'Don't let the bed bugs bite,' they said in unison, and then they both turned over and closed their eyes.

Connie spent the next five minutes wiping away the tears of laughter and envying her friends' marriage before hearing Hugh's voice come once more out of the darkness.

'Well, do you think they do it down there?'

Zelda sighed heavily and threw the blanket over her head.

Eric and Billy were lying side by side but each in their own camp bed, looking up at the underside of the stage. They could hear Randolph above as he turned over on the sofa and they watched as the clouds of dust drifted down. They could hear Arthur's snores, which made them both laugh as the noise went from a deep grunting full-grown pig up through the scale to a squealing piglet.

They had been talking quietly for the past hour or so. Eric had been on the defensive all evening. He couldn't stop talking about how Phyllis had made him feel.

'Why does it worry you so much?' Billy asked, out of the blue.

'What?'

'It's not important. She's hurt your feelings, that's all.'

'My feelings aren't hurt, I assure you,' Eric lied. He felt unsettled and all the defence mechanisms he'd relied on through his life were starting to fail.

'Perhaps I can stay with the Company,' said Billy, trying to change the subject. 'I could help Sam and Molly – learn how to change the scenery, or become an actor. Anything would be better than going back to the army.'

Eric wanted to keep talking about himself and felt annoyed that he wasn't the main topic of the conversation. He lay and sulked for a moment before realising that he was just falling back into his default position. Nothing and nobody mattered more than Eric Cornwall. Only that wasn't true anymore. Now there was someone else that he seemed to care about, and he could hear and feel his breath close to him.

Billy half turned to him in the silence.

'Well, I could always ask,' said Eric, feeling Billy's eyes scanning him. 'I'll talk to Randolph in the morning.'

'I'm not sure that will be a good idea,' replied Randolph, when Eric broached the subject the next day.

'He'd be very useful.'

'Yes, yes, I'm sure he would, but I have the feeling that not all the Company would be in agreement.' Randolph was trying his best to be understanding, but in truth he didn't need any more problems; this production was turning into a nightmare as it was.

'Have you completely lost your senses?' snapped Veronica, overhearing the conversation as she made her way along the corridor, 'or are you boys just ruled by your cocks?'

'No more than you,' Eric snapped back.

'Oh dear, how sad. And I thought we were friends.'

'You don't have friends, dear, you have victims.'

'It sounds like the Campbell-Bennett woman has been filling your head with stories.'

'You know you're a total bitch, don't you, Veronica?'

'Yes, I should hope so; I work very hard at it,' she smiled. 'I had hoped that you and I might make a good double act; it's so much more fun sharing the spoils with someone else, but it seems you're just like the others when it comes down to it,' she said wearily, lighting a cigarette.

Eric wanted to hit her.

'And falling for the soldier boy, how sad,' she continued, blowing out a long, tight plume of smoke. 'You know they'll put him against a wall and shoot him? That's what they do to the deserters, and then you'll be just another poor little war widow.' With a theatrical flourish she looked at her wrist watch. 'I might just have time to pop down to the police station before we start and then the local bobbies can come and pick him up; how does that sound? I expect they'll throw him in a cell and lay about him with their little truncheons.' And with that she walked off towards her dressing room.

'She won't do anything of the sort,' said Phyllis, who had been hovering further along the corridor. 'I shall lock her in that dressing room if she tries it, believe me.'

Eric forced out a smile.

'And by the way, Eric, they don't shoot deserters in the British Army anymore, and the British policemen do not hit people with their truncheons – this isn't America.'

'What the bloody hell is all this?' asked Arthur as Connie and Billy made their way to his dressing room laden with a woman's costume.

'It's your costume, dear,' Connie smiled, hanging the large, lacy black silk skirt on the rail that was screwed to the wall. The skirt on its own seemed to take up half the room. 'And these are your two underskirts.' They seemed to take up the other half.

'Two underskirts? What the blazes do I need two underskirts for?' Arthur looked them up and down.

'To fill out the top skirt, dear; it's quite fine silk and if there's no body under it, it will just hang down and you'll trip over it.'

Arthur sighed. 'And what are those?' he asked, pointing at the long, baggy white…

'Bloomers, dear. You have to have bloomers for when you lift the skirt. Whenever an audience sees bloomers, it never fails to get a laugh.'

'I can't possibly wear all that lot on stage, I'll sweat to buggery.'

'And here's your wig,' Connie continued, choosing to ignore his coarse language. 'I've dressed it quite tightly at the top so it won't fall off and given it these two granny pigtails that will hang down the front over your little jacket and lace scarf. And this bonnet ties under the chin.'

'I am not wearing all that lot and that's final.' Arthur stamped his foot.

'But it's the classic costume for the part, dear. I have it on very good authority that the jacket and skirt are the very ones that William Penley wore on the first night of the play at the Theatre Royal, Bury St Edmunds.'

The dress rehearsal went the way that dress rehearsals tend to do – badly. Veronica trod on Penny and Phyllis's lines quite deliberately during the second act, and when questioned about it replied that she was convinced that one or the other of them had dried and she was covering for them; wasn't that the professional thing to do? Phyllis decided not to counter her by accusing her of upstaging for the umpteenth time, thinking it best just to try to get to the end so they could be ready for opening night.

Arthur stumbled through his part word-wise and tripped over his skirts and cursed his wife loudly whilst pleading to Randolph to settle the matter. Randolph did settle the matter. He thought it all looked splendid and sought to flatter Arthur's ego by telling him that when the audience saw his first entrance in full costume he was bound to get a huge laugh and even a round of applause.

However, Arthur was not to be placated and stormed off into the wings, lit a cigarette and proceeded to lean over Molly and look at the prompt script, resting his hand on her leg. Molly leaned out of the way the best she could only to be engulfed in a nightmarish confection of black silk, satin and lace.

Relieved when the rehearsal was over, Randolph released the Company for a fifteen-minute tea break, 'Which is to be followed by notes in the auditorium. For what good they'll do,' he muttered, under his breath.

'Can't we have notes in half an hour?' Arthur asked fiercely. 'I have to get out of this bloody frock or I'll keel over.'

'It's not the frock that will make him keel over, it's the half bottle of whisky tucked into his petticoat,' Teddy joked as he and Sam went to collect Molly in order to go off for a well-earned cup of her mother's tea.

'Hello, sir,' said Molly as a rather short balding gentleman in an ill-fitting dinner jacket, complete with bow tie, came through the stage door as they were about to leave.

'Good afternoon, Molly,' said the man kindly, 'and who are these gentlemen? Perhaps you'd be good enough to introduce me?'

'Oh yes, sorry sir. This is Teddy – I mean Mister Shaw, and this is Mister Laine.'

'Pleasure to meet you both,' said the man.

'This is Mister Ripley, he was my teacher at school,' said Molly quickly.

'In that case, it's very nice to meet you,' said Teddy, holding out his hand. 'If I may say, you've done a fine job with Molly here. She's been a God-send – we couldn't have got to the first night without her. You should be very proud of her.'

Molly blushed.

'That she is,' said Mister Ripley, smiling benevolently at her.

"Must try harder" was the phrase that Molly always associated with Mister Ripley as he always wrote it at the end of every school report: "Molly is a good girl and well behaved but really must try harder."

'Your mother told me that you were helping these good people out. Well done, well done. But I don't think she will be able to help out with the little favour I've come round to ask.'

'And what favour would that be, guv'nor?' said Sam.

'Well, you see, as well as teaching at the local school, I am also on the committee that oversees the theatre and will be the duty manager for the next few evenings,' he stated, rather pompously, 'and one of my jobs is to get this piano here,' he said, tapping the old upright, 'into the stalls for the King.'

'The King; is he coming?' asked Sam, cheekily. 'I didn't know he played.'

Mister Ripley looked confused as Sam's joke flew over his head and landed with a thump on the floor behind him. 'We need to get it into the stalls in order that Miss Plowright will be able to play the National Anthem at the end. It's in the licence, you see; we have to play the King.'

'And you're in need of a bit of muscle to get it out the front, if I get where you're coming from?' said Sam.

'Yes. Four of us should be able to do it. You gentlemen and myself, plus one other. The wheels are quite sturdy but it's the steps down that tend to cause the problem. Perhaps this gentleman?'

It was the very moment that Arthur, relieved of his costume, and lighting up yet another cigarette, came around the corner from the dressing rooms.

'Yes, I'm sure this gentleman would help out,' replied Teddy, 'wouldn't you, Arthur?'

'Doing what?'

'Transporting this Joanna here into the stalls,' said Sam.

'Bugger off. How many times do I have to tell you people? I'm not a bloody stagehand.' And without pausing, he was out of the stage door.

Mister Ripley winced at the uncouth language and wondered if he should inform Molly's mother about it.

'Well, I'm sure this gentleman…' He was stopped in his tracks as both Teddy and Sam shook their heads and tapped their chests in unison as Hugh and Zelda appeared.

Getting the upright through the doors and into the wings did not present too much of a problem, other than a corner of it taking out a fair chunk of the doorframe. The wheels were sturdy and moved freely so dollying it down to the front of the stage took no time, but then came the tricky part of getting it down the steps into the auditorium without losing control and letting it fall into a splintered heap at the bottom.

'What we need to do is keep her upright as long as we can and then gently lower the front down onto the bottom step, using the underside as a fulcrum,' said Sam, having moved a great many heavy bits of scenery in his time and not a few pianos. 'You want the weight of the old girl to do all the work.'

'But how do we do that with only three of us?' asked Mister Ripley.

'Four of us,' said Molly, her confidence gaining.

Mister Ripley looked at her and nodded patronisingly at her. 'Of course, Molly.'

Molly decided that she didn't care very much for that look and that, no matter what, she was going to pull her weight and show him that she was just as good as he was – better even.

'Right then, Molly Malone,' said Sam, with a wink, 'you and Mister Ripley slowly push the Joanna towards the edge while Teddy and I take the weight on at the front; move her nice and slowly so we can hold her level, and when she's past the point of no return we'll lower the front end down and then grab the other end, and hopefully she and us will still be in one piece.'

This they duly did although the whole thing nearly came a cropper as they were lowering the back end and she crashed to the floor.

'Well, if she wasn't out of tune before, she certainly is now,' said Sam as they started to push her towards the side wall at the front of the stalls.

Teddy opened the lid and attempted to play a scale. 'There are quite a few duff keys, you know.'

'I wouldn't worry about that,' Mister Ripley answered. 'Miss Plowright can only pick out a tune on her right hand by using two fingers. Nobody will notice.'

23

Sergeant Green Investigates

'Sadly my bacon supply is running low,' explained Missus Hart, as she put down his plate, which contained a small rasher of bacon and a fried egg, in front of the sergeant. 'Between you and me, I had a very good supplier until a couple of days ago, but she's gone now.'

Green raised an eyebrow.

'Oh, me and my big mouth,' she laughed as she poured out his tea.

Spivs were everywhere, he knew that, and not all of them looked like Max Miller.

Leaving the house, having had his fry-up and a couple of pieces of toast and marmalade, Sergeant Green adjusted his cap and straightened his tunic. He'd go for a little walk, take in the area, ask a few questions. Nice and gentle now.

Stretching his muscles and trying not to show the pain he was in, he set off down the promenade with the gulls swirling and screeching overhead. A gentle breeze came off the sea and the salty air filled his lungs. Dunkirk hadn't smelt like this, that was for certain; there the air was full of burning oil and death. A bombed-out oil container a few miles inland had blown acrid black smoke over them. A black cloud with a silver lining – it was a life saver, acting as cloud cover, which helped to hold off the German dive bombers for a while at least, although some German pilots had been mad or brave enough to dive steeply through it and plough nose first towards the sand, before they would pull up and fly parallel to the beach at about fifteen feet, firing the machine guns, the bullets sending up plumes of sand or plunging into the backs of the British soldiers running for cover. Too many were destined to meet their maker in that way. The fortunate ones were carried off to the "the butcher's shop", as the field hospital was known to the troops.

As Green wandered the streets, his hands relaxed behind his back, he felt a certain sympathy for young Pryce not wanting to return to that carnage, but, he mused, the country was at war and the lad was in the army, and in the army you obey orders, no questions asked. Yes, he realised that sergeant majors yelling at the top of their voices left, right and centre was offputting to a lad with certain sensibilities, but these boys had to understand that without it there would be no bloody soldiers left to fight. You can't win a war if your recruits decide they don't like having bullets whizzing past their ears or seeing their mates cut down before they can grow some proper hair on their chins. *That's the price of war, Private Pryce, and we can't have you running away just because that sort of thing doesn't appeal to you.*

Making his way around the town, he stopped to have a chat to a few of the locals, nonchalantly pulling out the photograph and wondering whether they may have seen any young soldiers in the last few days? All very friendly, all very fatherly. Some of them asked him about Dunkirk. He'd answer as diplomatically as he could. It was a small setback, nothing to worry about, and the army would have boots on French soil very shortly, and then Jerry would know all about it. They'd smile and walk off happily, while Green shook his head. *Will we buggery; not a chance. Those bastards could be landing on that beach tomorrow and there wouldn't be a lot we could do about it.*

Throughout the morning his wounds made sure that he remembered them, and by lunchtime, he was tempted to drop into one of the local pubs and rest up, perhaps have a swift half. He wasn't a big drinker. He drank enough in the sergeants' mess to be sociable but most of his colleagues weren't his sort, so he would never hang around for too long. He wasn't impressed by bad language – the talk of ladies' breast sizes and the like. No, his idea of relaxing was to sit with a good book, perhaps take a perambulation around the camp and maybe have a chat with some young recruit to show that not all men with three stripes on their arms were ogres; get the lads on your side, that was the way.

'No, sorry Sergeant,' said the landlord of The Nelson Arms, 'I've not seen him, I'm afraid.' It was the same in The King's Head and The Crown and Anchor. Two half pints and a swift scotch later and he felt heavy and in need of forty winks so he crept back to his digs and gave into the urge to lie down and rest his body before continuing on his quest. No point in overdoing it.

It was around four thirty when he woke, bleary eyed and cursing himself for succumbing to that whisky. His shoulder ached and his leg nagged. *Will this bloody pain not go away?* Splashing his face in the bathroom, he shook his head to get rid of the cotton wool that seemed to have lodged in it. He made his way out of the house, took in a few deep breaths and ambled up the winding road towards the ruins of the bombed-out building.

'The Cliff Hotel,' said the warden who was guarding it, 'or it was, before the ruddy German bombers got it a couple of days ago.'

'Many killed?'

'The manageress, Miss Goddard, and the young girl.'

'Just the two?'

'Two's enough.'

'Yes, of course, two too many,' Green corrected himself.

'The girl waitress, Alice, poor lass – well, she's still under there somewhere, as far as we know. Old Ma Goddard, at least they got her out and to the hospital, much good it did her. Come to think of it, it was one of your boys that found her – heard her, had his ear to the rubble. Said he'd learnt it in his army training.'

Green was brought up short. *One of your boys.* He nodded his head.

'Those Jerry buggers just drop their bombs willy-nilly; they don't care. Some of the buggers machine gun us when they feel like it and all. Nobody's been shot yet, but they will be, you mark my words.'

Sergeant Green produced the photograph.

'You said one of our boys – I take it you mean a young soldier found the lady in the rubble?'

'Miss Goddard.'

'Yes, Miss Goddard. The soldier, was he in uniform?'

'No, civvies, I think.'

'Had you ever seen the lad before?'

'Weren't local, if that's what you mean.'

'I see,' said the sergeant, the photograph in his hand.

'No,' replied the warden, 'he was with them theatricals, as far as I know.'

'Theatricals?' Green raised his eyebrows.

'Down at the Regent. They've not been here long; putting on a play I hear.'

'Would this be the lad, do you think?' Green brought the photograph up like a magician asking if this was the card you first thought of.

He looked at it.

'Ah, that could be the youngster.' He peered at the photograph again. 'I can't be sure; only seen him once, mind.' The old boy shook his head and then nodded it for good measure.

24

The First Night

The Company crowded into their dressing rooms to get ready as Molly went around calling how long they had until the play started. The 'half-hour call', Sam told her, was thirty-five minutes before the start, which was confusing until he explained: the 'half-hour call' at thirty-five minutes; the 'quarter-hour call' at twenty minutes; the 'five-minute call' at ten minutes, and then what was called the 'beginners' call' came when you wanted everybody who was on stage at the start of the play standing by in the wings five minutes before the curtain went up.

'It's all logical when you think about it,' said Sam. 'The only trouble is you have to work out when to set off to get to the dressing rooms in time to knock on the doors and call out the times.'

'Act One, beginners please, Act One, beginners please,' Molly shouted as she knocked on the dressing room doors.

'Break a leg,' said Teddy, turning around to her as she popped her head round the door.

She stared at him. *Why had he said that?*

'It's bad luck to wish anybody in the theatre "good luck",' he said, seeing the confusion written all over the poor girl's face.

The theatre, she decided as she continued on her rounds, was a very topsy-turvy place. 'Act One, beginners please.'

Having done her calls, she made her way back to her stool in the prompt corner, adjusted her shaded lamp and opened the play script at the beginning: Act One. Sitting there alone, she suddenly realised that she had butterflies in her stomach; this was her first first night, even though, in fact, it was only just coming up to half past five in the afternoon.

'We have to finish so the audience can get home before the blackout,' Sam had explained. What would she do without Sam? She looked forward to seeing him every day and felt funny inside when she caught a glimpse of him. *Is this the feeling someone has when they are falling in love?*

'Are you there, Mister Tuppence?' Molly called up to the lighting perch, pulling herself back to the present.

'Ah,' was the reply.

'Good, well, standby, then,' she said, and pushed down the switch on the cue board in front of her. The red light came on. 'Is your red light on, Mister Tuppence?'

'Ah.'

'Break a leg, Mister Tuppence,' she called up to him.

'Ah.'

'And you,' said Sam, coming up from behind her and giving her a chased peck on her cheek. 'Enjoy it. And if Arthur Desmond makes a nuisance of himself, then tell him to stop and let me know, and I'll see he doesn't do it again.'

Molly nodded, her cheeks as bright red as the 'standby' cue light and as hot as a furnace. Frantically fanning herself with the prompt script, she turned back to the front and, putting the script back on her desk, hoped that she wouldn't have to prompt anybody with an audience out there. She tried not to think of Mister Desmond, who as yet hadn't got through his part without having to be prompted at least two or three times. She crossed her fingers on both hands, touched wood and mumbled a short prayer to the gods of the theatre, just as she'd heard Mister Laine do on numerous occasions.

'Dear Dionysus, Apollo and all the others I can't remember the names of, and God in heaven of course, please make sure they all get through the play from start to finish without any help from me.'

'How's the house doing, old girl?' She smelt the stale tobacco smoke and whisky long before he arrived. Not waiting for an answer, Arthur squeezed past her to look through the side of the tabs. 'There's no bugger out there – an empty house. Bugger me, I don't know why we're bothering.' He pulled the tabs back a bit further. Molly recoiled as he almost smothered her face with his body; she wanted to retch.

'My mother's out there,' she said, in the futile hope that this may stop his little antics for once.

'About twenty, by the looks of it,' Arthur continued, ignoring her.

'Put the tabs back, Arthur,' Randolph snapped as he stormed down the wing, 'we're not amateurs.'

'That's debatable,' Desmond muttered, winking at Molly and brushing his hand on her thigh as he sloped away.

Grabbing the material, Randolph closed the gap, but not before taking a sneaky look himself.

'Stand by everybody,' he called out in a loud whisper, as Mister Ripley popped his head round the door.

'Mister Laine,' he said, 'I think that's about your lot.'

'How many, do you think?' Randolph said, almost under his breath.

'About thirty-five; we lowered the ticket prices but you can't get blood out of a stone.'

Waving his hands, Randolph shook his head and started to shoo him out of the door.

'And you won't forget that we'll be having the King at the end,' Mister Ripley said, turning in the doorway.

'Yes, yes. Well, let's get on with it,' he said, turning round to the Company. 'Right, Molly, we have front of house clearance, so stand everybody by and break a leg.'

Molly cleared her throat and called out, 'Stand by, everybody,' even though Randolph had already said it once, before turning back to her bank of switches. Taking one last deep breath, she pressed down the switch below the red light, which brought up a green light, which in turn brought up the green light on Mister Tuppence's perch, which cued him to pull down on the big wheel at the end of his lighting contraption, making the house lights slowly judder out. Looking through the gap in the tabs (as ASM, she was allowed to do this and not be called an amateur), Molly watched as the theatre went dark and then, having turned off the green light in front of her, she counted to five slowly, giving Mister Tuppence time to move some other dimmer levers up or down and tighten them off (or so he had told her) in order that the corresponding lights would come up when he turned the other big wheel at the other end in the other direction on the cue.

'...three, four, five,' she counted quietly, and then switched the green light back on again. Mister Tuppence duly turned his other big wheel the other way as described. Then, grabbing hold of the sash that hung down from the fly bars above, Molly pulled on it and the tabs started to open, as smoothly as she could make them. At the same time the footlights at the front of the stage and the other lights, which Mister Tuppence had painstakingly hung in the auditorium, flickered into life and the stage became illuminated as Sam, who had snuck on in the darkness, went into his first speech.

'*I can't. I can't. I can't get the vein. I don't know how to say it.*'

And the play had started; no turning back now.

'Mister Laine?' called out the boy from the hotel as he came through the door into the wings.

'Shhh!' hissed Randolph as he stood waiting for his entrance.

'I've got a...'

'Not now. Go away, boy,' Randolph hissed again, waving the lad away. 'No visitors allowed backstage after "the half". Get out.'

'But I've got a letter for you. I told the postman I'd give it to you as it's addressed to the hotel,' the boy continued, holding up an envelope and feeling rather deflated, having done a good turn and getting no thanks for it.

Randolph sighed and half apologetically took the envelope from the boy. He shoved it into his costume pocket as he and Eric made their first entrance. Molly still laughed even though she had now seen the play a dozen times, which is more than could be said for the audience as they sat in stony silence.

'Dear God, they're all dead,' said Arthur, as he paced the wings mumbling to himself and taking a sneaky hit from his hip flask. 'What a waste of bloody time.' His pacing seemed to get more manic as the minutes passed.

'What's my first line, what's my first line?' he said suddenly, before rather hysterically pushing himself against Molly, his hand brushing her breast as he reached frantically across to turn the pages over.

'Don't do that, Mister Desmond; please, I need to concentrate,' Molly hissed, endeavouring to turn the pages back to find her place again.

'Don't be an old silly, girl, I need to see my lines.' His voice seemed to get caught in his throat and was slightly higher in pitch, and she noticed he was sweating even more than usual, making the stench coming off him even more intense. He flicked the pages back and forth as the words refused to come into his head. His free hand was now pushing heavily on the top of Molly's thigh and it took all of her self-control not to scream out. She wasn't going to give in to this awful man and she wasn't going to be the one who ruined the play.

Breathing heavily and muttering the lines under his breath, he pushed away from her and stormed up the wings, repeating his lines time and again, stifling a cough until his moment came.

'Jack, I say, Jack, old man...' he shouted from off stage before striding out towards the French windows.

Molly took a deep breath and did her best to hold back the tears. *He isn't going to upset me,* she thought. *I won't let him spoil things. I won't.* And with that, she put her finger back on the page of the script and listened for the next lihe, and prayed that Mister Desmond didn't dry in the meantime.

25

THE SERGEANT CLOSES IN

Sergeant Green entered The Cockleshell public house and made his way to the bar. John Stirling looked up at the uniform. The two young farm hands, who were back after serving a week's banishment, craned their necks to take him in. What if he was one of those recruiting sergeants they'd heard about? They slunk into one of the booths, out of harm's way.

'What can I get you, Sergeant?'

Green ordered a half pint. He'd made up his mind that he'd have no more than that until he got "fellow me lad" safely locked up for the night down the local nick.

'Don't see many of you boys in khaki up here,' said the landlord to make conversation as he poured the beer. 'Are you from that bunch in Yarmouth?'

'Now, now, sir, mum's the word,' said the sergeant, with a wink, 'we don't want Jerry knowing where our lads are, do we?'

'Of course not, Sergeant, very remiss of me. Any of us lot could be a fifth columnist.'

'You never know, sir, you never know. The Germans are a cunning race; they could infiltrate anywhere. You can never be too sure.'

Stirling nodded his head and poured the beer.

'Actually, I was wondering,' said Green as he picked up his glass and took a sup, 'if you happened to have seen any of our lads about here, recently?'

'There was a soldier boy up here the other day, weren't there, John?' the tall lad called, poking his head out from his hidey-hole.

'Really?' Green reached into his tunic pocket for the photograph. 'Would this be the lad, do you think?' He held it up as the two boys emerged to take a closer look.

'Could be,' said the smaller boy, not being able to remember much at the best of times.

'He'd just got back from France, I think,' said the landlord, as he looked at the photograph. 'Scared little rabbit; sat in that corner over there supping a half pint. Gone AWOL, as he?' He handed the photograph back.

Green decided to play it very calmly, so just said, 'Let's put it this way – think of me as a shepherd, just wishing to keep his flock together.'

'He was with those pansies,' said the taller boy, stepping forward.

'Pansies?'

'Actors, weren't they, John? Coming in here, taking over with their caterwauling.'

'They just happened to be here at the same time, that's all,' said the landlord. 'The lad came in for a quiet drink by himself and then slunk off.'

The sergeant sucked his teeth and nodded. 'Right, well, perhaps I should have a word with these theatricals. Come in here often, do they?'

'Well, they're all in the theatre now; The Regent, off the high street. It's their first performance, I think.'

Green nodded again and decided to say nothing more, slowly making his way over to one of the booths and sitting himself down out of sight of the bar, thinking about his next move. His instincts told him that this was his boy. "Sensitive type", the CO had said. Theatricals were said to be "sensitive types" from what he'd heard. Yes, it made sense. Birds of a feather and all that. This was his man, no doubt about that, so now all he needed to do was to haul him in. He'd need back-up of course; a couple from the local constabulary should do the trick.

'Oh, I can't spare two constables at the moment, Sergeant,' said his opposite number, Desk Sergeant Walker, standing behind the counter of the local police station.

'I won't keep them long. Having wandered about, I can't see that there's too much going on in the town of a criminal nature.'

The desk sergeant looked across the desk at the army sergeant. He wasn't over keen on having the army telling him what to do. Why should he hand over his chaps, just like that, no questions asked?

'I'll have to have a word with my inspector, but I warn you, he won't be happy about it; it's his day off. He never likes to be troubled on his day off.' Walker picked up the telephone on the counter and asked the operator to put him through to Inspector Turley at home.

Green bit his tongue. *No point in antagonizing. Stay calm.*

26

Arthur Desmond's Last Night

DONNA LUCIA *I have my niece with me, Miss Delahay.*

LORD FANCOURT (Charley's Aunt) *Miss Delahay!*

SPETTIGUE *Bring her. Delighted!*

LORD FANCOURT (Charley's Aunt) *No, no. I can't, my things… my things…*

ELA *That voice. (Running to LORD FANCOURT.) It is. It is… (He turns to meet her.) Oh! (She turns to DONNA LUCIA.) No!*

LORD FANCOURT pulls his dress over his head and falls into SPETTIGUE'S arms.

CURTAIN

Mister Tuppence started to turn the master wheel on his lighting board and the stage lights slowly dimmed as Molly made a grab for the sash rope and pulled on it to close the tabs. Reaching back, she flashed the green light twice as a sign that the tabs were closed and that the houselights and the footlights for tab 'dressing' could be brought up.

In the auditorium there was a light ripple of applause and a low murmur. Molly squeezed through the gap behind the tabs and the downstage end of the scenery and onto the stage to stand by to 'throw the line' for the flats. At the same time, Sam and Billy were unlashing the flats, lifting the stage weights off the braces, and spinning the flats around so the interior decoration was now facing downstage. Meanwhile, Teddy and Randolph each took an end of the garden bench and struck it into the wings, while Hugh, Zelda and Connie picked up the pots of foliage that had created the illusion of a garden. When a flat had been turned and moved into its correct place, Molly grabbed the sash line and lassoed it over the top cleat and laced it down and around the descending cleats onto the two adjoining flats; she looped the ends and tugged the line down, as tightly as she could, which miraculously bought the flats together to form a wall. Having dumped the garden bench, Randolph and Teddy returned to the stage carrying the sofa, whilst Connie and Zelda struggled on with the wing armchair between them. Hugh, not feeling able to carry anything of weight, was helping Penny bring on a few of the dressing props: a cigar box, a table lamp and a writing set for the desk, which Teddy and Randolph were now negotiating through the newly built French windows, along with a pouffe footstool and the Captain's chair that went with the desk (but which was never sat in as one of the legs was broken).

In her dressing room, Veronica was patching up her make-up and applying a new layer of lipstick whilst Arthur was standing on the steps outside the stage door, staring out into the alleyway, smoking and taking a snifter or two from his hip flask, which he kept in a little pocket that he'd forced Connie to sew into his underskirt.

On stage the final adjustments were made and the scene was set as Spettigue's drawing room for the third act. As Molly returned to her prompt desk, she looked up at the clock hanging on the wall above her and was thrilled to see that they had done the complete change in seven minutes – which was a great deal faster than the dress rehearsal, and meant that they could all take a breather before the final act.

'Do you think we should try to get the last act up early?' asked Phyllis, doing her bit by putting the antimacassars on the back of the armchair and sofa.

'Yes, I'll see what I can do,' replied Randolph, looking about the stage to double-check that everything had been set correctly.

'I do hope it picks up. Playing farce is difficult enough at the best of times, but an audience that's thin on the ground and half asleep is making it torture,' Hugh commented to his wife as he stood in the corridor, having done what he thought was his fair share of manual work.

'Perhaps we should all shout a bit louder,' said Veronica as she joined them.

'Are the masses back in their seats yet?' asked Arthur, closing the stage door and nearly getting his skirt caught behind him as he stubbed his cigarette out on the floor.

'I do wish you smokers would put your cigarettes in the ashtrays provided and not leave them on the floor for others to pick up on their shoes to take on stage,' muttered Hugh.

Arthur raised his eyes to heaven as Randolph popped his head round the door from the wings. 'The stage is set, everybody,' he said, clapping his hands. 'Stand yourselves by.'

'We've only had ten minutes,' said Arthur, wandering off down the corridor to take another swig from his flask.

'What does that matter?' sighed Hugh. 'Come on, we don't want to let them go off the boil.'

'Go off the boil, dear? That lot aren't even on a low simmer and the gas is about to run out,' said Veronica, lighting another cigarette.

Mister Ripley opened the stage door, rather nonplussed to find the entire Company turning round to stare at him.

'They're all back in; those that are staying, that is,' he said, rather nervously.

Randolph came forward. 'Those that are staying?'

'Yes.'

'Have some gone?'

'Yes.'

'Why?'

'Well, one or two thought that it had finished.'

'Finished?' asked Hugh.

'Yes.'

'How on earth could they think it was finished?'

'When the curtains closed and the lights went up, they thought it was all over,' Ripley answered.

'Didn't you tell them that there was another act?' asked Randolph.

'Oh yes, but they said that as they'd got their coats on they wouldn't bother.'

'Dear God in heaven,' exclaimed Arthur, opening the door to the wings and storming off into the gloom.

Molly, having made her final check that everything was set on stage just as Sam had told her to – check, check, and then check once more for luck – sat back on her high stool in the prompt corner and turned the page in the script to the start of Act Three.

Arthur Desmond took a quick swig from his hip flask as he leant against the back wall in the wings. Looking around, he noticed that only he and Molly were there.

'Let me check the dickie birds, old girl,' he said, charging up quickly, and without waiting he proceeded to lean over her and turn the pages of the script with one hand. His other hand quickly slipped onto her leg and pushed up her skirt, and roughly fumbled up around her knickers. She was trapped, petrified and engulfed in his skirts.

The stench of the fresh liquor made Molly feel sick. He had his full weight pressed against her back now, pushing her body forward against the desk. She tried to beat him off but she knew that her efforts were feeble. Still innocently flipping the script pages with one hand, he grabbed hold of the bottom of her knickers and attempted to push his hand inside – it was her worst nightmare; then suddenly it was over. She looked around to see Teddy with his hands around Desmond's neck, throwing him bodily upstage before starting to pummel him in the stomach with his fists, and then landing a perfect uppercut under his chin, which made Arthur's head jilt back and into the wall, making a sound like a large egg cracking against a bowl.

Molly retched.

Teddy was about to go in for another punch as the grotesque figure slid down the wall when Sam grabbed his arm.

'Enough, old chap, enough now,' he said, firmly putting his arms around Teddy, pinning his arms to his sides. 'It's alright now, you've done enough, I'd say.'

The adrenaline pumping through Teddy started to drain away as Penny took his hand and pulled him gently to one side. She held him close to her, trying to soothe him.

Phyllis made her way over to Molly.

'It's alright, my dear, everything is alright, I'm here,' Phyllis cooed, pulling Molly towards her. 'Did he hurt you, dear?'

Molly could not take her eyes off the body as it lay crumpled in the corner, looking even more incongruous in the full black satin skirt, blouse and bonnet, which now lay at an angle on his drooping head, his chin sitting on his chest – an Edwardian rag doll.

'I think he scratched me a little,' Molly replied to Phyllis eventually. 'I'm not sure.'

'Zelda has some ointment. We could go along to the wardrobe and clean you up,' Phyllis said kindly, but Molly shook her head.

'I'm all right, honestly I am.'

Phyllis nodded. 'All in good time, then.'

The others looked on, stunned, as Randolph came into the wings after having his usual last-minute visit to the toilet.

'Right, everybody, let's get this over with and… dear God.' He stared down at Arthur.

'He was interfering with Molly,' said Hugh in Randolph's ear.

Connie was standing stock still, looking down at her husband.

'I'm so sorry, Connie,' Zelda turned to her friend.

Connie said nothing.

'Teddy landed a haymaker on his chin,' Hugh continued.

'Is he conscious?' said Randolph to Sam, who was checking him over.

'Out for the count, guvnor, and some,' Sam replied.

Randolph had just about seen it all now. 'Well, this leaves us in a pretty pickle.'

'Shame. You'll just have to tell the audience, such as it is, to go off home,' said Veronica, ready to go back to her dressing room and change into normal clothes. She could do with a gin or two.

'No, don't do that,' cut in Eric. 'Billy could play it. Billy can play the part. You know it, don't you, Billy?'

Veronica had heard enough. 'I shall be in my dressing room,' she huffed, and she clattered off down the corridor and slammed the door.

'What do you mean, old chap?' asked Randolph.

Eric was rather excited. 'He knows the part, he's been going through my lines with me; he knows that part better than Desmond ever did, really.'

'Oh marvellous. What do we tell the audience? That Charley's aunt has turned into another person altogether?' scoffed Hugh.

'Dressed in all that lot, dear,' replied Zelda, looking down on the crumpled old lady lying on the floor, 'I doubt if anybody would notice the difference.'

'I really don't think that would work, Eric,' said Randolph, looking down at the crumpled figure and allowing himself to wonder.

'There's only thirty people out there,' Penny piped up, 'and most of those are fast asleep, so what does it matter?'

'Well, I think it is a jolly good idea,' said Connie, rather cheerily. The others looked at her. 'Yes, I think it would be a jolly good idea,' Connie repeated, grabbing Billy by the hand as he looked on.

Stuck between a rock and a hard place, Randolph was unsure what to do, but whatever it was, he had to do it quickly.

'What do you think, old chap?' asked Randolph, turning to Billy.

Billy stood stunned for a moment, peering down at Arthur and remembering how he had lain on his bed listening to the play, mouthing the words.

'Yes. Yes, I'll give it a go.'

'Oh, how wonderful,' said Connie. 'Zelda, dear, there are a couple of underskirts hanging up in the wardrobe, along with a spare blouse – Billy can use those – and I'll just take off Arthur's main skirt, jacket and bonnet.'

'And I'll get him some make-up,' said Eric, making off towards the dressing room.

'That doesn't surprise me,' said Hugh, before being given a filthy look by Phyllis. 'What?' he shrugged.

Phyllis shook her head and proceeded to help Connie to divest Arthur of his top skirt before Sam and Teddy carried his limp body down the corridor and placed him on one of the camp beds out of the way. As they lay him out, the hip flask fell from the pocket in his underskirt. Picking it up, Sam slipped it back in.

'He might need that when he wakes up,' he said with a smile.

For once, Teddy didn't reply. The man was beyond redemption as far as he was concerned, and he deserved all the punishment he'd metered out to him.

'I've never done anything like this before,' said Billy, as Eric applied the make-up and Connie straightened the skirts. 'We were just messing about.'

'Don't worry, you'll be marvellous,' replied Eric. 'Now keep your mouth shut whilst I put on some lipstick.' Stepping back, he admired his handiwork. In front of them stood, for all intents and purposes, an old Edwardian lady in a long black skirt, blouse and jacket, with a bonnet tied under her chin with a black silk ribbon, with plenty of Five and Nine greasepaint over her face and black mascara on her eyebrows. The audience, such as it was, would never know the difference.

'I've put a copy of your words for the last act in your handbag,' said Molly, 'so if you need them, you can always take a peek. Otherwise just say "line" or "yes" and I'll prompt you.'

Sam smiled at his protégé. 'A proper little stage manager you are, and no mistake.'

Molly forced a smile. Even though her heart was beating nineteen to the dozen and she felt physically sick, she knew she had to stay strong and not let anyone down.

'Break a leg,' said Eric, giving Billy a swift peck on the cheek.

'Yes, yes, break a leg, old chap,' said Randolph a little unconvincingly before getting himself in position on stage, ready for the first lines of the final act.

Billy stood by the door where he would make his entrance as Molly turned back to her desk and, crossing her fingers on both hands, waved them towards Billy.

'Break a leg,' she mouthed and then, turning back, she pushed down the red light switch, counted to five very slowly, and then switched on the go light and peered through the edge of the tabs to see when the house lights had gone off completely. Taking the sash in one hand, she leant across, switched on the green light again and started to pull open the tabs.

BRASSETT *There they go! Dinner's pretty well over now, and they'll all be in here pretty soon. Fancy old Spettigue getting me to come here tonight and butler for him. I suppose he's too mean to have a butler of his own. Well, all I can say is it's simply marvellous the way his lordship's kept it up! He's played the perfect lady something wonderful!*

From the wings, Eric, Teddy and Sam made unintelligible noises off, with Teddy conducting the proceedings.
    Hullo! What's up now?
    Teddy lifted his hand and they produced more noises off until he slowly lowered his hand and they quietened and then fell silent.
    Anyhow, if the worst comes to the worst, I've got his lordship's dress clothes with me.
    Eric nodded towards Billy and, taking a deep breath, he opened the door and walked onto the stage.

LORD FANCOURT *Brasset, get me a fly. I'm going home.*

He said his line in character and was off. Sam and Eric made their entrances as Jack and Charlie and pushed Billy around the stage to get him into the right place without the audience noticing. Nothing had changed as far as the people out front were concerned; the few who had laughed continued to laugh, and the ones who had slept through the first two acts continued to snore, unaware of any subterfuge.

27

AN INSPECTOR CALLED

'There's an army sergeant here, Sir,' Desk Sergeant Walker announced into the telephone to the Inspector. 'He says he's looking for a deserter and wants a couple of our chaps to go with him to pick the lad up.'

There was a pause while the Inspector said something to his sergeant.

'Yes, I would have thought that he'd have brought his own men with him, but there we are, Sir.' He listened again and then laughed. 'Yes, very good, Sir, the army is a law unto itself; very good. Well, the thing is, you know the score, Sir, and I'm not sure I can take two of our own men off their beats.' There was another pause as the Desk Sergeant listened patiently to his superior. 'Yes, Sir, that sounds like a good idea, Sir. Yes, I shall put that to him.'

He looked up at Sergeant Green. 'Inspector Pickering asks why you can't get two of your army chaps up from Yarmouth camp?'

Green closed his eyes and tried his best to stay calm. 'Kindly inform your inspector that I had, of course, thought of that, but came to the conclusion that by the time I'd got hold of the camp, explained the situation and waited for said soldiers to arrive, chummy boy would have had it away on his toes.'

'I'll explain that,' said the desk sergeant, trying to remember what Green had said. Luckily the Inspector informed him that he'd heard every word.

Every word of this Green knew to be a lie. Yes, of course he could involve Yarmouth camp, but then that would mean it would get around that Little Bo Beep had had lost one of her sheep, and that would never do. Inter-regimental rivalry was rife in the army and he'd not be thanked if it got out. "Keep it quiet", the CO had said, and keep it quiet he would.

At the other end of the phone, Inspector Pickering sighed, and even though he agreed whole-heartedly with his sergeant, he knew in the end he would have to agree.

'I hear what you're saying Albert,' he said, 'but there is a war on and all that and I suppose we shouldn't obstruct the army. After all, you can't have soldiers running off, can you? Who'd be left to confront the Germans, eh? Sort a couple out for him, there's a good chap.'

'I hear you, Sir, but the thing is…'

He turned around and cupped the telephone mouthpiece so Green couldn't hear him. *Come on, come on.* Green started to pace round the room whilst Desk Sergeant Walker quietly reminded his inspector that the only police car at the station was out of petrol and still had a flat tyre, owing to the fact that some local children fired airgun pellets at it whilst imagining they were elite British soldiers left behind in France to fearlessly fight the Germans single-handedly, using the police car as a surrogate German tank.

Putting down the telephone, the desk sergeant reluctantly informed the army sergeant that he would allocate Constables Fisher and Turnbull in the task of accompanying him to pick up the soldier. There was only one problem, and that was finding them out on the beat.

'The Inspector's on his way in his car to pick you up and then you'll have to go and find them,' said the desk sergeant. 'But I warn you, he's not happy, not happy at all. It's his day off and his missus won't be happy, and if she's not happy, he won't be happy.' He shook his head and looked down at his desk, sucking his teeth and muttering "no, no" and 'not happy at all" a few times.

After cruising the back streets of Haleston, it wasn't long before Constables Fisher and Turnbull were found and told to report to the front of the Regent Theatre straight away. Climbing onto their bicycles, they pedalled off, shouting across at each other as they went.

'Blimey, when I saw the Inspector, I thought I'd copped it,' said PC Turnbull.

'Why's that, Bernie?' yelled PC Fisher back at him.

'If he'd arrived two minutes earlier, he'd have seen my bike leaning on the wall of number thirty-three,' Bernard Turnbull replied.

'You still seeing that one on the quiet then?' PC Fisher laughed.

'Just for a cup of tea and a bit of fruit cake,' Turnbull replied.

'Oh right, of course, Bernie, whatever you say,' his old pal yelled back, stifling another laugh.

PC Bernard Turnbull blew out his cheeks and thanked the Lord above that he'd got away with it. He didn't want Missus Turnbull to start hearing any rumours – or indeed, the husband of number thirty-three when he came back home on leave.

'What's all this about then?' said PC Fisher.

'I'm buggered if I know,' PC Turnbull called back as they cycled on. 'Well, we finish our shifts at six so it can't be much.'

'Let's hope not, at least. Looks like it's coming onto rain as well.'

'Have you got your cape?'

'It's in my saddle bag.'

'Me and all. Looks like we'll need them before much longer.'

'You're to work under the orders of Sergeant Green here,' said the Inspector, when they'd all arrived at the front of the theatre, 'but no heroics, mind. I can't afford to lose my constables on some hare-brained exercise.'

Constable Fisher looked concerned. 'What sort of heroics, Sir?'

'Yes, what sort?' chimed in PC Turnbull.

The Inspector shook his head. 'Just be careful, that's all I'm saying to you. You're both experienced coppers.' And with that he got in his car and drove off, glad to be going home, although not so glad at knowing he'd have to face his wife's wrath for abandoning a job he had promised to do on his day off.

'There aren't going to have to be any heroics, are there, Sarge?' asked PC Turnbull.

'Let's hope not, lad,' replied Green. 'Now then, you two, listen to me…'

They listened and having been informed of the task, the two local bobbies exchanged glances, relieved; after all, they were only being asked to help arrest an eighteen-year-old deserter. What trouble could he cause?

'Constable…?'

'Fisher, Sergeant,' said Constable Fisher, coming to attention for no reason apart from that he thought he should.

'Relax, Constable, there's no need to dance about on my behalf,' replied Green. 'Now, lad, I want you to station yourself down that alleyway. From what I understand, that's where the actors come in and out.'

'The stage door, they call it, Sarge,' said PC Turnbull.

'Do they? Jolly good.' Sergeant Green shook his head. 'Now then, if this young lad comes out of that… the stage door,' he said, holding up the photograph, 'grab him.'

'Sarge,' said PC Fisher, saluting in that rather slack way that policemen did. Sergeant Green winced but decided to let it pass.

'Well, off you go, lad; he could have been out that door and halfway along the coast by now,' Green snapped.

PC Fisher turned, wondering whether he should have come

to attention first, but then marched off having decided against it.

Sergeant Green turned. 'Constable...?'

'Turnbull, Sergeant,' he said quickly, trying to sound confident.

'You'll stay with me, lad,' said Green, looking up at the theatre front and then leaning in to peer at the handmade poster: *The Laine Theatrical Company presents 'Charley's Aunt', a Comedy by Mister Brandon Thomas.*

'*Charley's Aunt*, eh?' He'd never been one for the theatre, himself; he liked to settle down with a good book. 'Well, let's hope they don't make us look like a bunch of charlies, eh?' he said, turning to the PC and pulling open the front door.

Green looked around him as he entered the theatre foyer. Hearing the door, Mister Ripley peered through the small box office window:

'Hello, can I help you?' he said as he leant down to see who it was. Green looked around, wondering where the voice was coming from. 'I'm afraid the performance is nearly over,' said Ripley through the small hole.

Green looked around him again and then noticed a face in the small window speaking to him.

'We're looking for somebody, Ken,' said PC Turnbull.

'Oh, it's you, Bernard. Hold on, I'll come out.'

'We're looking for this young lad, sir,' said Sergeant Green, stepping forward and bringing out the now dog-eared photograph from his tunic pocket as Mister Ripley appeared. 'You wouldn't have happened to have seen this young lad about the place, would you?'

Kenneth Ripley hadn't seen the lad but he'd heard about a young soldier hanging about with the Company.

'I'm not sure,' said Mister Ripley. He was a law-abiding citizen but he didn't feel comfortable; he didn't want to be the one to get the boy thrown back to the front line. Ripley liked to think of himself as a bit of a pacifist, although he had to admit, he didn't wish to be overrun by a bunch of Nazis. Being a primary school teacher was a reserved occupation, and having seen enough of his old boys reaching the age for call-up, Ken Ripley couldn't help remembering them in their short trousers innocently running about the playground. The thought that they were now in uniform or lying somewhere in a foreign field, as Rupert Brooke, so eloquently, put it, saddened him.

Sergeant Green nodded. 'You wouldn't object if the constable and I popped in the back just to take a look around, would you?'

Ripley knew he couldn't really refuse and hesitantly, opened the door to the back of the stalls, letting them both slip in.

As soon as he had closed the door, the schoolteacher made a decision; he had to warn the lad. He knew it was against the law, but he couldn't just... No, he told himself, he couldn't.

He made his way out of the front doors and around to the alley, where he saw PC Fisher stamping his feet with his arms behind his back.

'Evening, Les,' said Mister Ripley as he slowed down and tried his best not to look as if he was in a hurry.

'Evening, Ken,' said PC Leslie Fisher. 'What are you doing around these parts then?'

Ripley told him of his part-time job.

'You know you may have a deserter in there?' said Les Fisher.

Ken Ripley nodded. 'So the army sergeant said, but I've not seen him.'

Guilt washed over his face but Constable Fisher didn't notice as he looked skywards. 'Was that rain?'

They nodded at each other, paused, and then Ken Ripley nodded once more and disappeared through the stage door.

Constable Leslie Fisher stamped up and down the alleyway to keep the blood moving. He looked again. Yes, something damp had hit him on the nose. Blast; it was rain alright. He delved into his bicycle saddle-bag and took out his police cape and threw it across his back, fastening the brass chain link. It would help keep him dry for a while at any rate, but if it started pelting down and it got really wet the heavy serge would get even heavier, owing to the fact that the material wasn't in the least bit waterproof.

Mister Ripley popped his head around the door of the wings and whispered in Molly's ear.

'Molly dear, where's Mister Laine?'

She turned round. 'He's about to go onstage.'

At that moment, he noticed Randolph in the gloom, standing outside the scenery door waiting to make his entrance.

'Mister Laine,' said Ripley.

'I can't talk now, I'm about to go onstage,' hissed Randolph.

'But there's an army sergeant out the front looking for the boy.' Mister Ripley winked, but in the darkness Randolph couldn't see that. 'You know, the young soldier.'

Randolph paused for the slightest moment and then entered, and as he closed the door he nodded surreptitiously towards Ripley, perfectly in character.

'It's all right, sir,' Molly whispered back, 'he heard you, I could see that. Don't worry.'

Ripley thanked her and thought it best to return to the front of house. Nodding to Constable Fisher as he passed him again, he hurried down the alleyway as the rain started to fall.

On stage, as he stood waiting for his lines, Sam could make out a couple of figures standing at the back of the auditorium. They weren't members of the front of house staff as the theatre didn't have any of them. He thought they might be in uniform. Yes, one was a policeman; he was still wearing his helmet. Sam's gaze went across the top of the audience to the second man. Another uniform. Army, he was sure of it.

'Looks like the army's in town,' he whispered to Teddy out of the corner of his mouth.

'A sergeant,' said Teddy. 'I can see his stripes.'

Sam took another look just as the army sergeant beckoned to the policeman to start making his way down the side of the auditorium.

DONNA LUCIA *I shall have to talk to you very seriously before I give you this. (Shows letter.) Charley, I'll never forgive you if you deceive that sweet girl again! (To LORD FANCOURT.) And as for you, sir...*

LORD FANCOURT *Oh no, never again, I give you my word. I'll give you the clothes if you like, I've done with them. Miss Delahay has consented to think me over as a husband, and in future I resign to Sir Francis Chesney all claims to Charley's Aunt.*

Molly flicked the green go switch down, and as Mister Tuppence brought down the stage lights, Molly leapt at the sash cord and pulled the tabs together so fast that they billowed out over the first row of the audience, raising a cloud of dust off the top of the footlights.

28

THE CURTAIN CALL

'All in a line as rehearsed,' Randolph called out firmly.

'But there's an army sergeant out front,' yelled Eric, rather hysterically.

'Everybody must stay calm and take the curtain call, don't forget we're professionals,' Randolph continued.

'But what about Billy?' Eric wanted to get him away as soon as he could.

'Three bows, Molly, then bring the tabs in slowly, in a dignified manner,' Randolph called across to the prompt corner, ignoring Eric's hysteria.

'Three bows?' Veronica scoffed. 'We'll be lucky to string out one.'

Randolph waved to Molly and she began to open the tabs again to a smattering of applause.

Sergeant Green hovered by the piano, waiting for his moment. He knew he had to work fast.

Three painfully quiet bows later and Molly started to pull on the sash line to slowly close the tabs.

Green saw his moment and made his move towards the steps up onto the stage, waving over to PC Turnbull to move from his side. The sergeant's foot was on the first step when he heard it. The low rumbling bass sound from an out-of-tune piano. The sound was a prelude to something he knew only too well, having been in the forces for all his life. He froze and cursed at the same time as he heard the opening refrain.

God save our clunk-*cious King, long live our noble* clunk,
God save the clunk.

'That'll do,' snapped Green, turning back to the piano and grabbing Miss Bentley's hands before she could send the monarch victorious, and closing the piano lid.

'But there's the second verse; you have to play the second verse,' Miss Bentley answered. 'The King expects it.'

'Not today he doesn't,' Sergeant Green answered back, 'the King told me so himself.'

Turning, he made his way back to the steps as the tabs started to come together. Clambering up and onto the front of the stage, a sickening pain shot up his shattered leg and into his hip.

Miss Bentley shook her head and hoped she hadn't upset the King. Randolph gestured to Molly to chivvy up; so from the slow and graceful, the tabs suddenly took on a life of their own and billowed closed.

'Run, Billy,' hissed Eric.

'Everybody stand perfectly still, if you'd be so kind,' said the sergeant, fighting his way through the centre of the curtain material. 'In the name of the King, I order you all to stay exactly where you are.'

In the name of the King, thought Green. *Where on earth did that come from?*

They all froze as he appeared like Banquo's ghost, lit from below by the footlights.

'That's right, very good. Now, turn around all of you, if you please,' he continued, 'and I'll try not to keep you long.'

They all turned apart from Veronica, who was busily working out whether it was best to shop Billy there and then, but Penny grabbed her arm and whispered threateningly in her ear, 'Don't you dare. You try to destroy another person's life and I'll swing for you. I swear I will.'

Veronica paused with her cigarette halfway to her mouth, before taking a pull on it and turning slowly to face the front with the others – obedient, for now.

'How dare you come on stage like this, with the house still in,' said Randolph in a rage, which even he wasn't sure was genuine or not, but he sounded suitably affronted. 'It's completely unacceptable and totally unprofessional.'

But the sergeant wasn't listening. 'Come on, laddie,' Green snarled at PC Turnbull as he climbed onto the stage without the aid of any steps. Green turned back to the Company and regained his usual calm demeanour. 'My apologies for not following your professional etiquette, Mister…?'

'Laine,' answered Randolph, bringing his full pomp to the fore. 'Randolph Laine, and this,' he gestured with his arms, as if he had suddenly become Henry Irving, 'is my troop of players.'

Phyllis was full of admiration for Randolph. When it came to it, he would always put his Company and his profession first.

'Very good,' said the sergeant, not overly impressed. 'Now let's get these curtains open, shall we?'

'Tabs,' retorted Randolph forcefully.

'What?'

'They are not curtains, they're called tabs, derived from the word *tableau*.' Randolph was rattled and when Randolph was rattled, his pomposity knew no bounds. Added to which, on this occasion, he was playing for time while hoping some plan would formulate itself in his head to save the boy. 'They were named after the *tableau vivant*, which I believe means "living picture" in French. The actors would get into positions and freeze and the tabs would open to…'

'Whatever they're called, sir,' cut in Green, 'I'd like them open, now.' He did not like being messed around with and it was at times like this that the civilian population got on his nerves.

'Well, I'm afraid you'll just have to wait until the audience are out of the theatre as I refuse to behave in an unprofessional manner for you, or indeed anyone else,' replied Randolph, knowing that he had now most definitely crossed the line.

The army sergeant walked very slowly over to him and looked him in the eye. 'But you'll do it for the King, won't you, sir?'

'When the King arrives, I shall wait for him to ask me,' Randolph answered back.

'Constable, get these bloody curtains open. Now!' Green bellowed, the spittle exploding from his mouth and into Randolph's face. Randolph did not react. 'I suggest, sir, that you and your troop of theatricals listen very carefully to what I have to say. Is that clear, Mister Laine?'

Randolph nodded.

Sergeant Green turned on the ball of his foot and, with his hands behind his back, wandered to the other side of the stage and turned again to look at the motley crew in front of him.

PC Turnbull took hold of the sash rope and pulled, but the tabs stayed put. Molly gently took the sash from him and pulled on the other line, and they parted as the last of the audience slowly drifted out of the theatre.

'Thank you, Molly,' said PC Turnbull, when he realised who the girl was. 'I'd get yourself home if I were you,' he said in a whisper. 'Best not to get involved, I'd say.'

Molly nodded but had absolutely no intention of abandoning her friends. Above, Mister Tuppence looked down on the events, and Molly in turn looked back up at him as he leant on the guardrail. She felt so helpless. Poor Billy, the sergeant was bound to find him. He was there, right in front of him. It was only a matter of time.

'Now, everyone into line, just like you were when you took your bows; that would be the idea.' He paced along the front of the stage as if they were on parade. He took a few deep breaths to calm himself down. He knew, after all his years in the army, that when you're not in control of your emotions, you make bad decisions. Clarity was what was needed; clarity and firmness were the order of the day.

The Company, including Billy, who had pushed the bonnet firmly on his head and pulled the two black ribbons under his chin and tied the bow in such a way that it covered the bottom part of his face, formed a line along which the sergeant proceeded to walk. He was now completely in control and calm, his voice soft and gentle.

'Now then, I expect you're all wondering, in your innocence, what this is all about.' He paced, looking at the floor; his words seeming even more menacing through his quiet demeanour. 'A young soldier, Private William – Michael – Gordon – Pryce,' he said the names slowly, then took a pause for them to sink in before continuing, 'failed to return to his regiment last Monday. One week ago. We call that, in the army, going absent without leave; I don't like to use the word "deserter", as it sounds a little too harsh. AWOL. Absent – without – leave.' He continued to walk along the line, not looking at their faces. As he reached the end, he caught Molly's eye as she stared at him from her tall stool; he smiled a fatherly smile. He gave a slight nod of the head towards her before turning and starting to walk back again. Molly decided that she didn't like this man.

'Now, it has come to my attention that this young soldier was last seen with members of this –' he looked up at Randolph, 'what was it again? Oh yes, this troop of players.' He smiled into Randolph's face. Randolph stood still and firm, with just enough moral outrage in his demeanour to show the sergeant that he was far from happy with this treatment. Green continued on his perambulation, unperturbed.

'Now, let me make this clear: His Majesty's forces and the War Office aren't keen on one of their charges deciding that they don't wish to play soldiers anymore, just because it gets a bit rough.

Added to this, His Majesty's forces and the War Office aren't keen on civilians withholding information as to that soldier's whereabouts. They have a name for it – aiding and abetting a deserter from His Majesty's Forces – and it is punishable by a very long term in one of His Majesty's prisons.' Green turned again and stopped. He paused, before continuing. 'I trust that I am making myself very clear. I trust that you all understand the implications of what I'm saying. I trust that we can solve this little problem amicably. Any questions?'

Randolph decided that full-on pomposity should be the order of the day. 'When do you think my Company would have the time to befriend a young soldier when we have been busy all week rehearsing our play? Contrary to all you may have heard about this noble profession, a performance such as this takes a great deal of time, talent and effort.'

Veronica snorted and Teddy looked up to heaven – well, the flies anyway.

'I'm sure that it does, sir. I'm sure it does. And I would wager that after such gruelling work you would all wish to slake your thirsts. I'm sure I would. So, let me ask you this: were you and your merry band here in The Cockleshell public house last Monday when a fight broke out between some local lads and a couple of visiting actors?'

Randolph nodded.

'And would those visiting actors be part of this troop of players in front of me now?'

'Yes, I was one of them,' replied Teddy, standing up straight and giving his best Michael Wilding.

'And I was the other,' Sam piped up, full cheeky chappy, with a nod and a wink.

The sergeant turned and stared at them.

'Jolly good. Now we're getting somewhere.' Green smiled – at least, it looked like a smile – and continued to walk the line. 'I have been reliably informed by these local lads that a young soldier was also in the pub at the time and that one of the actors went off to look for him. Would I be right in thinking that the actor was part of this Company as well?'

There was silence. Eric thought about owning up but he didn't feel that he had the strength to stand up to this man.

'Come now, no need to be shy – the other two gentlemen owned up to being part of the fisticuffs. What's there to hide?'

Eric's pulse was racing and he threw a look down the line, catching Veronica's eye. He hoped against hope that she wouldn't snitch on the lot of them. She, in turn, reached into her bag, brought out her lipstick and started to apply it.

In her prompt corner, Molly was racking her brains, trying to work out a way to help; she felt so dreadfully useless and silly just sitting there. She looked up at Mister Tuppence, who in turn looked down at her, shook his head and stroked his chin. It was then that the idea jumped into her head. It could work. It was worth a try. Without another thought, she looked back up at Tuppence and pointed to the top of the ladder. He nodded, as if reading her mind, and moved off to meet her as she started to climb up to his perch. At the top and holding on to the rail, Tuppence bent down as she whispered in his ear. Straightening up and looking at her, he nodded, and said in his heavy Norfolk accent, 'Roight.'

Her heart racing once more, but for a very different reason, Molly climbed down the ladder, stopped and looked back up at him. 'I'll cue you,' she whispered.

Tuppence nodded and she could swear he gave her a wink and a smile. She had never seen dear Mister Tuppence smile before.

Going back to her stool, she sat and then, carefully and as quietly as she could, pushed down the switch. The red standby light came on. The light seemed brighter and she could swear that everybody on stage could see its red glow. She crossed her fingers on one hand and placed her other hand over the bulb, shielding it from the stage. It was warm to the touch and she just hoped that it wouldn't become too hot.

On stage, the sergeant was still pacing, looking at their faces, trying to wheedle it out of them. 'Prison. No bright lights and pretty costumes in prison.'

Veronica sniggered a little at the thought that he could equate what they were wearing with 'pretty costumes'.

'In prison,' he went on, matter-of-factly, 'it's hard graft; no more play acting.' He paused again, eyeing them up and down, looking for any clues; nothing as yet, but he'd get there in the end. 'So, I'll give you all one more chance. Give the lad up now. Tell me where I can find him and I'll be lenient with you all. I can't say fairer than that,' he said with a fatherly smile as he walked straight past the old woman in the black skirt and bonnet.

Veronica shifted, Hugh coughed, Zelda stood firm, Eric bit his bottom lip, Penny looked to the front, Teddy was calmness itself, Sam had a half smile on his face, Billy had his eyes closed, Randolph stood with his back straight and hands to his sides, attempting to look important, Phyllis was adopting her sweet little old lady look and Connie… Connie was making her way down the corridor, having been sitting with her unconscious husband, totally unaware that anything else was amiss. So when she pushed open the door into the wings, she had no idea why Molly, when she saw her, put her fingers to her lips and beckoned her to take a look. She let out an "oh" and asked Molly what they should do.

'Mister Tuppence and I have a plan.'

'What sort of plan?' asked Connie.

'I don't want to say, in case someone hears,' replied Molly.

'Right,' replied Connie, and she stood and watched the proceedings through the gap at the side of the tabs.

'I hope you all understand what I'm saying.' Sergeant Green was getting a little short-tempered now. He wanted all this over. He wouldn't mind having a sit down to rest his leg. The tension in his shoulder wasn't helping either. 'I wouldn't want you to be under any illusions as to what would happen if you don't come clean. I'm a patient man, but it's been a long few days and my patience is liable to start becoming a little frayed around the edges, so please don't even think about thwarting me.' He took some deep breaths and bit the inside of his lip to stop himself from wincing from the pain, which was getting worse. 'So you just tell me where Private Pryce is hiding up and we shall say no more about it, but…' He stopped. He looked and nodded his head. 'Make me force it out of you, and I'll throw the ruddy book at you, and I only ever read very heavy books.' His voice rose and the final three words came out loud and clear.

There was much shuffling of feet and looking down at shoes but still nobody spoke out.

He started to promenade again along the line. Something was nagging at him. He couldn't shake off the feeling that he may be being taken for a ride. He couldn't put his finger on it but as he walked the line again, he looked every one of them in the eyes. He passed the old woman again and kept going until he came to Phyllis. He stopped and looked closely at her. He mused a moment before starting on his return journey.

'Gotcha.' He placed his hands on Billy's shoulder. That was it, of course. It had suddenly dawned on him; the bugger was hiding in plain sight, and one of the old women wasn't anything of the sort.

At that very moment, Molly flipped the switch and the green light came on – BLACKOUT – as Mister Tuppence threw the large lever up on his perch above.

'Run,' rang out a voice in the darkness.

Green tried to hang onto the boy but somebody kicked him on the leg and he lost his grip.

'Put those bloody lights on,' he yelled in pain. 'Constable, get those lights on now.'

Turnbull turned but with his eyes not adjusted, he was unable to see a thing and immediately fell to the floor, banging his head on the side of the winged armchair.

Billy froze at first until he was pushed upstage towards the French windows.

'Run, lad, run,' Teddy whispered in his ear.

Suddenly waking from his torpor, he reached out for the French windows and, knowing the obstacles, leapt over the stage weights and braces and ran along the back wall towards the wings.

Eric took a pace to his right and felt the full force as the sergeant ploughed into him as he tried to follow. Another curse as he fell to the floor on his bad shoulder.

Meanwhile, Connie calmly tottered over to the door that led to the corridor and opened it for Billy as he stumbled towards it.

'Good luck,' she whispered as he went past. Closing the door quickly, she grabbed the heavy sand-filled fire bucket and placed it in the way.

Outside, the rain had started coming down quite heavily and the wind was whipping around the narrow alley, lashing it into PC Fisher's face as the stage door opened and a strange-looking old woman burst through it. Hearing the noise, Fisher looked towards it. Billy froze. The constable touched his helmet.

'Evening, ma'am,' he said, much to Billy's surprise.

Billy nodded and tentatively started to walk past him, thinking that at any moment, the officer would grab him. Unsteadily he walked on until he got to the main street and then he took off again, unseen by Les Fisher, who was too busy trying to keep dry and warm but to little avail.

Arthur Desmond had started to come to. His head was thumping and he felt sick. Through the pain he tried to fathom out where the heck he was. A sharp pain shot through his jaw. Pulling himself to his feet, another sharp pain shot across his chest and he buckled. Taking another stab at standing by using the make-up bench as a crutch, he pulled himself as upright as he could and made his way along the wall, pulling open the dressing room door. Staggering and half crawling, he slowly made his way along the corridor, the unstructured underskirt wrapping itself around his legs.

On stage, Sergeant Green had fallen for the second time.

'Constable, don't you have a ruddy torch?' shouted Green as he struggled to his feet again.

'Yes, Sarge,' Turnbull croaked, dazed.

'Well, turn the ruddy thing on then.'

'I can't, Sarge. It's on my bike.'

'So help me, God. Get those bloody lights on!' Green's pleasant demeanour had completely gone. 'What's the matter with you?

The matter with PC Turnbull was that he was only half conscious, his forehead having crashed heavily onto the corner of the chair. In the darkness he had fallen again over the small table, which was now on its side, and one of the legs had somehow gone up one of his trouser legs, which sent him over once more. He reached out to grab something and the something he grabbed was Phyllis, who, being used to making entrances and exits on darkened stages, had adjusted to the lack of light very quickly. Having fallen to the floor with the constable, she decided that she could detain him by holding onto him tightly while screaming hysterically in his ear, which, along with the darkness, only reinforced his lack of equilibrium.

Green eventually made his way to the French windows and stumbled through them. Turning to the left, he almost immediately stubbed his foot on something very hard – a chunk of metal. Ignorant of the workings of the theatre, he knew nothing about stage weights and braces that held up the scenery. He tripped into the wooden brace and fell, grabbing hold of it, hoping to steady himself, but having dislodged the weight from the brace it just swung on the hinge that fixed it to the flat and he crashed to the ground once more, the canvas and timber wall tilting back on him as he went down.

PC Turnbull picked himself up and groped his way until he found what he thought might be a door to get off stage and fumbled for the handle, but unbeknownst to him, a diminutive lady was on the other side of it in the shape of Connie Desmond, hanging onto it for dear life until she decided to let go, having lost the struggle, culminating in the door flying open towards the constable and making him fall back onto the edge of the chaise longue, which jarred his back, making him shout out in pain once again as he found himself back on the floor.

Sergeant Green rolled on the ground, having bounced off the back wall onto his bad shoulder, his army boots tangled in a tail end of sash that was now hanging loosely from the back of the stage flat, which in turn was leaning back into him.

Sam was making his way to the scenery door only to have the policeman grab his leg whilst endeavouring to get himself back up. Teddy was attempting to go through the French windows but the entire back wall had now badly buckled, having been pulled out of shape, and the flimsy French window doors had closed shut and jammed.

Picking himself up and cursing his injuries, Green groped his way along the back wall towards the door into the corridor, and pulling it open, he thrust himself headlong through it, only to crash into a shape coming the other way. Feeling the loose material that could only be that of a woman's skirt, he was convinced that he'd caught his man.

'Got you now, you bastard,' he said, keeping hold of him, only for the figure to scream out in agony and fall heavily to the ground. Sergeant Green wrestled him and yelled at the figure who he took to be Private Pryce to keep still, or he'd know all about it, and then he put his face up close to him to bark at him like a good, old-fashioned drill sergeant…

'Who the hell are you?' It wasn't Pryce, but another man in a bloody skirt who stank of booze and stale cigarettes. 'Where is he, you bastard, what have you done with him?' It was then that Arthur Desmond fell back, convulsing.

'Leave my husband alone,' said Connie, like a terrier snapping at the sergeant's heels, when she opened the door and saw them in the gloom.

Green was confused. How many old women were there? He opened the stage door and yelled at PC Fisher, 'Have you seen the boy?'

'No, Sarge, not a sign, just an old lady.'

Green flew into a rage. 'You fucking idiot, that was him!'

Oh God, thought Fisher, as his opposite number came out behind the sergeant.

'Well, don't just stand there, you dozy bastards; go after him.' Any thoughts of giving Pryce an easy ride had gone out of the window. The little sod was going to get both barrels when he got hold of him. The two policemen started to run along the alleyway and then paused at the top and looked both ways. 'Split up, you idiots, one each way,' yelled Sergeant Green as he made his way towards them as fast as he could.

The two coppers looked at each other, the rain dripping off them both. 'I'd get your mac, if I were you, Bernie,' Les Fisher advised his friend.

'I didn't bring it,' said Turnbull.

'Me neither. This bloody cape weighs a ton already.'

'Well, don't just stand there having a nice chin wag,' Sergeant Green bellowed as he passed them. 'Get a bloody move on.'

Behind them, Teddy, Sam and Eric appeared at the stage door and started to follow at a distance.

Molly called up to Mister Tuppence that he could put the lights back on, which he did. The sight in front of them was one of carnage. The furniture had toppled over, the small table was lacking a leg, and the dressings – such as photo frames, flower vases, lace coverings and antimacassars – lay all over the floor. The set itself was leaning at a precarious angle along the back wall and the curtains had been ripped off their pole.

Randolph sighed as he took in the sight but realised that there was nothing he could do about it at that moment, so he beckoned the others to follow him. Connie was kneeling next to Arthur's crumpled body, which lay on the floor in the corridor.

'Oh Christ, is he dead?' asked Veronica, rather shaken.

'No, he still has a pulse, I think,' said Connie.

Zelda knelt down beside her and felt for a pulse in Arthur's neck. 'Yes, I can feel one,' she said, looking up at the others.

'Shouldn't we call an ambulance or something?' said Hugh.

Penny stood back, out of the way. She wanted him to be dead. Dreadful, she knew, but he was an animal and he deserved all he got.

'Shouldn't we try to lie him down on one of the beds again?' said Hugh.

'Yes, yes,' said Randolph, 'we'll take him back to the dressing room.'

'We'll have to lift him.'

Phyllis had had enough. 'No, no. Hugh, go and get one of the camp beds, we'll lie him down on it out here.'

'Yes, yes of course,' said Randolph.

'Get you home,' grunted Mister Tuppence to Molly, as he made his way down the ladder from his perch. 'You none get involved. Get you home to your mother now.'

Molly had never heard him say so much before but she shook her head. 'I can't.'

'Get you home, girl,' he mumbled again. 'You mon get hurt. Your mum already lost your pa, she don't want to lose you too. You're too precious to get hurt. Get you home now.'

She could see the pain in Tuppence's eyes and the sincerity written in them.

29

THE CHASE

Mister Ripley peered through the rain-splattered glass doors at the front theatre as they ran off. The wind was strong enough now to rattle the doors and he was glad that he didn't need to go out in it. He'd been standing there ever since seeing an old woman run past, attempting to fathom out what she was doing running in the rain.

Billy ran down the narrow-cobbled alleyways, which were lined with tiny fishermen's cottages; he kicked the high-heeled shoes off and continued in bare feet, the edge of the cobbles stubbing his toes but the adrenalin coursing through him numbing the pain. The skirt, soaked through, was clinging to his legs, but still he ran with the bonnet tied up under his chin as it, too, started taking in the rain and fell back off his head and onto his neck. As he ran across the road towards the promenade, he attempted to untie the ribbons, but his cold wet hands couldn't shift the tightened knot. With the sodden ribbon pushing into his throat and the bonnet jiggling on his neck, he continued. What any nosy parker looking through their net curtains would have made of a woman dressed in Victorian clothes running along in the pouring rain in her bare feet was anybody's guess.

With PC Fisher having taken the town route, PC Turnbull made his way towards the seafront, running down the cobbled alleyways, having left Sergeant Green some yards behind. He cursed the fact that he was a little overweight, that his big policeman's boots weighed a ton and his cumbersome helmet banged about on his head, making the peak fall over his eyes as he juddered along the uneven ground. His serge uniform was already soaked through and getting heavier, which made running even more difficult.

As he reached the side of The Cockleshell he looked through the mixture of the heavy rain and the spray that was whipping off the sea, and could just make out a figure in the distance, heading towards the pier.

'I know where he'll be going,' said Eric to Teddy as they came along a parallel alleyway to stay clear of the sergeant and his men. 'There are beach huts on the front, that's where I found him; he was going to camp there. I'd say that is where he's heading.'

And he was. Billy Pryce looked around and could just make out the shape of a policeman in the distance behind him. Hoping not to be seen, he dived down the steps to the beach as the waves crashed onto it. Running along the concrete pathway, he tried to remember which hut he'd used before, trying all the padlocks and pulling on the hasps, but they were all firmly in place. This one; he was sure it was this one. Locked. The next, locked. Third, fourth, locked.

'Where is he?' yelled Sergeant Green above the sound of the rain as he reached Turnbull, cursing his injuries under his breath.

'Gone, Sarge,' said Turnbull as they made their way across the prom. 'He was over there the last time I saw him. Now he's vanished.'

'He can't just vanish, lad. Comb the beach. He must be down there,' Green said. PC Fisher appeared from the other direction.

Constables Fisher and Turnbull started down the steps as the waves crashed over the lower defences.

'I can think of better places to be,' said Constable Fisher.

'Hold on, Les,' said Turnbull when they were out of sight of the sergeant. 'Let me get my breath, son. I'm not as young as I was.'

'I could do without this ruddy rain,' replied Fisher as they both leant against the sea wall to rest, attempting to stay out of the worst of the elements as the water cascaded off their helmets and down the back of their necks.

Billy had reached the end of the line of huts, having had no luck. He must have missed it but he knew he couldn't go back. Leaning against the side of the last hut, he tentatively looked back along the line and could just make out through the mist two figures slowly making their way towards him. Trapped, he slipped back to the rear of the huts and squeezed behind them. *I might be able to make my way back unseen,* he thought. He pushed himself against the sea wall and started to inch his way back towards the steps, the two policemen passing him on the other side of the huts totally oblivious, half-heartedly trying all the locks and cursing the weather every few minutes as they went.

As he reached the last hut, back by the steps, Billy craned his neck to see if the coast was clear. Unable to make out a thing as the wind whipped the rain and seawater into his eyes, he decided to make a run for it and climbed back up the steps.

'Gotcha,' said the sergeant, making a grab for him as he reached the top. But Billy was ready and primed, just as he'd been trained to be, and firmly charged at Green, making him lose his grip long enough for him to break away and run off as fast as he could.

Green's legs had buckled and he'd fallen against the seawall, turning his ankle as he did so. A sharp pain shot up his leg, making him cry out in frustration.

As the two local bobbies made their bedraggled way up the steps, bemoaning the fact that they should be off duty now and sitting by a fire with a cup of tea, they were sharply brought out of their revelry by their persecutor's voice.

'Come on, come on,' yelled Green, as he saw them, struggling to his feet. 'He's set off towards the pier. Get after him.'

Eric made his way as best he could over the cobbles and was glad to get to the end of them. 'Come on,' he shouted, his legs aching like never before but determined to go on.

Neither Sam nor Teddy had any idea what they would do if they found the lad before this army sergeant got to him, but Eric was single-minded and they knew that they had to do or try something, however pointless in the end.

Having put Arthur on the camp bed, Randolph and the others changed back into their day clothes and, excepting Connie, made their way round to The Cockleshell. John Stirling handed Randolph the phone and he dialled 999 and waited and waited and waited, until having eventually got through, he was told that the nearest ambulance was over an hour away as the local one had broken down, and they weren't sure how long it would be before it could be fixed.

'Well, get one here as soon as you can; the gentleman has had a nasty fall and is completely unconscious.' Randolph put down the receiver and ordered himself a large whisky. 'Well, it wouldn't do to go into details,' he explained to the others as they looked at him.

Connie watched over her husband, adjusting the blankets.

'I don't know how I've put up with you, Arthur,' she muttered, wiping the tears away. They weren't falling because he was lying there; they were from years and years of pent-up anger. 'You've spent all my money and made my life a living hell, yet I put up with it because I loved you, or thought I did. All you've ever done since we married is despise me. Hate me. How has that made me feel, do you think? You don't care. You don't think about me.' She looked down at him and then, quite suddenly, she started to thump his chest with her fists, harder and harder and harder, thump, thump, thump, until he suddenly opened his eyes and stared at her in horror. She stopped abruptly and looked down at him.

'Connie,' he gasped.

She shook her head. 'No, I don't want to hear your voice again, never again. I want you to die; I want to be rid of you for good. You nasty, evil man.' And with that, she got up off her knees and walked out of the stage door and along the alleyway as the rain fell on her, drowning out her husband's voice as he called after her. *Thank goodness,* she thought, *thank goodness, thank goodness.*

Arthur tried to pull himself up but only succeeded in rolling onto the floor. Grabbing hold of the bed, he tried to lever himself, but it toppled over onto him. As it did so, a sharp pain ripped across his chest and through his body. He froze as the pain came again and then subsided as he lay on the floor, dead.

With the skirt clinging around his legs, Billy had reached the entrance to the pier, and pulling frantically at the loose barbed wire, he started to squeeze through. Halfway and he felt a tug as the skirts became caught in the barbs. Reaching back, he pulled at it, but the more he tugged the more the material wrapped itself over the wire. Sensing that the others couldn't be that far off, he made one more determined effort until the skirt came free, tearing a huge rip, that hung down as he stood and wrapped itself round his feet. Both his hands were rivers of blood as he bent down to tear away the loose material. Desperate not to be seen, he started to crawl along the boardwalk until he reached the first covered shelter. Peering through the side glass to see if the coast was clear, he took a chance and made his way towards the temporary bridge, his bare feet – also bleeding now – splashing across the boards.

On the promenade, the policemen stopped and attempted to shake the excess water off their uniforms and to catch their breaths.

'We've lost him,' said Turnbull, more in hope than expectation.

'I can't see him,' replied Fisher, leaning against the boarded-up box office window, where in better times holidaymakers could buy their tickets for the pier variety show or any of the other attractions.

'Don't stop,' shouted Sergeant Green as he reached them.

'Lost him, Sarge,' said Turnbull, trying to clear the water from the back of his neck.

Green looked about him and immediately spotted the gap in the barbed wire.

'He's on the pier.' Green shook his head. *The thieves in this town must live the life of Riley with coppers like these two policing the streets.* 'You,' he pointed to PC Turnbull, 'get yourself further down the promenade and look back to see if you can spot him. If you see him, blow your ruddy whistle as hard as you can.' Green had had enough of Constable Turnbull. The other plod couldn't be as bad, surely?

Bernard Turnbull wandered off. *If you see him, blow your whistle*, he thought. *In this ruddy weather, I'd need a foghorn.*

'Right lad, get your finger out and move that bloody wire out of the way and get yourself down that pier. I'll be right behind you.'

The last thing that Les Fisher wanted to do was crawl through barbed wire and run along the slippery boards of the pier. He knew them to be lethal in wet weather and he loathed the pier at the best of times. The gaps between the boards may only be less than an inch wide, but some of the boards creaked as you went over them; he could swear they they were in danger of giving way at any time and that thought was enough to bring on his vertigo and make his legs turn to jelly. Why hadn't he let Bernie Turnbull stay with him? He didn't have vertigo, even though he would have been too fat to squeeze through that barbed wire.

'For Christ's sake, lad, don't just stand there, move your backside.'

No heroics, the Inspector said. No chance, thought Fisher, as he pushed the coil of wire apart and ever so gently made his way through it. *I'm no hero.*

Running along in front of the beach huts, Eric could just make out a figure on the pier in the distance. The rain was teeming sideways in the wind and the salt from the sea was making his eyes sting, but he could swear that it was Billy attempting to cross the bridge. Looking back, Teddy pointed towards other figures, first one and then another emerging from the head of the pier.

PC Fisher was fighting his way into a headwind, when it suddenly changed direction and gusted ferociously around the pier's structure. He feared he'd be blown clean off it at any second. Hanging onto his helmet and with his cape billowing up over his head, he lost all sense of direction until the sergeant grabbed his elbow.

'Hurry up, lad, come on, move yourself,' he bellowed against the sound of the sea roaring underneath them.

This is a ruddy nightmare, thought Fisher as he saw the looming gap ahead of him, making his legs give underneath him.

'For crying out loud, lad, keep going. Come on, what's the matter with you? Over the bridge, lad.'

'Over, Sarge?' *What, over that? Me?* The thought of crossing the narrow boards with a long drop into the North Sea made him buckle. *No heroics, the Inspector said.*

'Go on, lad,' Green shouted. 'Over you go.'

Les Fisher shook his head. 'I can't, Sarge.'

Green tried to sound calm and encouraging,

'Of course you can, lad. Three deep breaths, then run across and don't look down.'

Another huge gust of wind and PC Fisher grabbed hold of one of the nearby lampposts, hugging it as if his life depended on it.

'For Christ's sake lad, get a bloody move on.'

Fisher clung on and shook his head. 'Can't we just wait, Sarge? He can't stay out there forever and there's no other way off here.'

'No, we can't,' yelled Green back at him. He had no intention of staying out in this God-awful weather any longer than needed. A good soak in a hot bath to ease his body was what he was craving. 'Get over there now, and that's an order.'

He can't order me about, thought PC Fisher as spray exploded over the side of the pier and poured over him. *I'm not in his ruddy army.* He shook his head again.

Green growled like a rabid dog. 'You bloody coward.' And with this, he started to cross the bridge himself. The boards were flimsy and he could feel them bending under his weight. Another gust of wind and he teetered a little and his leg gave out, but he managed to pull himself back before falling and then he was over onto the other side. Even he had a brief moment of fear, but he did his best to hide it.

Billy ran past the boarded-up variety theatre before turning to see if the others were close. No sign; thank goodness.

From the beach, PC Turnbull could just make out the figure but it was hopeless, the visibility was so bad; and the wind was howling with the roar of the North Sea so there was no way that the sergeant would be able to hear his whistle.

Green continued on down the pier as Les Fisher got onto his hands and knees and started crawling across the bridge on all fours, hanging onto the sides as he shuffled forward with his eyes tightly closed. He couldn't let that bastard sergeant call him a coward.

'He's going to try to hide,' said Eric, as he, Teddy and Sam ran along the prom above the beach huts. 'He has this place where he can hide, under the pier, but he can't go down there in this weather.'

Billy threw himself behind the rear wall of the old theatre and bent over to catch his breath. Out of the wind for a moment and making his way to the trap door, he pulled on the brass ring, which cut into his fingers, but his hands were too cold to feel anything. The wood of the trap door had swollen and it remained jammed in place. Kneeling down, he pulled again, harder this time, and felt it move a little. Desperate, he counted to three under his breath and pulled with all his might, until suddenly the door flew open, sending him head over heels, the skirt tangling itself around his feet. He tugged at the material to try to free it. He grabbed at the tapes that held the skirt tightly round his waist and attempted to free the knots, but they were now so tight and drenched in rain and seawater that there was no way they would budge. He tore at the skirt angrily but only succeeded in making matters worse as shredded and torn material flapped around him. Cursing, he crawled back towards the trap.

He edged his way to the top and attempted to get his legs onto the cat ladder but the frayed skirt made it even more dangerous than normal. He looked down at the sea below; it lapped over the platform, and then every so often a huge wave engulfed it. He knew it was madness but in his panic he had no choice.

'Hello, lad.' It was the sergeant. 'Can you hear me, lad?' His voice was carrying on the wind, which made Billy look around thinking that he was on top of him, but there was no sign of the man. Taking a deep breath, Billy placed his bare feet on the rusty ladder and, clinging on, started to lower himself down, the rust biting into him. The sea below boiled and foam rolled over the platform, but Billy knew there was no going back as he reached up and pulled the trap door closed above him. Clinging on to the ladder, he felt his feet slip on the fresh seaweed that had wrapped itself on the rungs and he slid down, the rust from the side of the ladder cutting into his hands. Falling onto the platform, he rolled along it towards the edge, the guardrail stopping him from plunging into the waters below. The wind dropped for a moment, just enough for him to gather himself and drape his legs either side of an upright of the rail, and he clung on for dear life.

Above, Sergeant Green stumbled around the corner of the theatre and, fighting the wind, hung onto the side rail and looked about him. The boy was nowhere in sight. He looked over the side, peering down into the water, moving his head to one side as the remnants of a wave hit him, taken up by a gust of wind. Turning back, he scanned the terrain. He turned the handles on the boarded-up doors at the back of the theatre, but they were firmly locked and bolted. Turning again, he cursed under his breath and looked about some more, wiping the seawater that was stinging his eyes and trying to keep his focus. It was then that he noticed the brass ring in the deck and some of the boards standing slightly proud of the rest of the decking. Leaping forward and grabbing hold of the brass ring, he pulled at it and the door flung open, sending him backwards, landing badly on his damaged shoulder. Gritting his teeth and shielding his face from the spray, he crawled back and looked down. Below him he could see the incongruous figure of Private Pryce, with black material whipping about him like a crow, his body wrapped around the outer railings with the waves crashing over him.

Weighing up the situation, Green knew that the boy wouldn't be able to hang on for long, so he'd need to move quickly to get him up and out of there. 'Hold tight, lad,' he shouted down at him. 'I'll have you out of there soon. Don't worry, lad, stay calm.'

Green looked around him and saw PC Fisher appear around the side of the theatre, very white, pasty and wet.

'Grab that lifebelt,' Green yelled as loud as he could. But even a voice as strong as his couldn't cut through the roar of the waves below and the wind howling around them. 'The lifebelt, get that bloody lifebelt,' he yelled again, pointing at the belt hanging next to Fisher on the wall of the theatre.

Les Fisher had to lean forward, nearly losing his footing as he attempted to understand. Cottoning on, he lifted the belt from the wall with one hand whilst hanging onto the drainage pipe with the other.

'Good,' Green continued, shouting and gesticulating. 'Now pick up the end of the sash rope that's tied to it and attach it firmly onto the outer railings, and then pass me the belt.'

Fisher, cold and petrified, closed his eyes and told himself to be strong and all would be well. Slowly and very sheepishly, his fingers totally devoid of feeling, he got down onto his hands and knees and crawled over to the railings.

'Come on, laddie, don't take all day or we'll lose him,' Green coaxed.

'I'm doing my ruddy best,' Les Fisher muttered under his breath, wrapping the freezing wet sash around and around before attempting to tie a knot whilst lying on his back and looking up into the rain. He pulled on it to make sure it was firm.

That done, Green beckoned him over. On his hands and knees, he made his way towards the sergeant.

'Right,' yelled Green down to Billy. 'Listen to me, boy, listen to me. I'm going to throw down this lifebelt and you're to grab hold of it and place it over that head of yours and down to under your armpits. Do you hear me, son?'

Billy didn't look up or respond to the sergeant's directions but continued to stare out towards the sea, rigidly holding onto the railings. Green gritted his teeth and hoped that Pryce would co-operate. Swinging his arm back as far as he could, he threw the belt down towards the boy, but the wind was too strong and a gust sent it off and over the side into the water. Cursing, Green pulled on the rope to bring the belt back up to him.

'Help me pull on this, man,' he bellowed over to the constable, who was crouched on the wet boards, trying to keep out of the elements the best he could. 'The bloody thing's stuck on something.' They both tugged at the sash rope and after a few attempts, the lifebelt jumped up over the platform edge.

Realising that he couldn't hope to land the belt near the boy, Green took the decision to climb down the ladder a little to get a bit closer to his target. He just hoped that his leg would hold out as he gingerly clambered through the trap and placed his feet on the rungs. He could feel them slipping from under his army boots, which were too heavy and cumbersome for the task. Gripping onto the ladder, he manoeuvered the lifebelt into what he hoped was a better position, and threw it out again.

The lifebelt hit Billy on the head and knocked him sideways a little, but still he refused to grab hold of it.

I'm not going back, he told himself *no matter what happens, I'm not going back.*

'Come on, lad, don't be silly now,' Green called down to him, trying to keep his temper, his shoulder stabbing him with pain. 'I won't harm you, lad. I promise that when we get back to the camp, I'll look after you; you'll be one of my boys. Nobody touches or harms one of Sergeant Green's favourites. Just a few days in the glass house and a bollocking from the commanding officer, and no more need be said.' Bullshit, of course, and they both knew it.

Pulling in the belt once more, he threw it, but again Billy didn't move from his spot.

Green decided to take a breather while he gathered his thoughts and tried to ease the pain in his shoulder.

Back on the not-so-dry land, PC Turnbull came to the conclusion that any efforts to keep an eye out for the boy were futile. He thought about attempting to get closer to the pier from the beach but the defences and the angry rolling waves put pay to that idea pretty sharpish. He wasn't going to risk getting washed out to sea for anybody. "No heroics", the Inspector had said, and the Inspector was his boss, not that ruddy army sergeant.

At the same time, Eric had run ahead as fast as he could along the prom. He had only one thing in his mind, and that was to save Billy. He hadn't a clue how he was going to achieve it, but he couldn't just let them take him away.

'Eric, what are you doing?' called Teddy as Eric started to scramble through the gap in the wire. 'Come back, you fool.'

But he wasn't listening and, forgetting all fear, he stumbled along the pier as the elements battered him. He didn't seem to notice the bridge and was over it and making his way towards Billy's hideaway in no time.

It was Constable Turnbull that stopped Teddy and Sam following.

'Now then, gentlemen, I wouldn't advise you going on there. It's a death trap in this weather,' he said, shaking his head and attempting to get some shelter from the elements under the awning of the ice cream shop. 'Besides which, it's private property and I'll have to arrest you if you step foot on it, and I don't want to do that.'

Green, having got his breath, turned to PC Fisher. 'Right,' he yelled, pointing. 'Get the other lifebelt, untie the sash and tie one end to the railings and give me the other end. Come on, move yourself, man.'

The last place Les Fisher wanted to be at the moment was on the end of this ruddy pier freezing to death, but he knew he had no choice and crawled over towards the second lifebelt.

Green knew he had to get this boy out of there and under lock and key at the police station soon. His body couldn't take much more of this; every move he made felt like he had a ton of lead hanging off him. He wanted to sleep but his pride kept him going; he wasn't going to lose the boy. Pryce couldn't hold on much longer down there; one more large wave could sweep him out to sea; Green had no desire to have to live with that.

Fisher crawled on his hands and knees back to the railings. The wind was getting even stronger, if that was possible, and he couldn't risk standing up for fear of being blown over the side. Lying on his back again and reaching up, he tied off one end of the sash rope and played the rest out as he crawled back towards the trap. Grabbing it, Sergeant Green began looping it through his army belt and around his waist.

'Now,' he shouted up to Fisher, 'keep this rope tight at all times and just feed it out enough so I can get down the ladder and grab the boy and get the lifebelt over him.' He said it slowly, as if talking to an idiot – which, in fairness, he thought he was.

'You're not going down there, surely? You'll get washed away.'

'Well, lad, it's up to you to make sure I don't,' barked Green, who was no longer the charming Sergeant Green, the squaddies' favourite, but a desperate soldier who was not about to have his honour damaged by a pig-headed conscript too stupid to realise that he was trying to save his life. 'Don't let go, for Christ's sake, and if you feel it tighten suddenly pull it back, do you hear me?'

'Yes, Sarge,' nodded Fisher, unsure as to whether he was up to this task. The sergeant was six foot and full of muscle and Fisher no more than five foot ten, cold, wet and in need of a bit of exercise.

Green cursed his army boots again as he slipped on the rungs below him, only saving himself from falling by wrapping his arm around the top rung quickly, jarring it badly.

PC Fisher played out the rope, trying to keep it as tight as he could, but it bit into his hands, which, along with the constant saltwater spraying over him, made them sting like the blazes.

Slowly climbing down, Green eventually placed one foot onto the platform as foaming sea water brushed over it. As he placed the other foot down, he felt his leg go from under him, slipping on the layer of seaweed. It was like ice and Green had to keep a tight grip on the ladder as his shoulder barked at him again.

Eric made his way along side of the old theatre, arriving as the policeman played out the rope down into the hole. He watched in horror as suddenly the rope tightened and the policeman was pulled forward towards the edge of the trap.

Les Fisher gritted his teeth as the rope bit into his hands. His feet slipped on the boards as the rain and spray bombarded him from all directions. Seeing a figure out of the corner of his eye, Fisher beckoned him to stay back as yet another gust of wind whipped around the structure. Eric could feel himself being pulled off his feet and hung onto the downpipe that was fixed to the theatre wall.

Beneath them, Sergeant Green was fighting to stay upright as the wind and sea water mixed together to create a vortex around him. He had both feet placed on the platform now but he was aware that letting go of the ladder while still standing up would be suicide. He lowered himself onto his hands and knees and, letting go of the ladder with his good hand, wrapped his bad arm around one of the rungs and hoped that he had enough strength in it to hold him, and that the policeman above had enough brains and strength to hang onto the rope. One-handedly, he started to haul in the lifebelt, which had been playing back and forth with the waves below. He couldn't risk letting go of the ladder to get the thing over the boy's head and it was obvious that Pryce had no intention of helping him out. More in hope than expectation, Green threw the belt like a hoopla at the fair. It hit the boy's back, knocking him forward slightly. He adjusted his grip on the railings, still not turning; refusing to heed.

Cursing the boy at the top of his lungs, Green started to pull in the lifebelt once more, but as he made a grab for it an enormous wave crashed into the end of the pier. Les Fisher looked up in horror as a vast wall of water came rushing over the railings and straight at him. He had nowhere to go as it broke and crashed down on him. The force threw him backwards into the wall of the theatre before the undercurrent started to pull him back towards the end of the pier and over into the North Sea. Somehow, he kept hold of the rope, which he had wrapped around his fist. It dug into his skin as it tightened; his body was at full stretch, his legs pulling away from him as he hung in the water three or four feet above the pier. Mercifully he crashed to the decking as the water subsided, leaving him stranded, lying full-length on the ground.

At the same time, Eric was thrown backwards and his body surfed along the side of the old theatre until he came to a juddering halt as, by some miracle, he ended up jammed under the bench in the corner of one of the shelters.

Below, Sergeant Green didn't see the wave coming and breaking above him so he wasn't ready for the vast deluge of water that funnelled its way down through the trap hole, engulfing him from above. He could feel the rope tighten around his waist as the force of the water lifted him, and before he could take any evasive action it washed him speedily towards the edge off the platform. His body crashed into Billy and crushed him hard against the rusted iron work before washing them both over the side and into the swirling undercurrents.

The rope around Fisher's hand had become a tourniquet, cutting deeply into his skin as it was pulled as tight as piano wire, before slackening off as the waves came back in, before tightening once more as the sergeant's body was thrown further out to sea. Fisher attempted to unwrap the rope from around his hand, but looking down on it he could see that the fibres were embedded into his skin; his hand was a mangled mixture of sea water and blood. The pain swept over him and, sobbing, he tore at his hand to free himself. He vomited as he saw the skin peeling away with the rope as he prised it off. Attempting to pull at the rope with his good hand, he crawled over to the edge of the trap entrance and stuck his head over to peer down but he was knocked back as the force of the water from another incoming wave boiled over the side of the pier. He lay on his back, exhausted, shaking from cold and the fear that the next rush of water would take him off. There wasn't another rush. He could feel the wind starting to die down and the waves ceased engulfing the structure so violently. It was far from calm, but the worst of the storm seemed to have blown itself out and the rain wasn't coming down as hard... or was this just wishful thinking?

Having got his breath, Les Fisher crawled back to the hole to look down. He could make out that the rope that had held the sergeant was now hanging over the side of the platform, but there was no sign of the man. What he couldn't see was the sergeant's limp body swirling about under the water below it and crashing against one of the rusting steel pillars. Private William Pryce's body was now way out to sea and would one day, more than likely, be washed ashore. One day.

At the pier head, Teddy and Sam stood waiting for some form of news.

'I've got a bad feeling, gentlemen, I'm afraid; yes, a very bad feeling,' said Constable Turnbull, shaking his head and squinting his eyes to see what he could see along the length of the pier. Although he couldn't make anything out at that distance, he'd been around the sea long enough to know that nothing good could come of this adventure; a fear, indeed, that was confirmed when he saw the bedraggled figure of his friend, PC Les Fisher, making his way towards them, his arms around the young actor. They both looked in complete shock as they crouched down and crawled through the gap in the wire. Both faces were crumpled, as if all life had been drained out of them.

'They're gone,' said Fisher as he helped Eric to his feet, 'both bloody gone.' He put his hands up to his face, his shoulders moved up and down and his entire body started to convulse. Bernie Turnbull then did something that he'd never done before – well, men don't do those sorts of things – he pulled his friend and colleague to him and cradled him as Les Fisher sobbed uncontrollably.

Eric looked up at Teddy and Sam, his eyes dead. Teddy moved towards him in an attempt to put his arms around him but he pulled away and, holding onto the railings, stared out to sea, shaking with grief.

'I'd get your friend dried off if I were you,' PC Turnbull said softly. 'I'm afraid that we'll be needing you and the rest of your… the others, down at the station later to make statements. The Inspector's not going be happy about this, I'm afraid. No, not happy at all.'

30

The Final Curtain

'So they'll be coming for us,' said Veronica when Eric, Teddy and Sam came into The Cockleshell with the news, having divested themselves of their wet costumes. 'Well, I'm not taking any of the blame for any of this, I can tell you.'

'No, of course not, Veronica,' said Phyllis archly as she took Eric by the hand and sat him down next to her. 'That's right, dear, you just think of yourself. Why change the habit of a lifetime?'

Teddy sat himself down next to Penny, who placed her head on his shoulder.

'I knew nothing good could come of it,' said Hugh, looking over towards the others.

Zelda patted his hand but in reality, she couldn't care what her husband thought at this particular time; she was too worried about her friend Connie, who – even though as far as they knew, her husband was still lying unconscious in the theatre – seemed totally unperturbed. She seemed strangely unconcerned that the ambulance would take its time to get there and no, she didn't have any intention of sitting with Arthur until it did.

'I'm sure he's quite comfortable,' she stated, when asked. 'Yes, quite comfortable, I'm sure.' Even though she didn't actually know he was dead, deep inside, she certainly hoped he was.

'Oh dear, this wasn't what I planned, not what I planned at all,'

Randolph fretted, throwing his whisky down in one go. 'I thought we could all just get together and have a jolly time.'

Phyllis patted his hand. There was a great deal of hand patting going on.

'Ah, yes,' Randolph said, patting his pockets and pulling out the envelope that the boy had given him earlier and handing it to Phyllis. 'Take a look at this.'

She looked at it. 'Mister N Laine?' she said raising an eyebrow.

'Norman,' Randolph replied.

Opening it, Phyllis pulled out the letter inside and read it.

> *Pebble Cottage*
> *Beach View Road*
> *Eastbourne*
> *Sussex*

Dear Norman,

I am sorry I have taken so long to write to you but things have been all rather up and down here. To be honest, more down than up, but I digress.

By now, you will no doubt be wondering where the promised funds are with regard to your little theatrical venture. The honest answer to that is still in His Majesty's treasury, where I fear they will be staying. Let me explain.

When you came to see me that morning and asked that I help you out, I – and I say this in all honesty – was more than happy to oblige and thought that with a little civil service chicanery, all could be arranged without too much fuss.

Unfortunately I was mistaken. My credit with the Accounts department was, it seemed, at a terminal level. In the words of Mister Macawber: "Annual income twenty pounds, annual expenditure nineteen six, result happiness.

Annual income twenty pounds, annual expenditure twenty pounds nought and six, result misery." According to Mister Harrison in Accounts, my expenditure was firmly in the misery column and had been for some time. Sadly, being a Knight of the Realm does not necessarily mean one is comfortably in funds – quite the reverse. The problem, it seems, was so bad that it had been decided, by those way above my pay grade, that my services within the civil service were no longer required and that I was to be given my pension without delay and put out to grass.

Therefore I write to you from a little bungalow in Eastbourne, which belonged, until her recent death, to Miss Finch's mother. You remember Miss Finch, I have no doubt. May I assure you that beneath that façade of imperious efficiency lies a woman of great tenderness, who, within the last month, has consented to be my wife.

So there, I'm afraid, you have the crux of the problem: the cupboard is bare. I am certain that this will come as a major disappointment to you but as I understand it, you theatrical types are used to finding ways to make ends meet and will have a jolly time muddling through.

In the credit column, may I add that should you and your little bunch of theatricals ever find yourselves in the Eastbourne area, do look me up. Tea and custard creams are always in abundance.

*Sincerely yours,
Perry*

The Haleston Lifeboat was sent off as soon as the "gods of the sea and all its elements" had sacrificed enough people for one day. Sergeant Green's body was found hanging under the pier, still attached to the sash rope, limply drifting like a lost rag doll.

'The force of the waves,' the coxswain of the boat, Harry Blow, said later, 'had smashed him into the pier structure so severely that his back had almost broken in half and was being held together by muscle and his army uniform.' They could find no sign of Private Pryce. Coxswain Blow gave his report to the waiting police inspector, having brought the lifeboat to shore. Duty done, Coxswain Blow took his crew off for a well-earned beer, which he did ritually after any call-out, and they all ploughed into The Nelson Arms and drunk to each other's health and their continued safety, bowing their heads for those lost at sea.

'Right,' said Inspector Pickering to Constable Turnbull, after he'd made sure that PC Fisher was safely tucked up in the local hospital, 'it's time to round up those ruddy actors. Bernard, if I get my way, I'll have the lot of them sent down for six months at least. What do you think?'

Bernard Turnbull wasn't really sure what he thought at first. He wasn't a vindictive person at heart and tried to think the best of people; but then again, as he thought of his "old mucker" Les Fisher lying in hospital, heavily sedated, and realised that the poor devil would have to live with the horrors of what he'd witnessed that day, he decided that he wasn't, on the whole, in a very forgiving mood. 'I'd give them a year each, sir, and a few lengths of the birch, if you don't mind me saying so.'

Inspector Pickering nodded sagely. 'You're right there, Bernard. Quite right. Now then, let's go and find them, shall we?'

'They'll be in The Cockleshell, sir, or that's where they told me.'

'The Cockleshell it is, Bernard. The Cockleshell it most certainly is.'

And, most certainly, it was.

'Right then, which of you gentlemen is in charge of the theatricals?' asked Pickering as he strode into the bar. He was in no mood for such niceties as introductions.

Randolph stepped forward and introduced himself and then thought he should get the defence in first.

'I think you should know…'

But the Inspector was having none of it. He'd had enough for one day – his day off.

'One moment, Mister Laine, one moment, if you please, sir. You'll have time to have your say when we get down to the station.'

'But the thing is—' Randolph endeavoured to continue.

'The thing is, Mister Laine,' the Inspector came back, he thought rather cleverly, 'the thing is that I don't wish to hear another word from you until we get to the police station., Is that understood, sir?'

Randolph huffed and puffed and then shrugged. 'I was just trying to save valuable police time.'

The Inspector looked around at the assembled Company. He had no wish to have to spend the rest of the evening going through all their statements, but he also knew that he had no choice. He had hoped to have a nice quiet evening at home listening to the wireless whilst nursing a nice little drop of whisky, having done all those little jobs his wife had wanted him to. *Yes, well, best not to think about all that. The best laid plans.*

'Right, let's be having you. The stations not far to walk, so let's be off.'

'One moment, Inspector,' said Veronica, standing up. 'May I ask why we are all being marched down to the police station like naughty schoolchildren?'

The Inspector turned. 'Madam, one of my officers is lying in a hospital bed with hypothermia and is in deep shock having seen two people drowned. So, with the greatest respect, I suggest you finish your drink and let's not hear any more about it.'

'I don't see what that boy soldier has to do with me. I said at the very start that he should have been handed into the police and be done with it.' She took a large drink of her gin.

Eric's rage welled up in him and he dived towards her, ready to, quite literally, scratch her eyes out. Veronica reached down for her handbag and calmly took out her handkerchief as Teddy and Sam held Eric back.

'I'm sorry darling,' she said, staring back at him, 'but if you think I'm going to be hauled down to a dreadful police station to take the blame for your little boyfriend's exploits, you can think again.'

Phyllis was on her feet and before anybody could stop her, she had brought her hand back and slapped Veronica on the side of her face with such force that it made her stagger into the table.

'Phyllis!' Randolph made a step towards her.

'No, don't stop her, Randolph.' It was Penny. 'Phyllis is right. The woman has no soul.' She turned back to Teddy, who put his arms around her again.

Veronica steadied herself and in defiance walked up to the Inspector. 'Well, come on, arrest me, if you must,' she said petulantly, putting her hands out. 'Put your handcuffs on me and march me to your police station and throw me into a cell.'

'*An empty vessel makes the loudest sound, so they that have the least wit are the greatest babblers,*' Hugh piped up. The Inspector stared at him. 'Plato,' Hugh explained.

Inspector Pickering was not amused. 'This isn't the stage. This is not one of your crime whodunnits.' He'd had more than enough drama for one day and he didn't need a bunch of actors to give him any more, thank you very much.

'I'm sure that we can clear this all up without resorting to the full force of the law, wouldn't you say?' said Randolph.

No, I would not say, thought Inspector Pickering. Quite the opposite in his view; a view that he now made known to them all in no uncertain terms.

'Quiet, the bloody lot of you,' he bellowed, his voice cracking with the effort. 'I don't want to hear another ruddy word from any of you until we get to the station. Constable, get this lot out of here.'

'But Inspector,' Randolph tried one more time, 'I really don't think we deserve—' He didn't get time to finish.

'Sir, the full force of the law is what you all deserve. Now, outside before I handcuff the lot of you.'

Out on the street the rain had abated, but the grey clouds filled the sky and had turned the entire landscape into a flat, colourless place. The Company shuffled down the pavement and into Church Street. Phyllis looked about her and was grateful that the town seemed to be deserted. The locals were behind their front doors, listening to the wireless, no doubt – *ITMA*, perhaps, or Max Miller… *Now here's a funny thing.*

Hugh looked up at the clouds, having heard a rumble overhead. 'Thunder,' he said. 'More blasted rain; if I get a chill it will be the last of me, I'm sure of it.'

Zelda had heard it all many times before and slipped her arm through his. *The silly old moaner,* she thought, he always had been and always would be but she loved him for all of that; yes, she had loved him from the first day they played as children back on the island.

Penny Rose turned up her collar and placed her hand back into Teddy's. It felt strong and comforting. She'd been such a fool, so selfish, and had wasted so much time.

Veronica stepped out with her head in the air as if bravely going to the gallows.

It's a far, far better thing, thought Phyllis, smiling as she looked back at her, before placing her arm through Randolph's. What would have happened if she hadn't introduced him to Hester that evening, so long ago? Life would have been so different.

Another rumble of thunder, thought Hugh. It would be raining cats and dogs in a minute, he just knew it. But then the sound changed; it was not a low rumble anymore but the high-pitched wail, trumpet-like – a Jericho trumpet. They all stopped in their tracks. Dear God, no. A German dive-bomber suddenly pierced the clouds. From both wings, bright lights suddenly appeared. Popping sounds like a thousand balloons bursting in the distance.

Randolph only had time to look up before the bullets ripped through him. Phyllis had no time to move at all. Zelda grabbed Hugh close to her as they fell to the ground. Teddy wrapped his arms around Penny and ran as fast as he could with her towards the shop doorway, but they could never outrun the hail of white-hot lead that passed straight through him and then into her, the fusillade strong enough to propel the both of them through the plate glass window of the newsagent's shop. Veronica and Eric froze and dropped where they stood. Connie closed her eyes and crossed herself before starting her journey to be reunited with her beloved parents. Sam, who had been at the back, had a split second to think and, diving low, threw himself into the recessed doorway of the shoe shop. The bullets smashed the glass an inch above his back, shattering it all around him as another burst of machine gun fire propelled a mass of bullets into his legs, shattering the bones like dropped crockery. Inspector Pickering wept as he fell and PC Turnbull, turning to run, was cut down before he could take a step.

*

Mister Tuppence insisted on digging the graves himself and the remains of the Laine Theatre Company were laid to rest in the far corner of the graveyard.

They were a funny old lot, he thought, as he leant on his shovel, having levelled off the last of the graves. *They never stopped squabbling; a proper old theatre of war, they were.*

Sam insisted on attending the funeral and Molly and her mother took it in turns to push him along in the rickety old wheelchair from the hospital to the graveyard. He bowed his head over the graves as the coffins were slowly lowered in, one by one. They were all there: Connie and Arthur Desmond, Veronica East, Eric Cornwall, Hugh and Zelda Munro, Penny Rose. Teddy Shaw, Phyllis Campbell-Bennett and Randolph Laine. Their voices echoed in his head. They would do so for as long as he lived, he was sure of that.

After the solemn ceremony, Molly and her mother, Sam Laine and Mister Tuppence made their way back to the theatre, where Molly informed Sam that they had one more thing to do. Wheeling Sam into the wings, they stopped, and Mister Tuppence brought over a single lantern on a stand and placed it on the footplate of Sam's wheelchair.

'Mister Tuppence and I made this. It's a ghost light. Mister Tuppence did most of the work, but I helped.'

Sam smiled up at her. What a wonderful girl she was.

Moving to the back of the wheelchair, Molly pushed it towards the centre of the stage and then, turning downstage, they stopped. At the same time, Mister Tuppence slowly started bringing down all the lights until just the footlights illuminated them. Sam waited for Molly to come and take the stand from him, but she shook her head. This was his moment. Gathering all his strength, Sam lifted the light stand and placed it down upon the stage. As he did so, Mister Tuppence dimmed the final light and then immediately brought up the solitary light centre-stage.

'It's to stay on now the theatre's going to be dark,' said Molly. 'You know all that, but this is a very special ghost light; I prayed to all the gods of the theatre and God in heaven and asked them to light Mister Laine and all of his Company up to heaven, where it will burn forever.'

'Lovely job,' said Mister Tuppence, from his perch. 'Lovely job.'